Forbidden love. Counter-culture. The shadow of Vietnam. Sexual revolution. Social unrest. Marijuana and LSD. In this intriguing coming-of-age novel by Larry Smith, *The Free Farm,* we journey back to America's turbulent late 60s and early 70s. Lee McCall leaves his steel mill town in the Ohio Valley to attend Ohio University, but the going isn't easy as he takes classes, works to support himself, and tries to form a utopia—a free living commune or "an adventure in group living" in an Appalachian farmhouse. Smith provides a unique window into Lee's life that is driven by idealism, a love of Emerson and Thoreau, and devotion to his beautiful partner, Sharon, who practices Zen, meditates, and can fix cars. Between college life and work, the troubles of his family back home, and the challenges of his new communal family, Lee evolves from a boy who left "a golden time when the world seemed safe and right" to a man with a global vision who needs to stand for something, embrace his destiny, and know where his real home lies. In this realistic yet often surprising and tender novel, a quoted line from "The Waking" by Theodore Roethke may serve as our guidepost: "I wake to sleep, and take my waking slow/ I feel my fate in what I cannot fear/ I learn by going where I have to go."

~ Laura Treacy Bentley, author of *Lake Effect*

Other Books by Larry Smith

Fiction:
The Long River Home: A Novel (Bottom Dog Press, 2009).
Faces and Voices: Tales (Bird Dog Publishing, 2007).
Working It Out (Ridgeway Press, 1998).
Beyond Rust (Bottom Dog Press, 1995).

Memoirs:
Milldust and Roses (Ridgeway Perss 2002).

Poetry:
Tu Fu Comes to America: A Story in Poems (March
Street Press 2010).
A River Remains (WordTech Editions, 2006).
Thoreau's Lost Journal (Westron Press 2002).
Steel Valley: Postcards & Letters (Pig Iron Press, 1992).
Across These States (Bottom Dog Press, 1985).
Scissors, Paper, Rock (Cleveland State Univ. Poetry
Center, 1982).

Biography:
Lawrence Ferlinghetti: Poet-At-Large (Southern
Illinois University Press, 1983).
Kenneth Patchen: Rebel Poet in America (A Consortium
of Small Presses, 2000).

Bottom Dog Press

The Free Farm

❧ A Novel ☙

Larry Smith

Working Lives Series
Appalachian Writing Series
Bottom Dog Press
Huron, Ohio

Bottom Dog Press, Inc.
P.O. Box 425 /Huron, Ohio 44839
http://smithdocs.net

Credits

Cover Photo:
An adaptation of David Woehr's
Appalachian landscape image
Cover Design: Susanna Sharp-Schwacke

This is a work of fiction. Only Stuart and Lois Brand are real people, and they have lent themselves to being fictionalized here in character. Their early work with *The Whole Earth Catalog* is inspiring. I thank author Peter Coyote for his telling account of commune life in *Sleeping Where I Fall* (Counterpoint, 1999) and for Rupert Fike's writing and editing of true accounts in *Voices from The Farm: Adventures in Community Living* (The Book Publishing Co. 1998). There is still much to be learned here.Under the "fair use" practice, 8 lines of Theodore Roethke's "The Waking" have been adapted here. This book also adapts fictional characters from my *The Long River Home* novel (2009) in this setting.

Acknowledgments

My thanks goes to the members of the Firelands Writing Center for their continuing support and input, and to my initial readers of Jeff Vande Zande, Charles White, Suzanne Smith, and my good wife Ann Smith for their human and editing insights. Laura Smith, Allen Frost, and Susanna Sharp-Schwacke at Bottom Dog Press and Bird Dog Publishing have helped this book along. I am indebted to June King and Dennis Horan my consultants on communal life who each shared their lives and memories.

Table of Contents

This book is dedicated to Ann.

"Think of community—
you think of together:
being—
living—
eating—
shitting—
freaking—
working—
it's not like we got to
get it together
we got to
see that we are."
—*Whole Earth Catalog*, 1968

In the simple grace of people
we all learn to survive.

Chapter One

Beauty and Travail at Twelve

My mother wakes me at five to do my paper route, then disappears down the hallway. I dress and go down the stairs as they all sleep, me rubbing cobwebs from my eyes as I go out the door, the town outside dead in the dark around me. At the foot of the hill my bundle is waiting. I cut the twine, glide them all into the bag, and as I walk, fold each paper into a fat stick that I toss onto the lost porches in morning dark. Mill and bird sounds, otherwise a quiet about the town.

At the top of the hill, under Mrs. Hinton's porch, I dig out my pack of Camel cigarettes and see I'm down to five after a month. Standing in the trees nearby, I light one and stare down the hill that I've just climbed street by street. Far below lies the steel mill spread out like a dragon of fiery light beside the long river. I breathe it in, the cigarette and smell of mill. A car passes. I start down the hill, dreaming of girls standing at their bedroom windows opening their thin pajama tops, throwing me a kiss, a wave, a look. A dog barks. Back home I'll eat the rest of Dad's oatmeal as my brother and sisters come down the stairs wordless in kitchen light.

Before me lies a day at junior high school watching the girls gab to each other as they lean against their lockers, skirts just at their knees, eyes looking out and past me, a kid with big eyes and ears, a seventh grader for Pete's sake.

I sit at my desk and listen. Outside the school building comes the roar of blast furnace, the heavy clank of trains shaking the classroom windows. Inside the study hall I lean my head against the words of my book and fall asleep.

"Lee, wake up. Lee McCall!" Miss Connors is pressing her fingers into my arm. I look up at her blank face—her call. "This is the third time this week, Lee. Do you want to go to the principal's office?" I call her bluff and shrug the shrug of the older boys. As she yanks me out of my seat, my books tumble onto the floor and for a moment we have the whole study hall as our audience. Her hand presses harder into my arm as she ushers me toward the door—her moving quick time, me slow. It is a kind of crazy dance we do till we get to the hallway.

Standing there, as we catch our breath, I notice her dark blue dress with a white Pilgrim collar; she could be pretty if she let herself. I sigh, "I'm sorry, Miss C. I been up since five delivering papers."

"Too late." She looks down at me and frowns. "Too late, too late," she chants like some bird, then tops it off with, "Young man. You're just too late."

At the principal's office, the school secretary, Mrs. Quinn, smiles up at us and nods, "What have we here?"

"A boy who would sleep through study hall. I've warned and warned him." In her defense, Miss Connors is new at teaching, and I can tell this is causing her more pain than me, at least for now.

"Okay, Miss Connors, you leave him here and Mr. Franklin will deal with him." And with that, she turns, and in her Pilgrim dress hurries back to monitor the rest of the tribe.

Sitting along the wall on that hard wooden bench, so like his paddle, I honestly don't fear Franklin's wrath. I'm ready for whatever my crime deserves. It's already earned me some attention. What I am really thinking most is how much I'd like another cigarette.

When Franklin comes out, a stubby guy in a gray suit, not much taller than some of us boys, I rise. "What have we here?" he asks looking right at me, though he must be speaking to Mrs. Quinn.

When she doesn't answer, I confess, "I fell asleep in study hall," and I wait.

"This here is Lee McCall." Mrs. Quinn says. "He delivers the morning papers." I look over at her. "I know the family," she says softly smiling at me. *Why is she saying this?* We wait out the moments.

"Lee," he says as he takes hold of the collar of my shirt and lifts me up and out of my seat as it dawns on me that my very life is in his hands. "Lee...Lee...my boy. You've got to stay awake and study hard. Understand, son?"

"Yes, sir," comes right out of me, followed by a quick. "I will." In truth I no longer want to be the rebel boy. I've been converted and called.

"I'm sparing you...this time, my boy. But I don't want to see you in here again. You understand?" I bow my head, and with that he turns and goes back into his room. The door shuts and I stand there a long moment before the bell rings.

Mrs. Quinn winks, I thank her and head back into the mad rush of the hall.

My best friend Kenny rushes up to me. "Man, did you get it or what?"

I look back at him just as Sharon Hatcher passes in her little red and white cheer leader's outfit. Wow. My God, why do they allow these distractions in a school building?

"Well?"

"Yeah...I mean, no, nothing bad happened. He just picked me up by my shirt collar and threatened me if I ever came in again."

"Man, you are so lucky. Really. I heard Johnny Sook got a good taste of the paddle just for goofing off in Peterson's history class."

"Yeah, well he gets whacked about twice a week. Now don't he?" We are walking towards English class when I realize I lack my books. I can't afford another trip to the office. The bell will ring in less than three minutes, so I make a dash for it. Miss Connors is standing in the doorway, and she is holding my books out to me.

"Hurry, now," she says, and we both smile at each other like we've been through something together.

The bell begins to ring. I can hear doors closing, feel the hush that falls as teachers begin. Mrs. Z is my personal favorite. And not because she knows my mother or anything, though she seems to like me right off. She is just a good teacher. Believe me, kids can tell. Maybe 'cause there's so few good ones. Mrs. Z knows our names by the end of the first week and will praise you before the class if you do something halfway right. But mostly, she loves the things we read and will listen as we tell her what we thought of them. You can tell, for her, things aren't already over; they are just begun.

When we read *Silas Marner,* I tell her how lots of kids have got it about that bad at home. I say, "Even though the story goes over the top with little 'Eppy in the Toe Hoe,' even so, it told how things is."

"*Are,*" she corrects, "How things *are*, Lee. And thank you for making a good point. Writing can exaggerate at times but still be true. Why is that, do you think?"

I remember the silence as we all think. Then Sharon has her hand up.

"Yes, Sharon?"

"To make us feel," she says softly but clearly—her pretty blue eyes and golden hair, her pale legs in the cheerleading skirt, more than I can bear.

Today, Mrs. Z is wearing a flowered dress, her hair cut short like my mom's. In the front of the room she begins passing out little booklets. She goes up and down the rows placing it into each of our hands and saying our names, like this is Christmas time or something. "These, boys and girls, are yours to keep." And a murmur goes up. We aren't used to getting things absolutely free in school, and especially not books. Our textbooks are all old as the hills, and with names in them going back to our parents' time.

"Students, listen now. A father and son, Emanuel and Henry Haldeman-Julius, print these up for you and for all the other boys and girls of America."

"You mean we get to keep these?" Myron interrupts.

"Yes, you do, and we'll use them here in class. Then...they're all yours to take home. What do you think?"

"Well, I don't see how they can make nothing on this."

"No, they can't and they don't want to, Myron."

I watch as Sharon bends over hers, reading ahead as always. They are poems, printed pretty tiny of course to fit the small pages which are soft and ivory colored. You can slip them into your shirt pocket. I don't know these two guys, but I can tell their names are Jewish, like old Mr. Stein who is also a Julius and a Jew.

"But how can they afford this?" It is I who speak out without raising my hand.

"I honestly don't know, Lee," she answers as though talking to me on the street or something. Actually I am her paperboy and have talked with her on the street when I collect on Saturdays. She lives up on Park Place, and I remember being knocked out that she is actually married and has two kids and a dog. I mean we never thought of teachers as being real people with a family and all.

Teddy gets to read the first poem aloud to the class. He is a terrible reader, but we all listen and wait for the words to come out like gum balls from a machine.

"I like...to see it...lap the Miles—
And lick...the Valleys up—
And stop...to feed itself...at Tanks—
And then—..."

That's as far as he gets because the next word is a doozy—"prodigious."

"Break it down into syllables," she says. "Pro—dig—ious" she pronounces for us. Teddy would have never gotten it. "Say it together, class: pro—dig—ious. Now," and here she waits and hopes, "Does anyone know what it means?"

No hands, and we all look over to Sharon who for once just smiles and shakes her pretty head. Back to Mrs. Z who hands Maryanne the dictionary, her finger pointing to the word. She has predicted our ignorance. "Yes," she says.

"Pro-dig-us" Maryanne mispronounced, "huge, vast, extraordinary in bulk, quality or degree—monstrous."

"That's fine, honey. Read on...Lee."

I am up. "Around a Pile of Mountains—
And [I sound it out] super-cil-ious peer
In Shanties—by the side of the Roads—
And then in Quarry pare..."

"Okay..." she stops me there. "Now think, kids, does anyone know what she's describing?"

We all look back over the words, "What does 'super-cil-ious' mean?" she asks. Silence again, and then Sharon slips out the solitary word, "Proud."

"I get it," I shout. "I get it."

All eyes are on me. "It's either a car...or a train," I say as sighs go up and laughter. Mrs. Z claps.

"Excellent, Lee, and since this poem is written in 1870, that should narrow it down." She reads the rest of the poem.

"It's a train," I say, closing the case. "It's a train," and I swear right then we can all hear the hoot of one down in the mill yard, and so everyone chuckles.

We read a couple more of Miss Emily's poems that day and talk them out together. One about death and a carriage...and one we all like that begins, "I'm Nobody...Who are you?" Mrs. Z ends by asking us all to write our own riddle poem for tomorrow and not to give it away too easily. Then she adds as she does at the end of every period, "Thank you, students. And don't you ever allow anyone to tell you that you are nobody...unless you want to be for a while...like Miss Emily."

*   *   *

Sharon is on my paper route, living in an old double house down at the end of Peeler Street where I pick up my bundle each morning, except Sundays. Only, her folks can't afford a paper. Her mother is usually all strung out with five kids running around the house, her old man Hank

Hatcher works part-time hauling slag and part-time sitting in Scaffidi's drinking away what's left of his pay. Funny how a smart beautiful girl comes from such a down under family—a rose among the weeds, my mom would say, or is it thorns?

Today is a sales day, so I stop to talk to Sharon's mom, trying to get a subscription to the *Post*, and I can see that same light in her eyes, standing there at the screen door looking out at me. She can talk well, too, when she takes a break from the laundry and diapers and things.

"Your dad's Del McCall?" she asks already knowing, and I nod yes. "We were classmates in high school," she adds looking me over closer. "Dated a couple times. You tell him ole Shirley says hello, you hear? But sorry, kiddo, I can't afford the paper," she almost smiles and turns away. I know Sharon is at cheerleading, so I don't bother peeking inside more than to see it is a shipwreck, toys lying around everywhere and clothes strewn across a beat-up lounge chair and couch.

That night sitting at the supper table, Dad smiles when I tell him, "Oh yeah, Dad, Ole Shirley down on Peeler says Hi." Mom looks around quick.

"Oh, no kidding," Dad grins, "Shirley Madden. Remember her, honey?" Mom's back is now a wall. "You know something, Lee? Shirley was our class valedictorian...but her family, the Maddens...well..."

"Well, what?" I have to know.

"Sonny, they were dirt poor, made us look rich. And well...rough, you know? Father drank hard and would take off for months at a time. Wonder Shirley ever made it through school, but boy she was smart."

"Funny," I say, passing him the baked beans he's pointing to. The rest of us have already eaten.

"What?" he asks piling beans on top of his mashed potatoes. He always builds projects with his food.

"Well, ole Shirley isn't doing much better these days, and her daughter Sharon—well, she's the prettiest, smartest girl in my class."

"Hey, you noticing girls now, boy?" he grins.

"No," I bark back. "I'm just sayin'..."

"Yeah," He nods over his plate and grins, "It's a funny world...only some of us ain't laughin'." It is an expression of his that ends many conversations, just when you think you're getting somewhere, like to Pittsburgh or a new idea, you have to turn and head back with, "Funny world."

The thing that is really eating me, and I can't tell to anyone, is how Sharon ignores me so. I mean she isn't mean or anything, but I can't seem to get the time of day from her, much less get up to bat. At night brother Dave and I lie there listening to this DJ on his clock radio for a half hour before sleep. You know, the old love songs from the Pentagons, "To Be Loved" or the Sky Liners singing "This I swear...is true—oo—oo" over and over again. It just about drives me crazy, lying there, eyes closed and seeing her sweet face and red lips and all. I have to turn my back to Dave and rock myself to sleep, if you know what I mean.

Wednesday in the cafeteria, kids are shouting like mad, the smell of melted cheese fills the room, getting on our clothes, but I'm going to do it. I've been working toward this for a month. I go right up to Sharon sitting there by the window with her girlfriends. I mean I go up to her and it spills out of me like pop from a can you dropped on the floor then opened. "Hi, Sharon," I say, and she looks up.

"Oh, hi, Lee. What's the matter?"

I must look awful. "It's nothing...I mean, nothing's the matter. I just..." (and here I take the longest breath I've ever taken in my short life) "...I just want to ask you something." She blinks those perfect blue eyes of hers, and I'm stuck again. "Well, see, the Scouts is having this dance...I'm a Boy Scout, you know. And we're supposed to bring a girl...so I'm just wondering..." It is just awful, like I'm asking her to donate blood or something. "Would you go with me?" I've never felt such a sharp pain in my chest. I can't think or breathe.

"Well, when is it, Lee...the dance and all?"

I begin to breathe again, I am in the old ball game, "Saturday...at seven...p.m....at the Methodist Church basement."

She smiles and a light comes on. Then sliding by me with her tray, so close I can smell her, she whispers, "I'll ask my Mom." Touching my sleeve, she adds, "And you call me, tonight, okay?" My arm is either dead or on fire, yet I manage to shake my head yes, and then she's gone. I think to say "Thanks," but in the din of the room, no one can tell.

Sharon's father answers the phone, and I lower my voice to sound more mature. "Who is this?" he asks.

"Mm...Lee McCall...the paperboy," I answer.

"We don't get no paper."

"Yeah, I know. I'm a classmate of Sharon's."

"Oh, it's you," he says and finally, "She said you might call...Here she is now. Boy, you best be good...or else, you hear?"

It seems strange coming from Mr. Irresponsible, but I promise, "Yes, I do and I will."

Sharon's voice is like music after his, and she sings to my heart, "Yes, Lee, I can go with you to the dance."

"Swell," I say, and I never say "Swell."

"But," she adds, "I have to be home by 9:30. Okay?"

A "Yep," burps out of me, and I think to add, "I'll pick you up at seven," then hang up—that short. I am doing this while standing in our closet with the phone in my hand shaking with disbelief and wonder.

That night in the kitchen when I tell my folks I am taking Sharon Hatcher to the scout dance, Mom drops a plate that breaks into a hundred pieces on the linoleum floor. "Del," she gasps, "You have to stop this...before it goes too far."

He goes over to her, stepping across the shattered dish and he actually puts his arm around her. "I hear you, honey," he says stroking her arm. I watch all this like it is a movie I'd come into the middle of. What's the problem with my taking a great girl like Sharon to a dance?

Finally Dad speaks up: "These are just kids, Jeanie. What—twelve years old and still innocent." That brings "the look" from her, that deep stare that can melt you, and he turns to me and, trying to make things seem normal, he asks, "Is this your first date, son?"

"Yep, it is." I am following his lead. "Just a Boy Scout dance in the church basement, and Mr. Smith and his wife will be there."

He meets Mom's stare now and turns his palms up, "They're just innocent kids, Jeanie."

She slams a knife down flat on the counter, "Yes, and you were once too!" Then she walks from the room and he glances at me, then follows Mom upstairs as I begin picking up the sharp shards of glass. My sister Janet gets the dust pan, while little Diane finishes her fries.

What is this? Is Mom afraid of losing me? Does she hate the Hatchers? I've never seen her quite like this. Oh, I've heard sharp words between them, even seen a dish or two fly across the room, but this is about me—and somehow I am standing in Dad's shadow.

Saturday comes, and I am wearing a white shirt and thin black tie, like I am going to a hip church or something. I show up at her house early at 6:45. We are to walk the couple blocks to the dance. It is raining lightly, so I carry an umbrella with me...Mom's idea. She's come around some. This is all new to me, but I drink up the specialness of it and feel it in my gut. Sharon's old man isn't home, and so her little brother opens the door. Inside are her sisters sitting on the couch and the old lounge chair. A general giggle goes about the room as I wait, and finally Sharon comes down the stairs in a blue flowered dress that just about breaks my heart.

Her mom comes out of the kitchen wearing an apron, and with a cup of coffee in her hand. "Now you two have a good time," she says, blessing us amidst the stares. "And be nice...okay, Lee?" She knows my name; they've been discussing me.

Outside, alone in the misty rain, I no longer hear the mill roar, just the touch of her voice, "Oh, watch your step, Lee," as we go down the broken walkway. At the sidewalk, I open the umbrella over her and she holds my arm as we stroll towards the church, like a scene right out of a movie. From time to time I can feel her soft breast against my arm.

I glide on air that night, even as we box step around the posts in that room. Mrs. Smith has decorated the place with some rainbow crepe paper, and at one point actually dims the lights a little. My brother Dave is playing DJ for the night, spinning 45s from home. And when he plays "This I Swear" and I hold Sharon closer, I realize I have never felt any girl's lower back before. I start to sweat a little, but she is light on her feet yet real and smooth, not like the bouncy girls from gym class, or the ones with heavy legs. Later we bop and even bunny hop, and do the hokey pokey and laugh. We talk about little things—other kids and school. She loves Mrs. Z's class too, and we both recite the poems we've written. I get her punch and look back to drink her in.

I could live on this planet with her a thousand years, but at 9 o'clock, Dave announces, "This is the last dance," and we hold each other close, her head on my shoulder...the sweet smell of her soft hair, her body swaying slowly with mine. I close my eyes. I want to be 21 and propose, then take her out of that house to our place in the country near a woods.

We walk home in silence. The rain has stopped. Outside her house I hold her hand a speechless moment, then say, "Thanks, Sharon," and she, "I had a great time, Lee." I float home and go right upstairs to crawl under the cover to dream of her.

*   *   *

This is how I'll always remember it—a golden time when the world seemed safe and right. Not the time of turmoil and pain that came about afterwards, like a curtain dropping on top of you or the slamming of a door on your hand.

Maybe I shouldn't have said it out loud like that at the breakfast table. But when Dad asks me how the dance was, I blurt out, "Great, oh just Great!" Then it spills out of me, "I love that girl." That is all Mom needs to throw another fit.

"Damn it all, Del. I told you it was a mistake!" Another plate goes to the floor—like a punctuation mark on her rage. And it is a Sunday.

No one speaks. No one eats another bite till Janie looks up then pushes a piece of French toast into her mouth. I glance over at the clock—Sunday school in 15 minutes. I go out the screen door letting it slap a goodbye at my butt.

Later that afternoon, Dad does speak to me. It is haircut day, and he taps me on the arm and points to the basement door. Down the steps where the coal cellar used to be is an old wooden stool and his work bench. He's rigged an overhead light so he can see to work. When I was younger, he'd cut Dave and me upstairs in the kitchen with hand clippers that pulled as they cut, and we'd have little nicks in our scalp while baby sister Janie danced around us. I like it better in the basement—the "men's room" Mom calls it—and we actually need the space and time together. Dad seems always to be working in the mill or on some friend's house.

This day he is stone silent as he stands with his back to me sorting out his clips for the electric razor, his scissors, and combs. I sit down staring into his back, then he comes around behind and shakes the apron over me. Near our feet are his toolbox and electric saw. I notice his hands shaking but sit in silence, still confused by the whole scene that morning. What does Mom have against the Hatchers?

Placing his hands on my shoulders from behind, he jokes, "Well, what'll it be, sir?" I am supposed to say "The regular," only today I say, "Some answers."

"Ah," he sighs, like I've stabbed him. "Okay, son, you deserve some." And as the clippers buzz around my head, he talks.

"Do you know when Sharon was born, Lee?"

"Yeah, we laughed about that. She's a month older than me. We're both Aquarians."

"Well, there's a story about that I have to tell you," he begins and stops the razor. He never does that. "You're both Korean War babies, see, 1950."

"Yeah," I answer, adjusting my feet on the stool rungs. "So...?"

"Soo..." he says, like that, holding a note then looking me square in the face. "There's no easy way of telling you this. You know you came along early, don't you?"

I give him a puzzled look.

"Your mother was still in high school when we fell in love." He starts to blush, "And, well, things got started before we were married later that year."

"No kidding!" I gasp. "You and Mom had sex and made me in some car or garage?" There, it is out. I've spoken the secret in basement light. He says nothing, but stares straight back watching me like a doctor would.

"Okay," I say, "So I'm a love child. I'm down with that."

"Good," he says and rests his hand on my knee. "'Cause that's only part of the story." The furnace clicks on with a 'foomp'—then the blowers start and I can smell oil or gas. Dad is actually biting his lip as he steps back from me. Christ, I think, what could be so bad?

"What did I do wrong?" I ask.

"Oh, it's not you...it was me." He faces me again. "You see, your grandmother Pullman ...well, she didn't like me...felt I was not good enough for her daughter. To keep us apart that summer she sent your mom to stay with her Aunt Tillie in Youngstown. I didn't see her for 3 months. God," he sighs, "I can't believe I'm telling you all this."

It would have been a funny scene, the basement confession of the father, only before me is his pained face and somehow my own fate with Sharon seems to hang in the balance.

He starts again, "Well, anyway, I felt lost and well...in despair. Do you know what that means?"

"Yeah, kind of...dark and hopeless."

"Right. That's it. I hope you never know such a feeling," he says, but I am already at the edge of it myself.

"Now, Shirley was married by then to Hank Hatcher, and he was off in Texas training in the army to go over to Korea."

Why is he telling me about Sharon's mom?

"And she and I had been, well...more than friends once. You understand? We'd get together and talk and share our lives. And one night when her folks were away...well...we shared more than stories."

"What are you saying, Dad!"

"I'm telling you the hardest thing ever, boy," he pleads and takes a breath. "Shirley and me, we made love, see. We was both lonely and hungry for something. And nine months later when I am back with your mom, little Sharon is born...She's a love child too, you see." He is standing beside me, his hand on my shoulder when it finally hits home. I take off the apron, throw it on the floor, and with half a haircut walk out the basement door. Down by the garage I stop running and go in. *Holy God, Sharon could be my sister! What somehow brought us together now pushes us apart.* My heart bursts in my chest, then a pain in my throat releases into tears.

I don't remember how long that I sit there crying on that dirt floor, breathing in the smell of gasoline, but when I finally look up, Dad is standing in the doorway.

Chapter Two

Marlene and Me

It took months before I was over Sharon, and my "despair" would have lasted forever except for one thing: Sharon and I became friends. Her mom must have told her the same story as my dad's—the perpetrators forced to take the witness stand. And though there was never any scientific "proof" of our blood ties, when we were around each other, we became kind of like sister and brother. A beautiful, smart girl as a friend—was a gift not a curse. Throughout junior high we studied together at each other's houses (mostly mine, though Mom watched us closely). We'd sit around the kitchen table talking and laughing, and one night she taught me how to fast dance real good while my sisters watched. All of us under bright kitchen lights dancing and laughing, but I couldn't do the slow dancing with her. I tried, and holding her close, smelling her hair on my cheek, was just too much for me—no way would I get drawn back in. When we entered high school, she often set me up with her girlfriends, and so that's how Marlene and I got together.

Marlene has this reddish brown hair which knocks me out, 'auburn' she tells me, and she usually keeps it in a pony tail. I'd sit in English class and just stare at her, check out the neckline of her blouse, her bare legs below her skirt, but mostly I'd watch her face and hair. She has the kind of female beauty that only gets better the longer you look. On our second date to the movies, I'm walking her home up what's called Hunky Hill, and I stop under a street light and tell her, "I think I'm in love with your pony tail."

She has this great laugh she'd been holding back on till then, and it's followed by our first kiss under that street light. Her father, Ernie, is Irish and works on the railroad with my dad. Her mom is pure Slovak and a great cook—cabbage rolls, pirogue, and these homemade sweet rolls she bakes on Friday nights. On those nights, I am there and inside their little house.

We are sophomores, sixteen, and both of us learning to touch each other in undiscovered ways. We hold hands, kiss good night at the door, and each time I stay longer, talk less, hug each other more, holding on to something real yet magical. After a couple months, I'm allowed in to sit with her late on the couch. And we explore, while her father snores down the hallway. One time I remember he gets up and goes into the bathroom in his underwear muttering something like "It's getting late, you two," but Marlene just rolls her eyes and presses her lips to my neck. I touch her breasts this night and get hard right there on the couch. Later I beat myself up over it and apologize to her the next morning, but she just smiles then gives me the deepest kiss we've ever made, right there at the school door.

I like her family a lot, her little brother and sister, but I do feel like I've invaded them, come not just to taste but to take their Marlene. She is smart, an A and B student, college prep. She watches the news at night and reads a lot. Thankfully my mom likes her, calls her "Sweetie" when she helps in the kitchen, fixing dessert or cleaning up. We are a couple, going steady. We go to dances, sit together in the stands, and hold hands as we go out the school doors. The fact that she's an Eastern Byzantine Catholic doesn't seem to matter so much. In our mill town no one gets off thinking they're that much better than the rest, except maybe my grandma Pullman, but heck, Grandpa works as a rigger in the mill alongside of my dad.

I've given up my paper route, sold it to Sharon's brother for five bucks, which he's long ago paid me. I cut grass for older neighbors now, and actually I've babysat a few times for my parents' friends and at the funeral home. Easiest job ever, 'cause the kids are already in bed. I watch tv, call Marlene on their phone, fall asleep, wake up as they come in the door and collect my pay. Then one night the little Fox girl comes sleepwalking down the stairs and yells when I stop her at the front door, wakes her up baby sister, and suddenly it's more than I can handle, so I call Mom, and Gretchen, Mrs. Fox, comes right over. Now Gretchen is a real looker, cute, with a nice little ass in tight slacks, a real 'fox' for sure. I check her out pretty good and wonder how the Foxes could ever be friends with my parents.

Like I said, Marlene and I go only so far—sexually, stopping at the gate though enjoying the ride that takes us there. And my affection for her is real. She is my girl and I her guy—though at times, we stand at our lockers and argue over what she said and to whom. She wants me to study more, hang out less at the pool hall. But we're a school couple, go to all the dances together, and are basically good for each other.

*   *   *

The summer before our junior year Marlene works as a playground teacher, and, because I've already learned to drive, I pick up this job delivering groceries for Pesta's market. I drive their old beater of a pickup truck, stick shift, buy hey, most cars are stick. Anyway, I'm working here at telling about our sex life, Marlene and me. On this scorcher of a day in August I pull up to this gas station out in the country out Ghould's Road, and sitting on a bench outside is this couple no older or younger than me or Marlene. As I sit in the cab checking off the order items I can see they are really going at it, making out like crazy right there in the sun. Kissing, yes, but feeling, and then she leans her head back as he slides his hand up her little skirt, and she just lets him, actually is urging him on by how she moves her little body. I start sweating, my chest pounding like it's me and not him out there. I close my eyes and the girl is both her and Marlene. Finally they get up and go behind the building, and me, I have to wait five minutes before I can get out and deliver any groceries.

This same week, I swear, I get an order from this trailer court out of town on Altamont Hill. I've never been there, though I've heard of it. Nothing fancy—trailers, not mobile homes. I find the right number, park in the driveway or yard, you can't tell. In the box is just some bread and eggs and well, women's napkins. So I go up to the door and knock, and pretty soon this really cute girl answers—brunette, dark tan, magic brown eyes. And holy Christ, she's in her baby doll pajamas, short and so sheer in the sunlight I can see through to her breasts and panties. I can't speak, but she motions me in—only she and I in that little trailer with just the sunlight through the dirty windows. I sit the box down on the counter and hold the bill in my nervous hand waiting for her to come for it. She takes it, looks up at me with those deep brown eyes, then turns and walks slowly back towards the bedroom. I'm so dazed, I follow her back, when suddenly she spins round and puts her hand on my chest: "Wait a minute, fella," she says, "I'm just getting my wallet."

I'm staring at her legs and still feeling her hand though she's moved it away. Finally I swallow my spit and take a step back to the door. Speechless, I take her ten dollars and make change. "Boy," she says smiling, "what just happened here?"

"I don't know," I answer, turn, and try to walk to the car. My brother is not going to believe this. I play this scene back in my head all afternoon—and that night in bed. But how come I lust after these two women and not Marlene? Well, yeah, I care about Marlene, maybe love her, but then why am I lusting after these other women? Is this natural? I don't tell any of this to Marlene, and I don't talk about Marlene to any of the other guys either. When they brag about themselves and drag some girl down, I'm quiet. Maybe it's 'cause I'm this love-child myself, and maybe I do love Marlene. I'm not sure. Truth is Marlene and I never have intercourse, though we come so close—only our clothes save us. That girl has the greatest back to just look at on a beach, and sometimes I let my hand cruise down her back bone like a boat. And her thighs—they're so soft and smooth, sometimes you just have to kiss them. And, okay, one day at Jefferson Park, in the sweaty back seat of Dad's Pontiac, Marlene's two piece swim suit slips off to the floor, but honest, I just drank her body with my eyes and hands, and we just squeezed each other tighter and went no further. I swear.

*   *   *

Then one night before our senior year begins, the guys and I are playing cards in our kitchen. My folks have taken the girls and gone over for dinner at Grandma's, and they've left me the place for our weekly euchre game. Kenny, Bobby, Jerome and I get together at each other's houses. This night we are listening to The Yardbird's *For Your Love* album and drinking tall glasses of iced tea. I've made a bushel of popcorn, and you can smell it strong and feel the oil on the cards. Anyway, this is the scene when we hear this knock on the back porch door...and I open to find Marlene and Sharon standing there giggling in shorts and halter tops.

"We're busting this party," Sharon announces in this low man's voice, brushing past me. "You're all under arrest!" And they stand there acting tough and so damn cute. I pat Sharon "hey" on the shoulder and then steal a kiss from Marlene.

"My gosh," Kenny yells, "I was afraid it was a panty raid!" Everyone laughs. Sharon makes like she's after him, and he calls, "Wait, I ain't wearing any." More laughs.

I bring a couple chairs in from the living room for the girls. Guys are great, but girls can be wonderful. Marlene stands at the counter leaning on me, stroking my sleeveless arm. The Yardbirds are singing "For Your Love," and I'm feeling really happy.

"What do they do anyway on these panty raids?" Jerome asks, taking another handful of popcorn.

"The college guys invented it, you see," Kenny says like he really knows. "They break into the women's dorms, and well, I hear it can get pretty wild." He grins over at the girls. "They grab panties out of their drawers, and well, some girls take them off and toss them to the guys."

"Kind of like a Tom Jones concert," Bobby says, and we all laugh.

"Hey, Ken," I ask, "Where'd you get to be such an expert...on college life?"

He actually blushes and lowers his head, "I read about it somewhere."

"Where?" Sharon asks.

"Yeah, where?" I want to know.

"*Playboy* magazine," he confesses to a round of laughs. "I really don't know nothing about no college. Do any of you?"

Silence, then Marlene speaks up, "Well, I know I'm going there, and not for the panty raids. I want to be a teacher."

Another silence, then Sharon says, "If I can get a scholarship, I'm going to that business college in Weirton."

We guys are struck dumb—none of us with a real plan beyond getting through our senior year.

"How about you, guys?" Marlene asks. "How about you, Mr. Lee McCall?"

I can't believe we've never talked about any of this or that she'd dare bring it up here in front of everyone. I know that left to ourselves, we guys would never discuss this, not while playing cards. "I honestly don't know," I admit looking around the room, ending by staring into Marlene's probing eyes.

"You should consider college," Sharon says. "You're really smart, Lee."

Bobby, who is our muscle man and the best athlete of our bunch pipes up, "Well, I'm joining the Marines. I figure I'll get drafted anyway, so I'm going to do my service now." He looks over at Kenny and me, "You guys registered for the draft haven't you?"

"Ugh, don't remind me," Kenny says shaking his head.

"Eighteen and ready to be wasted," I joke and look over to Jerome.

"Well, I hear Nixon's promising to end the draft and then we'll have an all volunteer army."

I look over at Bobby, "Sorry, man, but I have to say it. I know your brothers are all serving and I respect that, but I don't see how they'll ever get enough volunteers to fight in this dirty war."

Nothing, then Jerome says, "Well, I hear the mill is hiring, or I might go to work on the railroad like my old man, if I can get on. The army will have to come and get me."

Bobby laughs, "Oh, they just might, my friend," then looking around at all of us, "They just might."

Kenny sighs, "I don't know. I might go to Steubenville College, close to home. I'll ride out this, pardon me, lousy war on a double S student deferment." Then he gives a big grin, "To tell the truth, I don't know what I want to be when I grow up."

Then they all look at me.

"What is this, an inquisition?" I ask, only half joking. "You girls come over here in hot pants and halters to get our attention, then turn us into a bunch of egg-heads ...'considering our options' and all. I just don't get it."

"Lee," Marlene whispers sharply, but I'm feeling pressed and uncertain, so I ignore her. She shakes her pretty head at me.

Someone has slipped on an old Everly Brothers' album and "Bye, Bye, Love" comes on as I look straight at her, "Mar, I honestly don't have a plan. I can't see beyond starting school Monday. This is my life here and now...with you." We all wait a long moment for something that never comes.

"Gheez!" Kenny finally jokes, "Should we leave the room?"

We get back to the cards, and the girls actually pair up. They even win a couple hands but lose the round. Finally at 9:30, everyone leaves before my folks get home. Sharon waits on the porch while inside I kiss Marlene goodbye, but when I go to hold her, she's somehow stiff, and turns away.

"I'll see you at school," she says and goes out.

*   *   *

What finally breaks us up, I'm not sure. We're together that September of our senior year, then we start arguing in and out of school, less to talk about—and suddenly it's over, another curtain falls. When I drive over to talk, she meets me at the back door, hands me my ring, says we can be friends and she'll always remember me— need I go on? I keep calling and leaving messages for a while, then after a month, we both agree it was a good ride we shared and that we taught each other a lot. Mom is really upset about our breaking it off, and for a while I think she'd rather have Marlene as a daughter than me as a son. No question, I am really bummed out those months and drive my family nuts playing all the saddest songs I can find on Dave's record player, just lying in bed staring at the walls. Finally, I begin to think I'm getting over it when Bobby comes over and tells me from his car parked outside of our house that Marlene and Billy Matthews, the doctor's son, have done it, gone all the way. I am physically sick and puke right there on the sidewalk. Bobby jumps out and puts his arm around me, "You okay?" he asks.

"No I'm not," I say and groan or moan, I can't tell which I'm so dizzy sick.

"God, I'm sorry," he says and really means it, 'cause Bobby never says anything he doesn't mean.

That night in the back yard, I burn all her notes to me and all of our pictures while the mill roars on. Mom is looking down from the kitchen window at me talking to the night. It really hurts, physically too, a knife to the heart, and then her cutting them off by doing it with Billy Matthews. Ah, Sharon...Ah, Marlene...Ah, funny life without laughter.

Chapter Three

College Life

My brother is a better student than me, or I. All through school, he'd come along a year after me, erasing all my accomplishments with his achievements—my making the honor role with his being voted Outstanding Eighth Grade Boy, my making the basketball team with his starting his freshman year. I'm not really jealous of him, just have this smaller image of myself. We are the same height, for a while we both had flat tops, a real David and Ricky Nelson thing going on. My folks' friends still get us mixed up. Anyway, as the oldest, I am the first to go to college. It's been our dad's own lost dream, ever since Mom got pregnant with me when she was 17 and he 19. He followed Grandpa McCall right into the mill on the railroad, and though he never seemed to regret it, we know he's now giving us our chance to fulfill his dream.

Oh, I got the $200 scholarship to old Steubenville College that anyone in the top 10% of their class gets; Kenny took it and is using it. But again Dad had other plans. Ohio University down in Athens County was his, shall we say, suggestion. Grandpa Ernie was from around there, and it turns out he'd left Dad a little money to "get the boys a good education." I've been really so dumb about the whole thing, I just did what others wanted. "Go to college" had become my plan halfway through senior year, kind of in answer to Marlene's rejection of me, but I have no idea what I'll do once I get there. Mom has fought the whole idea, not our getting an education so much as the fact that all the family money will now be channeled into that, and not a new or even a better house. What can I say or do? I just filled out the forms and waited.

"Let him go to Steubenville College. He can live at home," she pleads. "He can still get his diploma." None of us knew then that it was called a degree, not a diploma. None of us knew anything about college, except what we saw in the old movies..."Joy in the Morning," "Where the Boys Are" –Hollywood stuff. Once I was accepted at OU, I got my list of "What to Bring to College," and we had a good laugh over that—umbrella, trench coat, a suit and sports jacket—I mean, we aren't hicks or the poorest folks in town, but I'd never owned any of this, except Grandpa's old suit jacket which had been cut down for me after he died. That list was a real challenge, but Mom surprised me here in that she went out and bought most of it. "We're good people, you hear," she said breaking the tags off my Sears trench coat. "And I won't have others looking down on us." To tell the truth, I came to love that trench coat, tan and with a plaid lining, and okay, I admit, I slept in it the first night.

The night before I leave, Sharon shows up to say so long. We sit out on the porch swing and talk for a long time remembering things, then she rises to leave but stops and turns around and gives me this warm kiss on the lips. "Take care of yourself, Lee," she whispers, "Write and call me anytime. I'll miss you."

Dad drives me down that first time. Four hours from home, a day's travel down roads that wind along the river and over what Dad calls 'hill and holler,' deep into real Appalachia. When we pass a road sign to McCarthur, he gets off Rte. 50, the main road, and we see cabins and shacks back in the woods. Driving down roads that look like paths, over creeks on homemade bridges, clothes hung out front on lines, he looks over at me and smiles, "This is where your folks come from...at least on the McCall side."

"Yep," I say. "I bet I'll meet some of them while I'm here," really hoping I won't. Hell, I'm going to college, not moving back into the hills. Back on Rte. 50, we near Athens following the Hocking River. "At least I'll have a river nearby," I say looking over at him and sensing a wave of missing home. All week I've been torn between anticipation and regret. Finally at the dorm Dad and I carry my two bags up two flights of stairs, and we discover that we've forgotten everything ...no sheets or pillows or lamp or waste basket. Mom had all of those things packed for us, but we'd left them in a box in the hall. And so we go out to find a Five and Dime, where we buy a sheet and pillow and waste basket.

"Maybe your roommate'll have a lamp you could share," Dad says as I catch him counting the ones left in his wallet. He has worn his blue suit jacket to the college, but he seems too large for the dormitory room, and he soon grows restless. So we go out on the front steps. We stand there breathing it all in, this college world. Then Dad smiles, squeezes my arm once, and says, "I best be getting back up the road. You'll do fine, son."

"Yeah, right," I say, then watch my father drive the old Pontiac down the tree lined street and out of sight. I stand there a long time, then turn and climb the stairs up to my room: two desks, a bunk bed, with my things already spread on the bottom bunk. I lie back and look over at the closet, my sports and trench coats hanging there like strangers.

Dad proves right, my roommate Tom does bring a lamp, but he doesn't share it or anything else he's brought, including the sandwiches which his family's 'maid'—can you believe it—has packed for him. I swear, wrapped in wax paper and cut into four neat squares without any crust. Later that night, before we go to sleep, I ask him, "Hey, Tom. Why did you come to Ohio U, and not some rich school back East?" He is from Pittsburgh and could have gone east or west.

He crosses his legs, sitting at his desk, and begins taking off his socks, then he sighs as if it takes great effort. "Two things, my friend." He has this thing of always numbering things for me like I'm taking notes. "One, both of my parents are alums of this place." I remember what alums means, though our family scores a zero on the alum account. "And number two, I didn't have the grades to go where I wanted, which was Brown University in Providence, Rhode Island. Does that answer your question, Leroy?"

"Oh, it's just Lee," I say, "Yes, it does...sufficiently, my good friend," the last a little joke to myself as I ease down into my pillow and sleep.

This Tom is a skinny kid about the size of my oldest sister, Janie. He's quick in his movements, always watching behind him, and spends most of his time searching for anything to do but studying: hanging around the rec room, playing cards and pool, watching the tube. Me, I'm so afraid of flunking out and losing my one chance and disgracing the family that I study harder than I ever did in high school. I read all my assignments, underlining everything, and even study in the library after dinner. Two reasons: One, the quiet, of course, and Two, the girls who prowl the stacks or sit across from me in short skirts with lovely legs.

When my dorm mates ask me my major, I say, "Not sure...General Studies for now." Back home, I'll tell them "Co-eds," then say, "College girls. I'm studying the women." When I finally call home to Sharon she tells me that Marlene has disappeared to some education school in West Virginia. "Good for her," I say like I don't care and try to mean it. Sharon and I are closer now; she writes me often and we talk on the phone once a week. And then one weekend at the end of September she comes down to stay with Patty Millhouse, from our class. Patty and I are two of the ten from our class who went on from Central High to college. She's studying nursing, and Jay her boyfriend is in the Army.

Anyway, Sharon really comes down to visit me, not Patty. And we do all sorts of things I've never done...hang out in bars listening to hard rock bands, dance into the night, and in the early morning, walk the streets of Athens, watching people. We sit outside a café on Court Street and make bets on who is college and who is local. It isn't as easy as you might think, 'cause the college kids from the suburbs up north take on the clothes and look of the locals.

It is marijuana time in Southern Ohio, and the townies are growing it on farms and woods and selling it on street corners. The cops seem to just look the other way down here, like it's another crop, and it is. On the night before Sharon is to leave, we smoke some that I buy from a guy at a kegger at a house on Congress Street. A crowd has gathered around their front porch and yard, and though we aren't invited, everybody is so stoned that nobody asks. Sharon is the cutest girl there, dressed in her flowered blouse and little Levi skirt that just covers her you know what, and guys keep coming on to her. Finally she comes over to me on the porch couch and sits right on my lap.

"You don't mind, do you?" she whispers in my ear, and I know I don't have to answer. I breathe her soft hair and feel her body warmth. I look in her eyes, and we are both sure we are going to hell. When the marijuana starts kicking in, we begin a laugh that just won't stop as we rock back and forth holding each other. "What am I going to tell them...back on the farm?" she asks which sends us off into another string of laughing. The Animals are singing "The House of the Rising Sun," and we both point to a sunburst over the front door and break up again. I love holding her, feeling her laughter, her warm soft breasts against my arm. We are being swept by a wave. It is the best time we've ever had together.

When the night has blown away, I walk her down the hill holding hands and we're trying to sing, like school kids. At Patty's dorm we look up to see Patty staring down at us. I think everyone back home knows our story of being half brother and sister, so we drop hands, wave to Patty and step into the doorway where I say good night and steal one sweet kiss from her so willing lips.

Walking back to the dorm, I am high and know I won't sleep. *What am I getting into...can I shut it off? Do I even want to?* I start to curse my dad and her mom for what they did to us, but then smile...without their love making there wouldn't be a Sharon. I lie back in bed, and *Ain't life sweet* becomes my mantra into sleep.

The next morning, I meet her and Patty at the bus station. It is early and none of us has had coffee. I want to scare some up at the little health food place next door, but don't want to waste the time away from her. She is wearing tight jeans and a little black jacket. The weather has turned cold in late September. Patty is talking too much about school, and I feel like gagging her. Sharon, comes close to me and touches my sleeve. She squeezes my arm and smiles. "Lee," she whispers, holding on, "You don't have to wait."

"What else have I got to do?" I ask, one of the lamest things I'd ever said. So I speak true, "I really love your coming down here. Last night was the best I've felt...ever."

"Me too," she says looking right into my dark eyes with her baby blues. I don't dare hug her, but I take her hand and hold it till the bus is ready to board. This time it's she who offers the kiss, one that goes beyond the 5 second rule and one I so willingly accept. Watching her bus pull out, I feel things pulling at me from all sides.

Patty and I walk down the hill to the campus together and without a word. I both love and hate this college town, living this college life.

Well, my concentration is totally blown after that great weekend, and it's not from the weed we smoked. I see Sharon's face when I close my eyes and on the bodies of campus girls. I can't help myself. I look down at my books and up again at the light, the windows, the clusters of orange and green leaves outside. Do I belong here where words and numbers and ideas mean so much? Couldn't I just move back home and take a job in the mill or on the railroad with my father and Jerome? What's to become of Sharon and me? The next night I take my marijuana bag down by the river which winds around this campus, and I sit on the bank and smoke a bowl alone while watching the waters flow and remembering that sweet, sweet night with Sharon and wondering where my life is headed.

*　　　*　　　*

I am struggling at school right now. Yeah, the protest of the war in Nam is heating up: protest signs on buildings, demonstrations on campus and there's been a national moratorium in Boston, and another's planned for D.C. I stand with the local rallies, and I know some guys who went to Boston, but my struggle is more about just being here at OU. It's been two months already and not once do any of my classes include my world. Here we are in the heart of Appalachia, and yet the university seems to turn its back on it. Only once in my intro to sociology course does the professor even discuss working people, or the "working-class" and then only to place them and me into our "socio-economic class." He asks us to write down where we think ourselves to be...upper, middle, lower, etc. Then he draws this big pie chart on the board—and describes each level. In his status driven vision I fall from average or middle-middle to maybe middle-lower at best. And this wouldn't have been so bad except for the hidden disdain in his voice as he talks of it. "Now what do these people need to do to rise?" No answer, so he asks, "How many of you are first generation college students?" And a reluctant show of hands rise, about a third of the class. "And you, my friends, by raising your educational level may move up a class to a better life." My own hand comes down as I think of what that might mean. *Would I no longer belong back home, would I lose my world, betray it for his so-called "better life?"*

I'm trying to swallow all of this down when a voice from the back of the room calls out, "Dr. Hunter." It's Ned one of the locals taking classes. "Can I ask you, sir,...which piece of the pie is the best?"

Hunter is taken back a moment, then responds, "Well, I'm not choosing for you," while raising his right palm to the obvious, "but you can see for yourself."

"Yeah, well, I'm just wondering," Ned says, "Tell me this, Doc, how you going to know that without first tasting each piece of the pie?" The hush that falls is finally broken by a laughter that borders on applause, and I look at grinning Ned as a new friend here.

Needless to say, this displaced person thing I'm feeling keeps me awake at night, makes studying calculus unreal, conjugating verbs in Spanish a senseless game. When we study the history of civilizations, the working people are seen as slaves or the "proletariat." And none of it fits the people I know, none of them sit around plotting revolution, calling themselves comrades or dreaming of rising up in the world. *Is college supposed to stir up all of this? And where do I belong?*

Tom doesn't help much with any of this. His rich, upper class world is safe, all he has to do is stay in school to be part of it. However, his own social deviance, a term from Soc. 101, might put him at risk. One afternoon I come back from class to find he's taken down his cork bulletin board and is pinning things to it—houseflies it turns out. Now, Tom is no biologist nor entomologist, and I see right away that his intention falls much lower than that. He is torturing them by pouring lighter fluid over their bodies and igniting them. I watch in disbelief and disgust, then yell, "Get your crazy Hitler ass out of here!" He scoops up his private holocaust and takes it out onto the yard where others gather and cheer. I begin to watch my back with him from then on. Sorry, but one way or another, Tom is not going to be my roommate by winter quarter—if I am still around.

When Sharon calls, we catch up on things—who she's seen around town, how Kenny and Jerome are doing. She's doing great at West Virginia Business College and has taken a part-time job at Nosset Photo Studio keeping records and setting up private shootings for the boss. When he asked her if she'd pose, she refused. "I wasn't going there," she said, "didn't need any job that bad." Sharon has been taking photos herself since eighth grade when she won the $20 prize for the Woman's Club essay contest. Before her old man could lay hands on the cash, she'd gone uptown and bought herself a good Kodak camera. She has dreams still.

"Are you seeing anyone?" I ask, holding my breath.

"No, not really," she says, "How about you?"

"Nope," is all I manage to say.

Then she tells me of a party she'd gone to with some of the girls from school. "Guess what...Lee, we were smoking pot," she laughs, "and listening to music when that song came on...'House of the Rising Sun' you know." There is a long silence on both ends, and I can hear her breathing.

"God, I miss you, Lee," she gasps. "When are you coming home?"

"Home and you are all I can think about," I confess and feel my own chest open, "I miss you so damn much, I dream your face." We both know we are crossing some kind of line saying this, but suddenly a free wind blows through us. "Sharon," I say, "I hate this place. I don't belong here. My roommate's a deviant, and they just want us all to be middle class morons and live in the suburbs. I don't belong here."

"No, Lee," she surprises me. "Don't give it all up. What I'd give to be there with you studying the whole world. I'm at a trade school here, and I know it's just two steps away from a job in bookkeeping or managing the lingerie department at Penney's."

"But I don't fit in," I insist. "There's no ground to stand on here." I am almost in tears saying this out loud to the person I care most for.

"Listen, Lee...Lee, take a deep breath," she instructs me. "I...care about you, Lee and we'll be together soon. I'll come down again or you'll come home for Thanksgiving. Hold on, please...please."

I take those deep breaths, but my heart is just bursting. I'm calling from the student union and the whole place frankly smells of hamburger. Finally "I will...hold on," comes out of me, then, "I'll do it for you. Oh Christ, Sharon. I care for you."

More silent breathing, then, "I have to hang up now, Lee. My dad's home. I'll write to you, tonight, I promise."

That night I smoke the rest of my pot and throw the bag in the river. Instead of laughter, tears come and a deep sobbing like I'd only known when Grandpa died in that hospital room. Back in my room I crawl into bed with my clothes on. Last night I heard Tom crawl into his bunk late with some muffled crying; tonight he is nowhere around, so I play his Dinah Washington album on his stereo..."What a difference a day makes... 24 little hours...." I feel like crying myself. I want a new day.

As the weeks go on, I see less and less of Tom. At first I assume he's been working on his books, but I'm wrong. He's been sleeping around, if you know what I mean. They keep hours at the girls' dorm here, figuring that will keep us guys in line, but Tom's sleeping around is in the guy's dorm. I pick up on something of this from the strange way others are treating me in the hallway or the cafeteria. There is no logic to it. "My roommate's a homosexual, not me," I want to yell at them, but they don't deserve a response. There is a real silence around the whole thing, a real closet to be sure. If I am getting these bad vibes, what must be happening to Tom? This is a big state university with some 10,000 men; some are bound to be gay, but it is still the 1960's and Ohio. Back home no one in my class ever "came out'"as gay, and if they had, they'd probably have their face smashed in by thugs.

Okay, so Tom is peeking out of his gay closet; it probably explains some of his other deviance and self-destruction. Listen to me, I'm beginning to think like a sociologist, but I'll admit I am rather ticked off that I'd been played along like this. So one morning when he is just coming in the door, I confront him, "Hey, man. Where you been? I hardly ever see you anymore."

He shirks, begins gathering his soap and shampoo for the shower. He looks even thinner, his eyes wider and wilder. "Don't worry, man. I won't be around much longer."

"Why, what's up?" I ask rising from my bunk.

"They're onto me," is all he says and tramps down the hall to the shower. I don't get him at all, you know, but I don't want to see anyone expelled. Only minutes later I hear yelling down the hallway, and go out to witness Tom running back naked with his face bloodied. He is cursing between tears, and I hand him my towel. His nose is bleeding; above his eye is torn flesh.

"You want to have that taken care of," I say, "We can walk you down to the health center."

"No," he mumbles, his face bleeding into the towel that Mom had bought me.

"Want me to get the R.A.?"

"No!" he gasps. "I can't afford another incident report."

He sits down at his desk and I stand over him. Ironically this is the closest we've ever been in our three months of living together. He isn't acting and I'm not afraid. I'd never known anyone openly homosexual before, but to me he isn't gay, he's Tom. And like me, he's struggling.

I cut class that morning to be with him, and we talk. He says he's known he was gay since junior high but told no one. In high school he'd found the theatre and friends. Though most kids knew, his parents didn't or wouldn't. "They were too busy with their stupid lives to notice," he says. "And I was still a virgin till I met Brad. At first we'd just kiss and hug...in the men's room at school. Then Brad and I started 'studying' in my room or his." He looks up at me, "You know what I'm saying?"

"Yeah, I get you," I lie 'cause I'm really getting a little dizzy from hearing all of this. It is so unreal to me and I try not to see it in my mind—two naked guys holding each other. I can't shut it out. All I do is sit there and listen for what must be an hour. All I can say is, when I look at Tom afterwards, he's a different person. The stiffness and pretense are gone from his face. In the worst of circum-stances we have bonded, two outsiders in a way. His rebellion has already cost him at school; as Dad might say, 'He'd cut the legs out from under him.' But strangely after our talk, I find Tom awake in the morning and we begin to walk to class together. He still disappears some, but often I do find him studying at his desk, so I begin to work with him. We decide that his best hope is to pass a couple classes this quarter and petition for re-admission.

In some ways college is like the military or a prison—full of expectations and regulations someone has already made for you. Both hang over your head pushing you on.

You go to college or Vietnam. You declare a major and they hand you a check sheet. And you have to do the walk when necessary, learn the scales if you ever want to play jazz, stay in college or be sent to Nam. I guess I picked up on this early on. My two infractions at OU so far are smoking pot and how I feel about Sharon. Both of these I keep hidden.

Chapter Four
College Work

Things continue for me at college with my one foot planted at home, the other barely on the ground of this new world. Soon money issues arise uniting the two. By October I've spent what I'd earned that summer. I don't want to ask my folks for any, so I put in an application to work the dining hall. Based on need alone, not skill (though none was needed), I am hired right away at the Kingston Dormitory hall.

When I walk into the huge kitchen, the older women cooks gleam at me in the bright lights and point to the front. I can smell tomato sauce cooking, steam rising from boiling pots of water. Then I meet Chance who's twenty-one and a college veteran of the football program. Right off he tells me how he banged up his knees in the summer practice a couple years ago and lost his scholarship. He's a solid looking guy with big arms which he uses to hand me my white apron. "This here is your work partner," and I look around only he's pointing to the large stainless steel dishwashing machine. Next we rinse and rack some pots, then run them through the machine which gushes like a miniature car wash.

"As they say, 'It ain't rocket science,' my friend. Any job you can learn in 3 minutes...foretells a limited future," he jokes, but he also sees how quick I get on with the machine. I start to fumble with some dirty dishes, "Hey, sport, spray them first. That's step number one. One of us will pull in the trays, separate the silverware into racks, then spray and slide the dishes and trays over to be racked. Second man racks then runs them through like I been showing you. Third guy unracks and stacks them. 1-2-3— Got it?"

I nod, watching him press the lever, then when the rack emerges through the steamy heat, juggle the dishes with his big hands into stacks on carts.

"Tonight, you can start at the end here. Murray will be in around five, just before we open. He's a local, enrolled in engineering. It's the three of us. One of us will help you tonight, but then you're on your own, brother. We rotate the positions, so you'll learn them all quickly. Oh, here's Murray."

Murray and I exchange raised-chin "Hey's," and he does not speak the rest of the night, he is short and thin, but man, is he quick. With both of their help, I have it down after 20 minutes. A week later I learn that Murray and my roommate Tom are close friends.

No, this isn't a career I am learning here, but in hefting those racks and shuffling the dishes, sorting spoons and forks and knives, I find something familiar—physical work. My body comes back as we move, handling the rush, doing what has to be done. All thinking is practical here not lofty and abstract. Here and now, anticipation and quick response. I feel at home.

Around seven, when we begin shutting down, Chance nudges me. "You done good, kid. You got a future in dishes." He is a real joker.

"I'll take it," I yell back over the machine.

Then he pokes me and points to the waitresses hanging up their aprons in the kitchen closet. As they stretch up, their skirts rise above the backs of their knees, oh so nicely. "We has our perks, my boy," he smiles and we laugh together.

As I walk back to the men's dorm, the work feels good in my arms, and I watch the leaves of brown, green, and gold falling all around me, transforming the campus lanes into a friendly world. The Halloween Weekend is coming that weekend.

When I tell Sharon over the phone the news about the work, she listens then just says, "That's great, but study hard, you hear." When I tell her the story of Tom, she asks, "What are you going to do about it?"

"Nothing, I'm down with it. He's just a kid, and my roommate."

"Well, please be careful, Lee," she sighs. "You're in a different place. You don't know everything, and ..."

"Yeah, I will be careful...for you," I whisper. "Listen, I'll soon be able to send you a bus ticket."

"Oh, that would be so good. But, listen, I can buy my own ticket. Let's plan it now though, so I can imagine."

"Well, come Thanksgiving we're at quarter break, and I'll be home a whole month."

"Maybe you can get a ride home with Patty?" she suggests.

"Yeah, I'll ask around first, and I'm thinking of just hitching it. I see lots of guys doing that with their little suitcase and handmade sign."

"Oh, be careful, Lee. I don't want anything to happen to you."

"Yeah, my sign will say 'Take me home safely to Sharon.'"

"Well," she laughs, "that won't go over well back here," then adds, "You're just kidding, right?"

"Yes, I'm kidding, but I wish to God that I could just announce it like that."

Silence connects us. "I miss you too," she sighs, and I feel joy and pain at once in my chest and throat.

Today I have to go pick up my grades from my advisor I've never met before, so I go and sit in his cramped office surrounded by his old books, as this complete stranger reads me my grades and looks me over the whole time. I have managed "B"s in everything, including calculus which I now hate, but an "A" in one course surprises him and me. "An A from Dr. Lombard in freshman Comp & Lit, that's quite an accomplishment, young man. I guess you're doing alright, especially for a first term freshman." And that's how he sees me, as another advisee; finally he hands me the slip of paper so I can escape.

The one class that I'm really into is the lit and writing, one of the most hated, with all that reading and writing. It surprises me too that I love it. I do. We read the classics of literature, then write about them in essays or "themes." We've read the *Odyssey* by Homer, a great adventure story, and I swear I am at the movies again in my head journeying with Kirk Douglas as young-old Ulysses. He too has his left his heart back home with his Penelope. And she, working on her weaving, is resisting those nasty suitors. I get right into it, or it gets into me. When we write about the quest theme, it all seems so obvious, and well, relevant. Next comes Dante's *Divine Comedy*, translated by John Ciardi. Heck the book even gives you notes to help keep track, but I begin to see students carrying those little yellow and black Cliff-notes, not to class but in the library or back in the dorms.

Dante's Beatrice, well I guess you can figure who that is, and me, I'm struggling through the rings of hell in life. I can taste the fiery hell smoke, see it all in the grit of the mill—monstrous blast furnaces booming their fire and Bessemer ovens casting out their orange-pink glow all over the valley. This eerie world of sin and sinners is all too real to me. Tom and I discuss it in our room, he protesting the rings, me questioning it, saying life all feels like limbo now. My essay on "Fire and Beauty" gets an A.

In truth, I've been writing most of my life, even before those poems in seventh grade. I'd been doing poems in a little notebook I've kept like a journal. Only Sharon and, well, Marlene for a while, have seen any of it. The poems are about the valley life, the places and people I know there. Of course, some of my struggles got into the poems, and some, sure, are love poems to 'her,' my Beatrice and Penelope. And here on campus I've become a letter writer, writing to all of my family and friends—Kenny, Jerome, Dave, Mom and Dad together, even my sisters Janie and Diane, and, of course, to Sharon. I start out writing with something I want to tell, and the pen will pause a moment, and after that I go on writing out my life for myself as much as for them. In the words on the page I find me and my path.

Chapter Five
Hitching Home

Halloween was really wild here, an Ohio Mardi Gras, with people in bizarre costumes and beer and pot everywhere. Then with the Thanksgiving holiday comes the quarter break. The campus has been alive with protests against the war, some I know are headed to another national moratorium in D.C., but I'm headed home with my suitcase and sign, "Home to Steubenville," the closest city to Mingo. Tom's parents have sent him a bus ticket, but it isn't clear whether he'll take it or try to stay in the dorm with the foreign exchange students. They not only don't get our Thanksgiving holiday, but also have no home to go to. So this Wednesday morning, I get a ride with some frat boys out of town to State Street and Rte. 50 East, where I sit my suitcase up at my feet and stick out my thumb in the cool November breeze. My sweater and hooded parka are fine till a semi blows past with a gush of wind that leaves me shaking in the autumn sun. I paint a hitcher's smile on my face and wait.

The first real ride comes from an older guy in a Buick, a salesman for textbooks who says he'll take me as far as Marietta. Big guy with a reddish face, lights up a cigarette every ten minutes. "Gotta quit, I know," he says, then offers me one. Rides aren't free, I soon learn, you're expected to listen to their life and to tell your own. This guy gets to the point rather quick, "So what's it like being on your own like that—lots of drugs and free love, huh?" Is he asking or telling me?

"Mostly I study and work," I say, staring at the dial of the car clock. "I'm headed home to my family," I add, putting the weight on the last word, trying to steer my own course here.

"Yeah, I'm not supposed to give you guys rides, you know—company car and all." He pushes the lighter in and slips another Pall Mall into his mouth. "But I do it anyway...give you fellows free rides and all."

I get it. I owe him something. "Well, grass is pretty cheap down here, and homegrown," I say, "and there are some wild parties, oh yeah, and panty raids." I have him with that and spin some fantasy fiction for him.

"No shit, kid" he says and gets quiet for a long while, painting his own lurid scenes as the car speeds along, rolling over these woody Appalachian foothills. And then he announces, "I'm bi—you know," grinning over at me like it's a real turn on or something. I stare out the window and let it pass.

Then outside of Marietta, he tunes the radio into some country gospel station, and I am almost asleep when I feel his hand on my thigh, "What are you...pretty good size?"

I sit up quick, push his big hand away, "Hey, man, I ain't into that." He puts his hand back. *What do I do now? This guy's a creep and won't stop.* "Let me out," I yell. "Let me out right here."

"Calm down, boy. I was just being friendly. I'll take you as far as Sistersville."

"No," I bark at him. "Let me out, right here at this stop sign." We are on one of Marietta's tree lined avenues.

"Okay, bub, if that's the way you want it," he says and stops the car quick. I push open my door, jump out and am standing there in the middle of the street as he pushes my suitcase out to my feet. "You're on your own from here, college boy," he shouts and drives off.

I stand there sweating and a little shaky as I watch his car disappear. Tom has been my gay roommate for three months now and not once put a move on me. This sap is trying to live his fantasies.

It turns out to be a long stretch into town before I can pick up Rte. 7 north. When I do get downtown, I get a quick pickup, but it's a city cop getting me for hitchhiking in town. "Where you headed?" he asks. I show him my sign. "Oh, a fellow river rat," he says and grins. "Get in, I'll give you a lift north, out of town." He motions to the back seat, and I take it. "You got to be carful, kid. Never know who's going to pick you up." I just nod.

My next ride comes about an hour later with a couple high school girls headed up to Wheeling for the Jamboree. They're dressed for it in gingham tops and jeans, but they giggle a lot and don't need me to talk, so I sit in the back seat and fall asleep. Turns out what had taken Dad and me four hours to drive straight, is taking seven hitching. Once I get close and into Bridgeport, I am really stuck. It's almost impossible to hitch in a city. My little sign and smile have no purchase near home, but hitchhiking is all about putting yourself out there and rolling with what comes. As I'm standing on the curb, I hear Grandpa say, "It's not the cards you're holding, son. It's how you play the ones you've got." In Bridgeport as night comes on, I am out of cards, so I call Dad from a pay phone outside a corner bar. He says he'll be down in about 30 minutes; I thank him and go inside the Lucky Star Bar and Grille.

"Can I use your restroom?" I ask the red haired waitress at the bar.

"You goin' to order something?" she asks, giving me the glare while she sweeps away some guy's plate. His abandoned ketchup and fries look real good to me, but I know I'm short on change and I plan to take Sharon out to a nice dinner tomorrow night.

"How about a coffee and an order of fries," I say, almost doing a pee dance there in the bar.

"That's all you want?" she asks like I'm being cheap. She seems a tough old dame, about Mom's age, but wearing too much makeup, for tips I guess.

I smile, "That's all I got."

"Go ahead then. It's in the back," and she motions toward a dark hallway past the bar.

When I come back, relieved and with clean hands, I see that my suitcase is now by a bar stool. I sit and fix my coffee with sugar and cream. It's so good to get off the road and to be close to home. I start to feel alright when the waitress sets a plate before me—a stack of fries and beside it a big open faced burger with lettuce, tomato, onion and pickles.

"The burger's on me, kid," she says and smiles for the first time. "I been there." At last I am back home and I want to hug her.

"Thanks," I say, then add, "The coffee's good too."

Turns out Gladys, the waitress, has a son over in Vietnam. "I hope he's eating good," she sighs, and I say I hope that too.

By the time Dad pulls up, I am out on the corner again, and I throw my suitcase onto the back seat and climb aboard. "I'm so glad to see you," I say from the heart.

"I bet you are," he says and pulls the car into the left lane for a quick pull around. "How long you been on the road?" he asks. I look at his face, watch his hands on the steering wheel.

"Eight hours," I say, "And I've already seen much."

"Oh, yeah?" he says as we head up Rte. 7 toward Martins Ferry and home. "You know that Lucky Star Bar and Grille has quite a reputation."

"Huh...for what?"

"Well, I don't know if it's still running, but used to be a *house*..." he looks over at me, "house of ill repute, if you get me."

"Didn't know that," I say then ask, "Hey, how'd you come to know that, Dad?"

He bristles a little, "From railroaders, son. Not from experience. From railroaders." We drive on.

"God, I love this old car," I say and mean it. It and Dad and Sharon are the closest I've been to home in three months. As we drive I give Dad the short version of my ride with Mr. Bisexual, and the cop who gave me a lift out of town. He just lets me talk, and we are comfortable being quiet together till I approach the question.

"Dad, I gotta ask you something hard. Please understand...I just need to know."

His grip tightens on the steering wheel. "What's up, son? What you need to know?"

We are already in Yorkville, so I have to get it out soon or we'll be home. "How did you and Sharon's mom know that you were the father?"

He jerks back his head, looks over at me, then pulls the car off the road and turns on the dome light. "Well, we had sex, see. I've told you that," and he swallows hard, uncomfortable like when he gave Dave and me the facts of life talk. "Hank, her husband was away in the service and your mom and I had broken up." He looks straight at me as if pleading to be let off. "When Sharon came along, I didn't know she was mine for a long time, years really. Then one day Shirley and I run into each other up at the swimming pool with you and little Sharon, and we're sitting along the wading pool when I say something like how cute she is. And like that, Shirley just tells me right out, 'This one's yours too.' I like to fall over right there into the pool."

"Jesus, what'd you do?"

"Well we never done nothing about it. That's just it. She was married to Hank and I to your mom. Hank was too dumb to figure it out, and so I just kept a watch out for Sharon, slipping Shirley some money every month when things was tough. You understand, son?"

"Yeah, kind of I do," I give him time to settle his breathing. "I'm not meaning anything here." It is my turn to swallow, "But how did you *know* then that it was only you could be the father?"

"Jesus, boy," he lets out an unaccustomed curse, then sighs, "Okay, I see where you're going with this now. And the answer is we finally had a blood test...and sure enough, the baby and I are the same type, and so is Shirley, her mom."

"Huh," I sigh. "And that was enough?" My gut feels tight and sick like I'd swallowed something bad, like glass.

"Yeah, guilty as charged. Okay now?" he asks to be let off, and when I nod, adds, "And listen, we don't need to bring this up again in front of your mother, right?" I nod and he slips the old Pontiac into gear and heads up the road toward home.

Mom is in the kitchen. The girls come gather round me, and little Diane actually wraps her arms around my one leg so that I almost stumble. I haven't felt that much loved in three months. Dave gives the chin lift and a "Hey," from the couch. I "hey" him back, and go out to the kitchen to give Mom a big hug. She is all cheery with a cupcake in one hand, an icing knife in the other. "Oh, honey, I'm so glad to have you home," she says in my ear. *I do have a home,* I say to myself as I've done all semester, only now I'm sure of it. "I have some hot dogs and beans on the stove for you and your father. He took off for you during dinner," she says and fixes Dad and me a plate. I look up at the clock. At 8 p.m. we sit down at the table, and my sisters watch as Dad and I eat.

I tell them some things about school, how you don't have to be in class 8 hours a day, how I'm working in the kitchen now making friends and earning some money. I do not mention Tom or the marijuana, though I do say Sharon visited once. Dad nods while Mom looks away. Then I take a deep breath and look at them all, "God, I really miss you all," I say and almost choke up. It's a regular "Leave It to Beaver" or Mayberry moment, but I just can't help it, a counterbalance to all that standing on my own I've had to do. Thank God, Dave comes up and punches me on the arm.

"So, bro, how was the hitchhiking, and how are the college women?"

"Later, man" I say, as the trip comes back to me like the taste of the onions on the burger at the Lucky Star.

Upstairs, I use the phone to make a quick call to Sharon.

"Hi, I'm home."

She gasps, then in a slow soft voice, "Why don't you come down and see me sometime?" Her laughter is sweeter than honey, and I sigh.

"Hey, I can run down right now and meet you outside your back door. What do you say?" I am literally shaking with hope she will and fear she won't.

"Come on down," she says, "And right away. Oh, I missed you so much."

I hang up and think of the easiest way to slip out. They can practically see Sharon's house from our back porch, though it is night. I go back downstairs, through the television room, and give Mom another hug. "I'm just going to slip out and walk around the block. Be right back."

Mom looks up from her tea cup kind of puzzled and says, "Okay...I guess. It's up to you. We'll have cupcakes and chocolate mint ice cream when you get back."

"Sounds great," I say and slip out the back door, down the porch steps; then I cut through the yards, leap the fence at the back, turn down the alley and end up at Sharon's backyard. It is still wild with weeds and the toys of her younger brother and sisters. I don't knock, 'cause we don't want any interference. As I stand in the dark, I can feel myself breathing and begin a little chant, "Calm...down ...Lee...Calm... down...Lee..." then I hear the door open and before me appears her face in the moonlight. Her clear cheeks glow with innocent beauty, her eyes brighten with starlight. We take each other's hands and can't help embracing, breathing into each other's bodies.

She begins to cry a little and I just hold on. The breeze says what we both feel, "I missed you so. Please don't go." She pulls her head back just a little to look into my eyes, and we fall into a kiss...her lips melting into mine. My head is vibrating, my heart pulsing. "I'm home," I say again and again. "I'm home in you." A mill whistle blows, a car passes, another, and we do not move, touching and tasting each other in this way that just can't be wrong, no matter what others think. Something rises from deep inside me. I can't explain it, but know it is truth.

"Sharon, I..." She touches my lips with her soft fingers.

"Don't say it, Lee. I feel it too. I do."

We drink up the darkness for a while, sheltered in the night, then I take her hands, kiss her fingers and whisper "Tomorrow." I turn and can't help running through her dark yard toward my house and family hoping not to stumble and fall.

I glide home above the grass and concrete pavement under the glow of the streetlight through the darkness of yards in a kind of bliss I'd only known a few times in my life, once after our first dance. I enter the basement door—the smell of fresh laundry and soap, the odor of oil and paint, shelves full of stuff untouched for years—our basement the hidden subconscious of our family life. I climb the old wooden stairs and enter the kitchen light where Dave sits at the table. He looks up. "Well, finally," he sneers, "we can have dessert, at what...10 o'clock!" Then he reads my face, "What are you so happy about? You got one of those shit eatin' grins," and whispers, "You been smoking pot?"

I laugh and grab him by the back of the neck, pretending to choke him. "I'll tell you upstairs, brother," I say as Janie and Diane come dashing into the room. Mom nudges Dad awake in his La-z-boy, and comes over and gives me another long hug.

"Look at you," she says. "So happy to be home with your family." And I am really, if that includes Sharon, and in this strange double way, it does.

Lying in bed on my side of the room again, I watch as Dave slips out of his clothes and crawls under the sheets in his Jockeys and Tee. I think of Tom for a moment, feel a little sadness, then look over at Dave again under his covers, and I let out a sigh. He tunes his radio softly to the night D.J. from Weirton, and we lie there just breathing the night while Dusty Springfield croons "The Look of Love."

"So what's up, bro?" he asks in our shared darkness. *How I need to tell someone, but at such a risk.*

Finally I whisper, "I think I'm in love."

"No shit," he turns to face me. "Who, some chick you met at college?"

Can I trust him? "You have to swear not to tell anyone, you hear?"

"Yeah, yeah. What's the big deal?"

I get up and go over and sit on the corner of his bed. Sitting there in my boxers and t-shirt in the moonlight coming through the window, I whisper, "It's Sharon."

He jerks himself up in bed, almost knocking me off. "No!"

"Shh...yes, it's true, and I can't help it." I sit there shaking my head yes.

"Jesus, man, are you nuts!" He is poking at my bubble with reality's sharp knife. "Don't you see how wrong this is, what a mess you're getting into? Christ, look in a mirror—the two of you even look alike."

I'll admit I jolt at this, but I take his wrist, "Listen, Dave, I know the risks and I can't help myself, see—we can't. Please, God, no word to anyone, till we can let them know somehow."

His face is a hatchet, and I don't honestly know what else to say, so I drift back to my bed.

"What are you going to do?" he finally asks in the dark.

I have no real answer, but I need to back him off. I smile, "We'll move to West Virginia, never have kids." He just stares at me, and I tell him, "I really don't know, but we'll work it out somehow, just don't tell anyone."

"I won't," he says and lies back down. "Jesus," he mumbles and turns his head away.

We both lie there a long time as song after song comes and fades away. At times I see her face in the moonlight, sense her next to me, the sweet smell of her hair and her firm softness held against me. At times I close my eyes, fall almost asleep till the faces of others appear—Dad and Mom, her mother, and her old man—and I jerk awake. *How will we ever work all of this out?*

Chapter Six

Thanksgiving Break

The next morning I rise early yet feel exhausted. I dress in this familiar room while my brother sleeps on. In the bathroom I wash the cobwebs from my eyes and go downstairs where Mom is already sitting at the kitchen table. She looks up at me.

"Oh, honey, you look awful," she says and starts to rise, "Are you sick?"

"Don't get up," I say and rest my hands on her soft shoulders. "I'm fine," I lie. "Just had a long hard day yesterday."

"Oh, Lee, I wish you wouldn't do that."

"What?" I face her. "What do you mean?"

"That hitchhiking thing, it's too hard and dangerous. You can't trust people that way anymore." Mom has always been guarded, someone who knew right from wrong quickly. And when she didn't get fairness from her friends she would cut them off, even her sister at times. I don't want to be one of those.

"Coffee?" I ask.

"On the counter there...in that new white Corning Ware coffee maker. I just love it."

"It's beautiful," I say and pour a cup. "How'd you get Dad to give up his old percolator?"

"Oh, it's still a percolator, but in this new designer pot."

"Where is he by the way? I know he has today and tomorrow off."

She looks forlornly at the back door. "Where he always is, down in that damn garage of his working on his pet project."

"What project?" I ask.

"Oh, you don't know! Your father has become a collector."

"He's always been a collector, Mom. That basement is a museum. A collector of what?

She pauses, then lets it out, "Old cars."

"What!"

"Yes, right now it's a Model T or A, I forget which. He picked it up from some guy in Amsterdam. He and Brownie hauled it here, and he's been spending all his time working on it...down there," and she nods again to the dreaded garage.

"No shit," I say.

"Watch it, son. Don't talk that way in this house. We're better than that."

"Sorry," I say and pick up a piece of buttered toast from the counter. "This I just gotta see."

My walk through the yard to the garage brings back the sweet taste of last night. Sharon would probably be at work by now. I'll pick her up at 4:00. Then as I go to open the side door of the garage, I find a vice grip for a door knob, one of Dad's tricks, use what's handy. There it is—black of course, Henry Ford's one color choice, and the interior covered with a blue tarp. Dad is unseen until I hear a grunt and see a light from under the car. I walk around to where his pant legs and boots stick out from the cardboard mat he's made. The garage floor is hard dirt.

"Hey," I call. "Whatcha up to?"

"Oh, good," he calls back. "How 'bout trying the brake pedal for me." His orders usually come like that in the form of a question. I climb aboard. The leather seat is still in good shape. "When I call, you push down the brake...the one on the left." We do this off and on for about 10 minutes, till he calls, "Okay, I think I got her" and slides out from under. Standing in standard dirty coveralls, he grins like a new father. "Well, sonny boy, what do you think of her—a beauty ain't she."

"Yeah, well it's kind of hard to tell just yet," I have to admit.

"Oh, sure, I can see that, but trust me, she's going to shine. Engine still runs. No speedometer, but she's probably got 100,000 miles on her. Your Grandfather Ernie owned one back in 1910." We stare at the car again. "Needs some mechanical work and a paint job, but she'll be set to go."

I was thinking *'Where?'* but I didn't ask. "Wow, Pop. I didn't know you were into repairing cars."

"Oh, this is more than that. She's vintage, son, a registered classic. Brownie and I are going to drive her in the parades, show her at car shows. That's the plan." He is beaming, such a contrast to Mom's dismay.

"How'd you come to know how to do all this, Dad? You been working on our cars for years, and I can see you're a regular mechanic."

He looks at me for a moment, then back at the Model A. "Well, I guess you never knew this, but I once planned on going to mechanic school up in Detroit."

"When was this?"

"Well, Lee, it was..." and he clears his throat, "right before you was born."

"Oh, yeah. I came along and changed everything."

He smacks me on the shoulder, "Yes, you did. You skunk," and laughs. "It's just how things turned out is all. Got to accept and go on—besides..." and he turns to pat away any regret, "wasn't none of your doing, now was it?"

I wanted to say no, and I wanted to say, yes, it's my business now too because I'm in love with that other little mistake you made years ago.

Later that morning I sit around the kitchen watching my young sisters eat their cereal as I make toast for them—covered with peanut butter and jam, something I'd learned in college. When Dave finally comes moping into the kitchen, I am tossing another slice to the girls. Our eyes meet and he just shakes his head, and grins. Mom and I drink another cup of coffee, then I show her my dishwashing skills.

"Well, they did teach you something useful at that school." She always calls it "that school," and I taste again her resentment at my draining of the family funds. Then she rubs my shoulders like she used to do. "You do well, is all I care," she says, a half truth we share.

I make her sit a while with Dave, while I finish up, then as casual as I can, while wiping the table with a dish cloth, I ask, "Mom, would you mind if I invited someone for Thanksgiving dinner tomorrow?"

"Well, who might you have in mind—your buddy Kenny?"

"Actually, I was thinking of asking Sharon," I say and walk toward the sink, but Mom takes hold of my wrist.

"Just her, or the whole Hatcher tribe?" she asks.

"Oh, just her." I wait, then maybe go too far, "She is...you know..." but Mom's eyes get sharp and she bites her lower lip. Dave glares at me.

"Yes, Lee McCall, I know..." she whispers and walks out to the pantry, then turns. "Oh, I guess it's alright. Did you ask your father?"

"Not yet, but I will. Thanks, Mom. Hey, when does he come up from the garage?"

"God only knows," she says.

I cover my joy by going out onto the back porch. I can see Sharon's house two streets below near the tracks. There are kids' bikes askew in our yard. The fall wind is pushing the leaves along, catching at the neighbor's fences where Mom's rose bushes hang without blooms. I stand there thinking: *I could rake while I'm home. I want to call Sharon, but know she is already on her way to work. What will I do today while she works? I could call Kenny. He'd be off school too and maybe hanging around his Dad's place.* In the old days I'd just walk over, tap on the door and go inside. Now, three months away from each other, and I feel the need to call first.

"Hey, man."

"Hey," he answers back.

"I'm home," I say. "Can I come over?"

"Yeah," he says, then pauses. "Hey, who is this?"

"It's me Lee, you jerk."

"I knew it, man. I was just putting you on. Since when did you have to call and ask? Come on over. I'm just hanging out here in the kitchen with the old man."

This too has to be a joke. He and his father, Frank, hadn't gotten along since his mother died in the accident. She and Frank were both drunk the night his dad ran off the road and rolled the Chevy over the hill onto the railroad tracks. Frank was thrown from the tracks, unconscious, but Betty took it straight on. It was in all the papers. That was two years ago, but his dad hasn't stopped drinking...at least not when I went off to OU.

I let everyone know where I am headed and get Dad's okay on Sharon's coming. I mean, what could he say, she is his what...daughter? This catches me again like a blow to the gut. I could take the car, but walk instead up Murdock Street, past St. Agnes Catholic School and church. Some of the nuns are out hanging clothes in the back yard. Though it is high fenced, I can see their hands pinning aprons or something on lines, and I can hear them laughing. The chimes are raining down from the bell tower just as the mill gives its noon whistle. At the corner, Mrs. Quinn is out sweeping her front porch and waves hello. I take a deep breath of back home.

Down St. Clair Avenue I can see right into the heart of the mill: huge cauldrons steaming, gondolas gliding one by one onto the car dumper, those great rust-red cylinders of blast furnaces rising like dinosaurs from the earth, scraping the sky. I just stand there a while and listen to the church chimes, the clashing of rail cars, the hoot of the noon whistle. My town, where I can put my feet down and know where and who I am.

At Kenny's house near the top of the hill, I knock on the old screen door and wait. Suddenly Kenny is there staring at me in his familiar t-shirt and jeans.

"Well?" I ask.

"Well, just come in, man. How the hell are you?" We smack hands, share grins, stop short of hugging—old friends still. He and I used to walk to school together from junior high on. If he were mad at me, I'd watch for him out the front window, and if he just walked on by, I'd beat it out the basement door, run all the way to school and be there to stare and grin at him as he came onto the playground. We'd been through a lot—basketball and track teams, taking girls to dances and we'd done the scholarship tests together; I'd been there for him during his mom's funeral and after when he'd sleep over at our house. He and I and seven other classmates were the only ones to go on to college or nursing school, though Kenny had to live at home.

As I follow him to the kitchen I stare at his square shoulders and wonder just how much I could lay on them.

"Frank's upstairs, drying out after a week of hard drinking. Sit down. You drink coffee or..." he looks up at the noonday clock—"You want a beer?"

"Coffee, if you've got some made."

"Always," he says. "So how've you been? How's life down in Appalachia?"

It's a slight put-down, so I come back with, "Ken, old man, see those hills outside your window there—what do you call them?"

He goes to the window, feigns surprise. "Well, I'll be darned, if it ain't West Vir-gin-i-a."

"Yeah, and those hills are the Appalachians, buddy. We live in App-a-lach-i-a!" We both laugh.

"Is that all you learned in three months down there?"

"How about you at Steuby-U? What you up to there?"

He sets our coffees down. "You take cream, right?" He pulls up a chair, "Oh, I'm doing the freshman core as they call it. But I'm leaning toward engineering—can you believe that, and I ain't talking about no damn trains."

"Mrs. Monday would slap you down for talking like that. 'Utilize your lexicon, young man.'" I mock her voice.

"Ha, you know, she was awful in class," he looks over at me, "but damn, her drilling grammar into our heads has saved my ass a hundred times. How about you?"

"Yep. I'm doing well in my writing, actually thinking of moving from possibly math to English as a major," I confess.

"What! You, McCall, a flaming English major...and what will you do with that?"

"I don't know—teach I guess, maybe write for a living."

He slaps the table. "Yeah, and next you'll be telling me you're a the-a-tre groupie! You know?" He points a sissy finger at me and draws back. I decide right then not to tell him about my roommate Tom. The phone rings and Kenny goes to answer it. I sip my coffee and wait. The kitchen is the organized mess it has been since his mom died. Dirty dishes are stacked all over the sink, the frying pan shows signs of a week of meals. A magnet for Len's Garage is stuck on the fridge right next to one for Steubenville College. Ken's older sister lives in Washington, D. C. now, so the curtains haven't been cleaned in years. Anyway, it's familiar to them, a place for getting by while Ken works his way toward a new life and his dad slides further toward the grave.

"That was Marlene, can you believe it? She heard you were back in town. Says she'll meet us uptown at the Horizon café on Fourth Street around four if you're willing." He looks at me puzzled like, says, "I got nothing to do, so I said sure. Is that alright?"

"Marlene...Are you putting me on, man? I haven't seen or heard from her in six months since that graduation party at the marina. How'd she sound...she after something?"

"Cool it. She's home on break, like you, from West Liberty College, says she's studying to be an elementary teacher. I've run into her a few times...lookin' real good...if you're still interested."

I take a breath. "No, I'm definitely not...still interested."

"Good," he says, "'cause I sure am." That feels okay but kind of weird.

"Well, I'm up for the café," I say. "Hey, I wonder if Sharon could meet us there from work at Nossets."

"Yeah, let's give her a call," and he holds up a bottle of beer from the fridge. I shake my head no, but he pops one for himself and sits down. "You and old Sharon still close, huh?"

He knows about the half-sister thing, so I nod, then in a sincere voice I half lie, "Yep, we stay in touch. What else did Marlene say?"

"Oh, yeah, said she had something real important to tell us all but wanted to do it in person."

He stares at me, and I jerk back, instinctively quick count the months—it's been a year since we've been together, and hell, we never really had sex. "What is that all about?" I ask. "We're meeting her at four, right? I'll give Sharon a call. Phone book still on the stairs?" Again, I'm pretending I don't know the number she gave me last night. "Hey, man" I ask, "We got a couple hours to kill. What you want to do?"

"Let me think, honcho."

In the other room, I find the phone book on the stairs beside a worn pair of shoes and someone's old socks. The carpet hasn't been vacuumed in forever. Mom would have a field day over here. I call Sharon.

"Good morning, Nosset Studio. How may I help you?" I love her voice.

"Hello, sweetheart," I deep breathe into the phone. "This is your lover boy." Now I am using a pretend voice to speak the truth.

"You're crazy," she whispers back.

"Hey, how about meeting Kenny and me for a drink at the Horizon Café... Oh, and Marlene will be there."

"Marlene...how is she? I haven't seen her in months...Hold on." There is a pause of just her sweet breathing then a mumble of words into the phone. "Lee, I have a customer. What time should I meet you?"

"Four—okay?"

"Yeah, I'll get off. And, Lee, I miss you already."

When I look up, Kenny is coming into the room. He throws me my jacket. "Okay, my friend, we're headed out the tracks to the creek."

We walk down Peeler Street, past Sharon's house, toward the railroad tracks; the whole town is built on a hillside running down to the Bottoms. At Clifton Avenue, we climb over the cable at the edge of the road and slide down the path through weeds to the tracks. At the old foot path we head out toward the woods, always keeping our ears open for possible trains. Soon we're standing atop the old stone railroad bridge looking down at Cross Creek. Some have jumped from here on a dare or when a train came roaring around the bend. And one kid did get hit by a train back in 1958, right here where we stand looking down. He became a small town legend. "Don't you ever go out on those tracks or you'll end like the Mason kid." And if we weren't listening, they'd throw in, "They brought him back in a bag...several of them."

I'll admit I'm thinking of him as we stand there for a while dropping stones into the swollen creek. An autumn wind turns the leaves left on the trees. Kenny pushes a bolder over the edge and says, "The Mason kid."

"Yeah," I add real solemn, and we move on toward the trees and safety. On the other side, we run down the path along the bridge supports and end at a fishing spot a hundred yards or so from the hiss of traffic out on South Commercial Street.

"Bare ass beach," he says.

"Yeah," I answer and find a seat on a log someone had dragged to the creek bank. Kenny lights up what looks like a cigarette, but is a joint.

He holds it out to me. "Hey, remember when we was kids and came out here to smoke my old man's Camels?"

I nod and take the joint from his fingers. I take a hit, then smile. "And I remember a couple times we actually smoked those hollow weeds along the bank."

"Smoked weed," he says like it's a song title or something. "Smoked weed," and we both laugh grinning at each other now. We sit inside time and watch the current ripples, floating sticks, maybe a fish jump out in the middle of the stream. It is a sunny day but cool, a good time for being quiet together. Kenny asks, "Hey, Lee, you think about Vietnam?"

"Yeah?" I say as a question, not sure where he's going.

"I mean the war and all, but do you ever think about being drafted...or maybe enlisting?" he asks.

"Yeah, and I do think about Bobby being over there. But, shit, the way I see it, this is their civil war and we can't win or end it for them. The U.S. is just another in a long line of imperialists. I'll tell you one thing, the protests are really growing on my campus, big moratorium in D.C."

"Wow, man, I see you've been doing some reading."

"Hey, I try to follow the news, even though I'm pretty much read out with text books and writing themes and stuff."

"Hmm..." he says and throws a stick into the stream. "Thank God for student deferments, right?"

"Oh, man, haven't you heard. They're starting a draft lottery next month. No more student deferments. If they draw your number, you're in Nam in a month."

"No shit, man! I'll tell you," and he takes a deep drag, holds, exhales, "I'll tell you, some days I just want to get it all over with. I'm tired of it hanging over me." He rises and throws another stick far across the water, "And some days I do feel guilty doing nothing, you know, while most of the guys from our class who enlisted or were drafted are already over there."

"Yeah," I say, "and one of them, Larry Fowler, was already killed in battle."

A long silence follows and we finish the smoke and just sit in the sun having our thoughts float down stream toward the river. Soon we climb the bank and take the path that leads out onto the road. The town dump where we used to go to shoot rats lies to the west, so we turn east and come out on old Route 7 near the old stadium. Kenny motions with his head, "Lots of good times there." I nod in the afternoon sun. At Flora's Bar and Grill, we grin at each other then duck in. Though only 18, we know we can count on old Flora for a draft or two.

"Okay, you boys," she greets us, moving toward us like a train. "You want to drink beer in my place, you got to give me a kiss." She's old but funny and it's almost worth it.

*   *   *

We arrive at downtown Steubenville a half hour early and so park Kenny's pickup in the Fourth Street lot then stroll the familiar streets—past the bus stop corner, Grand Theater, McCrory's Five and Dime where I'm happy to know the aroma of roasted peanuts still wafts out onto the street. This town has four movie houses and four Five and Dimes— McCrory's, Kresge's, Grant's and Woolworth's—where most of the townspeople shop. The big Hub Department Store across Market Street anchors the downtown. Two summers ago I worked there as a short order cook. Kenny and I glide through the swinging front doors and duck into the Men's Department where Kenny flirts with a pretty shop girl and I buy myself a man's corduroy hat for the journey back to OU. With the cold months ahead, I can see that my hitchhiking days are numbered. Come January I'll just watch the ride board to catch a lift back home to Sharon and my family.

"You look like a preacher," Kenny says and tries to knock the hat off of my head.

"Better than a bum like you," I laugh.

"Hey, old guy," he almost yells, "this here is Debby from my World Civ class."

"Hi," she smiles, and I remove my hat—dark eyes and smooth black hair, a real Valley beauty. We chat about schools, then she says she'll join us at the café after she gets off. Now Kenny has two to choose from—Debby and Marlene.

As we walk out through the revolving door, he pokes me, "Well, what do you think? Pretty cute. You interested?" *How can I tell him my only interest is Sharon?*

The café is a long, slim room with a bar up front—all Steubenville restaurants have bars. A waitress leads us to a round table for five or six in the back, and Kenny orders a pitcher of draft. Turns out our waitress is Marianne, a friend of Kenny's sister. Everyone knows everyone here, unlike college where friendships seem bound to dorm floors, classes, or other majors. Of course, small town familiarity comes with the price of town gossip.

At 4:05 exactly Sharon comes through the front door, surrounded by a beam of sunlight. My heart lifts with her beauty, races with her nearness. *How should we play this?* She holds out her hand to me and I take and shake it, though I want to kiss each finger and her tender palm. Though I hate this pretending, right now we lack the key to our relationship with friends. I smolder as she hugs Kenny.

"Hi, babe," he says. "Glad you're joining us. Haven't seen you since that crazy party."

"That was wild," she says and sits down between us. "Those guys from Weirton were looking for trouble that night."

"What guys...what party?" I mutter.

"Oh, I wrote you about that," Sharon says, taking my hand under the table and squeezing it. "Friends of friends from the business college. I invited Kenny for protection," and she smiles into my eyes while moving my hand to her lap—her cool skirt, her tender thighs. I lose all focus. Suddenly none of it matters except her being there. She squeezes my hand again and rubs my wrist. Kenny pours us all a beer and the waitress brings a large basket of fries and onion rings.

"It's on me," Kenny says. "Welcome home, Steubenville style," and we all laugh. There I sit cozy with friends and Sharon, just where I want to be.

"Screw OU. I'm ready to transfer to Steuby-U right now," I half joke.

"Oh, could you?" Kenny mimics a girly voice. Sharon beams as she casts me a wink. Her golden hair on a red silk blouse, her creamy cheeks and those intense blue eyes—she is my woman, my Beatrice and Penelope.

Here I am with my best friend and the girl I love in our world. And then the door opens and in comes Marlene. She too emerges through the light, dressed sharply in a flowered blouse and a slim skirt. Though my pulse increases, I am glad to see her again. She and Sharon hug each other, while Kenny and I stand waiting. She hugs Kenny then gives me her hand. *What is it about me that I just get hand shakes from women?*

"Let's sit," she says. "What I have to tell you will go easier." Her intense look has us all uneasy, as we sit. "May I," she asks, and takes a slug of Kenny's beer. "I don't know how to say this. It's about a good friend of ours." And we all just hang there staring as she begins to tear up. "Oh, it's Bobby," she bursts really crying now, and Sharon slides over to comfort her.

"Yeah...what happened," I ask, seeing Bobby's round face before me.

"He's gone...Bobby's gone..."she gasps.

"What do you mean, gone!" Kenny begs.

She swallows and spits it out, "He's been shot and killed in Vietnam."

"Oh, Christ!" I say, then Sharon starts to cry. Kenny starts saying, "No, no, not Bobby. Not our Bobby," over and over.

"Yes," Marlene gasps, "I'm so sorry that it's true."

There's a long silence when no one speaks, 'cause no one has answers for any of it. Finally Sharon turns to me and we hold each other tight in that little room. Let the others watch. If death can be this real, the need to hold to life is that much stronger. Truth has cut through us all.

On Thanksgiving Day Sharon does come for dinner, dressed in a pretty blue dress. Everything looks good on her slim curves. I walk her up from her house, and we stop in the garage to view my dad's Model A, but really to hold each other freely and kiss till our cheeks are pink. I love her face, touching her soft hair, holding her body next to mine. We go no further than that. As much as I love her wholly, I can't bring myself to touch her sexually for fear of where it might lead. Both love children, we know the cost. And somehow in the midst of the smell of oil and paint in the dim light we help each other get through our grief and pledge our love.

Finally we hear a knock and quickly separate. It is Dad come down to show off his car.

"Hi there, Sharon," he says, then, "She's a real beauty isn't she?" He is gazing at his car and I at Sharon.

"Yes, she sure is," Sharon answers for us, then she holds her hand out to him. He looks, then takes her hand, folds it in his own then hugs her. They both know their secret bond but have never really acted on it. Why shouldn't they touch, I think—they're family. And yet a side of me refuses to say that or to make any harder our loving each other. We are a triangle standing there, and I love all the sides of it.

"When's she going to run, Dad?" I ask.

"Ha, when she's good and ready, I guess. I been begging her to do just that for days now. She starts up, runs a bit, but then cuts out before she'll go."

"Sounds like the carburetor." It's Sharon who says this, and Dad who is grinning.

"Good girl. By Jove, she's got it!" he jokes. "Where'd you learn about engines, hon?"

"Well, my father's a truck driver, don't forget," she replies and shakes her shoulders. "All he ever talks about are engines and sports."

That word "father" hangs in the air a while. She has two fathers; we all know it, but we only acknowledge one.

"Let's go up to the house," I suggest, "before we all smell of Quaker State."

Mom has set out a relish plate and dip, and my kid sisters are already feeding like rabbits.

"Hello, Sharon. Welcome to our home," Mom says, standing at the stove in a bright yellow apron decorated with pumpkins and leaves. While stirring milk into the gravy, she says, "Dinner will be ready in a few minutes. Why not take her into the living room?"

"Oh, I'd like to help you," Sharon says.

"No, you two go on. I've got it all covered." Mom looks at me hard, as Diane runs over and takes Sharon's hand and dances her into the living room. And it hits me again, if it's true, then she's Diane's sister too—that double life we're all living, Sharon and I more than any of the others.

*   *   *

In the days that follow, we learn of plans to have Bobby's body shipped home. A memorial service will be held in mid-December. We all move in a cloud for some time as the distant death is brought home. During the days, I'd work around the house with Dave or hang out with Kenny at his place or down at Flora's bar; finally I call the Hub restaurant to see if they need me during Christmas, and they do. I start work next Monday.

That weekend Kenny, Jerome and I walk out the tracks once more to the Old Stone Bridge. We borrow a kid's little red wagon and drag with us this huge boulder from Bobby's front yard with his name painted on it in red. We pull it along the path beside the tracks, lifting it at times over rocks. The sun is almost down when we finally arrive at the bridge, then we push the boulder over the edge, watch it drop, then splash and drown in the waters of Cross Creek. It makes as much sense as Bobby's being dead—killed for no reason in some jungle the other side of the world. "For Bobby," Kenny says, then adds, "Fucking war," for us all. I don't notice anyone crying, but we do get to that deep quiet place inside. Then Kenny pulls out a bag of weed with three joints already rolled inside. We are about to light up when we hear the hoot of a train and run like mad down the path to the creek. We don't want to lose anyone else. What we do next is sit on logs by the stream and waste ourselves. We make a fire as night falls over us.

On Saturday Sharon and I drive the Pontiac to Jefferson Lake for a late fall picnic. By the time we get there, a light snow is falling, and so we park by the water and share our tuna fish sandwiches in the car. *There she is,* I think to myself again and again...*There she is, this girl I love.* I reach over and take her hand. She wipes her lips with a paper napkin then presses those soft lips to mine, both of us pressing, leaning into each other across the emergency break, holding on to all that matters. Away from home we find home in each other. I kiss every bit of flesh that I can see of her and some that I cannot. She wants them kissed.

Before heading back, she puts her head on my shoulder and begins to softly cry.

"What's wrong?" I ask, blinded by my own happiness. "What's the matter?"

"Oh, Lee, it's all so wonderful...and awful. I want to just let go when I'm with you." She folds her fingers into mine. "And I do. But I'm afraid that what we have is all going to break apart."

"How...By what?" I insist.

"By them—the others, when they know about us...our families, our shared father."

It is the first time she's actually spoken to me the name 'father' for Dad. It seems right yet stings. I search her eyes. "I know...it's hard. And I'm trying to understand how you feel."

"Oh, for you he's your dad and that's right and how it should be. For me, he's...well, the man who could have been my father all my life, and I'm not sure what he is now."

I take a quick breath. It keeps coming in waves, this sense of life's turning inside itself. Is she right? Could it all break apart and spoil this dream we share? I don't say anything. I have started the engine to keep us warm and the windows are fogging up, so I roll mine down a little, and we sit there silent, breathing together, listening to the snow falling softly on dry leaves.

One weekend in early December I ride down to Athens with John Woods who says he wants to take a look at the OU campus. I've left some things down there with Murray, and so agree. Once there he meets up with a girl and tells me he wants to spend the week down there. I'm pissed off of course, but he gives me $20 for bus fare. The next afternoon I hang out at that little veggie place by the bus depot on Court. When I board the Greyhound headed northeast, it is full of carless folks like me, young and old: a woman whose two kids won't stay in their seats, a guy in overalls with his tool box at his feet, a man in a blue suit with a Bible on his lap. I sit next to a Black woman my mother's age. We don't talk for miles as we roll past forests and fields, through mid-size towns. Then when the woman with kids get off, she sighs, "That girl got to get them kids to listen or they'll ride all over her." We each tell our stories the rest of the way to Parkersburg where she gets off, and a big quiet girl gets on and smiles at me with soft eyes. I say, "Hi," and disappear into sleep, waking only when we stop in Marietta. At the sight of the river, my heart quickens. I sit up and watch out the window as the bus eats up the miles bringing me closer to Sharon.

The day fades softly as a light snow comes on. Finally we are crossing the bridge to Wheeling Island, now over the new expansion bridge, past the huge Marsh Wheeling Cigar sign painted on that old brick building. And suddenly in the night there she is in her cute green coat standing under the streetlight outside the bus station. The bus pulls in, and she looks up to find me—snow falling lightly on her golden hair. Our eyes meet and we both feel that huge something linking and moving us.

I take her in my arms and kiss her soft, willing lips, holding her tight, as she whispers, "Beyond my dreams, Lee, there is you." An echo in my heart brings tears to my eyes as we stand together in this snowy night that we both want to last forever.

"It's so good and right to be together," I say. "I'm ready to move to Alaska to be with you."

"I know," she says and repeats, her own tears coming now...and I kiss her eyes and taste the salty sweetness of our life. *How do I deserve this?*

We stop at Elby's Big Boy for a coffee and sit tight together in a back booth talking slowly over our shared sandwich. I look over and just want to eat all of her. Her thigh is next to mine and she is wearing this red skirt of soft wool that slides a little above her knees. I let my hand touch her knee—the smooth curve over bone. She smiles shyly.

"Look at you, in red and green," I say, "You're a Christmas present."

She touches my cheek, whispers in my ear, "I'm my gift to you."

I swallow and sigh, "I accept," then take a quick breath and have to excuse myself to the restroom.

We drive up old Rte. 2 with her leg next to mine, her head resting on my shoulder, just breathing together as we roll along, winding around the roads of West Virginia towns, in and out of the light, steel mills and houses, river to the left, hills to the right. Then Sharon reaches over and turns up the radio. It is Patsy Cline, I swear, and she is singing that song. Both of us join her on the chorus: "Crazy...I'm crazy for loving you..."

We stop at home, say hi to my sisters, Mom and Dad. Dave is out with a girlfriend. I toss Dad the keys, catch Mom staring at Sharon. Then I walk Sharon home, our footsteps marking the fresh snow. We have to stop to kiss a few minutes inside the garage door, leaning on Dad's shiny black car. The smell of oil does nothing to the touch of her skin, the electric warmth of our two bodies.

At her house I don't go in, but we kiss long, then promise to be together everyday that I'm home. When I come in the door at home, Mom is cleaning the counters, putting pans away, and I begin to help when she grasps my wrist hard. "You're seeing a lot of that girl," she says, then whispers right into my face, "Beware. I'm warning you. That relationship is as wrong as when it all began." She bites her lip, digs her fingers in, and lets go.

"Okay," I lie. "I hear you...but Sharon and I are more than friends, you know.'

"I do. I just don't know how much more."

"I'm going up to bed," I say, leaving her with her pans and bitterness.

Dad looks up as I pass. "Welcome home, son."

"Thanks. I'm going up...long day." He nods. On the stairs I think this lyric to myself: *How could something so right be wrong?*

Money makes the next moves. Sharon is working days at Nossets, and I'm filling in at The Hub, slinging burgers, dishing up the macaroni, setting up plates at the hot table. I go to work in their white uniforms, come out wearing a map of spaghetti sauce or grease. At night we hang out at Kenny's place. Sharon becomes the best cook Kenny and his dad have seen in years, and I help clean up the place.

On the night Sharon meets with her girlfriends from school, I show up at Kenny's, and he takes my arm. "Okay, lover man. What the hell is going on?"

"What?"

He gives me the straight-on stare. "Jesus, you and Sharon. It's as plain as the smile on your face. Are you crazy or what? Where can that lead?"

Standing on the edge of speaking the truth, I am both relieved and afraid. "Yeah, we're together," I confess as he shakes his head. "Listen, man, we love each other and we'll do whatever it takes to keep it that way."

He draws a breath and sits down across for me. "Shit, man, this is deep. Are you two...doing it?" he has to ask.

"No, we are not if you have to know."

"Thank God for that."

It is my turn to stare back. "You have to promise to tell no one, till..."

"Till what?"

"Till we work this out. There's got to be a way. I'm telling you, this is the biggest thing in both our lives. Whatever the cards, we have to play them."

He stares back at me, reads my face, then says, "I'm square with that. Come on, let's go for a ride."

*   *   *

At Bobby's memorial on Sunday we see everyone. They hold it at the City Building, and the townspeople pour out for it. For some he's the local hero come home to rest, but for most of us, he's Bobby gone, a good friend wasted in a wrong war, part of this cloud of loss that hangs over things, from the loss of friends to the assassinations of Kennedy and King. Nixon has taken the war into Cambodia, the massacre of My Lai is in the news, but I do not mention any of this, not here in this town this night. Sharon and I sit near the front with Kenny, Jerome, and Marlene who shows up with her new boyfriend. We are all dressed up in suits and dresses, so after the priest and mayor speak and Bobby's mother thanks us all, we go out to the Hillsboro Tavern to drink away our sorrows. I'm not a drinker 'cause I've seen what it can take from a family, but this night I do let go. Before we know it, we are dancing to the pounding music of Buddy Sharp and the Shakers. The old bar is really shaking with the craziness of everything. Then Sharon and I step outside. She takes my hand and pulls me to her tight and won't let go. I take her head in my hands and ask, "What is it?"

"It's you," she says, "It's Bobby and the whole crazy loss of everything. I'd die if I would ever lose you." I hold her tight in the night air, then she lets go. "Okay," she smiles up at me, "I'm ready to go to Hell or Alaska whenever you are."

Chapter Seven
Transitions

Back at school, the month of January stretches out like a river, the place familiar to me now though my heart hurts for missing her and home. Work friends Chance and Murray have become a release from studies providing a place where I don't have to try to belong. Tom never does return to school, and after a couple weeks, I help the R.A. pack up his things into a couple boxes to be shipped back East. I hold onto his desk mat as a useful memento of a friend, but ditch the dreaded bulletin board. Also I keep a plaid shirt that I told him I liked once and know that he'll understand. And so I spread out in my single room as winter quarter opens a further chapter to my life. I did get a note from Tom, "Hey, man, thanks for being the one person I could count on. I'm okay here, got a job at a record store in Cambridge near Harvard, finding new friends. Ohio and that plaid shirt are all yours, my friend." It strikes me that despite all of Tom's sharing with me, I never once told him about Sharon.

When Dr. Wagner tells me that I have a gift for literature and writing, just like that, I switch my major to English. I register for a survey course in American Lit, second term writing, Spanish I, and for my science requirement, I choose biology. Actually Chance at work suggests it. "Do you know Charlotte Harris in biology? Man, I'm telling you, take a course from her, she's great." I'm on a new less travelled road here, though I can't really see further than my headlights allow.

Chance and I talk the war sometimes, and the student protests are rising, not just about the war but about the rights of students, women, and gays. It's exciting really, like we're on the edge of something momentous and it all might change. Our alienation from this war has united us into a movement that can't be ignored. One of the saddest days came when they do the absurd draft lottery. I meet Chance at the student union which is packed with young men waiting before the video screen to learn their fate. Student deferments are out the window now, and any male born between 1944 and 1950 is eligible or vulnerable. Each birthday is assigned a number for the day of the year. If your birthday number is called early, you're done for and in a month could find yourself in Nam or dead. And we sit here like ducks in a pond watching an old congressman choose our destiny by pulling a ball out of a jar, the way Mingo Mike used to draw bingo numbers at the movie house. The first number drawn is 257 (September 14) and a groan goes up. Then pretty much in a steady fire from a sharpshooter the rest are called. One guy walks past us toward the door, saying, "I'm a dead man. I'm going out and get stoned." Another guy yells out, "Bus headed north for Canada—anyone want to join me?" which gets a roar and our anxious applause. I am so sick of being the pawn to others, including this university, manipulated by design at their will. Everything's a fucking check-sheet we have to complete. I want out of the system. Only when they pass number 200 do any of us begin to feel any sense of safety. Chance is 201 (March 29th) though he probably wouldn't pass the physical, and finally I become number 224 (February 9th). We shake hands in the somber crowd, then hug each other and our fate.

Back in the dorm I wait in line for the phone to call Sharon. "I know," she says. "I watched it in my room. I love you." Her tears of relief pull my own. That night, someone paints "Hell no. We won't go!" in red on the ROTC building and a rally is planned for the park tomorrow.

Sharon and I have been writing each day and talking on the phone Wednesdays and Sundays, the longest day of the week. Putting pen to paper is my refuge. I begin to write and truth comes out as I scroll further into our life together. She keeps my letters locked in a box under her bed, and I show hers to no one. She actually writes better than I do, so clear and sincere, thoughts and feelings married on the page. "I walked out to the woods," she wrote yesterday, "at the top of the hill where you used to deliver papers. I stood in the fallen leaves and looked down the hill at the town, the mill, the river—the whole valley of our life. Then I took just a few steps back into the woods and just stood there in the stillness, listening till I noticed a small squirrel. She was carrying a pine cone to a tree where she gnawed her way to the sweet seeds inside...something I would have missed if I'd walked on. I was breathing the moment, Lee, you were with me. I started to think—*This is all a part of me,* when I stopped, *No, we are part of it.*"

I tell her on the phone, "Hey, maybe you should be taking courses down here, and I'll study business."

She says, "Yes, I just might, if I had a scholarship down there instead of here." Then she tells me she stops off from time to time to visit with Dad. "He's so in love with that car. It shines in his eyes. And he misses you, Lee, like his right arm."

At work tonight Chance asks me, "Hey, man, are you in love or something?"

"What?" I ask, sliding an empty rack his way.

"Are you in l-o-v-e?" he asks loud enough for the cooks to turn and listen.

"Y-e-s," I say aloud and turn to the cooks then back to Chance. "How'd you know?"

"Oh, man, you've got that drifty look in your eyes, and sometimes you don't hear what Murray and I say."

This is a joke, because Murray's a selective mute and only speaks of necessity. "Ain't that right, Murray?" he calls and is answered by a smile and single nod. Then Chance sings, "'You're not sick, you're just in love.' You know that song?"

"Yeah, I do, my folks used to sing it in the car on those long Sunday drives. What I'd give for one of those now." I look over at his big grinning face. "It's a girl back home," I confess. "I've known her since grade school. She writes me almost every day. She's blonde and has these great blue eyes that see right through you." From a dry river bed I've become a gushing stream.

"Okay, okay, now we know. Murray, see, I was right. Hey, guys," he calls out to us, "let's catch a beer after this is done and talk. Oh, I forgot...you freshmen can't drink real beer, now can you?"

He answers our chagrin with a big laugh, "Well, you can at my place."

I surprise old Chance in that I am not majoring in drinking like most of the freshman class. I do, however, have a small bag with me, and he gives me the nod to go ahead and smoke it. He lives in one of those old houses off campus. "These were miners' homes back in the 1920's," he tells me. "Small and tight and cheap." We nod sitting back in his bean bag chairs. "Most are owned by professors. It brings in good money. Lee, you should look into it for next year after you've done your freshman term in the dorms."

"Sounds like a plan," I say and grin. I have already spent my wad on telling secrets, and so just enjoy the marijuana ride and listen to Chance play a mean blues guitar. With each song he tells the tale of his finding it. A transplant to Ohio from Brooklyn, of all places, after high school he had hitched his way down South learning guitar licks on front porches.

"I'd just show up at a juke joint, follow some player home till he noticed me and was too tired to shoo me away. They'd call me out see, 'Come on, white boy, let's see what you got,' and I'd whip out my Gibson and play up and down for them. They'd just nod and then we'd jam together and I'd go beyond myself. You know the feeling, boys?" Murray and I sit back and listen, give our little nods and grins, and damn, he is good.

The winter quarter opens the world again. Though my heart aches, I am ready to move on. The leaves are all down when the Hocking River floods, closing the West Green. I've traded the flooding of the Ohio for the Hocking. Two dorms shut down and coeds crowd together for a couple weeks. And I meet my new roommate, James Odaffe, a foreign exchange student from Nigeria. The opposite of Tom, James is organized and devoted to his studies, and openly friendly. When we first meet he takes my hand and pulls me into a strong hug. "So glad to have you," he smiles generously, and I know this will be a new journey.

Right away my life begins to fall into a pattern of classes, work, and home, a triangle, though thoughts of Sharon run through it all. I can be studying at the lab table in biology and be back at Kenny's kitchen table watching Sharon cut her tuna sandwich into triangles and begin eating at the corners. I can be throwing the lever on the big dishwasher and I'm shifting gears in the Pontiac, Sharon's warm thigh resting alongside of my own. In American lit, we begin with the Puritans and advance slowly toward present time. Sharon comes into these stories as a character and voice. Again and again, I find myself taken by the way writing pauses to take in the world, to record and reflect the living. My own writing grows, not only in letters to Sharon and my journal, but in small poems I scrawl in a notebook then type up, breathing the lines, dancing the phrasing down the page. More and more I come to see how you have to believe something to write, and then the words you've written confirm the belief. It's a kind of devotion that breeds confidence. I believe in our love, and that faith feeds my love for work, this place, learning everything. Drawn by a light, I enter a threshold and pass through.

Dr. Charlotte Harris, my biology professor, is so young and pretty, unlike all the rest of my profs. The third week after class, she asks if I'd like to assist her with the lab. This hardly ever happens to a freshman, but what she meant for me to do doesn't take any great brain power; she has grad students for that. Basically I clean up the lab and set it up for the next group of Biology 101 students. I already have my university work permit, so it's an easy do, and I get paid. But honestly, the best part is working with Charlotte. I never knew anyone, except Sharon, to be so smart, and well, kind. College professors always seem on another plane from students, especially from a working-class guy like me. Oh crap, I sound like I'm buying into this whole educational hierarchy!

Charlotte is different. First off, she asks us to call her Charlotte, and secondly she doesn't give us orders and just disappear. She works beside us, scrubbing beakers, or like we're doing now, packing up the leftover frog cadavers in the waste packs.

"Lee, those have to be double sealed. Let me show you," and she takes the duct tape and rips off a strip. "Then you label each." She looks straight at me. "It's state policy when sealing animal waste."

I take the tape from her hand, do the next one while she stands there watching in her lab coat that comes an inch above her skirt at the knee, so that it seems the white lab coat is all she's wearing. Short hair, dark eyes, she looks really fine, but I honestly don't just think of her that way, though I will say she clearly holds attention in any classroom. She is the closest female friend I've found down here.

"So, Charlotte," I ask, "how did you get into this biology business, slicing up frogs and cadavers? I never knew a woman biologist." I actually never knew any biologist.

She steps closer to me, sighs, "Lee, I honestly don't have a good reason. It was an instinctive thing. I discovered it in high school and loved it. It may sound trite, but there really is this endless mystery about the animal world." She smiles as she is saying this, then laughs. "I know, I sound like a television science special."

"You do," I say and laugh with her.

"Have you come to a major yet?" she asks and puts down her notepad to and sits on one of the stools to really listen. She crosses her legs which actually seem to shine in the window light.

"Matter of fact," I confess, "I changed my major from math to English after the first quarter."

"Wow, that's a big leap. You must have found something."

"I did." Still sitting, she leans towards me. "I love writing—reading it and doing it." I hear myself say this and like it. "It's all real to me—putting life into words—I love it."

I am about to tell her of Sharon when two girls walk into the lab, and for some reason we both stand up.

*   *   *

My call to Sharon last night was just okay. She's been arguing with her dad about buying a car. He still takes half her pay, charging her rent for living at home. I wish she'd just move out, but she says she protects her brother and sisters from the old man's wrath. Her mom is smart but a washrag around him. I start to tell her about my talk with Charlotte but cut it short. Not good to be too up around someone who's feeling down.

After class, I begin cleaning up the lab by myself. Charlotte sticks her head in the door, waves, and says, "I'll be with you in a few minutes." I wave back. She's talking with an older guy who I think is the department head. I am almost done cleaning when she returns. "Oh, you did it all yourself. Let me do the set-up then." She seems a little shaky for some reason.

"What's up, Charlotte?" I ask, stepping her way.

"Biology Department business. I'm up for review."

I have no idea what that might mean. She reads my dumb look and says, "They're evaluating me for a contract for next year."

"You? You're the best teacher in the department. Ask anyone."

"Well, thanks, Lee. That's nice to hear, but obviously, they haven't gotten the message. You know, it's 'publish or perish' around here."

"What does that mean, 'publish or perish'? I've heard it but I don't understand."

She looks into my eyes. "Sorry. It's not your problem. I shouldn't be sharing all of this."

"No, I want to know."

"It means you have to not only teach and do research but you have to publish it somewhere, in certain journals. They have these professional journals in all of the disciplines. It takes time, and money to get it done. My research isn't ready yet, so I'm being warned."

She is not smiling and looks somehow scared, so I touch her hand and she doesn't pull away. "Listen, you're bigger than them; you'll survive this." The edge of a smile begins as she lets out a breath, and I hear myself offer, "You know what Mark Twain says? 90 per cent of what we worry about never happens."

We both laugh, and I ask, "What is your research about?"

Another gasp, and she sighs, "Genetic testing. I'm working on new tests for paternity."

It's my turn to gasp. "Wow, no kidding! This really is amazing."

She looks at me puzzled. "Okay, thanks, but why is it so amazing to you?"

I hesitate. *How much to tell her? How much to hold back?* Finally I blurt out, "Because I'm struggling with this very issue right now." *Oh, lord.* "This girl I know back home. Well, we're not sure who her father is, and it really matters." I settle for that.

"Well," and she too pauses. "I'm going to tell you this in confidence. I got into this research in part because I too am a 'love child,' and don't know who my real father is. My mom was, shall we say, promiscuous in her twenties, and so doesn't know for sure who fathered me." She looks into my eyes, "That's a poor choice of words; no one fathered me, she raised me herself."

"Wow, I didn't know this!"

"How could you? I don't wear it around on my lab jacket."

"Hmm. So why didn't you just do a blood type test? That's what this girlfriend's parents did."

"Oh, my!" she sighs. "Lee, blood type tests are no good for determining paternity. At best they're 30 per cent accurate. That means they're 70 per cent unreliable. My guess is they also did serological testing which was developed in the 40's. It looks at the serum for incompatible proteins on the red blood cells." I have to sit down. "Are you following me? This is a bit technical but I'll explain. A child's Rh, Kell and Duffy proteins are tested to help determine the father."

"I don't know. I don't think they did any of this." Here I am hanging at the edge of a cliff and a rope's being held out, but I have to let go of something to grasp it.

"Well, even if they did, Lee, it's only 40 per cent accurate. You see, there is no reliable test for paternity...yet. And that's what I'm working on, along with several other scientists."

I want to yell, I want to laugh, I want to cry. We do not know if Sharon is my half sister. We do not know! I take hold of both her hands. "Charlotte, I'm going to tell you a deep secret. I'm in love with this girl, and we think her father may be my own dad."

She gives a sigh but does not let go. "My God, Lee! You've been living with this not knowing." She shakes her head. "This is exactly why I'm doing this work. I want to help people like you and her to know. We deserve it."

"But what...there's no way of knowing?"

"That's just it, Lee. We believe there is. It's called HLA testing, Human Leukocyte Antigens. It also allows us to test for doing transplants and transfusions. The white blood cells are tested with attention to the HL antigens which are inherited from both parents." She reads my puzzled face, "Listen, you don't need to understand all of this now, just know that our reliability for paternity is measuring 80 per cent accurate." She looks straight into my eyes. "80 per cent. You can know, Lee. We can answer that unknown."

I am shaking and need to sit down, but I am already sitting. I stand up and Charlotte puts her hand on my shoulder. Out the window the afternoon light is falling over the snowy campus. I feel a little dizzy, and I tell her, "I have to call Sharon and let her know all of this."

She smiles, then looks dead on at me. "The thing is, our results and the test aren't official yet. To do it, we'd have to go outside our study, and that might jeopardize it."

"But can you do that? Would you? It's God important to us."

"Let me think a minute." Her pained face tells me this is taking a big risk for her. She walks away for few minutes and goes into her office, leaving me standing on the edge of a cliff. It's hard asking someone to sacrifice for you, but I'm lost without her help. Then suddenly, I feel her arms around me.

"Go on, make the call," she says, "We'll do it all in secret. I can run the lab tests myself. Go ahead, now, make your calls. I'll finish in here."

I want to kiss her. I want to jump for joy and get in a car and drive right home, but I have no car. And so I rush to the student union and call, first Sharon, then Dad. Though this test may make us blood family, it could also free our loving each other. Either way, I'm ready to walk through that door.

Chapter Eight
Testing

"My mother says no."

"What does she mean, 'no'?"

"Lee, she won't be tested."

"How can she say that?" I gasp, confused and hurt. "It's just a simple blood test. My God, and it can answer so much."

"I know, I've told her that. I've begged her."

Sharon is crying on the phone now, but I have to go on. I pause, then offer, "Okay, it's okay, hon. Just take a deep breath right now, please. We'll work this out somehow. God, how I want to be there with you."

"What did your father say?" she asks. "What did you tell him?"

"I just talked to him on the phone and told him there's this test to determine paternity and that you need to know, that you're asking him to do this, and so am I. At first he didn't answer, then he sighed and said yes, he'll do it for us. But we need to test all three of you to know anything."

"I'm sorry for this, Lee. I know you're right, and I'll talk to her again, I will. But I have to tell you that I'm scared too. How much do I reveal to her? And what if the test says yes, Del is my father? What will that do to us? "

It's my turn to take a deep breath now, and I look down the dorm hallway, all the closed doors. "I hear you," I say, "but we can face this together. And Charlotte is helping here even though she's breaking the rules to do this for us, you know."

"Who's Charlotte again?"

"Dr. Harris, my biology teacher. I told you about her. We're outside of her control group in her study, but she'll do it for us.... She knows about us."

"You told someone down there about us? I thought we swore not to."

"I had to, Sharon. If I hadn't, we'd never have known about this HLA test, and she'd never agree to do the test for us."

"It's me, my mother, and your father who will be taking the test." I hear a resistance in her voice.

"Right, I know that. But the test is for—us. It can free us to love openly."

"Yes, and it could lock us away from each other too. You know that, Lee."

"I do and I understand." I sense I'm pushing her to an edge. "Listen," I say softly, "I just believe the not knowing is hiding from the truth and it's already costing us. We have to go through this door together."

There is a long pause. I can hear her breathing; someone is talking. She must have the phone up in her room. "It's my mother. She's ready to talk some more. Oh, Lee, I do want to face it. I love you. I'll call you back soon, I swear."

How could something that's right be wrong too? How could not knowing be an answer to anything? I walk the hallway back to my room, past the doors open and closed. No one here knows what I'm going through. James is gone to his world history class. On the desk is his photo of Julita, the woman back in Nigeria that he's sworn to marry. I envy him, I do. He's away from her, but when his studies are through, they'll have a way to be together forever. I want this for Sharon and me. I sit down and try to write all of this but can't. I'm worn out from the inside...with excitement and now worry. This is a test for us all. I lean forward, rest my head on my arms and try to find comfort.

Sharon calls back an hour later after I've slept at my desk. "Call for Lee McCall," someone yells down the hallway. Let it be yes.

"Lee, she still refuses, and she won't say why. I can tell she's afraid of something, maybe it's Hank. 'This brings it all back,' she keeps saying, but won't give me a reason. How can she be so selfish? Damn it, she's only thinking of herself. What of my need to know who my real father is?"

"Honestly, I don't know. Something is hidden here. Something she doesn't want any of us to know."

"Yes, I agree. Oh, Lee, I'm ready to open that door and for me this test is a key to who I am. Am I being selfish in wanting to know?"

"No, you're not." It's hard but good to hear her talk like this with some determination to get things out.

"Mom and I had a fight, Lee. At first we sat on the couch and I tried to reason with her, but she got up and walked out into the kitchen. I followed her and said I'd move out if she didn't care enough to help me. She just stared at me and asked, 'Why, why would you do this to me?' She was shaking, Lee, but I said, 'Look at what you've been doing to me.' We were both crying by then, and I went to her. We sat down at the kitchen table and she reached over to me and whispered something you have to hear."

"What? What was it?"

"She said, 'I'm just not sure.'"

"Oh, my God! What did she mean by that?"

"I don't know. She wouldn't say more, but I could see she was starting to open up."

"She said she's 'just not sure' of what...whether to take the test or whether Del's your father? You see, that's what we're hoping for. Sharon, you have to get her to do it." I feel a dizzy lightness in and around me. "Tell her we'll do it without Hank knowing."

"Can we do that?" Sharon asks.

I think a moment, we're so close, and this is so tense. Then laugh, "If that doesn't work, we'll sneak some blood while she's asleep."

"Oh, I couldn't do that."

"I know; I'm only kidding. We McCalls are great kidders, you know."

"Yes, I do. Your mother especially. What does she think of all this? I don't think she likes me."

"We haven't told her. We can keep this under wraps till it's done and we know something for sure. Charlotte says it takes three weeks before we'll know the results."

"Lee?"

"Yeah?

"Just now, when I told her I'd move out, I liked saying that. I could actually feel it in my body. But where would I go?"

"That's easy—down here with me. We'd find a job for you at the university and you could rent a little place for us off campus. It could happen. A lot could happen and soon."

Even while we're saying good-bye, I'm planning a way to get home next weekend. I call Patty in hopes of hooking a ride, and she knows this sophomore Denise from Steubenville who has her own car and is going home. I make the call.

All that week I have trouble listening in class or at work. Washington Irving's stories seem childish. I skip Spanish because I haven't practiced my verbs and don't want to be embarrassed. During biology I'm plotting the scenario of confronting Sharon's mom. *Maybe my father would talk to her.* When Charlotte comes over and asks how things are going, I shy away, tell her, "We're working on getting her mom's cooperation." She touches my sleeve and nods.

At work Chance seems to understand. "I'll leave you alone with your thoughts," he grins, "but don't get anything on your apron." I laugh and swing an empty rack up onto the counter. He comes over and offers, "Hey, man, if you want to talk after work...I'll hang around." But I just can't, not yet.

Finally Friday rolls around and I meet Denise on the West Green. She lives off-campus and has a little '63 green Corvair. I'm passenger number three, so I say hi to her friend

Janice, then crawl in back and lean my head into a pillow pointed toward sleep and home. It's a cold car and January, so I wrap myself in my winter coat, think how sophomores can live off campus and have their own cars. If I'm still here next year, I'll do that with Sharon.

I wake around Sistersville, and they're still chatting away, so I just look out the window as mills and towns float by along the river. Janice is Black and lives on Seventh Street in Steubenville. "Hello, sleepy head," she says. Turns out she met Sharon at a party once. She turns around to eye me, then laughs, "That girl is datin' you? Man, you lucky."

"I know it" I say and laugh.

In front of our house in Mingo, Janice climbs out, then me. I thank them both and for some reason give Janice a hug. She's a solid girl and smells of lavender. It's around seven p.m. and the family is expecting me. Dave surprises me by coming out to the car to help me carry in my suitcase, says, "Hey, man, what have you gotten yourself into?"

"What do you mean?" I ask.

"Come on, I know something's up. Who all knows about you and Sharon?"

I look him square in the eyes, "Well, Mom doesn't, yet, so keep your trap shut. Dad does and doesn't know, just like Sharon's mom...the old conspiracy goes on. We need to get her mom to take this new blood test to tell if our dad is Sharon's father."

"Man, you really take it! You're plunging us all into some kind of whirlpool. I just hope we all come out safe and alive."

"Me too, Dave. I really do."

Inside they have waited dinner for me, and we all gather round the table for plates of beans and franks.

An hour later I'm outside Sharon's house. She comes out to meet me, and we embrace in the cold air. I taste her lips, press her head to mine, and we just breathe together there. It is windy and near dusk, and she's wearing just a dress and sweater. She looks into my eyes and begs, "Please go easy, Lee. We'll get farther that way. Come on in."

"Hi, Mrs. Hatcher," I say.

"Hi, Lee... and just call me Shirley, okay."

We all sit down at the kitchen table. Hank is out, and the kids are playing upstairs, though we do hear a thump in the other room.

"Mom, Lee's teacher at Ohio University is the one who would be testing us. He can explain it if you'd like."

She looks over at me, and I can read the tightness in her face as she says, "Oh, I don't think I can do this. I hope you didn't come all this way home just to talk with me."

Sharon and I glance at each other. "Well, yes, I did," I admit, "and to see my folks and Sharon. I'm just trying to help because I know how much Sharon needs to know who her father is."

Shirley looks down at her hands then up at me. "I know that your father told you about us already. He's Sharon's father, just believe that."

"Well, if there's any doubt, Shirley, this test would let us know. You understand? It would put this question to rest for her and us."

She pulls back from the table and says, "This brings up old stuff. I know your mom's never forgiven me. We used to be good friends you know, 19 years ago. And my husband Hank still hates your father." She stands up suddenly and walks over to the sink. She is literally shaking outside and in.

Sharon walks over to her. "Mom, all of that is 'old stuff,' like you say, and this won't change all of that, but don't you see, it could allow me know for sure that Del's my father. He and I might have a stronger relationship."

"No, I don't see. Just believe that he is. I've told you. Let it go."

"No, Mom, I won't. I can't. I'm asking this of you because of..."

"Yes, because of...what? Why? Why? Why do you need to know?"

Sharon is shaking too, but she takes a step back toward me and holds my hand, almost in tears, "Can't you see, Mom? Can't you see? Lee and I are in love." It comes out loud and clear, like a church bell ringing. I feel my chest release, my heart enlarge, as we all just stand there.

Suddenly the door comes crashing open. It's Hank from the other room.

"You little whore!" he yells, bolting across the room and slapping Sharon across the face. I try to get up to defend her but he pushes me down. "Stay there, you little shit. I ought to break your neck."

Shirley screams "Stop it! Stop it!" and tries to step between us, but he pushes her back against the sink. Some dishes come crashing down and I am up now standing between him and Sharon.

"Come on, Hank," I say "I'll take all you've got."

Shirley rushes toward him yelling, "Stop it! Stop it!"

"Get out of my house. Both of you!" he yells back, drunkenly sweeping us away with his arm. The kids have come down now and are standing in the doorway. He points to Sharon, "You, you don't live her any more, you hear, you tramp!"

Sharon, steps past me. "Go ahead, hit me, you brute. That's all you know." He steps back, and she moves forward, "I'm dying to get away from you. I only stay on to keep these kids safe." The youngest girl runs over to Sharon who takes her into her arms. "I'll go. But you do anything to any of them, and I'll have the police in here in a flash." Hank stares at us all mutely like a dumb animal.

I have never seen her so bold, her face flush, her eyes defiant. She hands little Gretchen over to her mom.

"Sharon is coming with me," I say and we brush past him and stand at the door.

Sharon looks back at her mom, her brother and sisters. "I love all of you," she says and we are gone, together out into the cold night.

We go into my basement and just hold each other a long time in the dark. We don't want to cause another scene with my folks, so I just borrow the car keys and we drive up to Kenny's place, hoping he'll be there. We knock at his door like Mary and Joseph.

He opens, and I say, "Ken, I need to ask you a great favor."

"Hey, come on in. Is that Sharon with you? Christ it's cold out there. Get in here."

Kenny's place seems a haven now; clothes and shoes and newspapers are still lying around, but it's warm and welcoming. His father is sleeping upstairs. We go into the kitchen, and Sharon takes off her coat and goes to the counter to make coffee. She's wearing that red dress I love, and I am so proud of her. Despite the awful scene, we've broken a shell and come out into the world.

Kenny looks right at me, and I say it, "We've told Sharon's folks that we love each other. Hank was there and things exploded."

"Oh my God! You guys are going through with it."

We both nod.

"I'm happy for you. Really," Kenny says. "And I'm worried too. Have you thought this through?"

Sharon and I look at each other, then she says, "We don't know everything yet, Kenny. It just came out, just now," and she turns to me, "but it felt good and right."

"Hank kicked her out of the house," I say like it's a prelude to something.

"Wow, this is big," he says, and without a pause, "You can stay here, Sharon...until you work something out."

"Will your dad be alright with that?" I ask.

"Are you kidding? He loves Sharon too. We all do," and he goes over to hug her at the sink. *What friends are for.*

He turns and I say, "Thanks, man, you're a life saver." Sharon comes over and sits on my lap, wrapping her arms around my neck. All of this drama has taken a toll, but to sit here with these two people I love gives me new breath. My folks are next.

An hour later I decide to go this one on my own, to leave Sharon at Kenny's place and drive down the hill to home, though what home is seems to change moment to moment. Sharon and I need to find our own place to be together. The cold air is biting as I pull the car up to the garage. The light is on, so I figure Dad must be here working on his car. I toot the horn and he opens the door. I pull the car in, and he is standing there in winter overalls bent over the old Ford's engine. He's rigged a large blowing heater to keep the place workable.

"Hey," I offer as I close the garage door.

"Hey, yourself. My gosh it's cold," he says and faces me. "What's going on?"

"Why? What do you mean?" I ask.

"Come on, son. You suddenly come home and disappear down to Sharon's house." He shines his flashlight toward me. "Your face says a lot. I just can't read it."

"You're right. A lot is going on. I just don't know how to tell it all. I'm glad we're down here alone before talking to Mom."

"I figured that. That's why I came down here, so we could talk. I'll spare you some of your pain by saying I know that something's going on between you and Sharon. I know you're more than friends. Anyone with eyes can see it. "

"Does Mom?"

"Your mom doesn't see what she don't want to. And she won't till you tell her." He looks me square in the face. "You're going to have to tell her."

"I know."

He puts his hand on my shoulder. "How could you get into this so deep, son? Didn't you know where it would lead? The church, the state, the town will all say it's wrong. What did you think?"

"That's just it, I didn't think, Dad. I fell in love, like you did once with Mom. Like any two people who care for each other." He does not take his hand away. We stand there in the dimly lit garage as moments pass. The wind outside is blowing as loud as his heater, a smell of gas and oil surrounds us, and my heart beats large in my chest.

"So, what's your plan?" he finally asks.

"We don't want to hurt anyone," I say looking back at him, wearing those overalls and understanding. "Hank threw Sharon out of the house tonight. She's staying up with Kenny and his dad for now. We're ready to face this, Dad." He does not move away. "We honestly don't know what comes next."

"Well, I know you don't need advice. But next you have to tell your mother and deal with that. "

"I know. I will tonight."

"Then, let me add this. If things work out with this test, I'd like to see you go back to college while Sharon finds a place here or there."

"God, Dad, you've been thinking harder than we have. I love your accepting this and helping us. Hank went nuts and Sharon's mom just cried. How is it you're able?"

"Well, Hank's a bitter man, and Shirley's, well Shirley. But listen, I've made my own mistakes, Lee. And you forget one thing," he stands close and swallows as his face gets flush, "I love Sharon too."

Up at the house, Mom is asleep in the lounge chair, an old Betty Hutton film playing on the television. Mom loves Betty's spunk, but her own has run down for the night. Janie and Diane are already in bed, and Dave is still not home. I hate to wake her, but it's time to talk.

"Mom...Mom...It's Lee. You fell asleep."

"Oh, Lee, I fell asleep," she says and tries to straighten in the chair. I push it gently forward from behind, then come around and sit on the couch beside her.

"What's the matter?" she asks, reading my face.

"I'm having a problem, Mom."

"With school?"

"No, not with school...with life. I have something hard to tell you."

She reaches toward me, touches my hand, "Go on, you know we love you, son. We'll deal with anything."

I almost back out at this point. *How can loving someone hurt others that you love?* "Well, I came home to persuade Sharon's mom to take a paternity test with Dad and Sharon."

"Oh, son, why do you keep bringing this up? It's done. It's over. We live with it."

I lean forward and take her hand. "Because, Mom...Sharon and I are in love."

She jerks her hand back in a gasp as if I'd stabbed her. "No...no...it can't be!" she keeps saying. "You can't do this, Lee. It will ruin us!" Her eyes grow wet with tears, and my own heart hurts, but I do not cry.

"Mom, I'm sorry. It just happened. Neither of us sought it, but we can't deny it any longer."

"Oh, God, what will we do! What will we do?"

I try to take her hand again, but she pulls away. "Listen, please, Mom. For now, we don't have to tell anyone. I'm going back to school. Sharon is going to find a place. Hank kicked her out."

"Maybe we should kick you out," she says cutting me hard, but I accept the wound. She is up from her chair, and I follow her into her kitchen. I take her arm and turn her.

"Mom, I love you. I'm sorry," I say in a breath.

"Give me time," she says, still gasping. "I need your father. Where is he?"

"He's coming up from the garage. He was giving us time to talk."

"He knows then?"

"He does."

"Give me time," she says again. "Oh, Lee...Oh, Lee" brings on tears.

These scenes have taken their toll on all of us. One more. I stop down at Sharon's place to pick up a suitcase her mom has packed, and she meets me at the back door. She too has been crying. I do not speak.

She looks into my face and says, "Lee, I didn't know. I didn't want to see. Tell her I love her...and I'll take the test." She steps into the cold to hug me. The first light out of this darkness, but bought at such a price.

Chapter Nine
Planning

Charlotte is glad at the news that we'll be doing the paternity testing. She comes over to me in the lab and puts her arm around my shoulder. She smells of lilac which almost defeats the chemical smell of the lab. I have never had a friend like her, a beautiful, smart woman. She looks right into my eyes and says, "Lee, we're going to have some news for you in about three weeks, as soon as I get the blood samples. I hope it's what you want to know."

"Whatever shows up, we'll deal with." I don't really want to get into all of the details of the visit home, but I find myself telling them anyway. "Sharon has moved out. Her father 'threw her out,' as they say back home. She's living with a friend."

"Oh my, Lee, this must be really hard for you...and everyone." Her arm is still around me, and we are standing close.

"It is," I confess. "But we're dealing with it. Sharon has two months of school left before she takes her test to be a public accountant. Then she's going to move down here."

Charlotte drops her arm. "No matter the results of the test?"

I look hard into myself and know the answer. "No matter the results. We love each other."

"Well, let's hope the results make it easier for you to do that. I know that it's the biggest decision of your life."

At work, Chance seems to know already. "Hey, I hear you had a good weekend at home."

"How'd you hear that?"

"Oh, I have my connections," he says and grins. "Charlotte and I are friends... friends of our friend Lee."

I'm struck that she might have betrayed our confidence. I stare at him.

"Don't worry, guy. She didn't disclose any of your dark secrets or who your secret lover might be. She's very professional."

I breathe easy but have to ask, "So, do you and Charlotte have a thing?"

"A thing...you call it? A thing...Yeah, I'd say there's a 'thing' between us," and he gives a big laugh. "She's great."

"Don't I know it, man."

"Hey, back off there, brother. That woman is mine." He punctuates this with a punch to my right arm.

"Ouch! That hurts. So you're dating an older woman."

He sets the big pot on the drying side of the sink. "Well, remember, I'm a senior and was off two years, so I'm a few years older than you, kid. Anyway, she's only four years older than me. Hell, man, we're both adults."

"Not a problem," I say and punch him back. "Go for it, man." Then we both turn to the stack of dishes that have been piling up at the window.

As the work slows, I ask, "Hey, Chance, if you were off for a year, how come you didn't get drafted then?"

"The leg, man—broken leg kept me off the team and out of Vietnam, though I never had to face a draft board," he says without stopping work.

"Oh, yeah, sorry. I forgot."

"Really bad break in a couple places, and even the Army doesn't seem to want cripples."

Sometimes I should just think before I talk.

We spray and rack, spray and rack, then make plans to meet at the protest rally up on the hill.

My other love is with American Literature, not a girl but two old guys, Ralph Waldo Emerson and his buddy Henry David Thoreau. Their ideas really blow me away. I get hooked into them, follow a path, lose my way, and have to go back and reread again and again, but they're truly revolutionary and wise. They see us and the earth together as one, a spirit and wisdom glowing in "each and all," as Emerson says. For them the writer's job is to witness and reveal this light. My own light comes on when I read them. Their prose is beautiful, and they wrote this stuff a century ago. So why, I wonder, hasn't the world caught on to this Romantic vision and changed?

Now, I'm not ready to move into the woods alone, but if Sharon were with me, I'd make it work. Maybe we won't have to move to Alaska, but to the woods of Southern Ohio, back where the McCall clan began.

About a week ago, I went into the Commuters Center and got a ride off the campus board to McArthur. It's only 20 minutes away. When I got there, I walked around the small downtown, found the cemetery with some McCall names on headstones. At the library a guy helped me with genealogy a bit, then gave me the name of Wilbur's son Harry still living in town. Wilbur would be my grandpa's brother, and Harry my father's cousin. I ring them up, and pretty soon Harry Jr. shows up, a guy my age in a plaid flannel shirt, with short hair and a mustache. His old Dodge sedan pulls up to the door, and he yells out, "Hey! You, Lee McCall?" I nod my head. "Get in," he says and he drives me out to the old McCall place, a small slat house on the corner of a great hilly farm.

"This here's the one acre we all started from, going back to Andy and Mariah."

"No, shit," I say. "Grandpa used to tell of this place. They had some hard times, huh?"

Harry looks over at me from the car seat, wondering how far to trust. "Yep, that's how they tell it."

Then I ask, "How did they survive with old Andy taking off like he would for weeks at a time?"

"Well, I asked my pap that once."

I wait, then have to ask, "What did he say?"

"'Mostly we didn't,' is what he said. "'Mostly we didn't.' You get that?"

Someone is renting the house now, but we get out anyway and walk around the place—a shed, wood pile, small garden, a pile of surface coal at the edge of the road—about how Grandpa described it.

"You work around here?" I ask.

"Hell, there ain't no work round here. This here's the poorest county in the state."

"Well, what do you do all day?"

We are back at the car, when Harry stops at the trunk. "Listen here, you're McCall blood, right, so just say no if you're not interested." He lifts the area of the spare tire, reaches under a plank and pulls out a black plastic bag. Inside of the bag, Harry picks out several clear plastic pouches. I recognize marijuana when I see it now, but I smell it to be sure.

"Where'd you get this?" I ask.

"Don't ask," he says. "I got my sources, but you're better off not knowing. Listen ...you interested?" he grins and spits tobacco juice on the ground.

"How much?" I ask.

"How much what...how much I got to sell or how much a bag?"

"How much for the two bags?" I ask wondering if I'm carrying enough cash.

"Fifty for each," he says and spits his chew out on the ground.

"Whoa, I didn't expect any of this," I try to laugh. "I don't have more than a 20 on me. I have more back on campus; I could come out another time."

"You know, cuz, you could sell this around to the college boys and triple your money." He pulls out his wrapping papers, spreads some of the pot on one, then rolls a joint, licks off the ends, hands it to me and lights it.

What the hell am I getting into? I'll smoke but I won't sell.

I smile. "Harry," I say, looking into his face, "Thanks, but I'm not brave enough to risk selling. Hey...but I would pay you the 50 if I had it."

He hands me the bag, throws the other back in the trunk compartment, and says, "I got nothing to do today. I'll drive you back to Athens, and you can get me the rest." So the McCall tradition of selling has moved from moonshine to pot, and though I'm not a seller, I am a holder and a smoker. Somewhere I read that the Transcendentalists smoked this stuff on their path to enlightenment, so now I'm also a follower.

After work that night, I walk down by the river, sit on a rock and smoke one, then just wait for a great light to come.

"Lee, I'm still here at Kenny's," she says. "I clean the place a little each day. They both work, and Kenny drops me off at Nosset's when I do. It's all working out. How are you holding out?"

She sounds good. "I'm okay. Miss you like crazy."

"Oh, me too, I do," she says and we share the longing.

"How are your classes going?" I ask.

"Good...boring. We covered all this stuff in high school. I can't wait to be done. I was wondering if maybe I could take a few classes down there at OU, then take the CPA test."

"Well, sure, sounds like a plan. I've been watching the paper for apartments or little houses off-campus. Chance says they open up at the end of each quarter. God, girl, it will be so good going through all this with you at my side."

"Lee, the gossip travels here in Mingo. Some people know about us, and I'm sure Patty will find out down there. How are we going to face those stares when I move to Athens? I mean if the test shows that...Del's our father."

"Gosh, those words sound strange. I'm praying that it won't. Besides, OU is a big place and people don't keep watch over everyone like they do back home. And I think we both know your mom is hiding something, enough to allow this test. How are things going at home?"

She sighs into the phone. "I talk to Mom and the kids on the phone, but I'm not going near that place with Hank there. He has no rights really, but according to the law, he does. I'm just staying clear."

"That's wise. Two things to remember: first, that I don't care what others think. And second, that I love you, and I'll face anything with you."

Silence seals it. Finally we both say "I love you," pause a moment, then hang up.

I get to work early, and Chance is already scrubbing the pots and pans. I put on my apron and he turns his head to ask, "So what you reading in American Lit these days?"

"I forget that you helped me choose all of my courses this term."

"Who's your prof for that?"

"New guy, I guess, Dick Snyder. Know him?"

"Can't say I do. What's he like?"

"Well, first day of class, he comes in a little late, longish hair and wearing a tan silk shirt with a brown vest and jeans. We all figure he's one of us, but then he lays all of his books on the front desk and begins to talk."

"The hip prof thing, huh?"

"I guess, but I like him. At first I figured he was a liberal democrat, like my folks, then an atheist by how he rushed though the Puritans. Then I started seeing him as a college socialist for all the leftist ideas he works into his lectures. Today when he talked for an hour about Transcendentalism and their communes, I could see a new light in his eyes."

"No shit. You must be into American Romanticism... Emerson, Thoreau, Margaret Fuller and those folks."

"You got it. Snyder is crazy about them, and to tell the truth, so am I."

"Count me in on that one," Chance says and hands me a drying rag for the pots.

"Well, you know, living in a mill town, I never knew such things as communes really existed...people living together with high ideals and then acting on them. Back home we all just worked to get by, you know. But we do stand up for our rights when we're pressed."

"Viva the Union!"

"Yep. But these Concord folks were real Romantic anarchists. They wanted to change the whole damn society by their example."

"Did Snyder tell about old Bronson Alcott and his disaster at Fruitlands?"

"As a matter of fact he did. He really knows his stuff, probably did his dissertation on it. He told us how Alcott and Lane set up this farming commune west of Concord with their families."

"Yeah, don't forget, I took the course last year, buddy. Both Alcott and Lane drag their families into it: vegan diet, no heated baths, no artificial light, no animal labor. And no real sense how to go about farming."

This is one of those really great conversations you sometimes have, and we're standing in the dorm kitchen. "Yeah, they didn't make it through seven months, and so little Louisa May later takes her revenge on her old man by writing her satire *Transcendental Wild Oats*."

"Gotta love her for that," Chance says, pushing me with his shoulder, and we both laugh.

"Right, but I have to tell you, man, I like this idea of a utopian farm commune. And that other one, Brook Farm near Harvard, was a real success at first, so I feel it could be done."

Chance stops laughing and moves closer. "Go on, tell me what you learned, Mr. Transcendentlist."

"Well, George and Sophia Ripley buy this big farm, see, and, though socialists, they sell joint stock in it. They set it up so profits are shared for equal work, and figure if everyone shares the work load, each will share time for leisure and great thought. It makes sense, you know."

"Let me quote Ripley, 'Industry without drudgery, and true equality without its vulgarity,'"

"Wow, how'd you know that?"

He looks straight at me. "I believe it, Lee. Physical work for a healthy mind and body. It's Buddhism really, like where everyone, including the main abbot, cleans the toilets. No one's better or worse than another. I'll take stock in that."

"You surprise me, Chance."

"Yeah, and sometimes I surprise myself."

"Okay, but let's be real here." I set down the dry rag. "It didn't last, and it didn't change the world."

"Right, but don't forget," he says, "they ran into two problems: they overbuilt and a fire destroyed them financially. And so what if they didn't really get the farm working. Their real income was from the school they ran for kids and adults. What did Snyder tell you?"

"Well," I try to recall yesterday's talk. "He said it was grander than Fruitland and with good people like Theodore Parker, Elizabeth Peabody...and that Emerson, Thoreau, and even Fuller visited Brook Farm and called it a 'grand experiment.'"

We've forgotten all about cleaning up. Chance asks, "Did he tell how Hawthorne was an original shareholder?"

"No kidding!"

"Yeah, and ole Nathaniel gets pissed off at all the labor they expect, and so he demands his money back? Read his *Blithedale Romance* on that one."

"Yeah, I'm going to ask Snyder about that." The kitchen is now open and about to serve dinner, but I don't want to stop thinking to work. "Chance, I'll tell you, this is the most exciting concept I've come to in my whole 12 years of public school and almost two quarters of college. And, you and Snyder are excited about it too."

"I'm with you, guy, 'cause what I really admire, see, is their willingness to act on their ideals. Look around, governments, religions, institutions—where else do you see that? You get a bunch of good people together who can break from the American way of violence and greed. Give good folks a new vision and, hell, man, they'll start a whole new stream of life in this country!"

"Christ, listen to us, we'll be running for office in a minute here," I joke.

"No way, man, no office, no officers, no kings, queens, bishops or rooks—just us co-op pawns sharing all the way." He raises a fist. This is the most serious I have ever seen Chance, and we find ourselves hugging each other just as Murray appears and the cookware starts coming up from the kitchen.

Murray looks at us funny, but I feel like dancing. Oh, I'm know Sharon and I will have some good talks about this. We've been running away from things too long, time we begin moving toward something.

Chapter Ten

Some Results

"Hey, Lee McCall...you have a call! Hey, that rhymes." Don the RA laughs to himself; the rest of us laugh at him, but I jump out of my bunk almost hitting my head and walk down the hallway to the phone. It could be Sharon, or Dad, or well, anyone from back home.

"Yeah, hello. Lee here."

"Oh, good, I got hold of you. I have some news."

"Hold on a sec, who is this?"

"Lee, this is Charlotte. I'm calling from my office."

"Oh, hello, Charlotte." She's never called me before. "I was taking a nap, so I'm a little dopey. What's up?"

"Lee," she almost whispers. "I don't want to tell anything over the phone, in case it's monitored. But I have some 'good news' for you I'd like to deliver in person. Can I come over there to your dorm?"

"Yeah, that would be great. When?"

"How about in 10 minutes? I'm all finished here and ready to head home. I'll see you at McDonald...right?" And like that, she hangs up. I head back to my room to put on some decent clothes, and it hits me...She must have the test results.

James is sitting at his desk writing a letter in his underwear. It's near the end of March, but he still wears the long johns he bought here in Ohio. "Yours is a very cold country," he tells me every time he comes in or goes out.

"What's happening, Mr. Lee?" he asks.

"Wait, what did you just call me?"

"Mr. Lee? I was, as you say, joking with you."

"Oh, that's funny, 'cause there's a song about 'Mr. Lee...Mr. Lee.'"

"Yours is a strange country. I never heard of a name that is just one syllable. You see how I remain an outsider in your country."

"Yeah, and sometimes I feel an outsider here too and at this college."

He doesn't get it and shakes his head, then asks, "Your girlfriend is coming to visit?"

"No, no, that was one of my professors. She's stopping by to give me some results."

"Well, indeed, you must be quite an important person. I have never seen a professor in the college dormitory."

"Indeed, I must be," I say in a mock British accent. He's really a good guy, and laughs. Then it hits me anew...Charlotte has the blood test results! My gosh, what a dope I am. What were her words? I think she said 'good news' or was it just 'news?' I go back and forth on that while I change into my jeans and Tom's old flannel shirt that I've been wearing to class all week, then I rush back down the hallway to wait for her.

"Hurry, my good man," James calls to me.

I sit waiting in the foyer on those awful plastic chairs, as though I'm in a doctor's office. And maybe I am. My mind's racing...*what are my results, what's my next move?* It feels like life or death. I'll call Sharon first, and then Dad and maybe let each of them break the news to the moms. I am so getting ahead of myself. I don't know anything yet. I get up and go outside to watch for her. Finally, a car pulls into the lot, a white Nova, almost new. It's hers. As I walk across the asphalt parking lot, she gets out of her car. She stands in the streetlight in this beautiful camel overcoat, a white scarf around her neck, like a model in a magazine. "Charlotte," I call, "I'm here."

"And I'm here too," she smiles and holds out her hands to me. "Where's best for a private talk?" she asks, and I point to her car.

"How about right here?"

"Fine," she smiles and rubs my shirt sleeved arm. "You'll have to get in quick."

I hold the door for her, and even in the midst of this confusion, as she gets in, I notice her long slender legs. I jump in the other side and rub my hands together. "Okay, what do we know?"

"It's good," she says. "Now listen, the results are as conclusive as can be made at this time that you and Sharon are *not* brother and sister."

I lose it right there. A heavy breath comes out of my chest, and my heart is pounding. "We're not?" I have to ask, my eyes warm with tears.

"Not even close, Lee. I don't see how they could have ever concluded this with so little evidence. Of course, Sharon's mother did declare it was true, and your father didn't deny it." I look over at her as she taps her finger on the papers in my hands, leans forward and says what I think, "My guess is she's hiding who the real father is because he's too close and she's afraid."

I take hold of her hands again. "Charlotte, I can't thank you enough. This is a real life changer for me and Sharon, for all of us really. And you made it happen." She has tears in her eyes too as we sit in the glow of the streetlight snow lightly falling around us. Something holds me back from kissing her in the dorm parking lot.

She pulls herself together, takes a hanky out of her coat pocket. "Now, we have to go over this once more," she says. "This is as thorough of a test as is possible, and the results are conclusive, but right now they must remain private. They can't be made public. It would jeopardize this study and perhaps my position here."

"I know. We all do. It could hurt you, and none of us want that. What can we do though?"

"Well, I guess I could write all of this down in a letter to be held in confidence. And I'm willing to call and talk with each of them."

"That would be so great. I'm just blown away by all this, really."

"What's important, Lee, is that now you and Sharon know. Isn't that right?"

"Yes, it is." I sit there breathing in and out, letting it all sink in.

"Do you think you'll marry the girl?"

I look out the windshield as snow flakes land and melt. "Marry? We're not ready for that, but live together...yes, as soon as possible." She doesn't ask, but I volunteer, "We've been practicing abstinence."

"Wow, good for you," she says, then pauses. "I've been doing that myself."

I'm surprised but don't go down that path with her. I get out of the car, shaking her hand once more at her window, then bend to kiss her soft cheek. "You're a savior."

She smiles, "A savior, I'm not...a goddess, maybe. I can't wait to meet Sharon." And she drives off.

"Hello, Kenny, it's Lee, can I speak with Sharon, please."

"Well, buddy, she'll be home in about 15 minutes. My dad is picking her up. And, Lee, I have to tell you, since she moved in, the old man has pretty much sobered up. Never thought I'd see it. So what's up with you?"

"Oh, nothing much...but I have to speak with her. I can't tell you till I've told her. You get it?"

"I dig it. I know something's going on. She's been hyper too...ups and downs. She should be here in 15, like I said. What else is going on?"

"Well, they haven't bounced me out of here yet, though they haven't made me feel at home either. And I met one of my cousins from down here. He gets me my supply of tea, if you know what I'm saying."

"Oh, yeah? They growing tea in southern Ohio now? And your cousin grows or delivers?"

"To tell the truth, I'm not really sure, but if you get your sorry ass down here someday, I'll share some with you, and it's fine tea, brews up real nice."

"Hey, till I do, enjoy, but watch out for the copperheads in the woods."

"Gotcha. So, hey, I'll call back in a bit."

"Gotcha."

I walk over in the snow to the student union where no one who knows me can overhear. So while I stand around and wait, I get a cup of hot coffee from a machine. When I worked that summer in the mill, a coffee machine wouldn't work for a couple weeks, so somebody picked it up and tossed it over the bank. I am thinking this while I'm also thinking I'd like to jump in a car and drive home to Sharon. This is something that needs celebrating.

"Hi...Sharon, we have the results."

"Oh, gosh, is it good news?"

"Yes, love, it is. The test results show that Del is not your real father."

"Oh, my God, my God, Lee, I can't believe it!" and she squeals on the other end of the line. Kenny is probably dying by now. "I love you," she says. "This wouldn't have happened without you and Charlotte. What if you hadn't gone to OU? Do you ever think about that? Don't." All the gates are down and she is just streaming with thoughts.

"Lee?"

"Yeah, honey, I love you too."

"Lee, then who is my real father? Can the test tell me that?"

"Someday probably, but I think that's a question you have to ask your mom."

"Believe me, I will." Still gasping for breath and thought, she says. "Oh, Lee, I love your dad, and I don't want to lose that bond...but now I have it through you."

I take a sip of my coffee and suddenly a plan appears. "Listen, honey, we're almost at spring break here. Charlotte says she's writing all of this up in a letter that she'll share with you, my folks, and your mom. But it has to remain confidential because it could compromise her study and job, or she's willing to come and share it with you in person. So, what if, I don't know, what if I drive home with her this weekend, and we can really celebrate Easter and our freedom together?"

"Oh, yes! Do that please. Oh, Lee...I want to give myself to you."

"Oh, Baby, those words are too much. I won't be able to think of anything else this week. But do yourself a favor...talk with your mom. Now that the mask is off, she just may share with you. She owes you that."

"You're right, but Lee, who else can I tell about this?"

"Well, really no one. I guess Kenny, but swear him to secrecy." There is a long pause while we try to take it all in, through tears I say, "I love you, and we are free to love wholly," then "I'm going to call my dad right now."

"Soon," she whispers, then hangs up. I dig out the rest of my quarters, take another breath, finish my coffee, and dial. "Hey, hi, Mom, it's me, your long lost son. How are things going?"

She sighs into the phone, "Oh, okay, I guess. My sister was here Sunday. It's been almost a year now since your uncle Homer passed away. Dave got a lead in the school play. The girls are fine. Did you want to talk with your father?"

"As a matter of fact, I do have some business with him to discuss. Is he there?"

"Are you kidding! He's always down in that darn garage...Oh, wait, I hear him coming up the basement steps. Hang on, honey....Del, Del, here, it's Lee for you."

His big voice comes over the receiver, "Hello, son, I thought you might be calling. What's the word?"

"Well, you were absolutely right. I do have news about the blood tests. You might want to sit down."

"Oh, brother, what now?"

"It's good news really, Dad, for Sharon and me. The test shows that you are not her blood father. And Sharon says to tell you how she loves you still."

"Wow, after all of these years! After all of these years, we finally know something." I can hear him taking a breath. "She's a sweet girl, Lee, and I love her right back, but you know what this means?"

"What? You're ahead of me here?"

"It means old Shirley's been lying all this time and that someone else fathered Sharon."

"Yep, it means just that. It couldn't have been old Hank home on leave could it?"

"Nope, we checked all of that when Shirley first told me I was the pop. Hank was away for 2 months of basic training in Texas, and she didn't visit. So unless he sent his sperm home in a jar, someone else did the deed, and I been carrying the weight of it all these years...especially with your mother."

"Here's the thing, Dad," I say in a lower voice. "We know it for sure from the test, but we can't make it public because it's part of Charlotte's study and not authorized yet. Can you live with that?"

"How do you say, I'm down with that, son? Anyway, I am. Hey, when are you coming home?"

"Maybe this weekend...and Charlotte Harris who did the test can meet you and explain it all. She wants to come." Of course, I hadn't asked Charlotte about this trip home, but she seems more than willing to follow through. "Hey, Dad."

"Yeah, what?"

"I love you for sticking by us through all of this. Do you want me to tell, Mom?"

"Well, no, son. I think I'd like to deliver that bit of news myself. But you bring your friend home to make it official."

*   *   *

Fortunately the next day the snow dies down, and the trip is set. Charlotte takes the wheel to Marietta, and I drive her up river to home. She is quiet through much of the trip, watching the winding road of Rte. 50 then grading papers beside me as I run her Nova through the gears. "That's the big Ohio River," I tell her as we roll north toward Sistersville, Bellaire, Bridgeport, all those river towns with great names, then on toward Martins Ferry, Yorkville, Brilliant, then home. We got a mid-day start, so the sun is slowly setting to the left over the Wayne National Forest.

"Well, what do you think so far?" I ask as we roll into Sisterville?

"It's lovely really, so deeply etched. Lee, this is strong country. I can see why you're attached."

"Yeah, it has great beauty and great ugliness too, can't deny it," And we pass the huge smoke stack of Powhattan Point. "Across the river in West Virginia you get a better sense of the mountains. Up river is Bridgeport and Wheeling."

"I knew a Bridgeport in Connecticut, close to where I grew up," she shares. The sun is setting as she slides all of her paperwork into her bag. "Are we close yet?"

"About an hour more," I say, then "I love these hills, can't understand why James Wright, Martins Ferry's poet laureate, wanted to escape them. *Green Walls* he named his first book. To me they're lush green arms."

"Hmmm," she answers, then asks, "Any more news from back home?"

"Well, yes and no. Sharon's talked with her mother and told her we're coming. She says she wants to hear it from your lips before she talks any more."

"Well, I'd say you and Sharon are the couple of the hour, but her mom sure earns a second stage...and your mother and father?"

"Dad's relieved though still working things out, and Mom's, well, almost penitent. She's been pretty hard on Dad all these years for his indiscretion."

"Well," she says, looking over at me, "this doesn't exactly erase that, you know."

"Yeah, but because he didn't father a child out of wedlock in our hometown, he's exonerated from a major indiscretion. It's the town's moral code."

"Yes, I agree, but remember, the town can't know any of this yet." Then she looks over to me, puts her hand over mine, "I'm glad we decided to do this in person, Lee. There's less risk to the study, of course, but it also brings me closer to you and Sharon. I can't wait to meet everyone."

We enter the early evening dusk in Martins Ferry where I stop for gas at an Amoco station. I insist on paying, though it takes my last dime. Maybe Ken or Dave will lend me some. When I get back in, I ask, "So, Charlotte, if you don't mind my asking, how are things with you and Chance?"

She gives a little start, "Hmm," looks over and puts her hand on my wrist, "I think, Lee, because he's still a student that I'd better not open that door with you. Okay?"

"Sure thing," and because I know she's wondering, I add, "He just said he thinks you're great."

"Well, I think he's great too," she says and leans back in her seat. She is wearing a soft blue woman's pant suit, her camel hair coat spread on the back of her seat. It is still cold in the Ohio Valley, 40 degrees, but the car is warm and close. She smells of a garden of lilac.

Unlike any visit back home...we come bearing glad tidings, if only all could enjoy them. We pull into the Holiday Inn on Stony Hollow Boulevard just north of town in Steubenville where Charlotte will be staying. My folks had offered to put her up, but it was getting a bit bizarre to imagine her sleeping down the hallway or waiting in line for the bathroom in our old house. I carry her bag to the front desk where she smiles, hands me the keys to her car, and says, "I'll see you in the morning."

I park on the street in front of our house, and Sharon comes rushing out the door and into my arms. She is so alive and warm and soft. She's crying, and all of the emotions of this crazy testing rush through me. We just hold each other in the cold night air. Then I take her face in my hands and kiss her lips, her eyes, her hair. "I never want to lose you," she says softly.

"You never will," my heart answers back, and when I look up, Mom is watching us through the front window and smiling. A block down the hill her mother is waiting.

That night, Sharon sleeps in the room next to mine with my sister Diane. Lying there, I listen, and their talking sounds like music.

The next morning, Shirley calls. Hank is at work, so Sharon has gone down to talk with her, while I go pick up Charlotte. In her hand she holds the letter from Charlotte explaining the results.

I'm having a second coffee with Charlotte when I get a call. I can hardly hear what she's saying. She's so excited or sad or both. Finally I say, "Let's meet at the garage," and she agrees.

Charlotte is seated at our kitchen table talking with my parents as if she were a long lost relative come home. Mom's a little shy, but offers her a homemade crumb cake she baked. Charlotte is drawn to Dad, who seems to be the universal father.

"Hey, folks, I have to run down and talk with Sharon. Something's happened."

"Oh, my, is Hank at home?" Mom cautions.

"You want me to come," Dad volunteers, fearing the worst.

"No, it's alright. She wants to tell me something, and I can't make it out on the phone." To Charlotte I say, "She lives just a block away. I'll be right back."

I tread through the snow and step inside the garage, turn on the light, and start up Dad's heater. I used to smoke cigarettes down here, kissed a few girls here too, but nothing like kissing Sharon. I look around. Dad's car is now a shiny black with new leather seat cushions. I think about sitting on them when suddenly Sharon is at the door. I go to her. Her face is flush from crying, but her eyes clear and loving. I hold her and don't want to let her go.

She pulls back. "She told me," she gasps. "It's Nate...Uncle Nate, Hank's brother, is my father."

I can't get the right words out.

"Oh, Lee, she was afraid Hank would kill them both, so she blamed your father."

"Jesus! I can't believe it!"

"You have to," she says. "It's the truth after 19 years of lying."

"Are you alright?" I ask, trying to read her eyes.

"I don't know. I don't know anything." She takes a quick breath and looks out at me. "The truth doesn't come with all the answers."

"No, it's hard, I know. But it lights the way out of the lies. We've been struggling so hard to be accepted and fit in, and now I'm beginning to question whether fitting in for others is even the right thing."

"I don't understand," she says, "but I know I love you," and kisses me fully.

"My God, Sharon," I say taking a deep breath. "We're free now...to love each other totally. We'll face anything together."

We stand there holding each other a long time without words, her body's lightness pressing fully against my trunk. We can hear the March winds above the distant mill roar, and in the small sounds of this room, the creaking and silences of this moment, we exist as one. Our bodies relax at last in soft breaths. Our long kiss and full embrace marry us.

Chapter Eleven
Making the Move

In May, the OU campus is shut down, the whole damn thing's under martial law. After the senseless slaughter of students at Kent State, then Jackson State, protests down here grow larger and more violent. When the National Guard comes onto campus, we sense we are the next to be sacrificed. And so the whole campus is now shut down like Kent, but a lot of us refuse to give in. At home we have no voice, and so many of us are hanging on down here waving our banners of protest at the government and the university. When Chance spends a couple days in jail for a sit-in at the administration building, I move into his place to take care of his dog Blackie. The final two weeks of May I'm wrapping up course work and typing up my term papers to mail to campus, two blocks away. At night we're standing in candle lit vigils with protest signs along the campus edge, facing down the guardsmen. It's a crazy time when fear and hope compete for space. Home seems a long way off, except for Sharon, who is working her way here day by day.

And so this June I do not go home. I take a job working with Chance in the kitchen of the Bagel & Deli Shop on West Union Street. When his buddy Clyde graduates and moves out, I move in with Chance and Blackie for real on Smith Street. Oppressed coal miners once lived in these old wood frame houses, where oppressed students now live. Sharon will be joining me here as soon as she extracts herself from home. My folks have been good about the whole thing of our being together. She eats Sunday dinner with them, and she and her mom are getting close again. "Things move on," I tell her, "how about you?" and she's almost ready. In a couple weeks, she starts a job down here working in the registration office. We talk on the phone every night after work. Things move on.

"I'm willing to do anything to be with you," she says, "though I'm not unafraid. You know, this living together is a big step for me."

"Yeah, I hear you, but it's the right step. Half the couples down here are doing it."

"Well, I know we've talked about this, Lee, but are you sure we shouldn't be legally married first, in case there are any questions? I'm willing if you are."

"Listen, honey, we couldn't say yes a year ago, and now since the results of the test, we've shared almost everything without that piece of paper making us legal. I hate to have others telling us what's right, and I can't stand honoring a government that is so wrong about so much. We make our life, and we live freely from our own inner conscience."

"Well, I hear you, I do, but I have to say you sound like whatever you've been reading lately or what you and Chance have been talking about. Remember I'm still living in our hometown, and for me, I just want to keep our love pure."

"So do I, Sharon. Believe me. I just don't recognize the right of church or state to rule in personal matters. When you move down here, you'll see. We're not meant to live under a microscope where every act is questioned by our peers. We're meant to live free, like Nature." We both pause a long moment, enough time for me to reflect. "I'm sorry, honey. I know I'm sounding like a lecture from old Waldo Emerson. Chance and I have been re-reading him this summer, and he's great. You should get to know him as I do."

There is another pause as we both recognize how awkward that just sounded. "Well, Mr. Intellectual," Sharon counters, "you may be surprised to know that I am reading him from that book you gave me. And I'm also reading Margaret Fuller right here in Mingo."

"Margaret Fuller—wasn't she in the class ahead of us?" I joke.

She doesn't laugh. "No, she wrote *Woman in the Nineteenth Century*—which I got from our own Carnegie Library. Have you read it?"

"Shut my mouth. I forget what a smart woman you are. I'm sorry, and I love you." We both laugh, backing away from our first near argument. "Listen to us," I say. "Oh, come down here and live with me."

"'Come with me and be my wife,' I believe is the line," she corrects, and we laugh again.

Blackie runs past me; Chance is coming in the back door. "You're wonderful," I say, "Chance is coming in. Do you want to say hi to him?"

"No thanks, just say hi for me," she says, and we both sign off with, "I love you and we'll be together soon."

Chance drops his book bag onto the floor, rubs old Blackie's fur, then comes over and tries to rub my head. I push his hand away. "Get out. You smell of grease."

"Boy, sometimes, you sound like a wife. That was Sharon, I'm guessing?"

"No, it was Charlotte. She wants you madly." I pay for that one with a punch to my arm.

"Hey, man, I gotta talk to you about something."

"I just got reamed for preaching Emerson to Sharon on the phone. She's reading Margaret Fuller, can you believe that girl! Somehow I never thought American Romanticism could reach into the Ohio Valley."

"Hey, watch out, you're becoming a snob to the working class, my man. The people—that's where it's at. 'Trust the divine light that's in everyone,' and all that. Anyway, what I want to talk about is more practical than all this."

He hands me a beer out of the fridge. "What? What is it?" I ask, knowing there's no way to stop him when he's onto something.

"Well..." he draws out the moment, "I think we both should get an earring. That's what I think."

"Holly shit, are you kidding me...earrings! Have you gone gay?"

"Now that's just stupid, bud. What you said is just wrong. We're both liberated men, sure of our masculinity...at least I am. Nothing wrong in hanging a piece of gold from one ear to show it. 'Free to Be You and Me'—remember that show? Old Rosey Greer singing 'It's alright to cry' for us guys.'"

"Yeah, as a matter of fact, I do. But an earring is a big step. Can you take it off when you need to?"

"What, the manhood or the ring?"

"The ring."

"And when would you not feel confident wearing it? Back in your hometown, with Sharon or your folks?" I can't tell how serious he really is about this. He loves the rhetorical argument.

"Chance, how serious are you about this? 'Cause I'm considering it?"

"Dead serious man. I already asked at the beauty shop up the street. Rose'll do it for $20, and that includes the gold ring. Come on, man. We can do it right now. I'll loan you the $20 if you need it. Come on, it will change you, man. It will help you to embrace the real you."

"Yeah, and we'll both become pirates and sail on the Hocking River." I'm ready to laugh, but he's not.

He holds out his hand to me. "Come, shake on it. Right here, right now." And we do.

And so ten minutes later we are walking up the street to the Cool Look beauty shop where Rose sits each of us down and asks, "Right ear or left?" We look back dumbly. "Gay or straight?" she asks.

"Oh, straight," we both say. Chance adds, "Straight but not narrow."

One at a time she freezes our ear lobe with an ice cube, then sticks a needle through. It hurts like hell, even if it's over in a moment. Chance jokes, "It's alright to cry," and I just grin. Then she sticks a gold stud in the tiny hole, washes it with a stinging alcohol. We're to keep that in for a couple weeks before we get our gold ring. I stare at Chance, then look at myself in the mirror. Such a small thing, but I do feel a real change. "You look good, man," he says, "I mean—really *bad*."

We step out onto the street and strut uptown to the burrito shop. Inside we watch to see if others are watching us, but only the cashier says, "Hey, you dudes look... like...real cool." We give her a good tip, munch our burritos, and decide to go see a movie.

Peter Bogdanovich's *The Last Picture Show* is playing, "Perfect," I say, and read the playbill aloud: "'A story of a small Texas Town, and youthful rebellion.' That's us, minus the Texas." Chance agrees. In line we watch for others to notice our ear studs, but no one seems to, except the girl at the popcorn stand who just winks and says, "Cool."

We are surprised that the film's in black and white, but ten minutes into it I become Timothy Bottoms' character Sonny. Chance leans over and says, "Hey, that's you, dude," and I nod. When Jeff Bridges comes on as Duane, I just nudge Chance, and he nods. "Yep, he's me." We forget about our new look as we get deeper into the grainy world of this film. Finally Chance says, "No one in that town gives a shit."

"They're all just lost," I say, though I admit it is the starkest film I've ever seen. And then this young beautiful actress comes on playing Jacey, the town debutante. "Who is that!" I say out loud.

"Don't you read the magazines!" the girl beside me whispers, "That's the model Cybill Shepherd." In the film she becomes a tormented bitch, but no one in the film or audience can look away from her beautiful face.

At one point, Chance, nudges me, "That actress ...she looks like your woman—Sharon," and I have to agree. Her fair features and smooth blonde hair, but mostly the way her eyes look into and through you. She's an awful person, the real opposite of my Sharon, but I love watching her. When she takes off her bra and panties in the swimming pool scene, I literally hurt for wanting Sharon. We have not made love yet, though we kiss deep and press our bodies hard together in the car, her bra slides off and I kiss her breast bone, her smooth tongue touches mine. But no, we have not had intercourse. She just started on the pill in June, and I know now that when she comes down here next week, we will.

Back outside, in the streetlights of Court Street, waves of others walk by, looking for a place to drink and mix. And they're in living color, most are smiling about something. And I feel different too, the way a movie can move you out of yourself, the way an ear stud can beckon you on.

*   *   *

Dave is driving Sharon down in the Pontiac for the weekend. And she's bringing some of her things for the move in a week. Our parents have to know what's going on, that she'll be moving in with me, but they don't ask. I guess that means they do and don't approve. So be it. We'll make our own way in this world. Dave says he wants to look the campus over, but to me really he confided, "Really, bro, I have much higher sights than this. I know I can get into Brown with a scholarship." Well, I looked it up, and that scholarship better be pretty big, 'cause Brown's tuition is 10 times what it is here at OU. I guess ole Dave is rising up in the world, yet I do know he's applied to OU as a back up.

Chance and I have had our little conversation about getting some privacy for Sharon and me while Dave's here, so he's taking him for a drive to McArthur to see the McCall place. I wrote out directions, and Harry Jr. will meet up with them. Chance and I have chipped in to share a bag of the homegrown from Harry, though I hope he doesn't try to solicit Dave into sales. Sharon and I will have our time together, and whip up a spaghetti dinner for when they get back, and Charlotte is to come over.

I can't wait to see and be with Sharon. I look around this place at the couch and chair by the front window, the bookcase stacked with texts and paperbacks, Chance's tape player on the floor over there, the used stove and refrigerator in the kitchen, our porcelain table and four chairs, and I know that she'll soon become a part of all this....and she'll make it hers too. It's all really happening. I've kept the earring as a surprise. I hope it's a good one.

They pull up the driveway around noon, and I rise from the porch couch to greet them. I hold out my hand to Dave, who looks at me odd. "What's up, bro? You need a hand?"

"No, I'm extending one to you," and to really challenge him I give him a man hug there on the steps.

"Hey, you got me confused with your pretty maiden here," he laughs, pulling away. And there she is in Saturday sunlight, dressed in a blue print shirtwaist, looking like a flower. Our eyes meet a moment before our kiss and embrace. She feels close and warm, and her sweet smell awakens this life we share...holding on to someone you never want to let go of...ever.

Finally she steps back. "Hi, there," she says, "Well, I'm here." And her smile broadens my own. She's more beautiful than Cybill Shepherd. "Your hair's grown longer," she says and brushes it from my eyes. We kiss again.

"Come on in," I say to both of them and beckon with my arm. Dave brings in their suitcases and sets them in the hall.

I hit the button on the tape player, and "The Best of the Animals" cassette starts up with, what else: "The House of the Rising Sun." Sharon chuckles and takes my hand, says, "Show me around our new home, honey," and we share another kiss while Dave pokes his head into the bedroom.

"Cripe, you're sleeping on the floor," he says. "You have no bed?"

"Well, that's how it's done down here, bub. Saves money, and everything's a reach away. Though I bet at Brown they come and tuck you into your bunk beds." I don't know why, but I do resent his going there.

"What's this thing?"

"It's called a lava lamp, kid, has wax in it that heats up and floats around in the blue liquid...It's really, cool." I look over at Sharon, "What do you think, honey, too much?"

She winks, "Hmm, we'll see if we get used to it."

"Chance's bedroom is upstairs. We got a bathroom on both floors, though the one upstairs has the tub and shower," and I wink at Sharon who smiles. My god, the blood is rushing through me. "Can I get you guys some lemonade? I made it an hour ago. This obviously is the kitchen."

"Hmm, not bad," Sharon says, "better than I had feared."

I pour us each a glass while they look around. "Come on out here. We have a backyard." We go out the screen door with a slam and into the rather rough backyard. "We cut it with a rotary mower, like the one we used to have," and I look over at Dave who sits down in one of the folding lawn chairs. "Maybe you can cut the grass while you're here?" I half-joke.

"Well, that's not exactly the kind of grass I was looking for down here," he says with a grin.

"You smoke?" I ask. "Mr. Intellectual smokes weed?"

"And you?" he asks. "I hear I'm going to meet up with a long lost cousin who supplies." Sharon looks over at me.

"Who told you that?"

"You did last time you were home, bro. You were a little high from being with Kenny, and you kept talking till you fell asleep."

"Well," and I shake my head, "we'll see what develops. Okay?"

"Good enough," he grins, says, "Sit you two down. Be here now—We have arrived."

Sharon rubs his hair and sits, saying, "Well, look who's taking over here."

"I'm just making myself at home," he protests, putting his feet up on the log we've placed before our fire pit. I look over at Sharon who sends me a pretend kiss, and we continue being polite to my brother when what we really want is to smother each other with kisses and sweet loving.

Fifteen minutes later, we do just that in my/our bedroom. I can't touch her enough, and she opens more of herself to me than ever before. "Slowly," she whispers, and while I begin to nibble at her tender neck beneath her soft hair, she squeezes my butt. I love this new boldness in her. I kiss her breast bone and she allows me to open her dress buttons slowly revealing her sheer lacey bra. My heart is pounding. Her skin is so smooth and soft. We are breathing hard against each other, our clothes on, but our bodies pressing together so close and long that we reach climax. Holding her tight afterward, I'm still gasping for breath as she gently brushes back my hair, starts to kiss my ear.

"What's this!" she gasps.

"Oh, that," I say shyly. "It's a stud for an earring." I am so in love with her, I don't want to offend in any way. "What do you think, should I do it?"

"Well," she says, resting now in the one chair in the room, "looks like you already have."

"Yeah, I guess so. Chance and I got a little wild one night. He has one too."

"So, you're a pair," she laughs softly touching my wrist.

"Come on, tell me, if it's too much," I protest. "I don't have to go through with it. It'll grow back in."

"You don't have to tell me about pierced ears," and she pulls back her hair to remind me of her own sweet earlobes. Then she smiles in that way only she can, "No, it's cute. And bold." Then she winks as she straightens her blouse, "Wait till Kenny sees it...or your mom."

I lean forward and she wraps her arms around my waist. I bend and we taste each other's lips again and again.

Later Charlotte shows up with a salad already made. She is wearing a sun dress and sandals. Sharon goes to her and they hug easy the way women do.

"I love your sandals. Can I ask where you got them?"

"Well," and Charlotte looks at me and winks, "if Mr. Handsome is willing, he could walk you there from here. It's Claire's Shoes and Boots up on Court Street."

Chance comes down from his shower and greets Charlotte with a hug and kiss. I seem the lone man out on

Charlotte's hugging; then Dave comes in from out back where he has parked himself since walking downtown. He knows everyone and just shakes hands with Charlotte. "Hey," she asks, "what's that you're reading?"

He holds up a slim black volume, "*Siddhartha*, by Herman Hesse. I picked it up from the used bookstore."

Though we all do the hip nod of blissful agreement, Charlotte speaks, "Wow, Dave, that is a great book, and a great find. I bet all of us have read it." Everyone smiles, except Sharon who shrugs her shoulders.

"Not this girl....not yet. Dave, you'll have to loan it to me when you're done."

"Oh, I'm almost done already. You can read it on the drive home."

"Oh," Charlotte says, taking Sharon's hand, "I thought this was the big moving day?"

"I wish," Sharon says, still feeling a little awkward, then smiling as she takes Chance's hand. "In a week...I'll be moving in with the boys. Ready for that, Chance?"

"I'm ready, if you are, hon," Chance says. "You can see how much we need a woman's touch around here."

I'm wearing an apron covered with sauce, but I lay down my spoon, take Dave's hand again and connect to our ring of friends. We look at each other, then Chance leads us in a dance around the kitchen table to Joni Mitchell's "Chelsea Morning."

"Let's hear it for the 'free to be' house!" he shouts, and we all raise our arms.

The next morning, we all rise around 10. Sharon has found the coffee and made us a pot. I actually smell biscuits baking. I could get used to this life. I rise from the bed, step over Dave's sleeping bag on the floor. He must be in the bathroom. Chance is also up and sitting in our lounge chair staring up at me. "Well, my man. Today's the day," and he winks. "I'll get the kid out of your hair and keep us away for a couple hours. You make hay...while the sun shines," and he winks large again. Everyone knows too much in this house, but I wink back and go out to the kitchen with Sharon who is wearing a light flowered robe over her pink nightgown.

I kiss her as we lean back against the sink and whisper, "I want you here always,"

She smiles, "You have me, don't you see….I'm yours."

By 11 o'clock, the guys have gone off in Chance's old composite car, made from the parts of several others, and Sharon comes over to me and whispers in my ear, "I'll go get dressed."

"Don't," I say.

"Oh, yes, I have to. I've brought something special for you." I try to swallow that lump in my throat and so go into the bathroom to brush my teeth and retrieve the two condoms I've bought. We've decided not to take any chances.

I'm standing in my shorts as I slip a Marvin Gaye cassette into the player and wonder if it will be long enough. "Ooo, that's nice," Sharon says from behind the French doors of the bedroom. "Come in when you're ready," she calls, while I try to hold onto my readiness.

Only the sunlight coming through the curtains—a lace echoed in her black negligee. She leans back against the pillows, as my eyes gather her in. My readiness appears in my boxers, and I move my arm over it; sitting beside her I begin working the rubber over me. Kneeling at her feet, I touch her ankles with my hands, then kisses. I stroke from her feet slowly gliding my hands to her knees and back again as she sighs. Her eyes beg my trust. I smile softly and continue moving my hands up her tender thighs, touching their softness, holding their firmness as she relaxes into coos and sighs. We move to the music and our breath, as gently I lift her gown. Her eyes are warm and close now as we kiss. She whispers, "I love you." My lips find her breastbone. She rises from her hips and my tongue grazes her tender nipples. I feel her heart beating with my own. We hold each other so, then I am above her as she reaches down to help me to enter. For a moment she jerks from some pain, and I would stop, but she whispers, "No, go on," and we begin moving to the divine rhythm of a love making. Our whole bodies are saying it now, again and again. I don't want to hurt her, yet I drive deep into her again and again. Finally, her sharp inhales, my deep exhales, and we release together, die into it to live again. *Oh, sweet day in the morning!* The curtains rustle and the music plays on as she kisses my neck while I lie inside her, breathing deeply.

We lie back. "Are you alright?" I whisper, and she kisses my forehead. She reaches down to wipe herself with a moist towel she's brought. We lie there just holding each other, gently exploring each other's bodies under the blanket, while the rest of the album finishes. Gaye is singing "How Sweet It Is to Be Loved by You," as we rest in each other's arms.

When I rise to get us a drink, she points down, where I've managed to keep my shorts on one leg. We laugh lightly and I smile, "Forgive me. I'm just a beginner." Then she glides up from the mattress and slips into the bathroom while I walk out naked into the kitchen. This bliss is beyond anything I've ever known or felt. I start the cassette again, and when I turn, she is standing there naked in soft sunlight, her slender, perfect body robbing my breath and words. She smiles, reaches her arms out to me and I press my lips deep into hers. Our sweet music begins again.

*   *   *

When the guys get back, we've showered and have lunch ready for them. They are both laughing and grinning like country boys, and I can tell they're still riding a high from whatever they got with Cousin Harry. I pull Dave aside and warn him, "You let Mom know about any of this, and you're a dead man." He looks up from his tuna melt.

"Do you think I'm nuts," he says and grins.

Chance holds up the bag he bought, but I shake my head, "Put it away, man, please. I don't want to scare Sharon." I go into the kitchen and talk her into walking uptown to shop for those sandals she admired. It's an easy persuasion, and we're back in the sunlight and easy happiness of this day. A young girl passes us on her bike. "That's you ten years ago." I say.

"How would you know?" she asks taking my hand in hers.

"Oh, honey, I've always watched you," I say and she squeezes my hand.

At the traffic light at the corner a bakery truck stalls, then gets it going. I'm showing her the town and we're in no hurry. At Claire's she finds the sandals in brown. I enjoy her trying them on...her skirt, her legs, her eyes, her skirt, her legs. Then the clerk, who seems to enjoy touching her calves, says, "These are real popular with you college girls."

"Oh, I'm not a college girl," she corrects, a little embarrassed.

"I'm sorry," he says, "I just assumed..."

"Yeah, you did," I butt in and add, "We'll take them." When he goes to ring them up, I offer to pay, saying, "It's worth it just to watch you try on shoes. My god, your legs are wonderful."

"Yours aren't bad either," she kids and pays for the sandals herself. "Soon," she says, "our money will be 'our money,' and we'll start a joint checking account."

"Can't wait," I grin proudly, waltzing out the door together.

We tour the rest of the shops on and off of Court Street, see the protest signs painted on buildings, then return to the house to find Chance and Dave still deep asleep. Chance's bootleg of the Grateful Dead's "Turn on Your Lovelight" is playing, and Sharon whispers, "Come here, you" and leads me into the bedroom.We lay down on our mattress love bed, in our clothes now, to nap togehter. Tomorrow she leaves me again.

*   *   *

Today is the day Sharon is moving in. I'm sitting here again on the front porch watching the sun come up over the hill. Dad is driving her down in Uncle Harry's pickup. I can just see them shuffling along Rte 7 with a travel chest, floor lamp, and a couple kitchen chairs from home all packed in the back. It's really good of him to do it, but he volunteered, said, "Listen, we hate to see her go, but I'll bring your Sharon

80 129

down to you." Funny how he's become more her father, now that we know he's not.

On the phone she tells me that her Uncle Nate met her for dinner at DiFrederico's, and they talked some, but she says, "There's no real father-daughter bond yet, if there ever will be. He's still just my uncle."

I tell her, "Down here, we'll make a whole new start. We have friends, and jobs, and we're free to make our own path. And we have each other."

She says, "Yes, but we are who we are, Lee. We can't just cut off the past." I know she's right, but I am too.

"We simply exist," I say on the phone. "The philosopher Jean Paul Sartre claims that 'existence precedes essence.'"

She laughs lightly. "And Sharon Hatcher claims that we are being and becoming as one. So you can tell old Sartre that our past is part of our being."

"Gosh, woman, where do you come up with this stuff?"

"Oh, right here in the Ohio Valley, where we continue to read and think and feel."

"You've got me there," I say. "You're romantic and existential and Buddhist bound in one lovely package."

"Thanks," she says, "I think and feel, therefore I am."

"I love you...and we'll be together in two days," I remember saying and sat there thinking over what she just said.

Today, the move happens. The sun is up and she'll be in my arms in two hours, for as long as we both shall live.

Dad toots the horn and I rush down almost falling over those old wooden steps. He and Sharon are standing in the yard stretching. They've made good time. I take Sharon in my arms and we kiss in front of Dad who stands there waiting, a nice grin on his face.

"Looks pretty good," he says, nodding at the house, "kind of like the houses on lower Commercial Street near the stadium." We shake hands in the front yard. Blackie comes running out and Dad reaches down to rub her under the chin. Chance has gone to work at the deli, so we have the house to ourselves.

"Come on in, you guys. I've got some iced tea ready, and there's a bathroom inside."

Dad laughs, "Oh, we stopped a couple times. Didn't we, Sharon?"

"Sorry," she says. "We did. I'm drinking water on this new diet."

"Diet," he smiles at me then looks at her, "Honey, believe me, you don't need a diet."

There's an awkward moment where no one speaks, then Sharon smiles and leans on his arm. "You're sweet...like your son." There is surprisingly little in the back of the truck, but we haul it in to make the house more of a home. The old kitchen chairs will allow us to have company for dinner. Charlotte and Chance will be joining us. I already have sauce simmering on the stove.

I watch Dad noting things about the house, planning repairs no doubt, and then I invite them to walk up the street to the deli where Chance and I work. We enter and sit at the little table by the window. Chance comes out from the kitchen to meet Dad and to talk with us. "You're staying for dinner, Mr. McCall?" he asks.

"Call me Del, but no, I think I'll get back on the road; get home about dusk."

"Oh, please stay over with us," Sharon pleads. "That's too long of a drive, Del." I also hate to see him drive back, though I'm uncertain of the sleeping arrangements if he stays. But in Sharon's words I hear a nice shift from being guest to "us" as hosts. She lives here now with me where we are making our place together. The obvious sometimes seems profound.

Before Dad leaves, he pulls me over, "Son, I know what's going on here, and I don't object, but I do want to warn you that someone might get hurt."

"Oh, I would never do anything to hurt Sharon, you know that."

"Yes, I do, but it isn't just Sharon I'm thinking of." I look into his eyes and he's serious. I go to shake hands, and he pulls me into a hug. Sharon comes down from the house to get her hug at the truck, then Dad climbs in and says out the window, "Be good to each other," and pulls out, waving to us at our home.

Chapter Twelve

Resistance

Charlotte has lost her job—let go or fired, it comes to the same thing. We are all in the kitchen when she enters and rather matter-of-factly states, "I've been let go....They didn't renew my contract." We all put down our forks. "Listen to this," and she reads from the letter shaking in her hand, "Dear Charlotte Harris, the Biology Department of Ohio University thanks you for your years of service to the university....Blah, blah, blah... At this time, we regret to inform you...that we no longer have a need for your employment. We wish you the best in finding a new position. Please turn in office and lab keys to the department secretary by 8 a.m. Monday." Her face is flush and we can see now that she is really upset.

"Son of a bitch!" Chance says for us all, rising. "Those bastards, they're getting back at you for standing with us at the anti-war protests. You should sue their asses. You should. We'll resist this."

She looks up to read the concern and conviction in our faces. Sharon goes over and hugs her, the unity of sisterhood. "Here, you need to sit down," Sharon says and pulls out a chair for her.

"But what about your teaching record?" I ask. "What about all of your research?"

"Oh, Lee, that's what really hurts. I'll have to begin again somewhere else. The research grant was through the university, so they *own* the research, and now that we're almost there with our results, they're shoving me out and turning their back."

Chance is pacing around the table in a ring of anger. "We're protesting this!" he pronounces. "We're organizing. I'll make some calls to Carl and Susan." He reads Charlotte's face and kneels at her chair and puts his hands on hers, "Is that okay with you?"

"Oh, god, I don't know," she sighs. "I doubt it will do any good, but what they're doing is wrong and people should know about it."

"If you guys had a union, they couldn't get away with this," I say, and they all look around at me.

"I wonder if we could get the classified help to protest with us. We backed them when the administration cut their wages." Chance is burning with a plan now. We all are.

Sharon asks, "Was anyone else let go like this?"

"I honestly don't know, hon. I just got this in my mailbox an hour ago, though they must have known about it for weeks. They didn't have the nerve to tell me to my face."

"The old pink slip on university letterhead," Chance says. "Those cowards! They run this university as if it were their private factory. Look how they shut it down back in May. I'd like to see the students shut it down now."

"They'll have policy and procedure on their side," Charlotte says.

"Yeah," I say, "and that's just more institutional bullshit they whip up."

"Wait a minute, guys," Sharon interrupts. "Let's give Charlotte a chance to catch her breath here. This has to really hurt."

"Thanks," Charlotte says, grasping Sharon's hand. "I am hurt, and I'm troubled, but I'm really angry too. I have two years invested in research I love...and their timing is just awful. The new quarter begins next month, and it's probably impossible for me to get a position elsewhere for now."

"Elsewhere!" Chance explodes, banging his hand on the counter. "Why should you have to leave!" He looks around the room for support, then back to Charlotte. "Don't they have to let you know this months ahead?"

"Yes, I asked my department secretary that. And they're claiming the closing of the university in May made it impossible."

"We're fighting this," he insists. "We'll get that lawyer, Ken Wilbur, who defended us arrested students, and we'll organize." Chance is all fired up, and we look over at Charlotte whose faint smile reminds us that we probably can't win against the machine.

By evening we are gathered in the basement of the United Church of Christ. Rev. Bob has backed us from the start. Though the university chose these two weeks before the fall quarter starts to make the announcements, we've rounded up a healthy crowd of 100 or more. Word has travelled fast, and we now know that Charlotte was one of 20 people let go without reason, including Dr. Snyder, my literature prof. All were instructors, most of them from the sociology and political science departments, and they all were ambushed by this move. No way yet to track all of the grad students who were also dismissed.

Chance rises to speak. "Listen, folks. Listen please!" He waits while they quiet. "Thanks for coming, all of you. I welcome representatives from the Black Student Union... our local NOW group...the Stop the War group...and from the campus workers' union."

Applause goes up for each, and someone starts a chant, "Bring it down. Bring it down!"

Chance waits, then starts again, "Hey, folks, I want to first call out all those faculty here tonight who've been wounded by this university hatchet job." A roar goes up mixed with applause. Sharon and I are on watch at the doors where we're to let people in who come late. He starts through the names, and each rises to applause.

Someone shouts out, "Hey, how do we know there are no university spies here tonight?"

Chance grins, "Well, this meeting is free and open, so I guess I'd just assume spies for the university and FBI are here, along with members of anarchists and the national SDS. Gauge your talk accordingly, but don't be afraid to speak out. We have a voice here, and we're not breaking any laws, are we Ken? This is Ken Wilbur, local public defender, who's working for us." Another roar goes up.

Ken, in shirt and vest with sleeves rolled, rises to speak. "Thanks, everyone. Thanks for coming and listen, you have the right to organize and assemble a campus protest. That's true. Just know that what you share here may be passed along, so I'd suggest some of the strategy be done in closed group."

"How about it?" someone shouts. "Has the university broken the law or not?" Another roar from the crowd, another round of chanting, "Bring it down. Bring it down!" Chance tries to quiet things, looks around, then says, "I guess this has turned into a public forum...is that alright with everyone?" Applause. "Ken can best answer that one."

"Sorry to be vague on this. We're going over the state and labor laws. Fairness and public opinion are on our side, though we've seen a backlash against protests since Kent State." A roar goes up. Ken waits, then declares, "I'll level with you. Against us is the fact that all of the dismissed faculty were on what they call 'term contract,' which the university has used to hire and fire at will. Any union worker has better rights." Someone starts a chant of "Union...Union...Union."

"Why can't students have a union?" someone shouts. "The Blacks have a union."

Kevin Robinson from the Black Student Union rises, takes the microphone and waves for attention. "Let me explain to you all. We are united with our brothers and sisters, yes, but we're not a labor union, and we got no collective bargaining. But...we do have power in union...in solidarity, brothers and sisters." A roar rises, and he goes on, "This here university's been forced to recognize us, see, and this fall we're launching a Black Studies Institute— right here, right now!"

The "union" chant begins again, and someone shouts, "Hey, don't the teachers have a union?"

Snyder stands up, "No, we do not. The best we have is the AAUP."

"Well, pardon my ignorance, but what that hell is that?"

Charlotte takes the floor, to applause. "Sorry, we're talking about the American Association of University Professors, a professional organization, but I can tell you about my brother's case in Illinois. It took AAUP two years to act and all they could do was issue sanctions against the university for its policies." The crowd boos at this. "It's a slap on the wrist, and by that time, all of us," she extends her hand toward the dismissed faculty in the front row, "will be long gone."

"We need some action now," Snyder speaks out again. "I think if we get the public and media on our side, the university could cave in on this."

"Let's march down to President Crawford's house...Let's build a fucking bonfire on his front lawn." I recognize Marv from the young anarchists' organization. He raises his fist and another roar goes up. His group is always ready to paint or burn something. I look over at Sharon standing at the other door. She's beaming, though her arm isn't raised with the others.

A group of 8 is formed to plan the next action in private. We're all to meet at the president's house tomorrow at ten. Chance brings up his guitar and with two other guys sings "Ohio" by Crosby, Stills, and Nash. Then Carl leads us in a chorus of "We Shall Overcome."

On the walk home, Sharon takes my hand and says, "I'll tell you something, Lee. I'm so glad to finally be part of something down here. Really, most of the time I feel like an outsider, neither a student nor a townie."

"You're a part of me," I say, "and a part of us," pointing to Chance and Charlotte walking ahead of us.

She stops a moment and looks right into my face. "I know, and I know we're right in this. I just hope we don't use our rightness to do something wrong. I don't want to see anyone get hurt."

"Me too, but I'd say some eggs have already been broken...and one of them is our friend Charlotte."

Chance and Charlotte have stopped at the corner facing the university gate. The National Guardsmen have gone, replaced by more campus police. I look across the street at what used to be 'home,' and it's no longer a friendly place. It's been taken from us, held captive, with new rules of governance. "It belongs to the people," I say to no one. "We have to take it back, free it and ourselves."

Later that day at home, we gather up poster board, tempera paint, and large color markers from the local five and dime; Sharon brings a yard stick to pencil in lines so our signs have some order. On mine I just write "Free the University." I look up at Sharon, "What do you think?"

She says, "That's good...but do you think it says enough?"

Still looking up at her, I say, "This is it, what we're really after in the end." She nods, and I fill in my lettering, saying, "The fewer the words the better."

Chance comes in, looks at my sign, and laughs, "Ha, you've got it, man. That's it. Free the university."

"What are you laughing at?" I ask.

"I'm just imagining it...what would a free university look like?"

"Well," Sharon says, "I probably wouldn't have a job working there, would I?"

"Or maybe a totally different job," I suggest.

"Yeah," Chance grins, "She could pass out condoms at the—free clinic."

She grabs him round the neck. "I'd like to put one over your head, you jerk."

"Which head?" he jokes, and with that I stand up.

"Okay, you two, break it up," I say and step between them, claiming my territory and woman in some primal male action. "We've got at least a dozen more signs to make."

Sharon kneels down and begins to work on one while Chance gets a beer from the fridge.

"I brought home sandwiches from the deli," he says, "We'll make that our dinner. We have some calls to make tonight to rally folks for the protest. It's grad students mostly, since the new crop of freshmen haven't arrived."

"Maybe it will all be free by the time they get here next week," I say. Sharon is finishing her sign. In beautiful blue lettering, it says, "Free the University. Free Yourself."

Next morning we show up with our signs at President Crawford's house a half hour early, and though we've agreed to just chant, march, and wave our posters, the anarchists already have a bonfire going on the front lawn. "Watch yourselves," Chance says to us. "Someone will get arrested for this...and those anarchists will be long gone. We're puppets in their work."

We talk it over with others and agree to stay. Charlotte, Snyder, and the other faculty are keeping away, so the voice is clearly that of the students and workers. Some of the organizations have their own signs. "We Want Our Faculty Back—NOW," "Rights to All Workers—Solidarity in Union." Some joker has a "No Violins" sign, and our "Free the University—Free Yourself" signs warrant a chant or two. Someone finally shows up with a huge metal burn barrel, and we try to get the fire into it, but it's already blazing, and someone's gloves catch fire. We mill around for an hour or so. Carl brings out the battery powered megaphone and leads a few chants. I guess we're hoping that President Crawford will come out on the lawn, but he seems to be stonewalling us. Someone says he beat it out of town and is up in Columbus meeting with other university presidents.

"Listen," a voice calls out, and we all look around. "This is the campus police. You are in violation of the campus code against unauthorized assembly. We're ordering you to break this up."

"It's Big Brother!" someone yells.

"Pigs!" is called out several times, then "Campus Pigs!"

Sharon looks around and grabs my arm. "I can't see who said that," she says. "Lee, tell them to stop, please," she pleads with me. I look to Chance who shrugs.

No one is using the megaphone right now, so I grab it and call out, "Listen, people, we know we're in the right here. But we need to keep it peaceful. Please." There are several boos to that, and Sharon surprises me by taking the megaphone.

"Please listen. The media will be here anytime. Let's not give them a chance to call us an angry mob or rioters." Only one boo, and the yelling quiets. "Let's stand our ground and free the university," she calls out and a real cheer goes up.

The police again: "I'm telling you all, President Crawford is not at home. You're going to force us to start arresting people if you don't cease and desist."

"Desist!" someone calls out. "Where'd you learn that word, Pig!"

"Oh, I hate this," Sharon says, pulling at my arm. "Lee, I'm leaving, going back to the house." She waits a moment for me to decide, then turns to walk away, and I stand there feeling dumb and paralyzed.

"Okay," I call to her. "I'll be home in an hour or so. I have to see where this goes." I feel really shitty watching her walk away alone, but she finds a friend, and I keep my eye on her till she disappears up the hill.

A reporter and photographer circulating the crowd are now talking with Chance. We've spotted a couple other photographers along the edge of the crowd, and someone whispers that they're FBI. The whole thing ends pretty dull with photos and interviews, no real response and no arrests, but we've appeared and made our point. Whether heard or not, we've gained our voice and taken a stand.

Back at the house, I find Sharon standing at the kitchen counter. She does not look back at me. She's making something for lunch. A large open can tells me it's tuna salad. She's really hacking at an egg when I touch her arm.

"Hey, are you okay?" I ask, but she does not turn, and when she does I see that she's been crying. "What is it?"

"Oh, it's nothing," she says, then facing me, "...and it's everything. Don't you see?"

I go to take her into my arms, but she stands off. "I see that you're unhappy about something. Please, hon, tell me what it is. I'll listen."

She lays the knife down on the counter. "Well, for one thing," she says, "it's the violence we saw today."

"What violence? Sharon, no one got hurt, no one even got arrested." It's the wrong thing to say I realize immediately.

"Didn't you see—the fire, the threats, that ugly name calling. It's all violence. It really bothers me that you don't recognize it." She is standing square in front of me looking right into my eyes.

"I'm sorry. You're right. You're better at seeing things like that."

"Yeah, well I learned it the hard way, living in a house where people yelling and hitting or bending the arms of children was all too common." I reach for her hand again. "Wait, I'm not done," she says. "I need to say one more thing. Let's sit down."

"I understand, really," I say and pull out our chairs. "But you've never mentioned any of this before."

"Well, now we're talking, aren't we? And I need to tell you something. I start to work at the university tomorrow."

"I know. Is that what's bothering you." Again I reach for her hand.

"No, wait. Let me get this out. I start to work at the university, but I'm not a part of this university that you want to free. It's not free to me. I'm still an outsider."

"Wow," I say, leaning toward her, and shaking my head. "You keep things inside a long time."

"I'm sorry, but I learned to do that at home."

"Okay, I'm hearing you. I love you. Tell me what you want to do?"

She smiles for the first time and lets out a breath. "I want to take classes, Lee. I want to be part of all the learning that happens here."

I'm struck dumb, by my own ignorance, "You mean accounting classes?"

She nods, "Maybe that, but I want to do more than keep records. I want to study things...sociology and psychology, philosophy and, maybe even literature." She sighs as though some weight has been taken off, some window opened.

I sit with this for some moments. "Okay," I finally say, "I'm hearing you and getting it. Listen, Sharon, we'll work this out somehow. I promise." I look over at this woman I love who's been hurting so, and say, "Baby, I see how I've been so wrapped up in revolution I haven't seen the real change going on around me."

"Oh, Lee," she sighs and comes closer to me. How could I miss the pain in her face and heart? Finally she sits on my lap, wraps arms around my neck, then whispers, "I love you, I'm sorry. I know I let things build." I just hold her in sweet silence, then she kisses me and slowly rises to finish the tuna.

I get up in a kind of daze and go sit on the couch by Blackie. I am petting her fury back when Chance comes in and plops down beside me. "What a day," he says, "Well, we'll read about it in the papers tonight or tomorrow." He looks right at me, "What's up, Bud? Seen a hungry ghost or something? You're pale."

I tell him softly, "Sharon wants to take classes."

He nods slowly, "Well, hell yeah, sure she does, why wouldn't she?"

"Thing is, I was blind to it, so caught up with our righting this university I couldn't see the pain of the person I most care for."

"And..."

"What?"

"Well, could be you get wrapped up in your own needs, man, like us all?"

He just sits with me on this, gives me time to take it all in, then picks up his guitar and starts softly finger picking. I look down at Blackie, then out the window when it hits me like taking off dark glasses inside a house. I've used Sharon as my rock against this college world, the same way I've used my family and home town. And though I love her and want her here with me, I kept seeing her as this refuge from the college world.

"Wow," I finally say, "It's so hard to swallow your own shallowness."

"Doesn't taste good, does it?" then he taps my knee. "It's not too late, my friend," he says nodding toward Sharon as he takes a sandwich and slips upstairs for us to be alone.

"Sharon," I say rising and moving slowly toward her, "I'm sorry I didn't see you clearly. You take classes, and, hell, we'll both work part-time to pay the rent and save for something bigger." Her eyes smile into mine and I add the rest: "I need you to understand. I don't want to close this university or shut it down; I want it to open for everyone, especially you."

We make our lunch and begin our plans.

That night, I rise in the darkness to go to the bathroom, stumble over Blackie, and return to Sharon on our floor bed. While I am gone she has stripped off the cover and is lying there looking up at me softly... slowly she slides her thin nightgown up and over her head. Her nakedness in window light is brave and close, and I bend to it, kiss her feet; my hands caress her smooth calves, gently glide up her legs slowly over her roundness, embrace her tender waist while I kiss the creamy wonder of her thighs. She does not resist, and I find myself dazed and ablaze with longing for her. She strokes my hair, twists, slowly rises and falls at the hips. I stroke and stroke all the glorious parts of her. For the first time, she holds her beasts and offers me her dark nipples, and I kiss then suck them till she writhes. Sounds deep and new come from her...from me. We join in this dance...and arrive, arrive, we arrive.

Chapter Thirteen
Complications and Re-Visions

August comes, and the university does not shut down, nor does it fold on the firing issue. 18,000 of us start back to classes that September, and among them is one pretty blond co-ed whom I know intimately. A meeting does occur, however, between our resistance committee and the provost and several deans. Gestures are made and the president issues a statement: "While we do regret the loss of some fine faculty, we must face economic realities in this time of educational crisis. We assure all that we seek to build better communications with all students and staff." And, get this, they want to create an auxiliary college for the community, which—This part just blows me away—they are calling the "free university." It all may turn out to be pure bullshit, but they had to be listening to have co-opted some of our ideas and our slogan. Classes will be free and taught by those who wish to volunteer; for now old Tupper Hall will be reopened and used. Closer to home, the cases of Charlotte, Snyder and other dismissed faculty continue with the lawyers, and may take a year or more to resolve. In my twentieth year I begin to recognize how hard it is to ever see or measure progress from within an institution, laced as it is with lies.

Sharon is excited though, taking night classes in freshman comp and intro to philosophy. The accounting course conflicted with her job at registration, and we do have to pay the rent, so I'm still at the deli. I got into Modern American lit, creative writing, and my first education course. I'm pulled by both writing and teaching, so why not marry the two.

Charlotte has had the biggest changes. She had to take a job working in a chemical laboratory for a perfume factory in Lancaster, Ohio, a 30 minute drive from campus. She's testing chemicals on small animals. Last week she moved in with us for now. The scene went like this.

Chance calls us to the kitchen table by strumming a chord on his guitar and singing "Meeting here tonight. Meeting here tonight." Like I said, he's good at using humor to relax tensions. "Well, folks" (It's only Sharon, I and Blackie), "I want to introduce our new house guest...ta-dum!"...and he hits the G chord hard, Blackie barks, and down the stairs comes Charlotte dressed in day-glo pink flannel pajamas. We all burst into laughter and wait for an explanation.

"I'm sorry," Charlotte pleads, "Really, he made me do this. I wanted to ask your permission first? And I am, asking."

Sharon and Charlotte do the girlfriend hug, and I too hug this fuzzy former professor of mine. "Whose idea was the pajamas?" I ask.

Chance laughs, "She kept protesting 'Oh, Lee will see me in my pajamas,' so I decided to get it over with right away." His grin spreads. "What do you say, guys, is it okay with you all?"

"Of course," Sharon insists for both of us. "I moved in here with Lee. Charlotte should move in with you, with us all. Then we women will take over."

"Sure it's alright," I add. "You'll just have to stand in the bathroom line with the rest of us. But please, do find some quieter pajamas. These will keep me awake at night."

Charlotte gives me a sisterly punch on the arm, and I pretend abuse, but just stand there amazed at how all of our relationships have grown.

Okay, I'll admit, the first time I see Charlotte running down the hallway in her blue panties, so tall and slender, her hair hanging down her bare back, I almost lose it. She glances around, and I am relieved to have the bathroom to step into, for several obvious reasons. *My god, we have these two lovely women living with us. What did we do to deserve it?* Catching my breath, I look in the mirror, tell myself I should see Charlotte as a sister, but I obviously don't. The mirror also reveals my sprouting beard. It's coming in light, but I enjoy stroking it, and right now Sharon doesn't mind, says it tickles, though I can see it chafes her pretty cheeks and sometimes her thighs. I guess I'm still finding myself here, bringing my off-campus self onto campus. When I think back a year to my coming here and look into this mirror here and now, I seem transposed.

"Who's doing dinner tonight?" Sharon asks, sipping her morning coffee standing at the kitchen sink in a sharp business suit.

"Me, I guess," I say, "Hey, where'd you get the outfit?"

"Outfit? Really, this is a Ralph Lauren's women's suit, courtesy of our good friend Charlotte."

"Oh, boy, now you're going to start wearing each other's clothes. How will I know which is which?"

She comes over and pinches my arm smartly, "You just better know who you're nuzzling, boyfriend. I heard about you catching her in the hallway."

"Gheez, do you girls share everything?"

"Our secrets, but not our lovers."

"My, aren't we saucy this morning...in your sharp women's wear. Do you want to call off work and work out some things in the bedroom?"

Her pretty smile turns down at the corners, all the message I'll get on that one, and with a goofy kiss, she is off to work. I check the refrigerator for supplies, and make a list of tomatoes, ground meat, and tortillas to pick up for the tacos I'll make tonight. Charlotte is up and gone before we wake most days. Chance is still asleep. So it's I and Blackie in the front room at 8 a.m. No class till 10, so I get out my notebook and pen, sit on the couch, and await inspiration to write. In creative writing, I'm the only sophomore among upperclassmen, and she's already starting the workshop practice. We're each to submit a writing to be runoff and shared with everyone. It feels like I'm kind of coming out of the closet with my writing, so to speak, so I decide to write the story of Tom's gay persecution on campus. It's something that needs to be told, and it's provocative enough to take the attention away from my weakness as a writer. The first line comes from memory, "Hey, man, where you been? I hardly see you anymore." Line by line it comes till it's grown: the ignoring parents, the boyfriend Brad, the sleeping around here, the bloody nose, moving out, ending with his note and flannel shirt. I tell it in his voice, him talking, and he comes alive to me again. First draft done by 9:30, I'll let it rest and trim later. I have to wake Chance and go to American lit.

Later this week I enter my creative writing class late. Twenty of us are seated around a U of tables. We're allowed to bring drinks in, and I enter with my mug of coffee. All eyes come back to me. I don't get it. Jane has already passed out the worksheet I see, and my poem "The Cost of Coming Out" is toward the front. Have they read it already? Is it that bad? Mary who sits beside me whispers, "We're with you, Lee. We just didn't know." I nod. Know what? Oh my god, I did this to myself. They think it's about me, that I'm the voice of the poem. Torn between wanting to deny it and to claim it as effective writing, when it's my turn to read, I simply say, "This is for my good friend Tom." Some acknowledge with a nod, but some shake their heads at my refusal to claim my own story. Jane commends my nerve and directness, says, "Yet, Lee, it begs for more graphic images to be fully realized," and we go on. I'll have to write Tom about this.

As the "Free University" gets started by October, some pretty open classes are offered: Yoga and meditation, cooking and vegetarianism, Appalachian music and folk art, along with some classes bearing more radical titles of "Revolution," "Socialist Thought," "Unions in Appalachia." Of course, the one that becomes instantly legendary is "Contemporary

Bullshit" in which the students meet the first day to have James the teacher enter, completely disrobe, and dismiss them. He tells them they're to do the same somewhere for homework and that they need not come to class any more, he will communicate with them through telepathy.

There's bullshit alright, but I suppose this is to be expected; there's plenty of it in the regular university. What surprises me is that Charlotte and Sharon sign up for a Saturday morning class with Dr. Li Wang on "A Taste of Zen." And it's not long before they start talking in this code of theirs. "Ah, beginner's mind," Sharon will say about something someone says or does, and Charlotte will just smile, "Infinite possibilities." Or maybe I'll start quoting something a professor has said, and Sharon smiles and says, "expert mind," like it's something wrong. Chance and I just grin and shake our heads. After the second week, they begin sitting on cushions together in our bedroom, meditating to a burning incense stick. What I do know is they've both become even more sweet to everyone and open to everything: birds, trees, rocks, us and themselves. Sharon begs me to read *Zen Mind, Beginner's Mind* by Suzuki, but I'm too wrapped up in my own writing now.

Chance and I take Dick Snyder's "Communal Living" on Monday nights. After class, we stop to talk with him. "Well, guys," he says putting away his notes. "I've taken a job teaching high school English in Pomeroy for now, till something happens with my lawsuit against the university. I feel like I'm biding time."

"Yeah," Chance says, "Charlotte's working at a lab in Lancaster, but she's taking this Buddhism course and says she can't kill another animal for research."

"A result of the 'free university' no doubt," he jokes. "She's a great girl. I'm glad she's standing with me and the few others. How about you, Lee, what's up with you?"

"I'm really digging creative writing from Jane Millhouse. Oh, and my girlfriend Sharon has moved in, so I'm really happy right now."

"I bet you are," he says, "Enjoy it while it lasts."

"What do you mean?" I ask.

"Oh, I'm sorry," he says looking up. "It's just...since being booted out by the university machine, I'm suffering some depression. I'm getting some counseling for it, but on my own tab, of course. Life's hard on we Romantics, and I'm finding it difficult to trust the good will of man."

He looks into my eyes, and I find myself reaching out to him. "Don't give up, man. Remember Thoreau. 'The revolution will come from within.' I'm into what you're teaching here."

"Up the Establishment!" Chance adds. "On to better models."

"Great," Dick says and smiles for the first time this night. He closes his briefcase. "Listen, let's talk more about this after class next week. I have to pick up Ingrid."

The conversation gets pretty good around our house now. We're all growing into something. Chance and I even sit meditation with the women now. Charlotte will light the incense stick, Chance will fingerpick soft chords on his guitar, then stop as we sit for maybe 20 to 30 minutes, one incense stick or two. I've not been smoking pot much lately because of it, something Sharon is glad of, I can tell; though on Saturday nights we still smoke one or two together rather than getting bloated on beer.

*   *   *

Right now I'm sitting outside of Tupper Hall in Chance's old car waiting for Sharon to be let out of her Saturday Zen class. We're headed to Marietta where Dad and Mom will be driving the Model-A in a Heritage Festival parade. We haven't seen anyone from home in almost two months. Wait, there's Sharon in her blue denim dress.

"Hey, Charlotte, want a ride home?" I call as they walk up to the car.

Charlotte's in jeans and a loose flowered blouse. She comes up to my window, gives me a nice peck on the cheek. "Thanks, Lee, honey, but no. You two love birds hurry on to your rendezvous with your folks. And tell them I said hello."

"Hi, Hon," I say, giving Sharon our 10 second kiss in the front seat. We caught ourselves doing the kiss and run one day, and she read to me from this article how the kiss between lovers should last at least 10 seconds. Not a problem, her lips so soft and sweet. I touch her bare knee beside me, and she touches my hand.

"Lee, we'll be late. Your dad said the parade starts at noon."

"Oh, yeah," I say and start up the engine, slip her into gear, and we are off down country roads headed east toward the Ohio River. On the way I remind Sharon about that ride I had with the salesman who asked about the size of my cock.

She reaches over and squeezes my thigh. "Can't say I blame him," she winks.

Just outside of Bartlett on county Rte 550, I have to pull over for a dead deer on the road. We both get out, each takes a leg, and we drag the heavy carcass off, careful not to get blood on us. "Who the hell, just left it here?" I wonder out loud. When we get in, the car won't start. No power, nothing, won't begin to turn over. I bang on the steering wheel senselessly, "Damn it. We're stuck. And I filled her up at the Shell station this morning."

"No spark....no fire for the gasoline," she says, and starts to get out.

"Wait, what are you doing?"

"Pop the hood. Let's take a look," she instructs.

I am such a dope with cars. Dad knew and did it all, and I was just his tool boy. I'd fetch what he asked for, hold the flashlight, hear him talk to himself but understood none of how it works, or doesn't.

She grabs a rag and wrench from under the seat, and looks at the wiring. "Distributor looks good. Battery cables are okay. Command wire seems alright, can't really know. Might be the solenoid itself," and she gives it a few taps with the end of a wrench. "Try it now," she calls, and I do. It fires right up.

"Get in," I call, but she's already slammed down the hood and is opening her door. I see she has gotten some grease on her pretty skirt. "Oh, honey, look," I say touching her skirt. "What'll we do?"

"Drive, my man, drive," she says laughing. "I think your folks will understand. We should be good to Marietta, if we don't turn off the engine...but, we'll need to park close to a parts store."

"Damn, you are good, girl. Where'd you learn all of this?"

"I told you, Hank's a truck driver, not good for much as a father, but I was always helping him fix things."

"Well, I was always helping my pappy too, but I didn't learn a damn thing," I confess.

"And I love you just the same," she says patting me on the cheek as I round the bend. About a mile down the road, she adds, "It's all cause and effect, you know, when you get down to it."

I grin at her, say, "Ah, expert mind," and we both laugh.

When we get into Marietta, the parade has already begun, and we park the car as close to downtown as possible and jump out.

A horse riding group in cowboy gear, a couple kids' drill teams, the high school marching band, an old fire truck, and finally there they are, a row of classic cars, Dad and Mom sitting up in some 1920s outfits she must have made. We wave and shout to them. They see us, and Mom waves, then makes a funny face, glaring at my beard I guess. Dad motions then shouts, "We'll meet you up 'round the corner in about 30 minutes or so." That should give us time to find a parts store.

"Since we don't have a wire tester," Sharon says, "I'm going to start with the solenoid. If that doesn't fix it, we'll get the command cable too." She turns to me and asks, "How much cash do you have?"

I open my wallet and shake out a $20. "Twenty bucks."

"I wish we had a tool box," she laments and digs out a screw driver and a pair of vice grips from the glove compartment. "This will probably do the job."

"God, you talk like my father," I laugh.

She shrugs, and we walk into the parts store. In under 20 minutes she has the thing changed using the makeshift tools. And she has me start it up several times in a row. Standing on the Marietta sidewalk she wipes her hands onto the car rag, and I spin her around. "You're wonderful," I say giving her a 20 second kiss. She bites my lip tenderly, erasing any trace of my inadequacy.

We stroll down the tree-lined avenue and find Dad's Pontiac and hauling trailer in a lot. I look around for a place to eat. "The Homestead: Family Dining" looks about right. We go in and get a table for four by the window where we can watch for them. "There they are, across the street," Sharon points to them and I dash out to help Dad load the Ford onto his trailer ramp. Mom gives me a hug, rubs my beard and laughs.

"You look like your great uncle Murray," she says. "Why are you letting that thing grow on your face?" She hasn't seen the earring, so I'm going to let that one slide.

"It's just for this fall," I say and give her another hug. "I've missed you two."

"Oh, how I've missed you," she says, "Your father's been...well, you'll see."

"Okay," I say, "You go inside. Sharon has a table for us. I'll give him a hand with the trailer."

"Hey," Dad calls, "Can you give me a hand here?"

"That's why I'm here," I say. "Tell me what to do."

He goes to shake my hand then pulls me toward him in a man hug. "Good to see you, son." Turning toward the car, "She's a bit fussy to drive, so I'll pull her up on the ramp. You guide me, then slide these blocks under her wheels once she's aboard."

It's a pretty simple process, and we're done in five minutes strapping her on, though I notice Dad's hands shaking as he runs the chains through the wheels.

"She looks good," I say.

"Who, your mother or the car?" he jokes.

"Both," I say. "Hey, you feeling alright, Dad?"

He doesn't answer—the McCall avoidance.

"Let's get something to eat inside," I say pointing to the diner.

"Wait," he says, grabbing my sleeve. "I don't want your mother to see this," and he slips me a wad of 50's.

"What?"

"Well, I got a promotion. I'm assistant yard master now, big time. I figure you and Sharon could use it...for a used car."

I look at his hands, his dark eyes, and don't know what to say. "Are you sure?"

"Yep, what's money for but to help you guys. We help your brother plenty at that school in Providence. Just don't say anything to your mother. Hey, how's the little woman getting on?"

I have to smile, hearing Sharon referred to that way. "She's doing fine, taking classes at the university now."

"Well, great. And who's paying for that?"

"She is, Dad. She's working at the university and gets a break on taking classes."

"Sharon's a fine girl. You better hang onto her. You're lucky to have each other." There's a long pause between us. Then he says, "Well, let's get us something to eat," and we enter the long room full of tables and booths. Sharon and Mom are seated together at one by the window. Sharon slides out and gives Dad a nice hug. While waiting for the waitress, I recount how Sharon just replaced our solenoid, and Dad grins proudly for her. Thankfully we all feel relaxed and at home with each other. We do not talk of Zen or communes or American lit. When I ask Mom when she's going to come and visit us, she doesn't speak.

Sharon tries to help. "Please, Mrs. McCall, you're welcome anytime."

"Well, I don't want to speak of it," Mom says. "But when you two are ready to get married, I'll come." No one answers that one.

On the drive home, I pull out the wad of fifties. "Here, count this, will you?"

Sharon stares at the roll of money I've dropped into her hand, "What's this?"

I grin, "Well, it's a gift...and I guess it could be our first car."

Sharon begins to get actual tears in her eyes.

"It's not just for us," I say. "They want us to be able to come home." And that just releases more tears. She's so strong and smart, I sometimes I forget what a tough family life she's had.

At dinner that night, Charlotte has made a grilled chicken salad, and we tell them of our good fortune. Chance smacks the table, "Just today, by gosh I met a guy wants to sell a VW bug if you're interested."

I look over at Sharon and ask, "How much we talkin'?"

"Oh, the whole car," he jokes, then says, "I think $800. It has lots of miles on it, but he put a new muffler on this year, and the tires have lots of tread."

"Wow, you gave it a good look over, huh?" I ask.

"Well, I was thinking of trading my old beater in, but you guys go ahead, if you're interested. I have the guy's number in my wallet."

"Well," Sharon says. "I guess we could take a look at it. I'd like to check the engine. The valves go on those VW's."

Chance looks up.

"She's not shitting you," I laugh. "This girl knows cars. She put a new solenoid on your beater in Marietta."

"What! She did? I'll pay for that. How much was it?" Chance asks.

"I forget. What was it, Sharon?" I say winking at her.

"Oh, I think $800 would do it," she says and cracks up at her own joke.

"Well, we'll be a family with three cars," Chance says. "My beater, your bug if you take it, and Charlotte's Nova. But listen, you guys, Charlotte and I have even bigger investments to propose. Shall we tell them?" and he leans back on his chair toward Charlotte standing at the counter.

"Maybe we should wait till dinner is through," she says. "I don't like talking money at the table."

"Oh, excuse my working-class crassness," he says, only half kidding.

She gives him a kiss on the forehead, "Oh, you're forgiven" and sets the large salad bowl on the table beside the fresh bread. "May I serve you, sir?"

After dinner, I rise to get coffee for Chance and me, tea for the Zen ladies. "Too bad we can't all drink the same thing," I joke for the fiftieth time. "So what's the big deal you were hinting at?"

They look at each other, deciding who should speak. Charlotte starts, "We're thinking of buying a farm."

"Holy shit, you weren't kidding!" I blurt out.

"A farm?" Sharon asks. "Wow! A farm—are you thinking of farming it?"

Charlotte looks at Chance then says, "First of all, this idea is just hatching, and we want to include you in all of it." She puts her hands over each of ours. "Listen, I pass near the town of Chauncey on Rte 33 every day on my way to work. And Monday I saw this sign, 'Farm for Sale Cheap by Owner,' so I just pulled off and followed county roads out past Millfield till I came to it. Believe me, it's well back from any roads, down a holler as they say, and up a rise. On the crest is this big white farmhouse with black shutters, oh, and several out buildings, including an old barn. Chance has seen it, you tell them."

"It's really neat, guys, in the rolling hills around there, a woods at the back end of the property. No one's lived in it for a couple years, but repairs would be easy. Everything done would add to its value. But we're not looking for an investment." And he puts his hands over ours now too. "Sharon, Lee, we're looking for a place to start a new way."

It's my turn to speak. "This sounds real big and really interesting. But, honestly, I have to ask what new way you're starting? None of us has time to do farming now."

"No, you're right," Charlotte says, "and I need to tell you that I'm quitting my job at that lab. I just can't kill another animal for commerce, not even for science. There's a small green house on the property, and I'd like to start with an organic garden and..."

Chance interrupts, "Okay, might as well get it all out there. We're thinking of a commune, a Free Farm Co-op among free spirited individuals, beginning with us and you two if you're willing."

It's taking a minute or two to sink in. "Well, would we still take classes?" Sharon asks.

"That would be up to you, hon," Chance answers. "With your new car, the drive to campus would only be 20 minutes or so. You could lead a double life on campus and on the communal farm."

"Wow, this is really big!" comes out of me. "A commune, right here in Athens County."

The word 'commune' seems to throw us into a deep quiet that we all just sit with a moment, till Chance speaks. "Listen, I swear, this all is just emerging here and now at this table, and we're all equal parts of it." And in a Chance style gesture, he has us all stand, join hands and raise them up. "To the Free Farm Commune of Athens County." We cheer, Blackie barks, and then, Chance and Charlotte kiss each other and then each turns to kiss us. And it's a full 15 second kiss.

Sharon and I look at each other somewhat dazed. Then almost as an afterthought, she asks, "Sorry to be the business mind here. I do love this idea, but how would we pay for it? None of us, I'm assuming, has money for a down payment."

Chance glances over at Charlotte and she at both of us. "I do. I've been working full-time for three years, and though I'm headed for unemployment, I have over $30,000 in a savings account."

"God, that's a lot of money, Charlotte, and really generous of you," I say. "Would you have to use it all?"

"Well, part of it's an inheritance from my grandmother, who was a spirited woman who'd just love this idea, so I'll use that $10,000 as a down payment on our place. The rest I'd like to leave untouched or keep as back-up for our adventure in group living."

That phrase also takes a moment of contemplation. *How would this all work out? How much would be shared and how?*

Finally I say something. "I wonder if Snyder would want in on this?"

Chance shrugs with a grin, "Yeah, and there's Carl and Susan, but whether they join us or not, we can do this. We can. We'll be creating a living alternative to the middle class way."

"Hey," I say, "If you can't fix the system, create a better one." Finally we join and raise our hands again like a giant flower. A blossoming has come to our table.

That night lying in bed I look over to Sharon, still awake, both of us filled with wonder and doubts. She takes my hand, whispers, "Let's do some deep breathing." I try counting them, in and out to ten, but can't get beyond three before questions pop back in. *Where's all this going? How's it going to happen? And what was that long kissing about?*

Chapter Fourteen
The Free Farm

This Saturday morning, I wake before dawn and lie here as light slowly spreads across the floor while Sharon sleeps. Thoughts of last night play back like a movie. How much is real, how much a dream? I turn on my side and look straight into Sharon's face—my guiding light. I want to wake her, yet I love looking at her.

The birds call outside, and her eyes open. I kiss her forehead and she wraps her warm arms around me. "Ginger Rogers," I say to her.

"What?" she asks yawning.

"Ginger Rogers, you're young Ginger Rogers, from *Flying Down to Rio*. Your eyes and hair, your dimpled chin and smile. You're so beautiful."

She lays back. "Lee, I'm not quite awake."

I kiss her hair, "I'm sorry. I used to think you looked like Cybil Shepherd, but now I see, it's really Ginger Rogers." She sighs and looks over at me.

"How about I'm just Sharon Hatcher for now?" she says, then "I love you," and we share a morning kiss. She sits up in her short tie dye t-shirt, and her bare legs fold into a full lotus position. "Oh, my god," she says. "I forgot all about yesterday. What a night that was. Are you ready to talk it over?"

I rise slowly, slide on my jeans. "Let me get us a cup of coffee. We have plenty to talk over."

"None for me," she sighs, "I'm going to just sit meditation."

Our next move of the day—we call this Robert about his VW bug, borrow Chance's beater and drive over to his place on East State Street. It's red, little or no rust, but has 100,000 miles. "It's in good shape," he says. "I got canned from grad school and need the cash. You dig?" We check the inside. "Hey, take her today for a test drive. I'll be here packing." We take him up on it and Sharon gets in the driver's seat. I wave goodbye to Chance's car parked on the street.

"Can you handle a stick shift?" I ask foolishly as she pulls out and heads down State and out onto the highway. As she speeds along, I tell her, "Today we can follow them out of town to the farm." Sharon nods and pulls onto Rte. 33, taking the turn like a race car driver.

"It's got lots of pep," she says.

"Like you," I reply.

"Hey," she says, as we glide along toward home, "I have a name for her if you're alright with it." I look over at her smile. "Let's dub her the buddha-bug, strictly lower case, but spiritual nonetheless. Okay?" I nod.

"The buddha-bug it is."

Back at the house, Charlotte and Chance are ready, and so we head out. Sharon finally lets me drive. As we turn onto Rte. 13 I tell her, "It's in Wayne National Forrest five miles off of here near Millfield."

She looks over at me, "Is that where the terrible mining disaster happened?"

"Yep, back in 1930," I say. "82 coal miners lost their lives in a methane explosion. The mine's been closed for decades. I drove out with Chance once, but there's nothing to see now but overgrown weeds and some abandoned timbers." Millfield is a crossroads, and we pass the village of East Millfield with its small hardware store, Hank's Drive-Thru, and Peg's Laundromat. We trail Charlotte's Nova east onto Sweet Hollow Road. "Mmm," I say, "sounds good already. I love these country names." Suddenly we are turning northeast onto LaFolette, and after half a mile, slow down, then pull up a dirt road driveway and out onto a rise.

"On a rocky crest, like they said," Sharon says, and before us sits a large white farm house, and all around it are fields and hills. We get out and Sharon points out what might have been a chicken coop and a wood shed beside what must be an outhouse. A barn that hasn't seen paint in a couple decades sits at the back of the drive, and beside it is the small greenhouse Charlotte spoke of. A rickety fence runs along some of the property. On the ground outside the main house lays a diminished pile of chopped wood. Grass and weeds haven't seen a mower in almost a year. I can see why it hasn't sold. No traffic, only the sounds of birds and October wind.

"Hey," Chance calls from the path to the house, "What you guys think?" Charlotte smiles to encourage us.

"Hey, back at you," I call. "I like the layout. Needs some work, of course, but lots of it is just great." When I look over to Sharon, she has disappeared behind the house.

"She saw a raccoon," Charlotte calls, "came off the front porch." We all grin as Sharon comes back around the corner, and we catch up with her.

"Well, you guys have the key," she smiles. "Let's take a look inside, now that mother raccoon is gone."

The door has to be pushed pretty hard, and the smell inside is probably from a nest of raccoons and who knows what else. "Keep your eyes open," Charlotte says, "where there's one..." Then we're met with bird sounds and the flapping of wings as two rain doves fly out a back window. Creaking floor boards echo my doubts, while Charlotte sighs aloud, "Oh, I just love it."

"Me too," says Sharon, and I and Chance stare at each other. We shrug smiles and bend to the wishes of women. And I thought they'd object to the filth. My mom would be dancing around in a rite of complaint. These are the new women.

"So, what do they want for it?" I ask.

Charlotte volunteers, "40,000, but that includes 10 acres of land, part of the woods and the two surrounding fields. We could give them $10,000 down and save the rest for repairs and back-up mortgage payments till the co-op idea kicks in."

Sharon says, "We wouldn't want it all to fall on you. We can each kick in a share toward the mortgage payments." She takes Charlotte's hand and slow waltzes into what looks like a kitchen. No appliances, only a sink, counter, cupboards, and a large window.

"Well, they do have electric," Chance says, "and I think natural gas. 'Course we'd have to turn all of that on. There's a well for the water, no telephone line, but then I'm not sure we should have a phone if we're going natural." It's still a question at this point, as the whole free farm is this unhatched egg.

We go from room to room and up the stairs, all of us wishing we'd worn gloves or brought a rag. I open a door, "Oh, thank god, there's a tub and flush toilet. The outhouse is just a relic!"

Chance opens the basement door, we stare down, but no one has the nerve to go down. Finally, Charlotte says, "The realtor warned there'd be snakes down there, and probably rats."

"Ah, Nature," I joke and watch relief come to their eyes as we close that door for now. No place to sit, so we go out on the front porch and sit on the wooden steps. After a minute I state the obvious, "It's a great view."

"Yes. It is," Sharon says taking hold of my arm. We look out at the autumn fields that run tan and yellow along the brown hills and up into the deep green woods. "We're both city bred," she explains, "but I know we could be at home here...don't you, Lee?"

"Oh, yeah," I say, half sure, half full of doubt.

We sit there feeling the quiet, then suddenly Chance lets out a yell, "Wa-hoo! Brothers and sisters, we got us a place!"

*   *   *

It's not until November 1st that we're able to move in—making an offer, closing the deal, paperwork at the bank and title office. The house officially belongs to Charlotte

Harris, but we've each signed a statement of partnership that Lew drew up for us. It's a co-op experiment in communal living—officially The Free Farm of Athens County. Its future is in our hands.

After our last Saturday class, we sit with Dick Snyder at the coffeehouse. He's excited for us, but warns us of the problems that arose at Black Bear Ranch commune in northern California. "You know the story? Well, Elsa and Richard Marley bought the place, the advertised it as "Free Land for Free People," and then they went down to San Francisco to raise the $20,000 from rich celebrities like Frank Zappa and the Doors."

"No shit, the Doors?" Chance says.

"Yeah, but by the time they got back, twenty people had already moved into the main house, telling them, 'Hey, we heard—'Free Land for Free People' so we moved in.'"

"So what'd they do?" I ask.

"Well, free spirited Elsa and Richard moved into the shed as a second building. That hard winter their limited survival skills pretty much thinned the herd for a while, but when the weather broke that spring they started getting weekend hippies dropping in for the drugs and fun. They were feeling their way in this. Then some fundamentalist hippie tribe came in and tried to take over. It hurt the group and finally the tribe were asked, then forced to leave." He looks up from his coffee cup, says, "We should learn from them," and with his "we" statement Chance and I know that he is in.

"What do you say, Dick," Chance asks, "you with us?"

"If you'll have me," he says, adding, "as soon as we can get out of my rent. Ingrid comes with me, of course. Okay?" We nod.

"Damn, this is exciting," he says. So with him comes Ingrid, his lover, a solidly built exchange student from Norway who turns out to be quite handy with a hammer and saw.

After a couple weeks of hard cleaning, the move is easy; the fridge and stove are delivered, and none of us has that much, except Charlotte with her books and equipment. Most of her clothes she's dropped off at the local Goodwill. "I'm done with that life," she says. "Give me a pair of jeans and a flannel shirt." We laugh, but I know I'll miss her looking sharp in her tight skirts and silk blouses. Blackie loves it here, roaming the fields, coming back with burrs or sometimes the smell of skunk. But thanks to him the raccoons never come back, and the rain doves move outside.

We have three bedrooms to divide among us, but we suspect that won't last long as word of the farm is travelling. Carl and Susan, from the protests, are planning to join us at the end of fall quarter...if we invite them in. That's one of the things we've had to devise a kind of natural selection that we collectively manage. I've traded my job at the deli for working at the drive-thru down in Millfield, a couple miles away. That way we'll get to know the locals and they'll see that we're harmless. I guess we're all keeping one foot on campus, except for Charlotte who is becoming kind of the mother of the house, keeping track of us all, working her garden in the greenhouse. Chance, Sharon and I work each day on fixing and building just to make some of it useable. Our hands grow callous from the brooms and hammers, shovels and rakes. Dick Snyder isn't much good at this, though he's better at gardening along side of Charlotte. "Do your own thing, but contribute," is our motto. They're trying to winterize the green house to keep some things growing, though we're rigging plastic shields instead of glass for now. We want to be as sustainable as possible, that's one of the new words around here—sustainable. The other is co-op. Each of us takes turns doing kitchen duties: cutting and cooking, and serving and cleaning up. Some of us want to go strictly vegetarian, but others of us (the men) hold out for meat three times a week. It's all working out.

This is until a moment ago when we had a scene. Ingrid shows up in the kitchen in just her blue silk panties, no top. Sharon drops the jug of orange juice on the floor and Charlotte gasps. I happen to be there and watch old Ingrid coming down the hallway, her body square but no fat on it, ample curves and…well, these voluptuous breasts. I enjoy the view then keep my head down in my oatmeal before the explosion right behind me.

"Ingrid, my gosh!" Sharon gasps. "Can I please talk with you, over here?" She must think it will be easy, but it's not. Ingrid stands strong before us, staring back at Sharon.

"But in my home, this is how it is. In Norway this is how we choose to do or do not dress. I'm doing nothing wrong in my own home," she protests to Sharon. Then she turns and reaches out to us, and I'm enjoying the view again. "Charlotte, Lee, what do you think? Is this not my home?" I can't help turning around if only to feign concern to Sharon. If I grin, I know I'll be cut off, though this is really a funny scene.

"Well, I hear you, Ingrid, I do." Sharon's a queen of listening, but this is a real test. "How about for now you slip on a shirt and we bring this up tonight after dinner?" I'm turned full around by then facing Sharon, and we all nod, yet Ingrid doesn't make a move, just stands there full figure, drinking a tall glass of milk. I watch a moment, but have to look away. Sharon glares my way then stomps right out of the kitchen without breakfast and goes into our bedroom.

Sharon stands there with her back to me, and I can see she's turned from anger to trembling. I go to her and begin to wrap my arms around her shoulders, when she stiffens. "No, stop, don't touch me," she says above a whisper. All humor is drained from the room. She is really hurt, but I'm blind as to why.

"That was really something out there," I say.

"Oh, do you think so?" Some anger flushes out. "I saw you get your eyes full."

"Sorry, but I couldn't much help noticing." I realize immediately this is wrong to say, but as I said, I'm dumb and blind here. "What's really bothering you, honey?"

And when she looks me in the eyes I see that hers are tearful. "I'll tell you something," she heaves sigh, "When I heard the word 'commune,' right away I thought nudism. Sorry, but we've all seen those flower child photos from California and Woodstock. I know you have. Well, right away, I said no, I can't do that. Lee, I'm a girl from the same mill town as you. I'm not a free love spirit like them. Are you?"

"God, I'm sorry. I didn't know." I hold out my hand to her, but she stands with her arms crossed. "Honestly" I plead, "I'm in love with commune ideals, the co-op alternative path, not the trappings of nudity and free love. Those are hippie things, I guess, though they've been around for a long time. And I don't think Chance and Charlotte are into that either, do you?"

She nods. Ah, we're agreeing, so I don't stop there. "What's really behind this, Sharon?"

She opens her arms and with trembling fingers unbuttons her blouse and bares her breasts. "These, for one thing. Just look at them."

"I am. And they're lovely." I say this while thinking this is the greatest morning ever, and I doubt I'll never be able to talk or write about it.

"Oh, God, you're such a liar. They're tiny, lemons next to Ingrid's god damn oranges."

"Grapefruits" comes out of my mouth before I can swallow it back.

She glares at me, folds her arms across herself, then turns and slams the closet door. She is dead serious about this, and I feel so lame, yet I can't bring myself to speak for fear I'll laugh.

"Lee, you just don't get it. It hurts that you see me and other women like this...like fruit for your eyes. And I hate to be compared with her."

"I swear I didn't mean it that way. You brought up the fruit. I'm sorry for what I said. I love you, Sharon."

She steps toward me, her blouse still open, and teary eyed says, "It's just that I've never developed fully as a woman. I've always had small breasts. And don't say you don't care."

The truth seems to get me in trouble here, but I go for it anyway. "God, Sharon, I love your breasts. I do. I've never kissed another woman's breasts, yet I know yours are perfect. I swear. I love all of you, body and soul, as you are."

Her eyes soften slightly as she grows quiet. Then slowly she comes to me, and I hold her safe in my arms a long time. The room is quiet and close, and I kiss her tender neck and then her breasts and she allows it. We both have nowhere to go but here.

Before morning work I write her a love poem. It begins, "I watch you move about the room/ in morning quiet, and each gesture/ teaches me how to feel again./ I kiss your slender wrist/ your tender skin./ Your body is a beacon to my soul..." I slip it under her pillow as I make our bed.

*   *   *

Dinner is a bit tense because we all know we'll be talking about commune rules tonight. I hate that word 'rules.' 'Principles,' we might think of it like that. Tonight Charlotte's acorn squash and fried tofu are not wasted on us, nor is the homemade bread, but dinner talk is short in anticipation of the big meeting.

Sharon and I clear the table, while others get coffee or tea. Chance gets a fire going in the fireplace. Charlotte has made brownies, and I have to ask, but she shakes her head, says, "No, just brownies. We need our clear heads tonight."

We sit around the fireplace on furniture or floor. Chance speaks first, the kind of elder of the group, though Snyder and Charlotte are older. "The meeting of the Free Farm has now begun," and he bangs the back of his guitar. Like I said, he's good at lightening things while moving them along. "This is the real revolution," he chants several times, then sets down the guitar to say, "I think we're here tonight to discuss some rules for this place."

"Principles," I say. "Let's call them principles; it's less restrictive."

"Though it may be the same thing," Sharon adds, sitting beside me on the couch.

"Okay," Dick says, rising to speak.

"Oh, let's just sit for this," Chance says. "Maybe we can pass a hat to whomever wants to speak, and the rest will agree to just listen till that person's through. Is that okay with everyone?"

We all nod at this, and Ingrid hands a toboggan cap to Dick. "Maybe someone should take some notes," Dick says. "I think we already have principle number one about speaking at meetings." Sharon gathers a tablet and pen. "What I wanted to start with is kind of funny, but it's a good warning. I've been corresponding to several of the big communes around the country... Morningstar in Sebastopol, the old Diggers Farm, and New Buffalo from Arroyo Hondo. It's my research, but now it's also practical for us here."

"This makes us sound like part of something big," Charlotte says, "and maybe we are." Someone starts clicking their fingers in approval, and a round goes up.

Dick begins again. "This is a letter from Peter Coyote who's at the commune in Olema. All are facing problems, he says. I know that we're considering having Carl and Susan join us, and they have, what, two young kids. Anyway, Peter's come up with what he's calling 'Some Pearls of Wisdom' for communes. They're a bit raw, but here goes. 'One: If you let the baby shit on the floor and then eat it, you'll have a sick baby *and* a shitty floor. 'Two: Free food doesn't mean that I cook and you eat all the time, asshole.'" Dick grins, "I think we're doing pretty well on these two. 'Three: It's fine if you want to take speed, just don't talk to me! I don't actually care that the insects are communicating with you.'" Everyone laughs at this, and some look over at me, though I've never done speed or dropped acid. Dick blushes a little as he continues, "'Four: I know the Indians used moss for tampons, but you're picking poison oak.'" Another round of laughter.

"I'd say we score pretty well on all of these," Chance says taking back the hat. "But what I'm hearing is he's talking to some of the young and maybe old drifters who fall into their commune. We haven't had those, thank god."

"Not yet," Dick adds, "but who knows, once the word gets out."

We all look around, then Ingrid says, "Well, Mr. Coyote does not speak of the question of wearing clothes— or not, if you like, and I do like. Please, all of us, I want to talk of this now." Dick hands her the hat. I look over to Sharon who's looking right back at me.

"First, I say that I respect and love my body, just as I do your body, I hope. In my country, in my village, in my family, we do not always need to dress at home...especially in the morning time. Today, I put on my best underwears, just because I know some of you are not used to this. And I tell you, I sleep totally without." I look at Chance who's looking back at me. We wink but do not grin.

Dick is the next to speak. "I want you all to know that I love Ingrid and trust that her naked body should not offend anyone. She's just being natural. As a matter of fact, we were thinking of disrobing for dinner tonight."

"Before, during, or after?" Chance jokes, but no one laughs, only smiles.

"Right now, if you'd like," Ingrid says suddenly standing up. Dick nods. Okay, I'll admit a personal bias, Ingrid naked—fine, but the thought of Dick standing naked here or anytime with his wanger hanging between his legs...well, sorry, but it's repulsive.

Charlotte takes the hat. "I know that customs vary in countries and families, and I think the larger question is what kind of family are we. Can we discuss that and come back to this?"

Sharon's turn. "Well, this is all new to most of us, but I'd say we are living like couples who are brothers and sisters. My gosh, that didn't come out right. What I'm saying is that we're siblings in general with a choice to couple. Oh, that's not it either. Does anyone understand me?"

I rise, take the hat, "I think Sharon's analogy to siblings is good," and I smile over to her, then add, "though it may prove restrictive if we're to find alternative lifestyles, here. It may be a starting point as a linking, but we shouldn't feel bound by it." A general look of puzzlement gradually eases.

Dick: "I think we should look to other cultures on this, say Native American, for example, the Cherokee who lived in these Appalachian hills. Men and women shared the work and raising of the children, and the man joined his wife's clan; marriage was respected but couples sometimes cohabited with others under tribal approval." We all stare over at him. "I'm just agreeing with Charlotte and Lee here that we should be open to new ways."

Chance asks for the hat. "This is really good, right? We've been so busy learning to survive and repair this place, that we haven't had time to develop our collective vision. I'm going to suggest something basic here, that instead of voting, we trust in consensus. We talk things over like this, hear all sides, and then agree together on an action or plan."

"Well, please to tell me how is that not to vote?" Ingrid interrupts, then says, "Sorry, I forgot the hat."

"Good question though," Chance says. "Can anyone explain it better."

It's actually Sharon who takes the hat in her hand, though she refuses to wear it. "With consensus, as I understand it, you work for a win-win solution and everyone is heard and then agrees to go along with it. It doesn't become an us-and-them thing, right?" and she looks around for approval. Nods and no questions.

Ingrid begins, "Well, okay," Sharon tosses her the hat. "This question of naked has us brought here. I feel it is Dick and I against you others. Am I not right? How do we make this consensus?"

No one speaks for a while, then Charlotte takes the floor. "I'm frankly okay with it as a choice…to wear or not wear clothes in and around the house."

Sharon and I look over in surprise, feeling the ground shift under us. Sharon interrupts, "Well, okay. Maybe as a choice…but how about some conditions, like cleanliness standards."

"Are we unclean?" Ingrid responds. No one is using the hat anymore.

"Oh, not at all. I didn't mean that," Sharon says. "But how about in the house wearing underwear? You can work naked outside or sunbathe all you want, but could you slip on panties or jockeys when around others inside, especially in the kitchen?"

Again, while the thought of Charlotte or Ingrid sunbathing stirs me, the idea of Sharon sharing her naked body I find a little disturbing, and again the image of Dick naked at the sink or sitting spread legged on the couch, makes me cringe. I take up the hat thing again. "Well, I like this idea...it's open and a compromise. How does this work? Do we vote or not?"

Chance is back at the helm. "No voting, Lee, just agreeing, and we haven't heard from everyone yet. We have to do that first. Dick, Ingrid, Charlotte...how is this with you?"

Dick looks at Ingrid. "I'd say we can live with this for now."

"Yes, we two can accept," Ingrid echoes.

"Wow," Charlotte smiles. "Our first real consensus. Write that one down, Sharon, please, along with speaking and consensus and Coyote's guides on eating, drugging, and not shitting on the floor."

Laughter and back to Chance, "Great. Now I think the next issue is accepting Carl and Susan and their kids Gracie and little Ned into the fold. Is anyone opposed to this? Do we need to talk it over further?" He looks around to each of us. "Okay, then we're agreed to live with them and our decision." Another cheer. "Well, what do you say—is that enough for tonight? Tomorrow night we can talk about television, the use of drugs and alcohol, and the sharing of the work." He looks around once more to nods. "Well, that's it, family meeting adjourned by silent consensus."

With that, Ingrid rises and strips off her t-shirt and shorts in lamp light. "Come on, let's celebrate," she calls out boldly naked, and Charlotte laughingly slips her blouse over her head, steps out of her skirt, then looks over to Sharon. I wait and watch, and yes, the blouse comes off revealing her beige lace bra which remain on with her panties. And she is smiling as the guys rise to take off their shirts, pants and jockeys. Chance begins to strum the guitar and we all dance wildly around the fireplace in a circle like natives. Laughter and song move us as we dance, and for just a moment I look out the window and wonder what the animals watching outside are thinking.

Chapter Fifteen
The Commune Grows

Last night's dancing continued for some time. A wine bottle or two got passed, Chance wore out his guitar fingers on his guitar, then we brought out the Marvin Gaye and Led Zeppelin cassettes. Someone passed a couple joints, and all of us got down to just our underwear, including Sharon. Some went further, so we now know that Ingrid's a real red head. Finally Sharon and I went off to bed where all inhibition flew away and we made love in new ways swaying to the music in our heads and with her astride. Today, Carl and Susan and their kids are coming out for another look around, so the clothes are back on. Though they can't move in till after December, we can begin to work things out with them now. Carl's blackness integrates our clan, and his being an engineering student should prove a great help with repair and construction. Susan's an education major and will be doing home schooling with Gracie. We got to know them during all the anti-war, anti-administration demonstrations. Though Nixon is President and the war rages on, we haven't given up on political change; we're just putting our chips and backs elsewhere working for people action. Our vision is clear and written on the fridge: "To act out our authentic inner life, and so change the way of the masses." Or as Chance says at each meeting: "We need to liberate the mind, people. Value over profit. Leave the wage-slave life behind."

While I buy into our extending the Romantic vision into today, I'm not blind to the fact we all still have one foot in this life, another at the university, and the gap between the two is growing wider. We talk about just dropping out and doing our work here at the farm, but it's the middle of winter, so we're hanging onto our day jobs and university. Like the Diggers out west, we recognize that part of our work is to take this free vision back from the farm and onto the streets. Come spring, we'll be growing vegetables to feed ourselves and others. Charlotte already has us gathering up restaurant castoffs and setting up free food tables back in Athens. We're developing a mission, in the good sense of the word.

Carl and Susan have just pulled up in their pickup, the kids squeezed up front. Okay, yes, I'm thinking that the truck can come in handy, but I really do like Carl. He knows how to get things done. Susan, I don't know well, but Sharon says she's fine. They come in and hug everyone, though Dick and Ingrid have gone into town. The little girl looks around. Susan is wearing one of those long flower-child dresses, has her long auburn hair down around her shoulders and is carrying the little Ned, about two I guess. She sits down at the table, slides her top down off her shoulder and begins nursing him. "Lunch is served," she jokes, while others smile and try not to watch.

"Hey, how's everybody doing?" Carl asks. "Looks like you're surviving out here."

"We are that," Chance says, "and today we're also your welcoming committee. We all agree that you're one with us if you want to be."

"That's great," Carl says. "Right, Sue?"

She smiles up at him, says, "Oh, we're tired of Athens life. No room to breathe, no chance for change or growth really. We dig this organic life."

"No objection to that here," says Charlotte sitting down beside Susan and stroking her hand. For a quiet moment we all notice something—we are all drawn to this breast feeding.

"Hey, let's have a look around," Carl says, and we guys lead him downstairs to check out the furnace and plumbing. It's dark and cold down there, but he checks things out and says, "It'll do." Next we take him back upstairs to look at the bathroom and floors. "So," he says in the hallway, "each of you has a bedroom. If you don't mind my asking, where would we be bedding down?" It's the most obvious question, though one we haven't answered yet.

"Well, buddy," Chance says, "we were hoping you might help with that. Downstairs is the one bedroom which Lee and Sharon have, but there's also that dining room we could convert into another bedroom for you guys. What do you think?"

"Can't tell from up here. Let's go take a look," Carl says. "We'll see what might be done."

"Sue, can you come over here?" Carl calls from the hallway, then explains, "Babe, one option would be to convert this room into our bedroom. What do you think?"

She gives it the look around, stares at the open door space. "Well, we could fit our double bed over there."

"What about Gracie?" Sharon asks.

"Oh, she sleeps with us together," Susan replies. "We sleep as a family." Silence, then she adds, "We'd need a door here for when the kids are sleeping, and we'd have to do something about those French doors."

"And we thought Carl was the contractor in this family," Chance jokes.

"Oh, I always check things out with Sue. She has this ability to envision things finished. Yeah, too bad they're not pocket doors, but if it's okay with the rest of you, we could replace them with wallboard and paneling or maybe easier just a set of solid doors. You can pick those up used at Harvey's outlet."

"That sounds good to me," Chance says. "And shouldn't cost much at all. Maybe, Carl, you could pick them out and haul them in your truck. We'll get them up for you in no time."

There is a hand shake on this, the way my dad would seal a deal.

Gracie sidles over to her dad and whispers something to him. He looks over to Charlotte, who says, "Okay, I'll take her," and holds her hand out to Gracie.

"Sue, you ready to take a look outside?" We walk up to the crest together. It is mid-November and most of the leaves have fallen, but our row of pines along the woods' edge is still green. We go over to inspect the out buildings.

"That's the old latrine," Chance says, "They put plumbing in the house about ten years ago. Barn down there; tool and wood sheds over here."

"I'd like to take a closer look," Susan says, "Maybe one of these could become a school room in the spring."

Sharon, walking beside Susan, sighs, "Oh, a school would be really nice."

Sensible Susan adds, "I wonder if there might be other kids in the area who would pay to take classes? It'll be Free in approach, but we'd have to charge something so it pays for itself. I'll have my teaching certificate at the end of this term, so we might start with a couple classes at a Free School this summer."

I watch the other smiling faces. "You know," I say in my least expert voice, "at the Brook Farm Commune in Thoreau's time, their school kept the commune going, till it burned down."

"Wow, a Free School at the Free Farm!" Charlotte says. "Gives me chills to think of it."

When Dick and Ingrid get back, we are ready for supper. Sharon and Charlotte have made a big stir fry of tofu and veggies. Susan has brought a loaf of dill bread, so we pull up a couple folding chairs and gather around the table. "We'll need to make this table larger, when you guys come on," Dick says. "Any ideas for that?" Everyone looks at Carl, who looks to Susan.

"Again, unless you're pledged to this porcelain table," and Susan looks around, "we might consider another flat door as an overlay."

"Yeah, I've seen it done that way," Dick says.

"And we can add the four kitchen chairs we'll bring," Carl says. "Lee, will you pass the bread, please?"

Ingrid keeps staring at Gracie and Ned. Finally she speaks, "Forgive my question, but is Gracie Carl's child?" A small gasp goes up, and everyone holds their fork for a bad moment.

"Well, if you're asking if he's the birth father, no," Susan answers while buttering Gracie's bread, "but he is her father now."

"I just wondered, because she seems to have no Negroid features. Am I correct?"

Charlotte jumps in, "Oh, Ingrid's from Norway," as though that explains her bluntness.

"Any other questions on genealogy or our sex life?" Susan asks.

"No," Ingrid glares back at her. "Not right now, thank you."

No one knows what to say about this edge that's arisen, so we change the subject. "Dick, what did you do in town?"

"Well, we went to see a new film at the cinema. Ingrid had heard that *Bob & Carol & Ted & Alice* was playing. It's very good, and quite interesting in a way. Maybe our group should go and see it together?"

"Who's in it," Charlotte asks. "Natalie Wood, Robert Culp, Elliot Gould from *M*A*S*H* and I forget."

"Dyan Cannon," Ingrid adds. "She's really hot in this."

"Oh, I loved *M*A*S*H*," Chance says. "Really gave it to the establishment, like Heller's *Catch 22* did to the military. What's this new film about?"

"Group sex is what I heard," Susan says, placing some more vegetables on Gracie's plate. We all look at Gracie, then Susan adds, "Oh, she's aware, if that's what you're concerned about. She's seven."

"How does it work out, the film I mean?" Charlotte asks.

"Ah, that's where I felt a little let down," Dick says. "This couple does some group encounter work, gets into 'just feeling' everything. Then they hook up with this other couple, and...well, you'll have to see the film. I don't want to ruin it. Let's just say it asks some real questions about relationships," and he pans each of our faces, "You know?"

Sharon is getting a little uneasy with all of this and so gets up to clear the table. I join her at the sink. "We have brownies again," she says. "Anyone ready for one?"

I look over to Carl and Susan. "Nope," she smiles, shakes her head, "...just flour," and we laugh again over this old joke.

After the table is cleared and dishes washed and left to dry at the sink, we gather in the living room for our meeting. Chance asks Sharon to review what happened at last night's meeting, and she sticks close to the group decisions: passing the hat to talk and working on consensus. "Carl looks to Susan, I think we're good with that. Anything else?"

"Well," Sharon adds, "we agreed on inviting your family to join us, and we talked about dress and undress here at the farm."

"Yes," Susan speaks up. "And what did you decide about that?"

"Dress is pretty much optional," Sharon says officially. "Except around the kitchen where underwear is expected for cleanliness. What do you think? Is this going to work with the kids?"

"Oh, yes," Susan answers. "We're raising our children as natural as possible. Carl and I rarely dress around the house." And so, at this point I suddenly see Susan in a new light, and completely naked. And okay, I'll admit I'm a little threatened by Carl's potential to humiliate us guys, yet I smile along with the rest.

"Well," Charlotte says, "another border passed. We're trying this for now. So, what's up for tonight?"

Chance holds up Charlotte's sun hat. "Who'd like to go first?"

"I'd like to say that we've come up with some visions today during Carl and Susan's visit." It is Charlotte who's speaking. "For one, we see how we can transform the dining room into another bedroom for their family, and two we see a potential in eventually making one of the outbuildings into a school...Oh, and possibly having other children come here to pay if they can for teachings by Susan and others." She looks around, "It would be a source of income as well as being open or free education. Personally, I love this idea."

Dick speaks without the hat, "When was all of this decided?"

Charlotte continues, "Oh, it wasn't or isn't. I'm sorry. We're not announcing it but laying it out there. I think they both are very practical ideas. How do you feel about it, Dick, Ingrid?"

Dick finally takes the hat into his hand, but won't put it on. "I'm okay with both of those ideas. But I don't see how they'll get two beds in there."

Charlotte reaches for the hat, "Oh, they're good with just one bed, they're practicing sleeping together as a family."

"Cool, I've heard of that, never seen it," Dick says, then grimaces. "Couldn't imagine sleeping with my parents!"

Susan reaches for the hat, "Well, that's the point. Many of us are alienated from our parents. We're hoping to stay close with our children all of our lives, and it begins now by establishing this early bond. Yet we're quite free with their activities. Anyway, we don't have a problem with the room or bed, once some repairs are made to the doors."

She hands the hat to Chance, who grimaces. "This hat passing is getting kind of tiresome, and nobody is putting it on. Maybe we could just pass something small, like that Canadian flag over there on the desk, or the wooden stirring spoon." I reach over and trade him the spoon for the hat, and he goes on, "So, has everyone had their say about the room arrangement? Do we have consensus? Yes, okay let's move on. Can we table the school idea for now, till it's closer to spring?"

Carl accepts the wooden spoon. "Susan and I want to thank all of you for, well, accepting us into your family. I never had so many white sisters and brothers." Light laughter. "We'll be living in town till after the holidays, but I want you all to know, we'll be out here working with you day by day to make all of this work."

The discussion goes on, and we get a lot done. We reach a consensus on no television, though I doubt an antenna could pick up much out here anyway, and no telephone, though it takes a while to agree on that one. For now, we're trying to go without to see what's necessary—Thoreau style. We'll continue with the food and garden rotations, though if someone is really good at something, they can trade with others. Work will begin on the doors and table, and with Carl's design help, we'll lay a floor in the tool shed, and maybe install a window. Ingrid volunteers for that project, though it's a little unclear whether she's drawn to working with wood or with Carl. Near the end, Charlotte and Sharon explain some yoga to us, something they've been doing in their Zen class. The two do some lovely stretches, arms and legs and tummies in beautiful display. We all do a few positions and agree to start a group practice the hour before dinner.

Tonight we do not end in our near naked dancing; instead we form the family circle holding hands and invite a spirit of caring by chanting the loving-kindness metta that Charlotte and Sharon have taught us. "May we be filled with loving kindness; may we be well; may we be free; may we be happy." Then we chant it for the world, and open our arms and hold our hands extended to all. Good vibes surround us, when Susan says softly, "Oh, I love this, and here's a variation I learned at a retreat: 'Even as a mother protects with her life her child, so with a boundless heart should one cherish all living beings.'" Warm smiles and silence fill our house.

Later lying in bed beside Sharon and looking up at the ceiling, we each clear our head by saying whatever comes, thoughts or feelings, while the other just listens. Eventually we slow down, then it's just sharing the silence between us. At times we whisper the names of the sounds. Before we fall asleep, I kiss her wrist, she strokes my beard, and we end in each other's arms.

*   *   *

"Lee, you have a letter," Sharon calls from the front porch. I'm helping to clear out the tool shed. We're taking everything out for now, moving it to the wood shed. Then we begin digging and hauling and leveling the dirt floor.

I yell back, "Who's it from?"

"Kenny. Come and get it."

"Alright, Baby, are you ready for it?" I try to insinuate sex into her mind.

"Okay, wise guy. I'll just toss it in the compost here."

By then, I am up to the porch and take the letter from her hand. I go to kiss her, but she quickly turns away, casting my kidding back at me. Without a phone, we count heavy on our mail. Mom writes me now and then, mostly about my sibs and relatives, and lately she says she's concerned about Dad. Sharon's mom writes the same kind of thing, and about our town. We share our mail. Kenny wants to come and visit around break time. "I hear you're a farmer now? What's that all about, buddy?" he writes. "How about meeting me in Athens and I'll follow you out. Call me if you're willing." This should be interesting, my several lives coming together like this—home, college, and the farm—and it will be good to see him.

He meets me at the bus station, though he's driven his own VW Bug down from Mingo. "Holy shit, you look like Jesus!" he exclaims.

"A little respect, my son," I trade back. We shake hands, then hug in the doorway. He looks around.

"You do look like a farmer, buddy. So what's been happening? Where's Sharon? You're still together I hope."

"God yes, couldn't live without her. She's in class right now. We'll get a coffee or something and pick her up in an hour. If you want, I'll show you the campus and the town. You look good, my man."

We leave our cars in the city lot for now and walk down Court Street toward the campus. He's noticing everything. "Still trolling for pretty women?" I ask.

"Hell, yes. Never saw so many, even in long coats, they're lovely, bare legs and leather boots. How do you resist, man?"

I shake my head. "Let's get a coffee," and we duck into the deli. "I used to work here, and we lived down the street in an old house."

"You know, the houses here remind me of home," he says, "some of them even leaning, most a century old. What's with that?"

"This is an old mining town, and good number of these houses are kept up for student rentals."

"So, big question—what's with the move to a farm? You're not a farmer."

"No, but I'm learning. We got fed up with the shit that was going down with the university, and so with two other couples, we bought this farm out near Millfield which we're running like a co-op. You know about those. Charlotte made the initial investment, but we all share the mortgage payments and live, well, like a family."

"Sweet Jesus, you're living in a commune!"

"Well, yeah...you could call it that. And it's really different, but I'll have to prepare you for all that on the drive out, but know this—they're all good people, the best."

At this precise point a young co-ed takes off her leather coat and is wearing the shortest leather skirt the law will provide, so I lose Kenny's attention entirely and most of my own. He shakes his head, "Man, why would you ever move out of this town! So many sweet women to look at and touch."

"You forget, I have Sharon. And there are bigger things."

"Yeah, right. You've got perfection with that girl, I agree. But I'm still shopping, brother, and the market's full of fresh vegetables and meat."

Kenny hasn't grown beyond Steubenville, but I'm hoping he tames down some before we get to the farm, where his male ego will meet a different kind of woman. Maybe Sharon will help.

Kenny fills me in on our friends from home—Marlene's engaged. Jerome was drafted in the lottery, though the war appears to be closing. The mills are running hard. "And your dad's been showing me how to do body work on cars. We did the fenders on that Bug of mine. But I have to tell you, he's been kind of jumpy lately, hands shaking on the tools so he has me do the fine sanding and stuff, which I actually enjoy."

I'm blindsided by this and don't know what to say or think, so I say instead, "Sharon knows to meet us here and should be coming any minute." Our sandwiches follow our cups of steaming coffee, and Kenny flirts with our waitress Darla. Why's he so horny? This won't go well at the farm.

Sharon enters and gives Kenny a hug and kiss on the lips, then takes off her green coat. She is wearing this white shirt of mine that she's made over into a dress, and it comes to her mid thigh.

"Wow, you look good!" Kenny says. "Let me have another hug."

"Down, boy," Sharon laughs. "My man is sitting right beside you."

"Oh yeah, that jerk. I forgot." We are back to our old ways of kidding about everything, but Kenny's talk about Dad worries me. We need to go home soon.

Sharon has a coffee with us and nibbles on some of our wrinkle fries. Then we walk back down Court to the cars. Kenny gets excited about the head shop and has to go in and look around. I give him the nod a couple times. I still have some of Cousin Harry's stuff hidden away. While he's looking around, I tell him "Oh, man I gotta tell you, this thing that happened the third week we were at the farm. The county sheriff shows up see, says he's come 'to inspect your plants.' And along with a plant expert he's brought a drug dog, a sniffer. Well, we say no and don't allow them into the house. So they go up to our greenhouse and pull out a dozen of Charlotte's plants. The inspector says, 'Yep, that's it, marijuana.' Charlotte is in town at the time, only Sharon and I are home, but they just ignore our protests."

"What happen, you guys get busted?"

"Well, the story even got onto the front page of the papers down here, probably satisfying some local resentment. At the drive-thru I'd heard our place called 'that hippie farm.' Anyway we just waited for the bust, and then the next issue of the paper prints a much smaller story, 'Local drug bust yields tomato plants.'"

"No shit!" he laughs as does the guy behind the counter.

"Yep, and guess what...There were no apologies from the sheriff."

"So that was you guys," says the guy. "We loved it. Let me shake your hand."

Kenny then buys a small pipe, and we head out. Sharon agrees to ride out to the place with Kenny so they can catch up on things. Before she gets into his car, I pull her aside, "Honey, I didn't get a chance to talk with him about how people might be dressed or not, and he's acting pretty horny."

"Well what were you talking about all that time?" She shakes her head at me, says, "I'll do what I can" and slips into his car without kissing me. This visit is already costing me.

I get to the house first, so I can give them a heads-up about Kenny. Charlotte is working in the kitchen, dressed, and Chance is up packing down the dirt floor in the tool shed-school. We bought a window frame from Harvey, but don't have the skills to install it. Dick and Ingrid are no where around. We're safe. So when Sharon and Kenny arrive, I'm waiting at the front window and go out on the porch to greet them.

"Wow, I'm impressed. I thought I'd find some shack in the boondocks, but you guys have fixed this place up."

"Yes, we have, so welcome to the Free Farm of Athens County, my friend." I take him out back to meet Chance while Sharon takes my hand and gives a cheek kiss, then goes in to help Charlotte with dinner. Though we're still feeling our way each day, our meals are regular and give us some structure. Chance and Kenny hit it off, and Kenny ends by taking a rule and level to the back wall, says he's done a window before in his father's garage. I leave them talking things over.

Inside the house, Sharon has put on a pair of cut-off jeans under her short dress. "We talked," she says, "but he is a bit randy."

"I know," I say, then mock sing, "How we gonna keep him out on the farm, after he's seen Athens?" She laughs and gives me a real kiss this time.

When Chance and Kenny come in, they wash up in the pantry, then stroll into the kitchen where Charlotte welcomes him with a kiss.

"Hey, he showed me how to sketch in for the window," says Chance. "When Carl gets here this weekend, we'll put her in. Our little school building is coming right along."

"School?" Kenny says, "What all are you folks planning?"

"Oh," Chance drawls, "a little revolution is all."

"Go for it, man," Kenny laughs. "We need us a revolution every now and then." He turns to me. "Say, brother, got any of that fine grass your cousin grows down here? Thought we might share some while I'm here?"

I look at Sharon then Charlotte and Chance. "Is it okay? We can take it out to the tool shed. But, hey, anyone's welcome to join us."

No takers but no objectors, though Sharon gives me that look. Since she's been doing meditation and yoga, she doesn't touch the stuff. I get high on life too, but I still dig my stash out from a floor board and we head up to the shed. It's late afternoon, and an autumn sun rests on the fields. The leaves are all down from the trees. We gather up some fire wood and light the fire pit. Sitting on a couple tree stumps we can hear birds and a light wind blowing. "This is nice," Kenny says, "and I'm glad to talk straight for a while."

"Before we light up, Ken, what do you think's going on with my dad? Is he sick or something?"

"If you ask me, it's nerves. He hates that yardmaster job, told me the men who used to work along side of him are playing him, and the bosses pressure him to get them in line. The stress is wearing him down."

"Did he tell you all that?"

"Yes and no. Your mom and I figured out some. He's too young to retire. What is he, not 50 yet. Says he'll work something out, told me he might move back to braking on the railroad, 'leave the bossing to the assholes.'"

"He didn't say that," I half-assert.

"Something like it, he did."

"Wow, I didn't know any of this. You're a good friend, man. Sharon and I are going to come home after Thanksgiving. I'll talk with him then." I realize how flat that sounds, and pull out my bag. We each roll one in the papers, lick the edges, twist the ends and light up. For now, time and worry vanish in the sweet smoke.

Sharon has to come up to get us for supper. It's cold, Ken and I are leaning together near the fire. We're in a kind of trance listening to the music of the fire. We grin up at her. "Oh, God," she says. "Lee, please pull yourself together. Ingrid and Dick are back now. We're doing yoga and..." She shakes her head as I grin up at her in the sunlit doorway. "Anyway, come on down for dinner. It's five o'clock."

Eventually I help Kenny up, and we mosey down to the house. The rest of them have finished doing the yoga stretches. Kenny greets Dick and smiles at Ingrid, who has removed her t-shirt and is using it as a towel for her naked body sweat. "Wow, what did I miss?" he says. Ingrid's chest has gained all his attention.

"Forgive him," I say placing my hand over his eyes. "He knows not what he does. This is Kenny from our hometown." Ingrid takes his hand, then gives him a kiss on the cheek, her breasts rubbing against his arm.

He looks over at me, smiles broadly and says, "Wooee, I gotta use the can." As I lead him away, he whispers to me, "Momma said there'd be days like this, but I never believed it. You got a gold mine here, buddy boy."

Ingrid slips on another t-shirt for dinner, and we all gather around the spaghetti, bread, and salad. Kenny has brought a bottle of Dago red from Frank DeVore, and it's passed around. Later Chance brings out his 12-string guitar, and Dick makes a fire in the fireplace which Kenny sits near and stares into for hours. When I finally tuck him into bed on the couch, he smiles up at me. "I like it here. That Ingrid babe is really nice, how free is she? I'd love to do her." Though his language hurts me some, I chalk it up to ignorance, but I'm still high enough to answer, "Hey, brother, tell me this...who's hotter Ingrid with her shirt off, or Sharon with that shirt dress of hers on?" He grins, rolls over, and probably dreams about making love to both.

Sharon is almost asleep, so I just lie beside her listening to the sounds of the house, feeling the air in the room, and thinking about the folks back home. I stroke her arm softly, whisper, "We need to go home for Thanksgiving," and she rolls over to hold me saying yes.

Chapter Sixteen
Back Home

Though Sharon is sorry to miss her Saturday Zen class, and I've had to work hard to finish my exams early, today we drive home for Thanksgiving weekend. Carl and Susan will be coming out and can sleep in our bedroom, so I stash my stash well, almost gone now. At noon we load up the car, give everyone hugs, tell them we'll miss them for Thanksgiving, then head down the gravel road in our little red buddha-bug. As we meet the main road, Sharon leans her head on my shoulder and says, "God, you know, this is our first trip home...as a couple." I nod to her, and she whispers to me, "It feels nice, almost like..."

"...like we're married." I finish her thought, and add, "I know." We grow quiet a moment. Marriage is a word we avoid like it's a deadly sickness one of us has. I kiss her hair and dare to ask it, "Do you ever think about it...getting married?"

Another long pause, then she says softly, "Sometimes I do...being married mostly. So much has changed in our lives this past year. Last Thanksgiving we were just coming out to others with our love."

"That's true. And now we're together down here, loving freely, both going to school, and living in our free commune family where no one is married, except maybe Carl and Susan."

Sharon looks over, says, "I'm not sure about them either."

"Well," I sigh as I turn out onto Sweet Hollow Road, "I am sure of one thing...our love for each other. I'd do anything for you...except hurt that. And I have to admit, I'm afraid doing the marriage dance to make it legal might just ruin it."

"We don't need it," she says pressing my arm.

"Yeah," I say, then kiss her soft hair again, "besides, we're doing everything married couples do...except fight and divorce."

She laughs, "Oh, I think we've had a couple little spats by now."

"No," I grin. "Nothing like our parents do."

"Do Jeanie and Del fight?" she asks. "I can't picture it."

"Oh, yeah. Not often, but a few times dishes have gone flying, and there was that week where we kids each carried messages between them."

"Hmph! Can't imagine it."

"Well, maybe you'll get lucky enough to witness it this weekend."

We're breezing past telephone poles and trees and I'm about to pull onto Rte. 13 north, when I hear myself say, "Honestly, Sharon, I love things the way they are, but if you ever want to be married, I'm willing to tie the knot forever...till death do us part." I slip the car into third, and we drive on, moving toward home, and though the weather looks like it might snow, we are warm together in our little buddha-bug.

It's a long drive, winding through small towns and along forests. After about an hour of chatting, Sharon slips on some soft music and sits in meditation beside me. She can sit up to half an hour now, and her stillness clears the space around her, so that I'm glad to be part of it. I try to do it while driving, and though I can slow my breathing, I can't reduce the road distractions, like that Greyhound bus that just whipped around us going 80 mph east on Rte. 40. I get back to my memorization. I've been working on my poetry lately, trying to get a feel for line breaks by memorizing poems, like we did in sixth grade with Mrs. Z. Only now, with meditation practice, I'm working to get the poem inside of me where I think it, breathe it, and feel it coming real. I'm using Theodore Roethke's "The Waking," because it has meter and rhyme, and rolls off the tongue. "I wake to sleep and take my waking slow/ I feel my fate in what I cannot fear./ I learn by going where I have to go." Mrs. Z. would be proud of me, and she might smile to know that next quarter Sharon and I are both taking the education methods class to help out with the Free School.

Near New Concord, Sharon pulls out a couple egg salad sandwiches from her back pack along with a little book. She unwraps and hands half of a sandwich to me.

"What you reading?" I ask.

"Oh, that novel everyone is reading, except you literary snobs, *Love Story* by Erich Segal. Charlotte passed it on to me, said it made her cry. And it does. Some really nice sections about these two college students who fall in love, then she gets this terrible disease."

"Oh, God. Please stop."

"Well, I might stop reading, though I only have a little ways to go. I just read the worst line in American literature."

"Oh, read it to me, please."

She gives me that look. "Okay, Mr. Smart Aleck, here's the line. At this really crucial scene, the heroine says to her boyfriend, 'Love means never having to say you're sorry.' Did you ever hear such bull?"

"Wow, look who's the critic now."

"Yeah, but at least I gave the book a chance. The writing's not that bad, but this idea is so wrong. Love means being willing to say you're sorry again and again. Oh..." and she closes the book. "Now I can't finish it. I'll pass it on to Susan."

"You're funny," I say and smile over at her. "Hey," I say, "you know I thought we were going to have trouble with Susan being bossy, but I'm really starting to like her."

"She's neat," she says and begins to eat her own sandwich.

"Yeah, but she and Ingrid still don't hit it off. In fact they seem to detest each other. I'm not sure why," I say this while taking the other half of my sandwich from her hand.

"You don't get it?" Sharon asks. "I'll tell you what I see. Ingrid is after Carl, and Susan and Carl are monogamous."

"Well, that's interesting. Our first conflict over free love."

She grows quiet. "Maybe not the only one," she says and lets that drop into my lap, like a match.

"What do you mean?"

"Oh, nothing....I took care of it," she says and gathers up the wax papers.

"Wait a minute," I drawl. "What aren't you telling me? Come on, girl...I'll pull this car over right now, if you don't tell me." I sound like my parents on a long drive.

"Well, promise not to get mad."

"You know I can't promise that."

"Okay then. It's good that we're away from there when I tell you that your ex-professor Dick has had his hands on my ass twice."

"Son of a bitch!" jumps out of my throat, and feels so right, I say it again, "Son... of...a...bitch!"

"It's over, Lee. I handled it."

"Where were you...what did you do?"

"First time was at the kitchen sink. We were doing dishes together when I felt his hand pressing on my shorts, so I turned away quick and put a wet sponge in his greedy paw. Then I left him with the dishes."

"Good! That was good. But that didn't stop him?"

"No, the next day we were cutting up vegetables for the salad and he acted like he was reaching for something, but instead slid his hand down my back to my butt. This time I had the cutter in my hand, so I pulled his hand around to the board and held the knife over it. 'You want to lose that?' I said, and this time he walked away."

"Son of a bitch. I didn't expect any of this, but you handled him perfect, girl."

"Yes, and you, Lee, have to trust that I can do that again. He'll get the message."

"Yeah," I say, "or we'll vote both him and Ingrid out."

"Can we do that?" she asks.

"I don't know, I guess we'd have to get a consensus, then ask or tell them to leave. I don't know how that would work."

"Well, I don't think we'll need to. I can control Dick. He's just a groper, and I've been pretty blunt with him. It's your friend Chance I'm a little leery about."

"I'm pulling off," I say and slow the car onto this gravel driveway near a small factory. I turn the engine off, look over at her. "Okay, what's he done?"

"Gosh, I'm sorry for bringing this up. I don't want to ruin anything."

"Oh, I want to hear this, believe me. I won't have you treated like some kind of love doll."

"Well, neither will I. Know that, Lee. I just don't know how to interpret Chance's long, hard kisses. He's done it three times now, where we're all being warm with each other and he presses his lips to my mouth and holds me hard from behind, so that it's clearly not just friendship. A woman can tell these things, believe me."

"Oh, I do. And to be honest, I think I've felt something like that coming from Charlotte too, and I don't know how to take it."

"Right."

"I'm really care for both of them...like family, but I'm not sure what this kind of affection is about," I say. "And I know I never kissed my sisters like that."

We sit there a few minutes while traffic passes us by, neither of us knowing the words to explain it. I take her hand and kiss her gently. Finally, I start up buddha-bug, pull onto the highway, and Sharon says, "I just hope this doesn't bring down the whole thing."

"Yeah. Let's have a hard talk with Charlotte and Chance when we get back. For now, let's focus on home."

At Bridgeport we make the big turn north and head up river toward home. Though we thought it might be closer driving this route, it's still the long four hours. If home is where the heart is, ours is here in the valley along this river roadway, with green hills on both sides. And yet, I'm beginning to feel home is both places—Mingo and the Free Farm. More than anything, home is Sharon now. By the time we pull off Rte. 7, the evening light is coming on. We stop first at my house where we'll be staying. Dave and Diane come out to greet us and to carry in our bags. They each have a good laugh at my beard. Little Diane has grown as high as the hedges now, and Dave is this college man with his hair cut short and combed. "It's called a Princeton," he says. "I see you're farming your own. Looks like the crop needs weeding."

"Where's Janie?" I ask.

"Oh, she's at church," Diane says, "practicing for the play."

"She's getting so smart," Sharon says, pressing Diane to her side. "We missed you guys," she adds, and we all hug on the front porch, except for Dave and me.

Mom sticks her head out the door. "Get in here, all of you. Let me get at you." And the hugging continues in the hall. It's nice to see her and Sharon be close like this.

"Don't even ask," she says to me. "He's down in the garage. But he wanted to know as soon as you two got in."

"I'll go get him," Diane says.

"No," I say, taking her arm, "let me surprise him." I go back out and walk along the house, down through the shadows in the yard. Mrs. Miller has cleared out her big backyard garden. I wish we had her working our fields, that woman could grow tomatoes on cement. I open the garage door and find Dad standing at his tool bench. His prized Ford is covered now with a tan tarp. He turns around.

"Hey, it's you. Welcome home. Come in here a minute will you."

Expecting him to be frail somehow, I see he seems as hearty as ever. We shake hands and he pulls me toward him, but there is something in his eyes. "I got some news for you."

"Oh, yeah, from whom?"

"From down your way actually, from Cousin Margaret in McArthur. I'm afraid, it's not good. Your cousin Harry Jr. is gone."

"'Gone'—you mean gone as in dead or gone off somewhere?"

"More like 'put away,' I'm sorry to say."

Though Harry and I aren't really close, this feels like a blow to my gut. Dad takes hold of my arm, stares into my eyes. "Listen, I hope to God you aren't involved in any of his dealings. Margaret says the feds arrested him for growing and selling marijuana."

I don't know how much he knows or how much to tell him, so I wait for more of the story. "Margaret is Harry's aunt, sister of my cousin Big Harry. According to her, it's Harry Sr. who was growing the stuff in an abandoned mine on the property. He'd run a wire from the house and rigged some kind of lights to make it grow underground. The boy is taking the rap for the father."

I look into his eyes. "I swear, I know nothing about this." He looks deeper, and I confess, "Okay, I did buy a bag of the stuff from young Harry, but that's all." He wants to believe me and so lets go of my arm. I have to ask, "How did they catch him?"

"Oh, stupid upon stupid. He'd come over into West Virginia, was selling the stuff in some old hotel in Parkersburg and got caught in a sting. It's just awful. They're back to doing what old Andrew did from his moonshining. Did I ever tell you, great-grandpa did time in the state pen?"

"Yeah, you have. And listen, Dad, I don't justify any of it, but I do know they were really hurting for work down there."

"No damn excuse," he says, and I let that stand between us. There's a long pause while he cleans the oil off of his hands with a rag, then says, "So, how are things with you and Sharon? I hear you're living on a farm now."

"Yeah, let's talk about that with everyone up at the house. Dad, I want to ask how you are doing."

"Oh, I'm fine," he says and turns away. "This is Kenny's old DeSoto he's fixing up. We did a fine job restoring the body. He wants you to call him when you get in."

I take his arm now. "No, Dad. Really, how are you doing?"

He looks back like I've touched a tender spot around a wound. "Can we talk about this later?"

"Dad, you know once we get around everyone, we won't. It's just you and me here in your garage. What's going on? Is it work or what?" I'm pushing but afraid to hear, yet I step closer and wait.

"Yeah, it's work mostly. They got me doing what I hate...bossing other men. And well, I can't do it well. I know it and they know it...the men and the bosses. It's the damndest thing. I feel trapped."

"I hear you," I say and nod.

"And now they want me to take an early buy out. Cripes, I'm not 50 years old. What am I going to do with the rest of my life...drive your mother insane here?"

"I hear you. This must be hard for you."

"Are you just saying that, or what? 'Cause it sounds like a recording, son."

"Give me a break, Dad. I don't know what to say or how to help, but I'm listening and I care. I do."

"I know you do, son. Sorry, but I've just been so damn edgy lately. My only outlet has been these cars and the church. You're mom's doing the best she can with me. I just have to figure things out." We share a silence, then he turns the lights off and we go out, walking through the yard up to the lights of the house.

Inside, Mom has set out a dinner of spaghetti and DiCarlos' Italian bread, a family favorite. Sharon has been cutting up the salad and looks over to read my face. I do the 'I don't know' shrug and ask, "Are we ready to sit down?"

"Okay," Mom says, "call your brother and sisters. I think Janie is back.

"Dinner is served," I yell loud enough so it can be heard upstairs.

"Well, I could have done that," Mom says and shakes a wooden spoon at me. Dad has given Sharon the hello hug. I notice he hugs her more easily than his own kids. Dave, Diane, and Janie come into the room. She waves hi to me and also gives Sharon a hug. That girl's just so lovable.

We are about to dig in when Janie says, "Wait. Let me say grace. I'll do my speech from the play. 'For each new morning with its light, / For rest and shelter of the night, / For health and food, / For love and friends, / For everything Thy goodness sends.'"

"Perfect," Sharon says and squeezes Janie's hand.

"Wow, did you know that's from Ralph Waldo Emerson?" I ask, while Mom dishes out the pasta.

Janie shrugs. "No, I just say it in the play. Who's he?"

"Only the greatest American thinker that ever lived," I boast.

"Says who?" Dave counters, the old rivalry still alive.

I turn on him, ask, "And who would you claim?"

"Well, how about Paul Tillich, for one?"

"Ah, a contemporary Christian theologian. You start with him, but where do you think he began? What are they teaching you at that East Coast university?"

"Boys," Dad cautions, "This is dinner time. You can wrestle with your brains later. Pass the salad down here, will you, please."

When we stop down at Sharon's place to visit the kids and her mom, we find the house in its usual chaos. It's seven o'clock and her mom has left Leroy, a kid of twelve, in charge. They are so glad to see Sharon, and she helps the girls get into their pajamas while I clean up the kitchen and Leroy tells me all that he's been up to. The kid likes me for some reason. Around nine, Shirley comes in from the bar where she has left Hank. "Oh, don't you two look fine," she says, a little high, "like a little married couple." She gives my beard a fake tug, "Yep, it's' real." We all laugh at this, especially Leroy. Sharon has made coffee, which helps bring her mom around. We catch up, them promise to see them tomorrow and skip out to visit Kenny.

It is Kenny who comes up with the idea. We're at his place, Sharon and I, sitting around his table drinking Budweiser when he says, "You know your old man is great with the body work. He's turned my piece of junk into a collector's car. He ought to think about opening his own body shop."

Sharon and I look at each other, then back at Kenny. "You've hit on it, man," I say out loud. "Right now he's feeling shoved out by the mill, and lost for what to do. That might just be it, start his own body shop in Mingo."

"I think that's a great idea," Sharon says, standing up. "Let's call him up right now."

"No, not over the phone." I say. "He hardly ever talks on it, and this has to be approached tactfully."

"Oh, you men are so...I was going to say sensitive, but I think it's more 'touchy.'"

"Ha," I laugh, "I think we pretty much share that with you women."

"God," Kenny lets out, "listen to you guys, doing the man-woman talk. You are getting old. Next thing we know you'll be married and arguing."

He lifts his Budweiser can up in a toast.

"Get out of here," I say and reach my arms around Sharon's waist. "We love each other too much for that."

"Well, I told you Marlene is engaged to that guy from West Liberty. Maybe she'll lead the way."

"Oh, I should call her," Sharon says, leaning her hip against me. "We women have to stick together in our marriage plot against you guys."

I don't touch that one. I'm beginning to feel that Sharon might want a ring in commitment, and I don't have the money for it or a clear understanding of how it would all fit with the Free Farm.

"By the way," Kenny insinuates, "What are the sleeping arrangements at the McCall house tonight? You guys getting your own bed?"

There's this pause as we look to each other for an answer, then Sharon speaks. "Your mom already talked to me about this. I'm to sleep in the girl's room, and, sorry, but you get your old bed. It's her house."

"Is that what she said, 'In my house...' ? Yeah, but we all know how I got started in a garage loft."

"I think that might be her point, my man," Kenny says and we laugh together. While I'm still trying to envision it, he adds, "We still have Sharon's room available up here...if you need it."

"Damn, I wish we'd thought of that," I say. "Don't you, hon?"

She gives me a nice smile, then says softly, "I think you'll be alright for one night or two."

"Not two," I plead. "Not two!"

"Oh, God, will you two try to contain yourselves," Kenny says, "I'm already feeling like the lone-man-out here."

"What do you mean?" I ask. "You have lots of women."

"Yeah, but none I really care about and no one as great as you, Sharon. No one who cares about me."

We pause on this, then sip on our beers. "Hey, let's order pizza," Kenny says, "What do you guys like on it?"

I answer automatically, "Pepperoni on half, tomato and onion on the other half."

"Gotcha," he laughs. "You forget, this is the Ohio Valley. DiCarlos' pizza comes by the slice, and all with the same delicious tomato sauce and cheese. I'll call it in, and we'll pick it up."

"Gosh, I forgot they don't deliver," Sharon says. "We are back in the old ways of home," she sighs.

"In more ways than one," I sigh loudly, stroking her arm. "...more ways than one."

We are getting our coats on, when the phone rings. Kenny says, "Wait guys, just a minute," then picks up the receiver. "Yeah, okay, yeah, they're here right now. Where is he? Okay, I'll tell them that." He turns to me with this graven look. "It's your dad, Lee. They think he's had a heart attack."

"What! Dad? Are you sure? Where is he?"

"An ambulance took him to Ohio Valley Hospital. That was Dave. He says to meet them up there."

I look around for Sharon. She is right beside me, and her face is as *grave* as I feel. I hate that word! "Can we go right up?" I ask the obvious.

She squeezes my arm. "Yes, right now, we'll go right up, right now."

"Can I drive you?" Kenny asks. I try to think but can't.

"Maybe not," Sharon says, "we might have to stay a long time."

"Right," Kenny says, then, "but I'm willing. Will you call me from there when you know something?"

"Yes, we will," she says, taking the keys from my shaking hand, "I'll drive, Lee. You take some deep breaths. It'll be okay. You're dad's still young and strong."

We drive over the back hills, on the way to the hospital. The houses pass but nothing registers except Sharon capable at the wheel. "Love, it'll be alright," she says again. "He's where he needs to be right now. I wonder what they did with your sisters?"

"Mrs. Miller, most likely; she's a good neighbor."

By the time we pull into the parking lot, my heart has quieted some, but walking into the bright receiving area with all the testing equipment, I feel a tightness in my neck, a burning in my chest. Dave is up ahead pacing the floor, and he looks around at us. His face is dire, as he says, "Hey, he's in there. They're running tests. We can't go in."

"Do they know anything?" I ask, then, "Where's Mom?"

"In there with him. They're running an EKG." I stare at his thin and anxious face and can't help hugging him. I just want to see Dad, and yet I'm afraid of what I'll find. Sharon tries to calm Dave by talking normal, while I look for a nurse.

"He's my father," I explain to the nurse coming out the door. "I need to see him."

She looks behind her toward the door where I know he is lying behind a curtain. She looks down at her watch. "I'd say, give it another 10 minutes and they should be done. Then you can go in."

Rules everywhere, even at death beds. I can't believe I thought that. "We'll be out here," I say, pointing to the waiting area. "Let us know right away." She nods and I go back to Sharon who has Dave sitting down now a vinyl chairs. It's just us and the four chairs and a lamp.

The waiting goes on for another 22 minutes till the nurse comes out. "I can only allow family members," she says and looks at Sharon.

"It's okay. We're his sons," I say. "And she's...my wife," more truth than lie.

When we enter the curtained cubicle, Dad is lying there looking helpless in a hospital bed with tubes in his nose and arm. Mom rises and comes to us, hugs me and Sharon, takes Dave's hand. "We don't know anything more," she reports. "He's breathing okay and resting."

I step toward his side, touch his hand. He looks up, and seeing him lying there so vulnerable and pale, I feel a sharp pain in my own heart—fear and love mixed. "I'm okay," he pretends. "You boys take care of your mother." I nod and feel as though I'm stepping back into my own shadow. I'm feeling so shaky, when Mom comes over to me.

"My God, Lee, you look pale as a ghost. Here sit down." And I do sit in the chair beside his bed.

Sharon comes to me, says low, "Put your head down between your knees. You're going to faint." I feel so useless and ashamed. I'm here to help and causing more pain and confusion.

It helps. "Now breathe deep and slow," she says stroking my shoulders. God, I love this woman. Still feeling the weight of loss, I look over at my brother, leaning against the one solid wall, his thin frame and troubled face, and I can't help thinking that if, God forbid, Dad should die, all of our worlds would tumble, especially his. Maybe I'm seeing myself in him, and in Dad, and in all who are suffering right now, which is really everyone. It clearly is the dark night of the soul, until the doctor comes in, an intern in a white coat.

"Well, Mr. McCall, I can tell you that you didn't suffer a heart attack." A sigh goes up from Mom. "But there is definitely something going on in your abdominal area. We want you to spend the night and do some more testing tomorrow morning."

"What do you think it is?" Mom asks.

"I can't really say, ma'am. You're his wife?" We all nod. "My best guess at this point is that it's an abdominal ulcer. I can feel something in there, and it may be malignant. That's just a guess. We'll find out tomorrow. Who's your family doctor?" He drops this "M" word on us meaning the "C" cancer word and has pretty much ignored Dad after the first question. Our relief moves quickly to this new concern.

Taking Dad's outstretched hand, Mom asks, "Can I stay here with him tonight?"

"You'll have to clear that with one of the nurses. We'll be moving him to a private room." He looks around, "Any other questions?" We are all too dumb struck to respond. "Well, if you'll excuse me, I have another patient who just came in with a gunshot wound."

By the time we leave Mom with Dad in his hospital room, it is one a.m. Someone has to take care of the girls. The drive home is quiet, no radio or talk. Though questions loom large in mind and heart, no one has answers. Finally when we get into Mingo, I say it, "He'll have to take a break from work now. He has to quit that mill job. It's too damn stressful, and stress causes ulcers."

"We don't know that it's ulcers," Dave says.

"Yeah, but we know his work is killing him. That's part of why we came home, Dave. Anyone with eyes can see it."

He moans, "You're right, I know. I just can't think anymore tonight. I'm exhausted."

"We all are," Sharon says, looking around to Dave in the back seat. "Let's get some sleep and deal with it tomorrow."

Mrs. Miller is asleep in the recliner chair. We wake her and fill her in; then she slips out. The girls are safe upstairs, tucked in bed. Sharon gives me a long kiss and goes up to them. Dave and I stand together in the quiet house. He looks at Dad's empty chair and says it, "I can't imagine him gone."

"No" I say, and swallow hard. We turn off the lights and go up together.

Lying in bed, thoughts stream through my head. I try some meditation, slowing my breathing into a steady rhythm. I'm greeting my thoughts and images and letting them go, like people walking past me down the street. Finally I fall off to sleep. The next thing I know, someone is touching my arm. Sharon has come to me in the night. She's leaning over to kiss me. I open the covers and she crawls in beside me. The touch of her body through flannel pajamas, the warm smell of her hair. We find our home together here.

Before dawn, a soft kiss, the gentle padding of her feet, and Sharon slips out and back into Janie's bed. I can't go back to sleep and don't want to wake Dave, so I gather my clothes and dress in the bathroom. I look in the awful mirror. *Who am I fooling with this beard? Who am I really? Son, brother, revolutionary, lover?* I go downstairs and start the coffee. Alone in the kitchen I face the fear that Dad might never come home from the hospital. It's a sick hard feeling in the heart and gut. I slip on my jacket and take my coffee down to his garage. It is early dawn now, so I don't need the light. I stand here in his space feeling more pain and trying to breathe into and through it. *Don't run from it. Give it space.* With his car and work bench and all of his tools so close around me, I breathe in the smell of oil and work and slowly begin to feel some comfort. I see his hands in all of this. This part of Dad will always live in us—his big heart, his caring attention, his working things through.

I close my eyes, then open them and go up to the house to prepare eggs and toast for my family.

Diane and Janie want to see Dad. We all do. So after breakfast, Sharon brushes their hair and helps them find pretty dresses to wear. She tells them, "We'll bring Dad some peace from home," and her calling him Dad moves my heart. In so many ways Sharon has not had a true father, even when we thought it might be Dad, and now beyond blood she's found him.

Dave and I sit in the kitchen drinking coffee and not talking. I start to do the dishes and find him standing beside me. "Let me do those," he says. "You made breakfast," and he takes the dish from my hand.

"We'll get through this," I say leaning into that belief. "Dad's in us, you know." He nods, and we share that knowing in the quiet room.

When we are done, Dave says to me, "We'll find out more today, and we'll deal with it. Even if it's cancer, people survive it these days." I nod to this brother of mine.

Sharon comes downstairs in her slip carrying that great red dress of hers and a dress for each of the girls. She smiles at me, gives me a kiss, then says, "Sorry, Dave, but these dresses need ironed."

"Well, don't be," he smiles broadly. "You're lovely in you slip." And she is, as I bring out the ironing board for her.

"I love you," I say. Beyond my loving and longing, she is family.

At the hospital, we find Dad in a new room. He is still lying in bed but propped up by pillows now, Mom sitting beside him. She gets up to hug the girls. "My, don't you look pretty," she says. "Who dressed you?" And they both look up at Sharon. Mom embraces her too, whispers, "Thank you, honey. Did you bring his pajamas? He hates these hospital gowns."

Sharon hands her a bag with the pajamas, says, "I also brought you this blouse, in case you want to change into something." Mom looks over at her and almost cries.

"Come here, you two," Dad says in his regular voice. And Diane and Janie are all over him. Dave and I wait like pillars at the end of his bed. Dad looks better. His color is back, his face relaxed.

"They ran some tests already this morning," Mom says. "We should know something soon. He seems to be out of pain." The worry is on her face still, as she asks, "Did you all have breakfast? There's a cafeteria downstairs."

"Mom, we did," I say. "Everything is fine at home. How are you doing?"

She winces and takes my elbow, "Let's go out in the hallway a minute." It is there she lets down, and thank goodness, Sharon is with me to accept her tears. The two women I love most stand together sharing the same pain. I rub their backs and swallow my own tears. "I'm just worried...for him," she finally says. We stand together, but I can't breathe. I need to walk down the hallway. At the end is this great set of windows looking out over the whole valley, the grand bowl of hills and sky, the long river running steady through the middle. The red-gray of steel mills seems dwarfed somehow by the wholeness of this vista. Houses nestle up and down these hills; lines of streets with them flow down to where Route 7 cuts through, connecting all. The sun is spreading on everything. Down the hallway in the room, Dad lies awaiting his fate from doctors, yet strongly willing himself back into this world that we love and endure.

We celebrate our Thanksgiving Day there in the hospital cafeteria with plates of steaming turkey and dressing, mashed potatoes and gravy, green beans and cranberry sauce. Dad comes down in a wheel chair, joining us in the pajamas that we brought, and we can't help laughing at ourselves and our little circle. "Where's a camera when you need it?" he says. We all smile, knowing that whatever comes, this image will remain with us always.

Chapter Seventeen
Working Things Out

Two days pass while Dad is treated with antibiotics and antacids, and we get a course in anatomy and physiology. While several biopsy reports show no clear signs of cancer, because of the severity of the pain and what they're calling gastrointestinal bleeding, they pull us together in the hallway. Dr. Too-Busy looks down at his chart and speaks, "Well, what we suspect is a perforated peptic ulcer here, and so our best course is to operate right away." We all stand there like sponges trying to absorb this when he explains, "We'll be removing part of his vagus nerve to stop the acidity flow." Then as if reading us our rights, "Of course, as with any surgery, there is some risk."

"Of what?" Dave asks bluntly.

"Well," the surgeon looks up from his chart to say it, "there are of course multiple complications that could arise. I could list them, but as with any operation and more to the point, of death."

This doesn't seem to register at all on Mom who asks, "This ulcer, doctor, is it caused by stress?"

He looks over to her, "Not the cause, Mrs. McCall, but certainly a factor in its severity." Then he check marks something off the chart, probably our meeting, and adds, "Sorry, I have to run along to an appendectomy." Now, I know I'm being pissy, but it seems to me it's not a person but a disease he's treating. He exits, leaving us in a painful silence.

The operation is scheduled for today. We're all up and ready. Mom and Dave, Sharon and I will go up, while Aunt Liz stays with the girls. There's a quiet yet anxious air about the house as we have our coffee and toast in the kitchen. Mom's eating nothing.

Sharon and I have been cursing the lack of a phone at the Free Farm if just to let people know what's happening. Our weekend trip has now stretched into a week. She does call the registration office to report off, and I call the Millfield drive-thru to tell Frank I won't be in. I ask him to relay this message to anyone from the farm who comes in. We've already put a letter in the mail, but our plans change from day to day, if not hour to hour.

The trip to the hospital is quiet, though nerves are on edge. For some reason, Dave drives us slowly through downtown Mingo past the old stores and shops, Weisberger's Clothing, a few people out on street corners, Al's Sohio station, past the city building, Town House bar, then up onto Rte. 7. Immediately the familiar brown hills rise up to the left; to the right—the mills, railroad, and river. "It all feels like Dad, doesn't it?" Dave says.

"Yes, it does," Mom answers from the passenger seat, then almost in tears adds, "Listen, I want you to know your father and I are proud of all of you, and that includes you, Sharon."

While Dave and I are still wondering where this is coming from, Sharon says, "Jeanie, he's going to be alright. He's a strong man, and he'll get through this."

"We all will," I turn round to say as Dave heads us up Adams Street, past the old church on the corner, across from the cigar store where people play numbers and catch the bus, then on past Kroger's up the steep hill to the hospital. All these rows of old houses that we've passed twice everyday for a week now seem part of Dad's treatment.

At the hospital in his room, we're able to see Dad briefly. He's looking tired of it all, but puts on a big smile for us. We each hug him, like he's the precious cargo that he is. "Thanks for bringing your mother," he says, and we smile. When they haul him away on a cart, we mosey over to the waiting room to make ourselves as much at home as possible during the long waiting.

We all have brought books: Dave, *Brave New World*; Sharon *I'm Ok, You're Okay*; and me, James Wright's beautiful poems in *The Branch Will Not Break*. Funny how we carry around these little signs about who we are. Mom finds a *Good Housekeeping* magazine at the gift shop and looks away from the television where a couple kids are watching *Sesame Street*.

The hours pass, and we sit there, taking in all the details of this nearly bare room and knowing that at any minute the doctor could come in with the worst possible message. We all try to appear normal so that God or Death will pass over us. Finally the doctor does come in; Dad has survived the surgery and is being moved to intensive care. Mom's allowed in to sit with him, and we return to wait again. Dave now falls asleep in the waiting room, so Sharon and I go to the cafeteria to get a tea and coffee. We slide a couple cushioned chairs next to each other before the windows facing that valley vista. I touch her soft hand and she looks up from her book, so I ask, "What's your book saying...Are we really all okay?"

"Hmm, not easy to answer," she says. "Honey, it's more about how we see ourselves and others. But, yes, under it all, we really are okay. Do you really want to hear it?" I nod. "Well, let me read you the four outlooks: first *I'm Not OK, You're OK;* second, *I'm Not OK, You're Not OK;* third, *I'm OK, You're Not OK;* and last, *I'm OK, You're OK.*" She looks over at me. "Lee, it's that fourth view that we're after." She smiles generously, "Do you get it?"

"Oh, yeah. I know people in all those categories, don't you?"

"Well, yeah. But the real question is where do you find yourself?"

"Hmm...not easy to answer....Different at different times. But it includes how I see the world that matters. Like

'I'm okay, the world's fucked up,' or it's 'I'm okay, the world's wonderful.'" And I smile back at her, "Do you get it?"

She winces slightly, "Are you making fun of me?"

"No, honestly, I'm not. Just saying that sometimes our view of the world shapes us, or maybe we shape the world. I'm a little confused."

"Well, you're confusing me now. You know Dr. Harris helped develop transactional analysis, which is about people being with people. You're bringing in the whole world."

"I'm sorry, really." She looks into me with those sincere blue eyes, and I confide, "Okay, one thing I want you to know is that you are more than okay with me. And when I'm with you, I'm more than okay."

"Hmm, I hear that," she says, "but I'd be fine with just 'okay,' really."

I nod, "Well, I guess I'm basically an 'I'm okay, you're okay' guy, but when I take it into the world, I get messed up."

She leans toward me, places both her hands on my arm and looks into my eyes, "Lee McCall, you are not messed up. You're okay, you hear, and I love you."

I get up and kneel down before her, right there in the cafeteria. "You're really something, you know. I want a whole life with you." I lean forward and kiss her long before everyone in the room. Then I shake my head, and say, "I can't believe we're having this really great conversation sitting in this room waiting to hear from my father's ulcer."

An hour later, we visit Dad in pairs. He's all hooked up to tubes and monitors yet tries to smile. He whispers, "I just want to go home." Mom has already told us it will be a week of procedures and recovery, but I don't say anything, except that I love him. Sharon hugs him and lays her head on his shoulder, and whispers, "I love you too, Dad. You're okay."

*　　　　*　　　　*

Today we are headed south to Athens. Dad is still at Ohio Valley, but Dave will be home till January; we'll check in with him, and he has the phone number at Frank's drive-thru. Dad will be on medical leave for six weeks, and Kenny's already been shopping around for garages that Dad might someday rent. Last night when I said good-bye to Dad in his hospital room, I realized something...for years each time I'd been saying good-bye, I'd quietly feared it might be our last.

It's been two weeks, and Sharon and I both need to get back to our other home and face our life at the Free Farm. Sharon takes the wheel for the first two hours as we head down river. She's a good driver and we 'talk of things that matter' as Simon and Garfunkel say. I sleep sometime during the first hour as we head south of Bridgeport. Then I wake as we slow into Powhatan Point, stare out the window a moment then ask, "So, hon, how are we going to approach this free love thing back at the farm? Carl and Susan might be there, and I think we can count on them as a couple."

"Oh, boy," she says. "Honestly, I think we should first talk with Charlotte and Chance privately. They're our deepest friends, and we started all of this together."

"You're right. I'm just avoiding that close confrontation, I know it. It's because they're so close, I don't want to ruin our relationship."

"Yes, but what is that relationship?" she asks, making the big turn west onto Rte. 78, a new way home. "If we can clear that up with them, we'll be better able to deal with everything."

"Okay, we'll do it," I say, and for a while I watch her at the wheel and together we watch the trees fly by as the car gobbles up the road. It's an old road but new to us. Finally I say, "You know this 'I'm okay' stuff you're reading?"

"Yeah, what about it?"

"Well, there should be one that says, 'I'm not okay, and that's ok,' cause sometimes that's how I really feel, not okay.'"

She startles me with, "No, Lee, don't do that! I really need you to be okay. You're the most okay thing in my life." She is so shaken by this she pulls off the road. The car is still running, her foot on the clutch, her eyes now pleading with me. She reaches for my hand but grips my wrist instead. "Please, for God's sake and mine, don't fall apart on me."

"Well, I'm not really. God, I'm sorry. Listen, I was just trying to work something out with you. If it hurts you, I'll stop." We are staring into each other's eyes and I see her tears welling and it hurts my own heart. "I wouldn't do anything to hurt you."

"It's just...just that we've gotten through so much together," she says breathing hard. "I depend on you, Lee. You're half of me now. And you know some part of me has been broken for a long time, but not you, and not your family. You make me stronger."

I honestly don't know what to think of all this, her needing me so much, her need for all to be okay. I reach my arms around her and pull her toward me in our little car. We hold each other for a long while, till our breathing becomes one. A few cars pass, a light snow begins to fall, I can feel her relaxing and finally she takes my handkerchief and whispers, "I love you," then sits back.

"Sharon, I swear we'll heal our wounds together."

"I'm sorry," she sighs. "I'm alright now. God, we better get moving in this."

The snow is falling through the trees and beginning to stick on the road. It's pretty but begs us to travel on. "Do you want me to drive?"

"No," she says. "I'm fine now, honestly," and she takes a breath, pulls out in first gear, second, third, we are rolling again. For a while neither of us talks, trying to absorb what just went on, a side of her I hadn't seen or she hadn't dared to share. I try to be thankful for it, but am a bit dazed. I too depend on her being strong, yet we need to be open if we're to be whole. I'm just blown away.

And then she asks, "Honey, before all this, something was bothering you. What was it? I'll listen now, I promise."

"It's nothing, really. Let's let it go."

"Come on, please, tell me."

"Well, okay." I search for the right words. "Like you, I'm torn between these two or three worlds we're living in...back home with family, working things out at the Farm, and taking classes at OU. You're the only one who's with me in all three. And sometimes I honestly do wonder—am I me in all three or am I three different people?"

She touches my hand with her gear shifting hand. "For me, you're one person, the Lee I know and love. What are you for you? What am I?"

"Hmm, I've no problem with your being you, but I do feel stretched, maybe torn, between these worlds, and I don't like it."

We ride on, these questions hanging there in the car air. Suddenly a pheasant flies out of the woods; Sharon tries to swerve to miss it but doesn't—hits it hard really. We hear the clunk, ca-chunk of it under the car. She squeals, gripping the wheel, cries, "Jesus, what have I done?" hits the breaks and pulls off the road.

I don't answer but crank my neck around to see it lying there in the middle of the road, large and motionless. She asks it: "Would you go back and take a closer look—please?"

I grimace to myself but hop out the passenger side and stroll back toward the bird. There's no hope, this bird is dead. I look around at the woods then use the edge of my shoe to scrape it off the road and into the tall grass, her body now a bundle of feathers in the weeds. I stare down at her and for a crazy moment think of Dad and almost throw up.

Back at the car, I announce the "no hope" for the bird and ask to drive. "Come on, you've done your shift and need a break after that...accident." I am sure to call it an accident, no culpability or she'll go into a lament to last the rest of the day. She gets out and as we are about to pass, I take her by the shoulders. "Not your fault," I say, but saying it seems to open the debate. "We're good," I add. "Let's head on, maybe make it home for lunch."

"Wherever 'home' is," she laments.

"Oh, please, don't you start doing it. One of us is enough."

She looks straight at me, "If home's where the heart is, mine is with you." We kiss in the cold air then jump into our car.

As I drive, the sky is getting gray as snow starts coming down hard. Not a blizzard, but a heavy fall. An inch or two by the time we get to McConnelsville. At an old service station, I stop for gas and a coffee while Sharon uses the rest room. The bearded guy sticks his head out the door and asks if I need him to pump gas. "Heck, no. I'll get it," I say and begin pumping, the wind whipping at my face and hands. I stop at $10, what Mom slipped me as we left, and I go inside. Sharon has my cup of coffee in her hand all ready and a large bag of chips.

"This should hold us over to Millfield," she smiles.

"You folks headed south?" the guy at the counter asks. "Hit pretty hard with this snow I hear. Fellow in here come up from there 'bout an hour ago says 6-8 inches already."

"Thanks...I guess. We gotta get home," I say, then ask, "How much for the coffee?"

"Oh, hell, on a day like this, the coffee's free. You folks take care, you hear." I hand him the $10 for the gas and we walk out to our car in the snow. All of the curved folds of the car are now lined with snow. It's become our Christmas vehicle, red and white. Fortunately there are no real hills till the forest around Burr Oak Reservoir. The snow is just so heavy right now, it's getting harder to see. Beetles are not known for their warmth, and from time to time, Sharon has to scrape ice from the inside of the windows. We look at each other. Can't stop, no good going back, and so we push on. The car rides so low, all the drifts take us for a moment, and at one icy crest, the wheels just slide, then the car spins all the way around once.

"Wooee!" I shout as we come to a stop. "That was something!"

"Wow!" Sharon gasps. "You handled it just right, didn't try to break or steer it, just let it come around. That's how to handle things, relax and come alive. Zen master Suzuki would smile on you."

I laugh and we continue, both of us excited and fearful at the same time. I don't want anything to happen to Sharon. We have some bread from home and a blanket in the back seat, but Lordy, I just want to get somewhere safe. We glide along through Bishopville and into Glouster, the biggest town so far. I look over at Sharon. "What do you say, want to stop or go on?"

"Oh, God, I'm so lonesome for our own place, but I just don't know. What do you think, hon?"

"I think we pull into this Sunoco and ask about the roads ahead." And we do pull off and park beside the garage bay. "Come on, let's run inside where it's w-a-r-m for a c-h-a-n-g-e."

She laughs, "Why are you spelling?"

"I don't know, feels like there's a great mystery about this trip. Come on."

Inside the little room are several people in warm coats and hats standing around gas stove near the pop and coffee machines. "Howdy," a woman in blue overalls says, "What can we do for you?"

"Ah," I say, "we just filled up in McConnelsville, but we'd sure like some hot coffee and advice."

"Help yourselves to the coffee. What you want to know?"

"The roads. We're headed to Millfield. Are the roads passable?"

She grins and looks out at our buddha car. "All depends now on what you're drivin,' don't it?" I give her the nod, and she smiles broadly, "With that little thing, what you call it, a 'bug,' I just can't say. A truck would make it, four wheeler definite. Got good tires?"

I sense she's not trying to sell tires but help us out. Sharon answers for us, "They're good, bought a few months ago. Anyone come up from Millfield lately?" she asks and looks around at the watching faces.

"Girly, I did 'bout an hour ago," says a dark man my dad's age, sitting in one of those plastic lawn chairs along the window. "Took me an hour to make it up here." He looks into her face like that of a lost daughter, "Honey girl, I give you a good chance a making it. Just stay on Rte. 13 for now, no county roads."

"Well, thanks much," Sharon says and looks over at me. We both know we'll have to drive on county roads after Millfied, but we'll take our chances when we get there. The closer to home, the better.

"You stay safe now," the woman calls to us as we go out the door, "But I don't see how you will" as the door closes.

"Them's real good folks in there," I half joke with Sharon.

"They are, really," she says. "Don't know us from Adam and Eve, as they might say. You want me to drive?"

"No way, I got it. You're my sidekick, Calamity Jane." Right away I'm sorry I said that word. I start up buddha-bug and head off on Rte. 13 south. No road out here runs straight, except for the new highways, and they're a long way off. Soon we come into Trimble, then Jacksonville, small towns with paved streets that get plowed.

"Did he say it took him an hour from Millfield? We're doing great so far." Just as I say that, the wheels go into a slide and we both swallow our breath; just as sudden they find traction again, and so we push on. Immediately the snow gets stronger, the drifts higher. Up ahead is a truck we can follow. He has his lights on, and I turn mine on too. Safety in numbers, and he's leaving a trail for us to follow.

No question, it takes an hour to get to Millfield, and by then we are tired and hungry. "Let's stop at the drive-thru. Okay? It would be good to check in with Frank anyway, and we could get something to eat."

"Yeah, let's do it," she agrees, then adds, "You know I do understand the not having the distraction of a telephone at the farm, but I sure do hate not being able to get in touch with our family there." I nod.

Getting out of the car in the parking lot, my legs and back ache. "Woo, that was the hardest hour. And we still have a stretch to go." Inside is warm and bright. We walk past the racks of bread and cookies, chips and peanuts. In the back is the sandwich rack. "Gretta makes these up each morning, so they're still fresh," I say and pick up one of the ham and swiss, another of turkey and mountain jack. I offer them to Sharon and she takes the turkey. We are pouring ourselves a coffee when Frank comes out from the back wearing his weather coveralls.

"Well, if you two ain't a sight for sore eyes!" he says and shakes our cold hands with his warm burly one. "But, I'd say the sore eyes is yours. Been driving long in this stuff?"

"About 6 hours, I'd say. Should have taken us 4."

"Well, hard to say what should or shouldn't be, ain't it? You got to take count of the weather. 'Cause it won't take no count of you." We all laugh at this and begin to feel almost normal around him. "Come on back here. We can sit and talk. Unless you got some place to go?"

"Well," Sharon says, "looks like we're not going any place right away, but we do want to get home sometime today."

"Let's see, you guys live up north off a Sweet Holler Road. I hear it's almost a foot deep up there. Now that's a county road and the plows probably got to it, but north of that is LaFollette, that's township. No telling if it's open. You could stay here tonight if you like. I got a bunk back here." He reads our sad faces, "But if you want to give it a try, I'll tell you what. I'll call up Chris Miller out your way. He's got a snow plow and could meet up with you when you get to the turn north."

"Oh, that would be wonderful," Sharon says, rising to thank him. "But isn't that asking a lot of him?"

"Nah, he's a vegetable farmer. What's he got to do, sit around watching *Green Acres* reruns? Honey, I'll give him the call, and we'll let him decide."

Frank goes out front; we eat our sandwiches, and Sharon slips on the sweater she brought in from the car. Frank sticks his head in as Sharon is stretching up, grins at her then me, and gives me the thumbs up. We wolf down our sandwiches and coffee and head out, thanking Frank and promising him I'll show up for work all next week. The car has gotten cold again and we have to scrape the windows once more. After 10 minutes, we head out.

The car moves along, slowly cutting through the snow all the way to Sweet Hollow, like he said, and then we're at the turn-off north, but no Chris Miller. The east-west snow plow has stacked the snow across the northern road, blocking us. I get out to look around when we hear the roar of a truck. It has to be Chris, who else would be out on these roads. I see the headlights, then make out a large truck, not a pickup, and on the front, sure enough is the snow plow. A husky guy gets out in the middle of the road. "Hey and hello," he shouts, "I'm Chris. Guess you'd be the hippie farmers from up the road."

That's probably how Frank described us, or how we're known in this neck of the woods. "Yeah, I'm Lee and this here is Sharon. Boy, are we glad to see you." He takes off his gloves long enough to shake my hand.

"Oh, yeah, I been seein' you folks afore going up and down the road in this little bug of a car. And I seen your missus too down at the drive-thru. Glad to know you." And he shakes Sharon's hand.

"Gosh, thanks for coming out on this treacherous day," Sharon says, and I know her smile is worth a thousand dollars. "How can we repay you?"

"Well, I ain't done nothin yet, honey. But you're neighbors, and your being safe and warm is thanks enough." He looks at the snow blocking the road. "This ain't nothin.' Course we don't know what we got ahead. Lee, you can just follow me through," then he grins, "unless you and your missus want to help me lift your little bug up onto my truck bed." We both do look around at his truck, then realize he's joking with us. "Ma'am, you can ride with your husband or up with me in my truck. It's up to you."

"Go on," I say to Sharon. "It's safer up there and no doubt a sight warmer." I realize I'm starting to talk down-home as she smiles at me, then boards the truck.

Chris makes three swipes at the snow block with his plow, and we have our way through. I have trouble keeping up with him in old buddha-bug, which I've begun praying to, but it's great following his taillights into what's become early dusk. He's fine all the way along the hollow road but stops at our gravel roadway that runs up the hill to the house. He gets out and comes over to my window. "Lee, I see it's gravel and pretty steep. You folks don't own a tractor I suspect. I'll tell you what. I can give the drive a swipe or two, to get you off the road, but I think this may be as far as she wrote for tonight."

"This is just fine," I say and jump out. When I go over to Sharon in the truck to tell her the situation, she jumps out. Turning to Chris she says, "Oh, gosh, Chris, this is great. I can see the lights from the house from here. You did it. You brought us home. How can we repay you?" She goes right up to him and plants a kiss on his ruddy cheek.

"Well, that's pay enough," he grins. "I'll get over here tomorrow and plow your roadway...if I can count on another kiss like that." He turns to me, "You and I will just shake hands."

We manage to get sweet buddha-bugoff the road, then I wave so long to Chris and gather up our suitcases and bag of food supplies. The snow is about 18 inches deep, and soon our shoes are wet and full of snow, but we plow our way steady up the hill toward the lights of home.

Chapter Eighteen
Returning to the Farm

By the time we reach the house, a pink-blue twilight has gathered all around us. Sharon and I are breathing hard from the snowy climb and ready to set our burdens down. She smiles up at me and says, "Look, your beard is full of snow and frost. You're the winter man."

"And you're my wintry maiden. Come on, let's get inside and melt these wintry clothes." You know you're tired when your coat is a burden. We push through the pantry door, and standing before us are Charlotte and Chance.

"Come in, dear ones," Charlotte greets us with a loving smile. "We watched you coming up the roadway. You're home. You've arrived." There are secure hugs all around, but we sidestep the kissing.

"We missed you guys," Chance says, his arm around Sharon's back. "Come, have some pumpkin soup with the family. We're just sitting down."

"Great, we brought some Italian bread from home," I say and pull a loaf out from our shopping bag. "Who's all here?"

"All the regulars, not Carl and Susan though," Chance says, still holding close to Sharon, "and we have some new friends for you to meet."

We are still shaking off the snow and warming our limbs as we enter our bright dining area. Dick and Ingrid wave to us, but immediately we notice three young faces smiling our way. Dick announces, "This is Bruce, Jenny, or Thunder as she likes to be known, and this here's Marsha, or Sky. They've come out from OU to live with us." It is one of those moments you can't prepare for, like sliding off the road or being whacked by a board. All you can do is smile and wait to comprehend. "They're art student drop outs—Can I say that?—who want to join us in seeking a new way."

"Hi," I say as they each rise and embrace us. Chance brings in more chairs.

"Yep," the tall one, Jenny or Thunder, says, "We're abandoning the sinking ship of America, including the university."

"Well," Chance says, "Welcome aboard. Let's eat."

"Come on over here," Charlotte motions to us, "We're doing buffet style now for most meals," and she begins dolling out soup from the kettle into large bowls. "See the new table Carl and Chance have made?"

"Yep," I say, still dazed. I look to Sharon who is hugging Charlotte, then I glance down at my soup and fully expecting a snake's head to come rising up. It's all just too much to take in, and so I do the next best thing...pull up a chair and pass the bread. "This is DiCarlo's famous Italian bread from the Ohio Valley." The strong crusted bread is quickly ripped apart.

"How was your drive?" Dick asks.

"Oh, it's a long story," I say shaking my head. "Twice as long and treacherous, but our buddha-bug brought us home."

Sharon adds, "And we met this really great guy, Chris Miller, from down the road who snow plowed us up from Sweet Hollow Road. He says he'll come back tomorrow morning and do our roadway."

A cheer goes up. "That is good news," Ingrid says. "We are okay here, but...how do you say...our supplies are getting low."

Chance admits, "We weren't ready for this," and looks around. "Was anyone?"

"Well, I guess Chris was," I say smiling. "He farms most of the year and during these hard winter months, he drives a snow plow. All I can say is, Thank God or Buddha for him. Oh, and he thinks we need a tractor."

"What for?" Bruce asks.

I turn to read this new face with its short ponytail. "Well, for one thing, to reach the road from the house," I answer. "And for another, to maybe plough fields in the spring."

Sharon speaks up, "Say, I know now's not the time or place, but since you asked, I want to lay this out there for later...I think we need a phone for emergencies and basic communication." She reads some faces, then adds, "I can't tell you how hard it was not being able to reach you all."

Chance nods, "Okay, this is good. Let's talk this over at our meeting this evening. It's clear no one is going anywhere tonight. We can all sit around the fireplace and, as Ram Dass says, 'Be here now.'"

"I loved the dancing last night," Jenny says. She has night black hair cropped shorter than any I've ever seen on a girl before, and strong dark eyes. Marsha seems shy, doesn't look you in the eye, and just smiles at everything. She's a pretty girl I've seen holding posters at a couple protests. I smile at both of them and can't help playing out the dancing scene that went on here last night.

When we are all about finished eating, Sharon asks of Jenny, "Well, how long have you all been here? Where have you all been sleeping?"

Dick jumps in, "Oh, sorry about that. They've been here, what, four days, and, well, we didn't know when you guys were coming back, so...they've been sleeping in your bed. I hope that's alright."

"All three of them?" pops out of Sharon's mouth.

"Yep," Jenny-Thunder drawls, "we're bi-, if you know what I mean. And so yes, we sleep together."

I watch Sharon's face turn to stone, and finally Marsha speaks, "Oh, we'll clean up in there right after supper. We didn't touch any of your things." She looks sheepish at Bruce, "At least I didn't."

"Your lava lamp," Bruce says. "I just love it. It puts me to sleep at night with my arms around these two lovely maidens."

I admit, I am denying and desiring the images of them naked together in our love bed. It's a strange mixed feeling, and I avoid looking at Sharon who I know is studying me.

After dinner, Sharon and I find a chair in the living room. She sits on the arm and I stroke her back. We are both somewhat in shock yet trying to be cool about it all. "Let's give them 15 minutes to clear out," Sharon says softly. "I'm so tired. Aren't you?"

I sip some after-dinner coffee and look up at her. "You know it. What a day this has been...starting in Mingo with family, then that long drive through snow, and now this muddle of who are they and where do we all sleep." I turn to Chance, "So, buddy, where is the triangle going to sleep tonight?"

"Triangle—? I get you," he grins. "We've been talking about their fixing up the basement like a bedroom. But we'll have to do something about the mice and snakes."

Sharon gives a shiver, and Chance comes over by us. "We're in the midst of transforming the dining room area into Carl and Susan's space, but for now I guess they can lay their sleeping bags on the floor here at night and scrounge around during the day."

"Or, they can sleep in our room with us," Dick volunteers, but Ingrid gives him a stony stare and pulls on his arm.

"Dicky Bird, I don't think that would be a good idea," she says rather insistently.

No one answers that, then Chance nods, "We can tell them the plan." First he leans over to confide in us, "They're really nice. Free spirits, really. They just arrived one day after Thanksgiving in that beater of a pickup. It runs though and it's been good for hauling. You weren't here, so we decided to give them a trial period. We can talk about it tonight. I gotta help Charlotte with the dishes. Sharon, how about you tell them the plan?"

"Sorry, but I'm not going in there, till they're out," Sharon says, "You go; I'll help Charlotte."

We all pitch in with the cleaning up and moving, and once Sharon and I get back into our den, we open the window a few minutes to air it out. Sharon pulls out new sheets from the bureau. "Our mattress," she says a little sad yet determined. "Let's just turn it over for now. Come on, grab hold of the bottom." She can really go at a job, like my mom, and I'm good at taking orders. Soon she stands in the doorway scanning the place and I put my arms around her from behind and kiss her neck. "Oh, Lee," she laments, "where are we headed here?" For a moment I flash back to the car and the driving through dark and snow.

"Wherever it is, we'll get there together."

Chance and Dick have made the fire in the fireplace.

Marsha-Sky and Jenny-Thunder come out in babydoll pajamas, Bruce is wearing his white Jockeys and a flowered shirt. It's too cold to go naked, at least for now. When Dick comes back down with Ingrid, we realize we are having a pajama party, and I look to Sharon, who shrugs and we return to our room. She chooses her flannel granny gown and I wear the dress pajamas I wore back at home. Mom washed everything before we left. Charlotte surprises us in her short black peignoir under a sheer robe. "It's all I have," she smiles, "Chance bought it for me." The men smile at this and at her long legs, and no one complains.

"This is beginning to look like a Playboy party," Bruce says and we all laugh.

Chance brings out his 12-string guitar to help soothe and enliven things. First he does some soft finger picking, then moves into Simon and Garfunkel songs, ending with "The Sound of Silence," kind of our commune theme song. We all sing along moving from "the vision that was planted in my brain" to the crowds of people "talking without speaking;/ listening without hearing," rising with "And the people bowed and prayed/ to the neon god they made," then closing with the prophets words on subway walls amidst the "sounds of silence." It's just a great song, and Marsha-Sky surprises us all by having a great soprano voice.

Finally Sharon begins, "Well, if possible, we need to have our family meeting." Charlotte hands her the wooden spoon we're still using. "First off, I want to present the idea of getting a telephone—for emergencies and basic communication. It was really awful not being able to contact you all, with or without the snow storm."

Reading the puzzled faces of some, I jump in, "I know we said we'd do without technology, but we could have some basic understandings about how such a phone might be used. And we could make it an unlisted number."

I pass the spoon back to Chance who says, "Let's hear some thoughts on this. We'll need to come to some consensus."

Surprisingly there is little opposition, then Charlotte speaks, "I hear you both, and I know most of us are watchful of the impact of technology. That's why we didn't get a phone to start with. But we do have electricity and several cassette players. Can we use such things wisely or will they take over? I'm not sure."

I take the spoon. "Well, none of you know this, but back home my dad had emergency surgery for bleeding ulcers, and the point is...if we hadn't been there, they couldn't have let us know, and even though we were there, we couldn't let you know. It might sound strange, but your knowing and caring energy could have helped Sharon and me, maybe even Dad." I look around and people are nodding, so I go on, "And on our really torturous drive down here we could have called you from gas stations and the drive-thru in Millfield. Even if you couldn't be there to help, your knowing would have made us feel less alone and strung out. I know we both are for it, and yes, with some basic understandings."

Bruce speaks out, "Well, man, I know I'm a newbie here, but I have to say, there you go with the rules and regulations. You know?" And then he stands and turns the spoon into a microphone, sings, "'Freedom's just another word for nothing left to lose./ Nothing, I mean nothing, honey, if it ain't free.' You dig it?" Thunder-girl claps, then stands up and takes Bruce by the waist and begins dancing to some unheard music.

"I'm with you, man. Freedom...This is the Free Farm," she shouts. "Leave the old ways behind, start fresh, naked and new. Freedom... 'It's good enough for me and Bobby McGee.'" With that she slides her gown over her head, and it is just cold enough to make her small breasts perk.

Sharon is weary yet she rises at the couch and takes the spoon from Bruce, "Well, nice tits, girl, and that's a great song, Bruce, but neither are proof of a way to live our lives." They stop gyrating and stare at Sharon, who's on a roll. "We need understandings between us, and yeah, we need some discipline too so we don't...well, so we don't shit where we eat." She really blows me away with that line from her mom. Marsha who's been smiling through all of this suddenly frowns and holds up an afghan to wrap around her sweethearts.

Ingrid bolts out, "I too am with Sharon on this. We need some kind of order or we have the chaos." Dick is still shaking his head, like he's pondering.

"Okay," I take the spoon. "What I see here is a house full of similar minded friends trying to work out a new vision, but think about it. We also need a survival plan if we're going to be around in a year or more. Dick, tell us, isn't the lack of discipline what brings down most communes?"

"Hmm," he says, nodding yes before the fire, so I hand him the spoon. "You're right, Lee. Historically those less practical have not survived, and I hear that Black Bear and Drop City are both struggling with so many drifters and weekend drop-ins that they may not survive. I guess the question before us is whether a phone is a practical tool or part of a net of mass culture. We've put away television here. Will we start to believe we need it now?"

Finally Chance takes the floor, "Hey, this is all good talk, really, good interaction. It's bringing out some of our vision and I guess our 'mission.' I for one have to admit that there's a lot we don't know about farming or surviving in these hills or in a commune, but we're moving in the right direction. Who knows, one day we may even lead the way by our example. So, yes, we do need tools—a truck, an axe, a level— you know what I'm saying? Maybe a telephone is just another basic tool we need to survive."

Charlotte speaks, "I agree, and I think the real change is not the things but how we look at them...our perception. The telephone in itself is not evil, if we use it wisely. I say we give it a try and mindfully watch to see what happens."

A thoughtful quiet follows, and it's Charlotte who asks, "Bruce and Thunder, are you okay with this? Sky, you haven't said anything. Do we have a consensus to try out the telephone?"

Speechless till now, Marsha-Sky finally speaks, "I was wondering who would pay for it."

"Well, like most things here," and Charlotte looks around, "I imagine it would be shared. Those who have jobs and a monetary income would share the cost. Those who don't would contribute work at the Free Farm or Free School. Am I right?"

Sharon, whose face has gone from pale to red and back a couple times tonight, speaks, "Well, that sounds good to me, but honestly, if no one else is willing, Lee and I will pay for the phone." This surprises me, but I keep quiet as she scans the faces then adds, "I feel that strongly about it. Let's please give it a try."

Chance stands with the spoon, and like an auctioneer asks, "Okay folks, once...twice...three times...We...do...have...a...consensus! Okay, we'll give it a trial period for what—a month?—and watch what happens. Who wants to call the phone company?" And the absurdity of this last statement hits us with a roar of laughter.

I volunteer, "Once we get the road cleared, I'll drive down to Frank's place and set it up."

The meeting goes on a little longer and we eventually reach consensus on using the living room area as a temporary pad for the newcomers and to begin work on the basement as a fourth room tomorrow morning.

Chance wraps things up with "Well, sounds like this meeting's at a close. And I hate to ask this, but does anyone know how to clear out the varmints from the basement? I think we need to start there."

"What kind of varmints you talking about?" asks Bruce.

"Oh, your regular rats and snakes," Chance says, grinning at Bruce, "but we're planning to ask them to leave before you move down there."

We look to our resident biologist Charlotte seated on the floor, "Well, I'm a researcher not an exterminator. But whatever we do, let's not just kill them. Right now they have a kind of balance going on down there. It's we who are taking over their space."

No response, and then Sharon volunteers, "I'll ask our farmer friend Chris about this when he shows up tomorrow."

"Agreed," Chance says and thumps once, twice, three times on his guitar. "Let's gather round for the family circle." And here we are, nine of us in our lovely pajamas, some more lovely than others, holding and raising our hands in a sign of unity declaring our new slogan, "Free to be...Unity in diversity...The Free Farm."

"Well, we danced last night," Chance says, "What say we just mellow out tonight," and he picks up his guitar and begins playing a new song, "Stairway to Heaven," with some of us singing along on the chorus.

Soon Bruce and Thunder are stretched out on their double sleeping bag before the fire, their bare legs intertwined. Sky is kneeling by Thunder, stroking her arm. Bruce calls out. "Hey friends, we still have some tabs of the acid we brought. We're going to do some here by the fire. You're welcome to join us...Mi casa, tu casa."

Dick and Ingrid are already headed upstairs, his hand on her bikini bottom; I look around at the trinity on the floor, with Chance and Charlotte lying near them on the couch, holding each other before the show. The music of The Grateful Dead is now playing, and Sharon is already standing at our bedroom door, looking beautifully exhausted. Tonight we'll just hold each other and be warm inside the storm.

Before the birds are fully awake, I hear the sound of a horn and the gunning of an truck engine. Our friend Chris is out there plowing the roadway to our house, farmer's hours I suppose. *I better go move the VW.* I find my long underwear, pull on jeans and a heavy wool sweater over my shirt. In the pantry I put on the coffee, then grab the highest boots, scarf and cap, then I head out into the cold air. The sky is purple gray as the sun creeps up the horizon. *What is it I'm to ask Chris? Oh yeah, the snakes and rats.*

"Hey and hello there, partner," he shouts to me from beside his truck. "I pushed your little car back a ways to get in here. I think she's alright there. How you all doing?"

"Oh, I'm good. No coffee yet at the house, but..."

"Well, here, have some of this," and he pulls out a metal thermos bottle, pours some into the lid. "Margo had this ready an hour ago. We can share and use this lid for now." And I do drink of it...strong and black.

"You're a savior, man," I say looking up at the path he's already made into our roadway.

"No, I'm a sinner, not a saint. But sometimes I find a way to help, and that helps me as much as you. So thanks back at you. You drink that, and I'll get back to work."

I hesitate but call to him, "Hey, Chris, before you start, I've got a question for you." He turns around and walks back. "We're having a problem with snakes and rats in the basement."

He grins broadly, "Well, what's the problem? We all live with the snakes and rats. They got here first you know."

"Yeah, I can see that. But we have some new folks moving in and ..."

"Say," he interrupts, "if you don't mind me asking, how many folks you got living up at the ranch there now?"

I can deny him nothing, so I say, "Right now there are nine of us. And three of them need to make their bedroom in the basement."

"Must get mighty close up there with nine adults, huh?"

I don't answer. He strokes his chin. "Let me think a bit. We had 'em in our house when we first bought it. I reckon it's garter snakes and rats that's your housemates— striped and a couple foot long?"

I shake my head, wishing I could write all of this down.

"You know, if you take out the snakes, you'll just get more mice and rats. Those snakes are controlling the tribe right now. So what you have to do is work on both together." We both lean back on his truck out of the wind, the morning light coming on over the pines. "Here's the plan. Go to Lou's hardware and get yourself some glue traps for catching rats. Now, this is important. You take those traps and tack each onto a board. You got plenty of scrap wood I suppose, or I can get you some. Next thing you do is you tie a rope to each board. You don't want it to get away. Now then, you want to place the board against the wall where snakes is most likely to slither along. But don't place it near no pipes that the snake can get hold of or he'll break free. You see, the glue is first for the rat, and then it's for the snake." He studies my face to see if I'm getting all this, then goes on, "You got a dog I see. Well, you want to keep her out a your basement while you're doing all this. Let's see, where are we? Oh, now's when the rope becomes real handy for transporting the snake away, see. And don't take me up yonder to these woods or she'll be back in a couple hours. Put 'em in your car trunk with a pole or somethin' and haul 'em on up to the forest there." He looks me in the eyes, "You gonna 'member all this now?"

"Yeah," I nod watching the mist of my words rise, "I'll write it down soon as I get inside. So what...we just leave the snakes there tied to the boards?"

He grins again, "No, son, if you want to be kind to the snake, you bring yourself some vegetable oil in a bottle and pour it over her, then wait a little. She's work herself loose and get free unharmed. You all into freedom and Nature loving, ain't you? And besides, you'll need your board and rope for the other snakes you'll come up against. I suspect you got a nest of them down there by now, but plenty of rats as bait."

He watches me a moment, then adds, "And know this, my friends, you can try to control everything, but those rats and snakes will keep coming back."

I'm still shaking my head about all this snake knowledge when he says, "I'll come up the house and take a look if you want, after I'm done with this? Only, I think you got her all down."

I nod, hand him his cup back, and he boards his truck, looks out the window and shouts, "It'll take a week or so. Get lots of traps. You can release the rats that survive... though they say they make a good stew." He watches my eyes enlarge, then has a good laugh and guns his engine.

Up at the house, Charlotte stands at the counter in a short silk robe, her bare legs kissed by morning sun. She is drinking a mug of hot tea, a big pot of oatmeal cooking on the stove. "Good morning, honey," she smiles. "Come give me a hug. I'm so glad you're back." We hold each other a minute till she laughs, "My gosh, you're so cold."

"And you're so warm," I say falling into her warmth, then stepping back. "It's good to be home," I add, clearing my throat. "We so missed you guys."

She looks right at me and smiles, "Here, get some oatmeal. It's ready. There's granola beside the stove. How's the work going on the roadway?"

"He's moving right along. Great guy...we should invite him in, but I'm not sure how dressed people will be when they come down." She smiles and nods. "You're covered nicely," I say, then look over toward the living room, "but Thunder will probably appear tits first. Chris is a good guy, but he's human and could carry stories to town."

While my oats are cooling, I go to our room and peak in. Sharon is awake and sitting meditation like a Buddha nun at the back window with a candle and sweet incense burning. Vanilla, I think. She looks peaceful, so I don't bother her and return to the table to sit with my pen and journal.

228 ✃

"Charlotte, our farmer friend gave me instructions on how to remove the snakes and rats with glue traps. I have to write it down before I forget."

"Can you do it without killing them?" she asks, pulling a chair up beside me.

"Yeah, that's the best part. The glue traps and rat, then the rat traps the snake, and we haul them both out on a rope and release them in the woods...up by the forest."

"Like that and they're gone? Wow."

"Well, not that easy, really. He says rats and snakes will keep on coming. We have to be on our guard."

I notice we are both drinking from our mugs when Marsha-Sky comes out from their room naked except for the pink panties hanging from her hand as she heads for the bathroom. "See what I mean," I whisper to Charlotte. "You never know what's around the corner here."

"Yep, it's kind of nice in a way," she says, "as long as it's innocent like this just now."

"Yeah," I decide to open that door, "but how do we know when it's not, innocent I mean?" I'm looking right at her.

"What do you mean, Lee?" she asks, touching my hand.

I swallow, "Well, I don't know, like hugging you right now at the counter. You look, pardon me, absolutely delicious, and I'm a man, but I'm also your close friend. Where do I draw the line...You understand?" How I wish Sharon were here to help me explain.

Charlotte looks a little puzzled, but leans close, "Listen, Lee, why do you have to draw a line? I'm a woman too; can't we respond as man and woman and still be close friends?" She leans into me so I can feel her breath as she opens her lips to kiss. Her robe opens to reveal her golden breasts. My loins and my conscience burn, and I jump up. *Anyone could come into the room, including Sharon.*

"Please, Charlotte. I just can't." She draws back, closes her robe. "We do have to draw a line someplace because...because our feelings for Sharon and Chance tell us so." I read the pain in her eyes. "Listen, I love you as a sister, Charlotte. I do, and I love Sharon as...well, as a wife."

Thank god Sharon doesn't enter until this very point. "What's going on?" she asks stepping toward me while looking over at Charlotte then back at me.

"Charlotte and I were clearing up some things," I say. "Things you and I talked about in the car."

"Oh, my God," Charlotte moans, "you two have been talking about our relationship without Chance and me!" She gasps, "What have you been saying?" This time she's staring right at Sharon who releases a heavy sigh.

"We've been saying what Lee just said, that we love you deeply as brother and sister, but nothing more. We can't, and we won't." I think it's this last sentence that sends Charlotte out of the room in tears. "Charlotte," Sharon pleads, but she is gone already, no doubt, to talk with Chance. Wordless, Sharon and I look into each other, our moment of relief vanished into long minutes of concern. *Will the Free Farm come tumbling down?*

Chapter Nineteen
Work and Play

Sharon and I go back to our room to talk things over, but instead, she starts in cleaning up the bedroom with me following her around the room. Outside in the proverbial 'crack of dawn' we can hear Chris's truck ramming the snow into a passageway, and I have a promise to keep—work at the drive-thru in two hours. Finally we face each other; I take her wrist lightly, "Sharon, let's talk."

"Okay, Lee, tell me please, what comes next? We've confronted the issue with Charlotte now, but I wish I'd been there to help you explain."

"Me too, believe me. Honestly it just came up. I walked in from outside. She was standing at the sink in her little nightgown; we talked some, and I guess you could say she came onto me, and I had to resist."

She drills her eyes into mine. "What did she do? What did you say?"

"We were talking about nudity here at the Farm and where to draw the line when she says she'd be happy to erase the line, that we are man and woman and sex is something natural to share. Something like that, and then she tries to kiss me. That's when you came in, right when I was telling her how I loved her like a sister and needed to have that line."

Sharon nods her head slowly, says, "Okay, that sounds fair. It had to be said. What do you think, will Chance come down?"

"Yeah, he will. Soon I hope, so we can get this over with and move on—one way or another."

"Oh, honey, it won't be that quick. If they don't ask us to leave outright, we'll still have to crop some of those feelings they've allowed to grow." She brushes back my hair with her soft hand. "And that means more hurt."

"Jesus, though, when you think of it...where would we go?"

She looks me square in the eye, says what we both know, "Back home."

There's a light knock at our door. "Hey, can I come in?"

"Sure, come on in," I say and go to open the curtained French door, but Chance has already stepped inside. Some impulse moves me to hug him, my best friend, but I hold back, read his face for its hurt or anger.

"Wow," he says, looking at me then over to Sharon. "I guess you guys had a real scene out here this morning."

"Is Charlotte alright?" Sharon asks stepping toward him, but he backs away.

"That's hard to say. Depends on what you mean by *alright* I guess. We're both really in a spin over this. She might come down in a little while, but let's us talk."

"Well," I take a breath, "I know that we both..."

"I know...you love us like sister and brother. I heard all that."

Sharon steps closer, "And we do, Chance. You're our closest friends. But it's not a romantic or sexual love we feel."

"Yeah, well, I think Charlotte and I are into making a new kind of love, one that's free and without boundaries or explores beyond them all. Damn, I thought that's what we were doing here." He looks right at me, "I guess we all have our own meaning for free."

"And for love," Sharon says.

There's a long silence as we feel the wound between us deepen. Then he digs further. "Do you remember back when you two thought you might be brother and sister yet you were willing to love each other as lovers? Was that really you?"

I want to defend but stop, look over at Sharon. Her lips are thin and tight, her eyes stare straight ahead, then she slowly shakes her head. "Wow," she sighs. "You must be really hurt to go at us with this."

"Damn right, we are," he says. "We feel betrayed."

"Chance," I say. "You're using the axe instead of a scalpel here. Don't you hear? We're all hurting, man. I understand you're upset."

"No you don't." It is Charlotte who's been standing outside the door listening. She enters the room, says, "You're the ones pushing us away."

Sharon steps closer, pleads, "Listen please, let me say something," then gathers her thoughts with her breath. "Lee and I have found something deep and lasting in each other. It's the strongest thing we've ever felt, ever. And yes, we once were willing to break any taboo to keep it, short of having a child together." Tears come to her eyes now and I'm helpless to stop them. "But we don't have to do that now, we...Lee, help me, please."

"We're a couple that's meant to be. We love each other like husband and wife. It's as real as this house or the sunrise outside. And we hope it's as lasting." They're silent looking across at us, so I go on, "Please, I know you're hurt and angry, and I'm sorry for that, we both are. We love you. Listen, this wound we're all sharing had to be treated for it to heal."

We each look around for some place to sit, but there isn't any, so we stand like four pillars among what might be ruins. Silence in a dim lit room, then it's Chance who speaks, "Well, I know our bond is deep, and that we're testing it now. But, hell, we've done all of this together, the four of us. We know that, and honestly we do see how you love each other. Who could miss it." He looks over at Charlotte, reaches for her hand. "Maybe we even envy you that."

We're standing there in our little room as the sun breaks through curtain lace, and we feel each other's presence. We've come to a quiet place in our friendship, and we measure it with our breath. Finally, Sharon says softly, "Next to each other and our family, you guys are our deepest bond. Any pain we cause you, we feel ourselves. Please, we want to go on."

"And so do we," Charlotte whispers.

We hear birds outside, the others coming downstairs.

"And so do we," Chance whispers.

I take Sharon's hand and we step across this river to embrace Charlotte and Chance as the family we've become.

In the kitchen others have gathered round the warmth of the stove. Charlotte had put in a pan of biscuits. I break the morning chatter to tell them about Chris working outside and that I'd like to ask him inside. "Do you think you could just cover up for half an hour, while we meet and thank him. He's done us a big favor."

"Well, then, let him look," Thunder says, grinning as she lifts her t-shirt. There is a slight snicker, and this flashing has me momentarily at a loss for words.

"Yeah, well, he's a good guy and probably would enjoy that," I say. "But think of how it might sound back in the diner in Millfield," I add. "These folks are our neighbors. I doubt they'd understand such freedoms."

"Okay, okay," Thunder says, "I'll slip on some shorts."

"Thank you," I smile as the others lift fresh biscuits to their mouths.

I grab one and open the back door to see that the snow plow is just a few yards away. He's pushed the snow back and into the bank. The road out and in is almost clear, so I put on my snow gear and head out. The wind has died down, and a nice light falls over the field of white drifted snow. It is "lovely, dark, and deep," and Robert Frost could be stopping by any minute to visit his brother Jack.

"Chris!" I yell above his truck's engine. He backs off and rolls down his window.

"Yeah, what's up?"

"This is looking great. Here, I brought you a warm biscuit. Hey, come into the house when you're done, okay, and meet the folks."

He takes the biscuit, bites into it. "Mmm, that's good, just what I needed. Yeah, I'd like to meet your family. He holds up both hands, yells, "Give me 10 more minutes."

"What can I do to help?" I yell up.

He grins, "Mostly just stay out of the way for now. Then clean up around your doorway there."

When I go back inside, the kitchen is full of robed housemates, many with sleepy faces. I meet Dick and Ingrid coming down in their underclothes. "What's up?" Dick asks. "I see you got the roadway cleared. He woke us up."

"Yeah, a snow plow will do that," I grin. "And he's coming in. Would you two mind throwing something on?"

They look at each other and their bare limbs, "Sure, no problem," Dick says and goes back up for shirts while a sleepy Ingrid brushes past me.

Across the room Sharon and Charlotte are seated close on the couch, actually holding each other, and I let go a sigh—two women I love, friends again. Chance is stoking the fire, adding more logs to heat the thin clad. The others are seated around the table chatting softly. It's a good scene for Chris to come into.

I go out again and grab the snow shovel and clear the doorway searching for a place to throw the snow. When I return to the warm pantry with him, I tell him he can leave his boots on. He does and laughs, "Well, partner, your little beehive smells like home. Woo, good to be inside."

"Yes, it is. Let's meet the folks and have a cup of coffee."

Sharon comes over to greet him, Blackie at her side. "Hi, Chris," she smiles and says, "I might as well pay you now," and leans forward with a kiss which he accepts. "Wow, you're cold," she says and asks, "Did you have breakfast?"

"Yep, and nope," he says, patting Blackie who's sniffing at his crotch. "I had eggs at the house couple hours ago, but I wouldn't mind some of those oats I smell and another biscuit please." He turns to me, "Say, you folks got some nice space in that old barn. Ever think about raising chickens? I got a few layers I could pass on to you."

We all just look at each other, as he shakes hands with everyone and tries to catch all the names. When he comes round to Chance, he sees the guitar and asks, "Say, you play that thing?"

"Yes sir, I do," Chance says. "How about you, you play?"

"Oh, I play some, but I'd like to hear you." Chance slips the strap on and surprises us all by doing a chorus of "Big Rock Candy Mountain" throwing in country licks and bass runs.

"Damn, you're good, man," Chris grins and claps his hands. "How'd you like to join our scrub band tonight? All of you should come down to Martin Weather's Barn Dance. We call it a human be-in band...some got instruments, others make them out a scrub boards, buckets, anything you can name. What do you say?"

We are all dumbfounded, looking at each other for an answer. Finally, Chance extends his hand, "Yes, brother, we would. Name the time and place. We could use the break from each other in this weather."

"I reckon we all could. These winters get long, and we're just at the mouth of it. The Weather barn is down there just where Sweet Holler Road turns north, where I met these two last night. Martin's got a heated barn for his cattle and hogs, and we clear out an end of it for makin' music and dancin'. You girls dancers?"

With that, Thunder rises, grabs Sky by the hands and they do a couple turns in their t-shirts and shorts, while I watch Chris' grin grow. "Damn, girls, you can dance with me anytime...anytime my wife's not around, that is. You all come down 'round 7 o'clock tonight and we'll make us some sweet music. We'll have pizza and beer. You all just bring yourselves." He's awakened something in us, and with that he rises. "I got to get back on the road, running the snow plow in town for a few stores." He looks over at me, "See you at the drive-thru later, my friend. We can talk more about those chickens."

When he closes the door, I turn around to a sea of smiling faces.

At the drive-thru Frank already knows that we're coming to the barn dance. "Bring that pretty little girlfriend of yours will you," he says, "Oh, and somethin' to play. We all just make the best music we can. It's all part of the fun."

"Well," I ask, "how do you folks get there in the snow? I mean Chris had to plow us out this morning."

"And he'll do it for others if they need it. It ain't a question of *if* but *how*. We all manage to get there each week one way or 'nother 'cause we need it these long winter months. A man can go crazy cooped up you know." And with that he pulls me closer by my shirt sleeve and whispers, "You know that farm you folks is livin' in...went empty 2 years." He looks around then leans toward me, "One reason why is old John Miller hanged hisself right there in the basement. Got up from watchin' 'The Defenders' one night and without saying a word to the wife, went down the basement stairs. She thought he was workin' on something, but then she didn't hear no sounds for a long, long time, so she goes down them steps and there he is hanging from one of them beams stretched out like a side of beef."

"Jesus, Frank!" I pull back, "Did you have to go and tell me all that!"

"Well, what's wrong? Ain't no ghosts up there no more is there? You folks musta chased 'em out with all your good spirits."

"Well," I sigh, "I'm sure going to struggle with knowing this now and not telling the others. And, believe me, they won't want to know. Three of them are moving down to that basement next week, soon as we get the snakes and rats cleared out."

"Oh, you probly got the snakes when you all started heatin' the old place again. They no doubt came in and was sleepin' till you folks started warmin' 'em up. Good luck on that one." He eyes me, then points to a load of potato chips that just came in. "You get to work unloadin' that; I'll go up front and relieve Gerty on the register."

I'm stuck in a kind of stupor for a while, unloading but forgetting my count, seeing basement images of ropes and bodies I don't want to. One thing about me is I tell everything, always have, but I don't want to ruin anyone's future with this tale of the past. *Damn him for telling me this.* Someone honks in the drive-thru and I go out, forgetting my count again.

When I get home, Sharon greets me with a long kiss at the back door. "Hey, this is like old times at your Mom's place," I say.

"Did you hear anything from home?" she asks, taking my coat.

"No, I didn't, but I did call the phone company. They'll be out Monday morning, weather permitting."

"What's up here?" I ask, sitting down to remove my boots. She steps between my legs up close, and I am cupping my hands around the backs of her knees, then her warm thighs. Her black tights are smooth and tight. I glide my hands slowly up and down her thighs, then over her smooth curves and up her inside her blouse to her bare back, feeling that smooth canal of her spine, the flat plane at her base. I press my face into the warm flesh of her stomach. She leans over to kiss the back of my neck, and I want to forget everything but her. We're like this a long moment, then someone yells something from the kitchen that we don't quite hear. I slowly rise and whisper to her, "We're so lucky to have each other."

"Yes," she smiles, "but, honey..." and she kisses me again, "...luck has nothing to do with it." She pulls back as Sky passes in a paisley blouse.

"Lee," Sharon says, "You wouldn't believe it. People here have been talking all day about that music thing tonight. All these free thinking intellectuals are just dying to get down with the locals."

"What are they saying?"

"Oh, you wouldn't believe that either. They're wondering how to dress."

"You're kidding. Well, Frank says to be sure to bring some kind of instrument to play. Do we have anything?"

"Hmm...let me think. You have an old harmonica in that shoebox of yours. I suppose I can turn a coffee can into a bongo drum." She turns around, "I better tell the others about this. That'll keep them busy till it's time to go." I stand at the basement door, watch her disappear, happy yet aching to tell someone about the corpse from down there, but I don't...for now.

Everyone is already dressed for the party, like it's a shindig or something, and I guess it is. The women are wearing bright print blouses and skirts, the guys are in flannel shirts and jeans. Some of them have dug out kerchiefs for their necks. "Well," I shout, "looks like we're headin' for a hoedown!"

Chance laughs, "A regular jam-bor-ee!"

"Yahoo!" I shout, "I better get dressed."

Before going to the bedroom I go over to Charlotte, kiss her on the cheek, and she gives me a quiet hug. I don't kiss the other women. In our room Sharon has slipped off her tights and is standing in her short denim skirt, and I whistle. "I know they're going to enjoy you in that."

I grin, but she frowns. "Is it too much? Maybe I should wear the tights."

"Up to you, I guess. Kind of depends on how warm that barn is." I watch as she slithers back into her tights. *God, I love watching her dress, and undress. Greatest show on earth.*

We eat bowls of hot steaming chili and warm wheat bread. We're down to three cars now since Chance's old beater died outside of Nelsonville. He and Bruce were on a run for some moonshine that Bruce had heard of when the car's engine just burned out. He and Bruce had to hitch rides back in the cold to Frank's, another reason for a phone.

"Let's see," Chance says, "Nine of us can pack into two cars if we squeeze a little." And we do, gathering up our homemade instruments and bundling for the cold. Sharon and I drive with Sky and Thunder squeezed tight in the back seat of buddha-bug. I keep my eyes on the road.

The barn is great, a large white building with a regular slide door. Inside is warm and bright; someone has made a little stage to one side. The cattle have been moved out to a second barn for tonight, and someone's done a lot of sweeping, though the ripe cattle smells remain. Sheets of pressed wood board have been spread on the floor for dancing I suppose. We're early, but Chris comes over with a stout young woman with curly hair. "Hey and hello," he calls to us. "Glad you all could make it. You can set your instruments down on the stage." The girls carry them over. Then Chris turns around, "This here's Margo, my better half." She smiles, steps toward us, and Sharon and I each give her a hug.

"Your husband's been a life saver," Sharon says for us.

"Oh, he's always ready to help out others," Margo nods, then adds, "'Course he seems deaf to my own requests."

"Margo here teaches first grade over to Nelsonville." You can tell Chris is trying hard to relate.

"No kidding," Sharon says, taking Margo's hand. "We're thinking of starting a free school up at our place. We should talk."

Chance and the others have arrived, along with some of the farmer friends. We are definitely overdressed, but everyone just laughs and shakes hands. Some set out food on a long table. Frank shows up with a keg of beer that he taps, announcing, "Girls and boys, the suds are flowing." Then he points to three young boys standing near, "But not for you younguns." Two guys with guitars and two more with a bass and a fiddle are tuning up, so Chance goes over with his guitar. Margo and Charlotte shake hands then hug. She and Chris introduce us to a lot of the others, farmers and their teenage kids; the little ones are at home or sleeping up in the house. Rings of talk go round as we all mix, and by the time the music starts, we no longer feel like aliens in a strange land, but neighbors among friends. Everyone sings "You Are My Sunshine," even the Triangle, and the dancing begins with an old fiddle tune "Keep on the Sunny Side." Bruce and Thunder rush out onto the dance floor. They watch the others some, then begin high stepping everything, exaggerating so that you can't tell if they're trying to learn or mocking the others.

We stand and watch, when the bearded band leader announces, "Okay, all a you not dancin' is playin', come on now, pick up your instruments and let's go on 'Big Rock Candy Mountain.'" Before he starts, Margo whispers, "That's our mayor," and then we are off slapping drum skins and shaking rattles; I pull out the harmonica and play softly trying to catch the key.

Hank comes over to slap me on the back, "Thatta boy. You're gettin' it."

I stop a moment, "Well, I gotta work on it some."

"Hell!" Frank laughs. "This ain't work. This here is play."

When we're not playing, we're dancing, square and round, and even some boogie-woogie. Chance puts down his guitar after a while and grabs Charlotte round the waist. At one point a young red haired girl steps up to the microphone and sings Tammy Wynette's "Singing My Song." She and the song are so damn beautiful; I stand transfixed till I feel a sharp poke in my back. It's Sharon waking me from my reverie. It's a slow song, probably a fox trot, and couples get close up and lean into each other. The Triangle have gone outside, probably to smoke, but I'm holding Sharon real close, feeling her breathe against me, and together we smile over at Charlotte and Chance, Dick and Ingrid, our free family.

*   *   *

A day later I am down in the basement with Chance cleaning out old junk, carrying it up in boxes and bucketfuls. I'm also looking around for the hanging beam which I do and do not want to find. It's when we sit on the stairs to take a rest that I spill the story of old John Miller hanging himself there. Chance reads the nervous sweat on my brow and knows I'm not making it up. "Christ!" he says, "What do we do now...keep it to ourselves or tell the others?"

"I don't know," I say. "I held onto it for 24 hours. It's something big and bad to know."

"Shit, man!" he says and kind of shivers. "I do wish you hadn't told me that. Let's knock off a while and get out of here."

The next day, I am working at the drive-thru when Chris comes in from snow plowing. He still has snow all over his cap and coat. He ducks inside the door. He's a pretty big guy, about 220 pounds. At the dance he told me he's 33, and he and Margo have no kids. For some reason, I let on that Sharon and I are married, maybe because it feels like we are.

"Hey and hello there, fella," he calls to me from the front of the store. I wave and motion him back where I'm stacking things.

"Where you coming from?" I ask.

"Out on East Millfield Road, the Kreb's farm. Had to get Tom to the doctor down to Athens. Heart attack, but he's doing okay. I been up a while, plowing some of these parking lots. Do a little, earn a little each day."

"You still have some snow on you, partner," I say and brush off the back of his shoulders. "Hard day?"

"No, not really, though I was afraid for Tom and Mary Sue. She dropped the kids off to her sister's place and followed me in their pickup. You know, people come to hate this snow, but to me, it's my work." We both nod to this, then he takes my arm, "Say, I forgot to tell you the other night. I hear old man Miller's giving up the farm for good now that his wife's gone."

"Hmm, she died?"

"Nope, took off with a traveling salesman," he says, watching my eyes get big and can't help laughing at his little joke. "Gotcha," he says, then, "I shouldn't laugh at the dead. Anyway, I'm tellin' you this 'cause he's got a small tractor for sale if you folks is interested."

"Thanks, Chris," I say, setting the last bag on the rack, "I'll ask up at the house and get back to you. How much we talkin' here?"

"Oh," he drawls, "'bout 800, I spose. Say, I hear you got a phone now. If you got a phone book, you can look him up, it's John Miller out on East Millfied Road where I just come from."

Something kind of rings a bell, and then I ask, "Say, is he related to the John Miller that lived at our place?"

He gets a dumb look on his face, then grins, "Hate to tell you this, but your place was last owned by the Carter sisters. John Miller's lived on his farm nigh to 50 years."

"Well, damn," I say, "I heard from Frank that he hanged himself in our basement," releasing the cat from the bag along with my frustration at keeping silent about the suicide.

Chris just looks me in the eye, and his grin gets wider and wider. "Well, damn yourself, boy. You just been had by Frank Sloan, one the biggest tale-tellers in these parts," and he slaps me on the back. I try to laugh, but manage only a fake smile, because mostly what I want to do is go in the back of the store and shoot old Frank with the shotgun he says he keeps in the closet, or maybe that's another lie of his. "You been had, my friend," Chris says again, chuckling. "Don't take it so hard, it's the way down here." I nod but do not understand.

When Chris leaves, I'm so mad at Frank and myself that I grab my parka and tell Rita up front, "I'm out of here. You can tell the old fart I've gone home to bury the ghost in my basement."

Chapter Twenty
Learn by Going

We have a nice Christmas with Carl and Susan sharing their kids with us. Chance brings in a tree from the woods, one we dug up and plan to replant. We decorate it with an assortment of trinkets we've brought or made: sparkling bracelets and necklaces, paperclip and paper chains, and strings of popcorn and cranberries that we made one night. No electric lights this year, just the sunlight in the daytime, candles beneath it at night. If anything, we're a resourceful bunch. New Year's Eve we all just lay around the fireplace, all of us stoned on some good grass Bruce scored in town. It was the first I'd had in months. At midnight Bruce set off some fireworks in the front yard. I can't remember anything else.

By mid-January we've set up our six chickens and one rooster in the barn and now rotate the chores of feeding and gathering. We also get together the $800 to buy John Miller's used tractor, and Chris hauls it over and shows us how to drive it and how to plow fields and our own roadway. When I ask if he just did this so he wouldn't have to do it anymore, he grins, "Listen, my friend, you'll find plenty uses for this old John Deere come spring and summer. You're farmers now, you know, till you make it or give it up." Not sure what he meant by that.

The members of the Triangle now live in the basement. After we chased the snakes and rats and most of the junk out of the place, we white-washed the walls, then each of them painted a mural with day-glow images...a porpoise for Sky, a dragon for Bruce (to eat the snakes I guess), and a naked goddess with small pointed breasts for Thunder. I've come to think of the three as our teenagers, though I'm only 22 myself. Sometimes I wonder if they're just looking for a place to crash, but then they throw in and work alongside of us. There's lots of smoking and free loving going on, but they keep it pretty much to themselves, especially when Carl and Susan come out with Gracie and little Ned. University classes have started again and we've seen Susan on campus each week at our education class. She'll graduate in June with a teaching certificate, and we'll all be her aides if we can get the Free School up and running by summer. That's the plan, and Sharon loves it. Yesterday she told me, "I think teaching is my thing." It's strange how on campus we've now become the college commuters, and though Sharon now has a plan, I'm just taking classes with no degree in mind.

My writing has been coming along though, and I've even sent off some things. *The Whole Earth Catalog* out west printed one of them, though it was just this long description of our Athens Free Farm. I was paid a ten dollar bill which they sent in the mail with a copy of the latest edition. Actually I think writing nonfiction is my thing; it's good work, pulling facts and ideas together in new ways, seeing what lies behind and bringing it to light. It turns writing to good use. It's part of this big *Whole Earth* thing that's rocking the world of publishing and culture. You can't really describe it. With it's outer space view of Mother Earth on the cover, it's cosmic and revolutionary, visionary and functional. You pick it up and realize it's like nothing else. You have to reorient yourself...it's a book, a magazine, a how-to handbook, a practical catalog of ways to start a whole new wave of thinking and living. Like I said to Chance, "This is the alternative we've been looking for." I bought the two earlier issues at the used bookstore with my $10, and brought them here for everyone to read. Chance knows one of the guys, Gurney Norman from Kentucky, who helped edit the last couple issues from out West. But it's the brainchild, as they say, of Stewart Brand, a biologist, artist, and freethinker from California. Back in '68 he and his wife Lois started it as the Whole Earth Truck Store, an actual Dodge truck they drove around the country visiting campuses and communes like ours and selling "tools" for building a better world. They settled in Menlo Park outside of Stanford, hung out with Ken Kesey and his Merry Pranksters, and began launching this series of catalogs to provide "access to tools." In Brand's words it's all to help the reader "find his own inspiration, shape his own environment, and share his adventure with whoever is interested."

Well, I'm really into it; like I say, I've found my own thing. I just hope they can keep the revolution going till I can catch up. Charlotte actually went to school with Brand and first put me in touch with his crew. And, get this, he's coming to OU this spring to speak at this year's Earth Day.

Things are moving along pretty well then, and we're learning where we have to go by doing it. We make mistakes, but then we learn from them. We had to do the schoolhouse floor twice to get it level, and we're still running electricity out to it with a long power cable from the house. Chris knows a guy who'll do the wiring come spring thaw. He and Margo have been out a couple times for dinners. Thing is, the Triangle doesn't like him. Bruce does an imitation of the way Chris walks and talks slow and country, and last night I had to tell him to stop, but he wouldn't, so I lost it and grabbed him by the arm. "Stop it, you A-hole. This guy's helped us survive through the winter."

"Oh, yeah," he says, "You call it survival. I call it compromise. We're becoming just like them."

I don't let go of his arm. At least we're wrestling with words, not fists. "How come?" I ask. "How come it's always us and them with you three?"

Thunder turns and faces me, "Now damn it, wait a minute, Mister Know-it-all. We're with you here. We do the work, by God." She steps toward me, "We're no more separated than you and your pretty woman are."

I turn to Sharon. Thunder turns to Sky. They both stare up at us from the couch. It's the drama of an open fight that draws attention. I let go of Bruce's arm. "Okay," I say. "I didn't mean it like it came out. I just can't accept your making fun of our friends."

"Oh," Bruce says, "and you don't make fun of us, calling us the teenagers? I hear you and Chance talking." He's got me there, and I just wait it out, honestly thinking *Here's the rock in my path that I have to learn from,* when Chance comes over from the kitchen.

"Say, guys, can we settle this someway? How about old fashioned apologies and a handshake, huh?"

While part of me wants to put my fist to Bruce's face and shake Thunder by her bony shoulders, another part feels the ugly anger burning through my body, the stupid tension in my neck and just wants to lay down all weapons. We're at the edge of something, and the moment stretches long for everyone in the room. Sharon's face is pleading something to me, and then she rises, and takes two steps into the middle of the room. Suddenly she opens her arms, "Please, everyone," she says softly but firmly, "Before someone gets hurt, can we all just try something... please?" No objections, and she really means it. "Right now. Let's take some deep breaths. Stop what you're doing and just put your hand on your chest...Feel it, that tension burning? Now let's breathe into it...Okay, nice deep breaths. Now in...and hold-2-3-4, breathe out...2-3-4-5-6. In...and hold-2-3-4; out...2-3-4-5-6..." I look around and we are all doing it. She keeps it going till we all lose track of time and place, then stops, waits, "Now take a deep cleansing breath"

"Wow!" Thunder sighs, "a natural high."

Sharon puts her hands together and does a small bow to us. "Namaste," she says softly, "I see the light in you."

Sky nods back, says, "Where did you learn that?"

Sharon smiles at her, takes her hand, "Oh, at that Zen class Charlotte and I took at the Free University. We did lots of deep breathing, didn't we?" And she looks over to Charlotte who takes her other hand.

Charlotte says, "Like I've been saying at meetings …we ought to do group meditation every day, morning and night." And there's this silent consensus of nodding that goes round, and I look over at Bruce and extend my hand.

"Sorry," I say as we shake.

"Sorry, man" he answers, and we both let go of something ugly and go off to our rooms.

Back in our bedroom, I touch Sharon's arm. "Honey," I say, "that was really something you did out there."

She smiles as she slowly unbuttons her blouse, "Not me, but we, and I know we can do more."

*   *   *

The next morning Carl and Susan show up with the kids. We're done with morning meditation and are all gathered around the table slurping up the oatmeal, spreading Margo's apple butter on our toast and sipping from hot mugs of coffee and tea. I think the mornings are best, before thinking and doing run our lives. Gracie has her hair up in little pig tails and comes straight over to sit on Sharon's lap. Susan places Ned on the couch for a diaper change. We all look away. Carl is talking something over with Chance, as this sense of sunlight and family comes into the room.

"Hey, Gracie, I like your hair," I say, flipping her tails up in the back. She pretends to smack my hand.

"Don't do that, please," she looks around, "I'm a woman, you know."

We all try not to laugh, and Sharon gives her a hug, "Yes, you are a woman. And men need to respect us, right?"

Gracie gives a big nod, and I steer away from that issue, even though the sides are pretty even in the room.

For some crazy reason, Thunder comes over and wraps her arms around me from behind. "Don't worry, honey boy," she says in a mocking way, "You're still loved and respected." She has never done this, but I do like the feel of her firm breasts pressed against my back. I twist around to face her, smell marijuana on her breath, and just grin, then I walk over to where Chance and Carl are planning the day's work.

We're doing some shelving in the dining room turned bedroom, and there are things in the truck to bring in: lamps and small tables, a box full of kids' toys. It's only February, but they are beginning to move in. They've gotten out of their lease and want to move along with us in this grand adventure. "We feel so out of it," Susan says, "coming here just on weekends, like we're drop-ins."

"Oh, you could never be that," Charlotte says rubbing Susan's arm as she nurses little Ned. "You're part of us."

"Well," Susan says, "a part of us needs to take a shower. Ned threw up all over me in the car. I think he's coming down with something. Do you have any peppermint or chamomile tea?"

"I'll make some," Ingrid says over by the stove. Dick's been away a couple days, at some literary conference in Indiana.

"Here," Sharon says, "I'll take Ned. You go and shower."

"Can I borrow someone's clothes?" Susan asks.

"Oh, you weren't here," Charlotte says. "You're in luck. We've started a new thing...a clothes bin in the pantry area. Anyone can just toss in things they're not wearing on the shelves...there's one for men, women, and other. Just pull something out of there."

Carl, Chance, and I begin carrying in boxes from the car. Pretty soon, Sky and Ingrid join us, while Susan showers and Sharon watches baby Ned. Thunder has put on their Joni Mitchell tape, and I again hear "Woodstock," their theme song since first meeting each other there in the mud and music, as we've heard a hundred times. On my next trip in, "The Circle Game" is playing and Sharon is dancing in the sunlight with young Ned in her arms. On the next trip, I walk in to discover Susan standing naked at the clothes bin digging for an outfit. It's the first time I've seen her nude body. She's a little shorter than Sharon yet nicely shaped. She's bending over and I see how full her breasts are, her buttocks round and sweet. She pays no attention till I let out a very soft whistle sound. She turns, holds a flowered blouse of Sharon's against her breastbone and smiles back at me, her dark nipples showing. I grin and let out a breath. The family grows.

I'm thinking I might need to take a break right away when Carl walks in, lugging the kids' toy box, and I give him a hand—he at one end, me at the other while Susan watches. "Hey, no bedding this trip?" I ask.

"Not yet. We left some things at the other place. We won't move in till next weekend. Then it's home sweet home." He looks over at me, asks, "Hey, are the folks here still down with our moving in?"

"Yes," I say quick, "we could use a little sanity around here sometimes."

"Oh yeah? Well, don't forget we're bringing two kids into the mix. How are you and Sharon doing, anyway?" he asks while sliding the toy box into the corner of the room. "Any thoughts of marriage, or don't you feel you need that?"

"As a matter of fact, we feel more and more like we're already married, especially here at the farm where there's some exchange of partners going on." I stop there, probably have gone too far.

He says softly, "Yeah, we've sensed that, Lee, and we're okay with it. We just want the same respect for couples if they choose...and we do, you know."

"Well, speaking for Sharon and me, we honor that gladly, but we've had to struggle some for it here." Carl is so damn nice, and I've just been eyeing his pretty wife. I have to get a handle on this nudity and sex thing, I know it. I feel like a double cheat in saying all this about fidelity to him, yet I do mean it.

He puts his arm around my neck, says, "Thanks, brother," and I sense he means it; then surprises me with, "Hey, listen, I know Susan likes to share her natural beauty, and I'm okay with that. It's just a look, don't touch thing. Okay?"

"Oh, hell yeah," I say a little too loud. "She just caught me by surprise. And she is beautiful."

"Well, the feeling's mutual on that," he says, then as we step toward the door, "Just remember how sweet Sharon is, Mr. Lee."

I nod as we start back out to the truck, but am not sure exactly what he means by that. Susan is dressed now holding Ned as she comes into the room followed by Sharon. "It's looking good," she smiles, "don't you think, honey?" and in this case the honey is Sharon.

"Well," Sharon says, taking me by the arm. "I guess we're lucky we've got these strong men to carry things."

"Yep, we are," says Susan smiling. We watch while she moves a couple things around, then comes over and says, "Let's talk together some about the school." Carl heads out to the truck, and Susan asks, "How's your Growth and Development class going?"

"Great," we both say, then I, "It's the most practical course I've ever taken by far. But heck, I started with calculus as a math major. This course is all about people and relationships, not words or numbers or ideas, and let's face it, people are all around us."

Sharon adds, "It'll be so good to have Gracie and Ned here to care for and watch them grow. I was imagining that we'll start the school with the early levels, maybe pre-school to fourth grade. Right?"

"Well, yes, in a way, but seriously," and Susan looks up, "one of the first things we need to throw out is grade levels. The person comes first. We'll treat each child where they are and work developmentally—Montessori approach but with our twist on it." Susan looks right at us, "If you don't mind my asking, have you two ever thought about having a child and starting your own family?"

Sharon and I are thrown back by the reality of this question. As close as we are, we've not talked of it. "Wow, you are direct," Sharon says, "I guess we're so focused on our commune family and classes that we haven't approached this. Mostly we've been trying hard not to get pregnant. I'm on the pill, you know."

"I'm sorry if I started something here." Susan says, touching Sharon's arm. "I'll butt out of it. It's just that you're such a loving couple, and childbirth is so rewarding, I wondered...Oh, I'll shut up and go see what Gracie's up to. We'll talk more about the school later."

She leaves the room, and Sharon and I stand in our puddle of ignoring, neither of us knowing how to step out.

Chapter Twenty-One
Questioning

Spring comes early and strong, the lion mixed with the lamb—showers filling the ground, daffodils blooming around the house, strong winds bringing songbirds from their new nests. Though things are moving along well with plans for the school, and we're now a family of 13, there are some deep rumbles of change. Susan brings up the first issue after breakfast when the Triangle has already headed into town.

"Can you overdose from LSD?" she asks, and looks over to Charlotte our resident scientist.

"Well, that's a little out of my area, but from what I've read, I'd say no. What do you think, Dick?"

"No, definitely not. Oh, you can get so high you might hurt yourself, but it won't kill you." He looks back at Susan who is sitting at the table nursing Ned, who's almost three now. "Why do you ask?"

"Well...I hate to say this, but they're starting to scare me a little. The other day Thunder couldn't stop talking. She was really flying, babbling about Woodstock like we were all there. She'd stripped and was running around wildly outside. It was all I could do to get her back into the house. Remember, Sharon?"

"Yes," Sharon answers. "She was kneeling naked talking to the grass, and we helped get her up and inside to lie down."

"And Bruce...Have any of you seen him lately?" Susan asks. "Yesterday, he was lying on the front porch couch trying to speak to me and Gracie, but he couldn't get any words out, just sounds, none of them with vowels."

"I saw him like that," Chance says. "It's pretty sad, because he thought he was being brilliant, moving his hands like it all made wonderful sense, you know? The problem is you never know how stoned you really are." He pulls up a chair and sits with the rest of us at the table. "I guess the questions are two: are they bringing anything to the family and are they likely to hurt themselves and us."

"Wow, you know," Dick says, "I don't want to turn anyone away, but they don't seem to be with us most of the time. Where do you figure they get their money anyway?"

Chance lets out a sigh. "I didn't want to say anything, but I've heard that they're dealing in town, Bruce and Thunder anyway. They hang around the coffeehouse and the bus station. That truck of theirs hasn't run for months, so what...they borrow our cars to go into town and deal."

"Oh, shit," I say. "I'm not down with that. I'm not. And when they do get busted, where do you think the cops will stop...right here at the farm. I say we have to do something."

Sharon looks over at Chance, "Why did you wait to tell us about this?"

He twists in his seat, then stands. "I don't know. I wasn't sure at first, but I should have. Charlotte and I have taken a few acid trips ourselves, thanks to them. We're not hooked or anything, but we are...'complicit' I guess is the word. Like you were, Lee, getting your grass from your McArthur cousin. You know?"

"Ingrid and Dick, you want to check in on this?" Sharon asks. "It's a big decision if we ask them to leave. We'd need a full consensus."

"Oh boy," Ingrid says. "I really like them, I do. But I do think they are a little crazy. I agree with Lee, I see the problem they put us into. What do you say, sweetie?"

Dick looks up, says, "Well, I've done a few trips too, but just to know what it's like." He squirms in his seat, "I'm torn, but I do think they could bring us all down. How about we start by confronting them."

"You mean, a kind of intervention?" Sharon asks.

"Well, more of an ultimatum, wouldn't you say?" Dick answers.

Chance speaks up, "Well now, I'm not sure how 'ultimatums' fit with a freedom commune."

"Yeah," I answer, "well, there are lots of communes who aren't around anymore because they only stood for freedom and nothing more."

There's a stillness after I say this, and I'm kind of embarrassed till Sharon says, "Come on, Lee's right. We have to stand for something, and as open as we might be, we're also about values...like growing without chemicals and buying local, like not making waste or using up resources, like having compassion for every living thing."

Susan nods her head, "Like caring well for children, and for the poor among us, and for mother earth. I really want to grow things here for ourselves and others." She pauses and looks around then adds, "You know, I'm glad to hear all of this. We just assume it, but we need to say it out loud from time to time like this. If Carl were here, I know he'd be with us on this. We need to move from being against things into freedom and discovering what we do believe in."

"Wow," Chance says leading a collective sigh.

Then Sharon says, "I can't tell you how good it is to share like this. I feel more healthy and sane."

"We all do, honey," Susan adds, looking around. "We all do."

"Well..." I say slowly, "what brought this all up was concern for our friends downstairs and their use and possible sale of drugs. I say we confront them when they get back this afternoon. No waiting around."

Charlotte joins me, "I agree, but let's do it with compassion and conviction." There's this collective nodding we do, then she clears her throat to get our attention, "Before we all take off, I have something to announce," she says. "I know everyone is planning on going to hear Stewart Brand talk next week. Well, I've a surprise for you. I've talked with him on the phone, and he and Lois want to come out to visit the Free Farm."

"No shit!" jumps out of me. "They're coming here for real!" I feel like a kid.

"Yes, they are. And, Lee, he said he remembers that piece you wrote for them and wants to talk with you."

"When...when did he say all of this?" I have to ask.

"Last night around 10 p.m....7 their time. You and Sharon had already gone to bed, so I waited to share this, then forgot. Sorry, but yes, it's real. All this talk about values reminded me."

Ingrid speaks up: "Excuse me for asking this, but who is this Stewart guy?"

"Ah," I sigh, "just about the greatest alternative thinker we have going for us today. His work is...oh, just suffused with ecology and good sense. He's the guy who started this *Whole Earth Catalog* I've been urging you all to read."

Dick chimes in, "Ingrid, I've told you about him. Matter of fact, I quoted him in my Indiana presentation. Let's see: 'Civilization's shortening attention span is mismatched with the pace of our environmental problems.' He's right on, and he and the people out West are making a new way outside of the American profit motive."

"How is he going to do that?" she asks.

"By making a new path—alternatives." I say, "By not following but creating. Oh, I could quote whole passages of these books of his."

"Go ahead. Let us hear one," she says.

"Well, how about this: 'Information wants to be free. You own your own words, unless they contain information. In which case they belong to no one.' Can you dig it?"

She looks at me hard then nods, "I get it. That's beautiful and now I cannot wait to meet him. Charlotte, thank you for inviting him."

"Oh," she laughs, "he invited himself. He's very direct but also sweet. No bullshit gets by him or Lois, his wife."

They break into smiles and chatter as the gathering dissolves. I take Sharon aside. "Honey, this is big...it's what I want to do—work for Stewart Brand and *The Whole Earth*."

She's taken aback a little but smiles. "Wow, now it's you who's flying high. But okay, I hear you. Tell me how would you do that?"

"You mean research and write? Isn't that what we all do now, here in our courses? I'm ready to do it for real and share it. All my life I've wanted to do something practical and visionary, make something that helps, like my father. Hell, 'Access to tools,' is their slogan. And I can do this work anywhere, but especially here near the university. It's what I'm meant to do, do you see?"

She pats my cheek, then kisses it, no need for words.

*   *   *

We each find our tasks, like we're in Montessori school. I'm working with the tractor filling up the roadway with new gravel, strong repetitive work, and I'm halfway finished when the Triangle pulls in. I wave them on, then park the tractor by the big barn and follow them in. We have this old school bell that Chance has rigged up by the back door to call folks in, and I ring it three times.

"What's up?" Bruce asks, tossing his jacket down the cellar stairs. I look him straight in the eyes, and for a change, he's there. That's good.

"We need to talk," I say. "Come on into the meeting room."

"I'm going to get a drink," Thunder calls. "Do you two want one?"

Sky follows her into the kitchen, says, "I'll get mine. Do we still have that green iced tea?"

"Tea?" Thunder laughs, then mimics sales talk. "Tea, my friend, is what we've got. Come and get it." It's an inside joke for them, but I catch on.

While the others are gathering, I ask, "If you don't mind my asking, where are you getting your tea these days, and by tea I do mean weed?"

"Why, you want some?" Bruce asks. "I keep a stash in the basement wall, and, good buddy, all you have to do is ask."

"I know you carry and deliver. Just want to know where it's coming from."

He looks at Thunder and Sky, then at me, "Let's just say I don't have to go far for weed here in Millfield."

"Okay, then, you're getting homegrown from the farmers?"

"Let's call them growers, some of them. And along with any tobacco curing in those old barns of theirs, you'll likely find some hidden weed. You get me?"

Everyone is seated now in the living room. "I was just asking Bruce where he gets his weed, and he says it's all local grown."

"Not too surprising," Chance says, looking over at me. "You had your own source for a while."

"But, Bruce," I say, "I have to ask why would they trust you?"

"Ha! That's the real kicker, man. It's because of you. They know you're friends with Chris and his little woman, and they see you at Frank's store, so they trust us. They think we're related or something."

I am not happy about being a silent accomplice to this dealing, but I just nod. Everyone has gathered by now and Chance asks the next question. "What about the LSD you guys have stored in the basement. Where'd that come from?"

"Hey," Thunder interrupts. "What's going on here, some kind of inquisition? Besides, the basement's the perfect place for it, it's cool and dark, and anyway, it's none of your business. It's our thing. And it's us doing it, so how about you all stand clear, alright?" Her face is getting flush, something none of us has really seen.

Charlotte steps in. "Okay, let's relax. We're getting excited. You want to take a deep breath here. "

"No, I don't want to take a damn breath here. You take a breath."

"Bruce," I ask. "In a general way, can I ask where you're getting your tabs? I don't think it's from the farmers."

"No, man. I don't care. Hey, any good chemistry major can make the stuff. It's not illegal."

"Oh, yeah, it is in the U.S. since 1968." It's Chance this time. "And I think I speak for the group in saying this. You're using it is, well, tolerated, but your selling it is not."

"Why, because you want it for free? Is that the kind of freedom you believe in?" Bruce is heating up now. "You've dropped acid, most of you, and you've gotten high from it. So what are you saying...we're free to use and give away, but not to sell? And where do you think we get our money? You want to control that too? Fuck this freedom of yours."

Charlotte gives it another try. "I can see you're getting upset. Listen now, we do care about you, and we didn't want it to go down this way. But yes, we've talked and decided we don't want to be, well, a drug house. We're asking you to stop selling."

"Jesus Christ!" Thunder takes the floor now. She looks over to Sky. "Can you believe this shit!" Sky just shakes her head. "You're treating us like whores, and you want sex but we can't sell it."

Susan finally speaks. "That's not it at all. I'm telling you most of us feel that it's wrong to deal, it's taking advantage of others, and when the drug bust comes, and believe me it will come, it could bring the whole farm down. We have a right to defend that."

To everyone's surprise Sky answers this. "Well, please just hold on a minute, let's look at some facts." She steps forward into the circle. "Since Doctor Hoffmann invented LSD back in 1938, it's been used for health reasons, like cluster head aches, which I suffer from, by the way. And it's been proven nonaddictive, and despite rumors, does no lasting damage to brain cells." She looks around at our faces and continues her lecture: "All kinds of folks have endorsed it as a spiritual experience...Alduous Huxley, Timothy Leary, Ken Kesey, the Beatles, even your friend Stewart Brand was part of the experiments with it at Menlo Park." She is really cooking on this. "Only once it became part of the counter culture did government get involved. Listen please, it's part of the alternatives you've been preaching here."

This is more than we have heard Sky speak, ever. "Wow," Charlotte says. "I appreciate your telling us all of this."

"And it kills off the ego," Sky adds, "lets you get out of your body and self, to see things better, clearer, more real."

"Okay, but that's a perception, Sky" Sharon says, "not a fact. And the drug is an hallucinogen which creates that very sense of enlightenment. And it does have its side effects. I've read up on this too, and given the right conditions—a safe place and reasonably stable mind—it can maybe give you visions, I agree. But given the wrong conditions, it can distort a person's senses and their basic judgment. Lots of accidents and injuries have happened to users. You know that." No one objects. "And if someone's in a bad place, I mean physically or psychologically, they can have a pretty awful trip and maybe do harm to themselves. There are cases of prolonged psychosis and flashbacks that can come on anywhere."

"Oh...but that's why you do it to-geth-er with friends," Bruce speaks out. "Like us here at the farm. Listen, we know we've got the worst room down in that cold, damp basement, but it's a good place for tripping, and we do it together. Like Thunder here, she's manic-depressive, I think you all know that," he looks over at her and she nods. "So she only takes it when she's manic. We help her with that."

Susan interrupts, "Okay, that's you three, and you seem to have worked that out, but if you guys are selling, you don't know how it will be used. And I hope to God you're not selling to kids. Because they're not ready for this, and it's wrong, wrong, wrong. And please tell me that you guys are staying away from crystal meth."

"Okay, Mom, we hear you," Thunder jumps in. "You know we can't really tell where the stuff is going or how it will be used, anymore than Frank at the drive-thru can know how the alcohol he sells is used. We're just making the product available." She looks around for some kind of affirmation. "And I can personally say that I've never sold to anyone not in high school or older."

"They're still kids in high school," Susan objects.

"Oh, I've sold to kids who've sold to other kids," Bruce objects, "You can't stop that. I mean I'm not God, you know."

"Yeah, but you're acting like one, putting this stuff in the hands of children." It's Sharon now. "Understand this. We're not against your using, but we do object to your selling."

"Yeah, sister Sharon," Thunder snaps back, searching our faces, "and what are you going to do about it if we don't stop?"

There's an ugly pause, then finally Dick steps up. "Listen, we've taken a consensus, and if you continue to sell drugs in town or anywhere for that matter, we're forced to ask you to leave."

"Didn't you hear anything I said?" Sky pleads looking around at us. "Are you the judge and jury here?"

There's another long silence, then Chance speaks up, "I know it's hard for you. It's hard for us too, believe me. We care about you guys, but we also stand for some things, and one of those things is not selling drugs to kids. Like Susan said, it could cause damage and bring down this whole house and farm. So, it comes down to this—we're asking you to stop or move on."

"So that's it?" Bruce asks. "We're out of here if we deal and deliver?"

"I'm afraid so," Chance answers back opening his palms to them. "It's your choice now." Bruce looks around at Thunder and Sky and motions to them with his hand, and the three of them gather and walk out of the room, leaving this huge vacuum of silence. We are all feeling pretty old, troubled but relieved, and then Ned cries out from the other room.

At work that day at the drive-thru, I ask Frank about the local marijuana growers. He's sitting at his desk in the back room working the books and doesn't answer me at first. I ask again, "So do you know there are local growers or not?"

"Of course, I know, Lee. This little store of ours hears everything. One time or another during the week just about everyone comes in here for somethin' even if just the local gossip. What's the problem, son?"

"I don't know, just wondering who put my younger family members onto it."

He stops whatever he's doing and looks up at me, serious though, "Well, that would be me, I guess. I told Bruce where they could get the stuff."

"You? Well, do you know they're selling the stuff in town, to kids maybe, and they're also dealing LSD?"

"Listen, I don't know nothin' bout no LSD or selling to kids. They're not getting that out here, I'm sure of that. These are local farmers growing the weed they sell, yeah. It's just another crop here in Athens County. And the way small farms are disappearing lately, it's what keeps many of them going."

He's standing up now facing me, pressing the moment, and I don't really know what my next move is. "I hear you," I say, "But, Frank, it's all breaking the law and we're afraid it all might come crashing down on us."

"Huh, I hear you too. And on that score, I guess I'm a dealer myself, only in legal alcohol, but I'm never sure where it's going when I sell a man or woman a six pack. You know? It's the buyer who makes that choice. Hell, my papaw used to sell moonshine on the streets of Athens."

"Oh, my god," I almost laugh, "so did my great grandfather, the one who lived in McArthur. We've got more in common than we knew."

"Well, I'll be damned," he drawls, then says, "Lee, I want you understandin' somethin'. I got nothin' to do with the LSD or any other chemicals they might be dealing. I'm strictly organic, and I don't sell none of it here, 'cause this little burg needs this store, and so do I and my family." He waits before sitting down, leans forward and asks, "Now, are we down with that?"

I rock back and forth on my feet a little, trying to feel my balance like I'm at the end of a diving board, and then I let out a breath and say, "I'm down with that," and get back to shelving the chips and salsa.

Chapter Twenty-Two
Other Roads

I run into the Triangle one more time the following week in the coffeehouse by the bus station. I've been dropping in there after my creative writing class on Thursdays. They are sitting around a table in the back, and at first I look away. I'm really uneasy about meeting up with them after they moved out, but they motion me back. They're sitting with this long bearded dude I've seen around campus, the Pipefitter they call him. I think because he deals in hash pipes at his little head shop up the street.

"Hey and hello," I say pulling up a chair. "How's it going?"

Sky stands up and gives me a warm hug, and I'll admit I do miss her. Thunder doesn't even waste an expression, just stares over at me, then gets up and puts her arms around old Pipefitter, and sits on his lap. She's wearing this little mini that doesn't cover her, but she doesn't seem to care. "Hey, Lee boy, this here is the fourth piece of our little puzzle." I nod to Pipefitter who by then is nuzzling his face into her breasts. "We're headed out west. You want to join us, partner?"

I know I'm being put on, but I try to keep it cool. "Sure, when's the bus leaving."

"Oh we have our own little bus," Bruce says with a grin. "Or Mr. Magic does, I should say." I catch that they've redubbed our pipe maker, so I grin and ask. "You can do that, just take on a new name when you feel like it?"

"Oh, yeah, man," he smiles back at me. "Do what feels right for you. That's cool."

"Bruce," I say because it's my last chance to ask him. "How come you never took on one of these magical names like Sky and Thunder or Magic here?"

He looks at me kind of weird, then nods, "Because, man, I already did. My real name is Rodney." I try to keep a straight face as he goes on, "And, hey man, you see that VW bus parked down the street at the corner? We're taking it all the way to the ocean, hope to stop nowhere but Marin County. Mr. Magic's from Sausalito, and he's packing up his shop and we're heading on-the-road and out of this hick county."

So the Triangle has become a Quadrangle. I don't know what I feel, just that I am happy to see them moving on with a new vision. "I'm real glad for you guys. I mean it." They smile back but no one has anything more to say, so I ask, "Hey, you sticking around to hear the guy from *The Whole Earth* tomorrow?"

They look at each other, then nod. "Yeah, I guess we will," Bruce says for them all. I look over at Marsha-Sky and wink. There is nothing more to say, so I stand up.

"I'm going to get my cup a java and head out. I'll tell the others at the farm."

"Yeah," Thunder says, "you do that." As I'm walking away I realize that these will be the last words we ever say to each other. "Have a good trip," I call out but I'm really thinking *Have a good life, because I'll never see you again.* Then I add, "You all take care," pick up my coffee, and I head out the door.

Back at the house, I go into our room and lie down to steal a nap. Then suddenly Dick comes rushing in. "Lee, Lee, you're the first one I thought of." He gets flush in the face when he's really excited.

"Yeah, what's up?" I ask, trying to wake up and recover some curiosity in the day.

"Well, I just got a call from your friend and mine...Stewart Brand. He wants to know if we can pick him up at the Columbus airport tomorrow afternoon."

"You are shittin' me! Stewart Brand wants us to pick him up?"

"Yessiree, he does. I've been writing him, and he remembered your piece in *The Whole Earth*. They keep track, you know. It's a very low key grassroots kind of operation. See, the journalism department here was to pick him up, but he said no, he'd rather meet up with friends. Told them it's a Native American thing, that it's always best when a friend comes to welcome. I told him we'd be more than glad to do it. So, can you get off to do it?"

"Hell, yeah! I'll quit my job if I have to. Who else is going?"

"Just the two of us. His wife Lois is coming along, so we have to leave room in my little Chevy." He slaps my shoulder and says, "This will be really cool. Just be careful how you tell the others, okay? Remember, he did ask for us."

Sharon is almost as excited as I am at the news, and the family instructs us to invite them out to the farm. "We all want to meet them, you know," Chance says, "not just you lucky dogs." We promise them that we'll bring them back if they are willing.

The drive to the airport is cool, and it's good at times to get out of town. Dick talks some about his trip to Indiana, says, "Now, I beg you not to say anything, Lee." I agree. "But I wasn't just there to present a paper, I was interviewing for some jobs."

"No shit," I say. "So you and Ingrid are thinking of leaving the Farm?"

"Well, I am, yes. I don't know for sure about Ingrid. You'll have to ask her."

"Hmm," comes out of me like I'm humming, and I ask, "Well, aren't you a couple?"

"Yes and no. Honestly, you're the only one I've told about this, not even her. And who knows, nothing might happen. I'm waiting to hear from Indiana University at Bloomington." He looks over at me, "Lee, I love to teach, and I'm really pretty good at it. I know I'll never get back on at OU, so I'm having to move on."

I'm sitting there nodding, trying to take it all in, when he says, "Listen, I love you guys and it wouldn't be easy to leave."

"Well, we wouldn't want to lose you. You've been with us from the start."

We are both quiet for a while, feeling our way into this possibility. He reaches over to play a cassette, but says one more time, "Please, don't say anything about this to anyone back at the Farm."

I hate these secrecy pacts. "Hmm," I say again and let it go as Bob Dylan sings "If Not for You" from his *New Morning* album. "God, I love this song," I say to change the subject.

"Yeah," he agrees and we both just listen.

When we get to the airport's arrival dock, I run in, while he parks the car. When he joins me, I tell him the flight is an hour late and hand him a cup of coffee, the way he likes it, black.

An hour later this couple that can only be them walks up the airport ramp, and we smile and wave like old friends. They're both sun tanned, in jeans, flowered shirts, their backpacks for luggage strapped to their backs. Stewart is tall, blond, and moves quickly. Lois has dark hair in pig tails, and this really sweet face, soft eyes looking at you through dark rimmed glasses. "Hey and hello," I call to them. "Stewart and Lois, we're here from the Free Farm."

Dick and I extend our hands, but they come right up and hug us. "Thank God," Stewart says, "we were afraid we might be met by a committee."

"Hey, you guys," Lois smiles, "thanks for driving out here. How much of a drive is it?"

"About 90 minutes. No problem though," Dick says, "I'm Dick Snyder, and this is Lee McCall, as you probably already guessed."

We head down the walkway, "Are we running late?" Stewart asks.

"Who's keeping time here?" I ask, trying to be cool, then add, "Welcome to Ohio."

"We don't usually fly," Lois says. "Our truck transports us."

"Yeah," Stewart says, "We were in Ohio back in '68, doing our Whole Earth Truck Store, and I believe we stopped in Athens. Didn't we, hon?"

Lois just smiles and tilts her head, "You know, we travelled so much back then, different town every couple days, staying with whoever welcomed us. Good times, but all kind of cloudy now."

"Well," Stewart laughs, "we were high much of the time, you know. It does erase a lot of what happened...kind of a good thing, if you know what I mean."

We're having a light laugh at this, when Dick says, "You folks wait here. I'll go get the car."

"No, are you kidding, man?" Stewart says, "We can use the walk. I hate being cooped up in that airplane air with no place to walk but to the toilet."

I offer to take Lois' backpack, but she waves me off, "No thanks, it's attached to me, so I really don't feel it. Let's walk."

"So," Stewart says as we head out in the March wind, "you folks are growing things, I hear, including a commune. How's that going?"

"Good," I say, "I wrote that piece about it in the 1970 *Catalog.*"

"Oh, yeah, good writing. I remember it. But I'm asking about now. When you're working with alternatives, things can change in a day."

"Yeah, you're right, they have," I say, "mostly for the better. I guess we've made a few mistakes."

Dick chimes in, "We had to ask three members to leave recently."

"Well," Lois says, "as you might know, that's pretty common, and never easy."

"Yep," Stewart says as we reach the car. "Learn from your mistakes, then they're not mistakes. Communes are the best places to make all those wishful mistakes, to get your nose rubbed in your fondest fantasies."

I'm still thinking that over when he opens the door, "Sometimes a mistake works...that's gravy, and an obligation. The *Catalog* was a mistake that worked. Hey, mind if I ride up front, Lee? I like to watch the road get swallowed up."

He continues talking, and I realize it's like reading the *Catalog* where each page is an education. He might be practicing his speech on us, but I love it. He's talking now about how formal education, government, and the church have failed us and themselves. "Their defects outnumber their gains," he says, "We've got to take it back to the individual, create a realm of intimate, person power. That's where the individual conducts his own education, finds his own inspiration, shapes his own environment, and shares that adventure with whoever's interested."

I'm just digging it all seated close beside Lois in the back when she reaches up to rub his shoulders, says, "Okay, Stu, take it easy on these fellows. They've hardly had a chance to speak."

"Oh, my gosh," he says and slaps his knee, "I'm sorry, guys. Just got all this stuff running through my head for the talk tomorrow. I get going sometimes, and a new place like this draws it out of me."

"No, that's fine. I'm digging it really," I say. "I haven't heard anyone talk with real vision for a long time, except maybe in Dick's American Romanticism course when he'd talk on communes."

"Oh, you get paid to teach this stuff?" he chides Dick.

"Well, I used to," Dick says, "but that's a long story. I got canned by the university along with some other faculty protestors. Right now, we're fighting that in court,while I'm doing my work at the Free Farm" Then he thinks to say,

"And Lee here was once my student, now he's my friend and cohort."

"That's super," Stewart says, "And, Lee, let me ask what you're studying now?"

"Education and writing," I say sounding like the sophomore that I am.

"Cool, man," he says. "Those are my interests, along with photography and design. Though, I'm a biologist by training. I hate that word, 'training,' like we're dogs or something. Lois here is into math and education. But you gotta make your own path, Lee. Major in nothing and everything."

"I remember in your article," Lois says to me, touching my arm, "you were setting up a Free School. I'd like to hear about that, maybe see what you've done."

So they are planning to come to the Free Farm. "It's still hatching," I say, "but we'd love to share ideas and show you what we're up to. Susan is really guiding that. She and Carl are part of the commune with their two kids Gracie and Ned. And you'll meet Sharon and Chance and Ingrid, and I guess you already know Charlotte."

"Oh, yeah, ole Char was quite a beauty in the biology department at Stanford. I was really into her, but she not so much," he says this while turning around to look at Lois, "I told you all this, remember?"

"Yes, I recall you're telling me of 'ole Char,'" she says and laughs to let off any tension. "Those were the days when you were taking classes one day and LSD the next in the drug studies. That was before we hooked up."

I have to ask, "And old Charlotte, was she in those experiments?"

"Not that I remember," Stewart says, "but then I don't remember much from that time. It was wild, opened me in ways I can't explain, ways beyond words that are still showing up in this work we're doing. Do you folks trip much at the Farm?" he asks, a touchy question for us right now.

"Some," I say. "This is marijuana country you know. Lots of that going on, second largest crop in Athens County."

"And you grow it at the Farm?" he asks, looking over at Dick who's steady at the wheel.

"Mmm, not really. We're more into vegetables and building the community right now," Dick says.

"Ah," Stewart sighs, "it's all community, all of it." He spreads his hand to the houses we're passing, "All of us. We are each other." There's a long pause after he says this, while we open to the idea. "Say, I see you've got a tape player there; would you like to hear this new one by the Dead? The boys just dropped them off at the Truck Store before we left town. It's called *American Beauty* and fits just right for this land we're driving through, mixes bluegrass and rock, Jerry on steel guitar, David on mandolin. It's really wild and sweet at the same time." He slips it in and the harmony of voices rings out, and for the first time on the drive, he seems to relax. We all do.

Then somewhere near Lancaster, between songs, he says softly, "Lee, while we're staying with you all at the Farm, I'd like to see some more of your writing."

By the time we reach Logan, Stewart is asleep. Lois and I watch the road glide by or talk softly in the backseat. "He couldn't sleep on the plane," she says snuggling up to me. "Tell me, where are you from...originally?"

"Up north of here in the Ohio Valley, a steel mill town near Steubenville," I say just above a whisper.

"I've heard of it, and your folks, what do they do for a living?"

"Mom takes care of the house and my two younger sisters, and Dad's a brakeman on the railroad at Weirton Steel. Oh, and he's also an auto body man. You know, I sent him a copy of the *Catalog*, and he loves it, said he's ordered some stuff."

"Is he Del McCall?" she asks.

"Yeah, how'd you know that?"

"Well, he's ordered over a hundred dollars worth of things. It's a small operation really, and we notice things. So, you're working-class smart, and that's why you're so grounded. I typeset your article, and I remember how it was strong on place and really practical. You took our tools metaphor and applied it to your Farm commune. I liked that, and so did Stu."

"Well, that's great, 'cause I'd like to write for the *Catalog*, research new things and help spread word of them."

She takes her glasses off and looks up at me with dark brown eyes. "Let's talk with Stu about that. Do you mind?" she says and lays her head on my leg. "I'll just catch a cat nap." And I lean my head back against the seat, look up at the sky and think, *Wonder of wonders, I couldn't have even dreamed it like this.*

Outside of Nelsonville, Stewart wakes up, looks around at me and Lois in the back seat, smiles then turns around and flips the Dead's tape around. "Truckin" comes on, and I watch as he starts rockin' to the music. It's a great scene as we pass along the Hocking River and railroad, looking out into the forest; the sun streams in and for me right here and now it feels like the whole earth is rockin'.

Lois wakes up as we roll into Chauncey, gives me a kiss on the cheek and straightens her blouse. She looks out the windows at the hills, "We're almost there," I say.

"What Native Americans were here, Lee? This looks like our kind of country." And I realize her tan skin and black hair are natural.

"Well, some Iroquois went through here, but mostly Shawnee and Cherokee made villages here. But way back it was the Adenas, the mound builders."

"Oh, my God," she gasps. "The Serpent Mounds! Stu, did you hear that, we're in mound builder country."

"Maybe that's what I've been feeling; this is spiritual land, fellows. Say, how close are we to your Farm?"

"About 10 minutes," Dick says.

"Oh, yeah! I can feel it...can't you, honey? A spirit in this land. Wooee!"

I don't know if I should laugh, but I know I feel giddy inside, so I answer back. "Wooee!" and then we all laugh in good spirits.

At the house, I rush in and let Dick show them the way. Sharon is standing at the kitchen counter cutting up carrots and celery. "Honey, they're here! Stewart and Lois are here...and they plan to spend the night."

"Wow," she says and smiles at me. "That's great, but where are they going to sleep?"

I know I'm rushing things but I have to say it, "I thought our room. We can take out some things we need to get dressed in the morning. I'm really sorry. None of us knew. I wished I could have called but we were in the car."

"I wish you could have called too," she echoes. "But come on, let's grab up some things. Fortunately the bed has new sheets."

Charlotte comes in from the back door, and I turn to tell her, "They're here, Charlotte. Dick's bringing them in. And...they're staying the night."

"Great! I'm dying to see old Stu. What are you two up to?"

"We're going to give them our room. We'll sleep in the basement or on the couch. I gotta help Sharon clear some things out."

In the bedroom, for some crazy reason, I grab Sharon, spin her around and really kiss her lips.

"Hey, thanks..." she says pulling back a little, "But what's this all about?"

"I just really love you, and I'm feeling so darn happy right now. Come on, you have to meet them."

"In a minute," she says. "You have to give a woman more than 90 seconds to rid up a room. You go on, I'll be right out."

"Are you sure?" I beg, and she nods, picking up my dirty socks and underwear from the floor. "Wait, I'll do that," I say and stay to help. We can hear the others talking in the kitchen. Chance has come in from the garden.

When we've cleared and gathered up enough, we go to the door, but Sharon takes me by the arm. "Honey, what's really going on?"

"I don't know, I guess I'm high from meeting them, and he said some great things in the car. They both did and they're interested in my writing and my working for them. It might be a way for me...not so much to make a living, but to do something right with my life. It feels as right as my being in love with you."

She doesn't let go of my arm. "Lee, would you have to move out there? Would we?"

"No, I think I could do the work right here in Ohio. Keeping the Farm going would be part of it and reporting its progress or decline. But gosh, I'm getting way ahead of myself. Nothing has really been offered or settled. And, hey, I wouldn't ever leave you for this anymore than I'd go off to Nam. We'd go off to Canada first—together."

Now the kiss is to me, and I accept.

The clan is sitting around the kitchen table chomping on celery and carrot sticks. Stewart is talking, and people are laughing. Ingrid comes down in t-shirt and panties, and Stewart gives her a long look. I introduce Sharon to Lois, and they take the back packs into our bedroom. Carl is taking a nap with the kids, and Susan's drinking peppermint tea at the table.

Chance is grinning at Stewart. "Well, Stu, we're all going to be there tomorrow. The Farm supports *The Whole Earth* and Earth Day." I'm wondering why I'm the only one who calls him Stewart? "Say," Chance asks, "This is March, and I thought Earth Day was in April?"

Lois answers this one, "Well, I guess you haven't heard the new slogan...'Earth Day is Everyday.' We brought some t-shirts with that for you guys."

"Besides," Stewart says, "It fit with Winter commencement here. So we're stretching things a bit. Then he turns to Dick to ask, "I was wondering if you folks use computers."

We look at each other, and Dick shakes his head.

"It's the way things will go," Stewart says. "I'm sure of it...One day we'll all have our own computers sitting on our desks at home to do the new work. They're really just another tool."

"Yeah, well, sorry, but they're technology," Susan disagrees. "Something that can impose itself on us and our whole way of thinking."

"You're right, in a way," he answers, "but it can work the other way around. We can use this tool to create change. We're already using it to print up the text for the *Catalog*. It's all in how you view it, then how you use it. Besides, I think it really can be good for the environment."

"I'm surprised to hear this," Susan says. "I thought it was all back to the Earth that you were practicing out there."

"Well," Stewart says, "You know what the *Catalog* says, 'We are as gods and we might as well get good at it,' and I'm thinking of adapting that to 'We are as gods and HAVE to get good at it, if we are to survive.'"

"Stu," Charlotte asks. "How'd you come round to this big vision thing? If I remember back at Stanford you were doing the LSD testing, smoking pot, taking photos, and only occasionally showing up at the bio lab."

"Ah," he sighs loudly, "ain't life grand. It's got so many surprises for us. And I don't know if that LSD didn't just open me up to this new potential. Hell, I was in the Army you know, and it could have ruined me, but instead it taught me organizing. It's how you view things or how you don't that makes the difference."

"Stewart," I ask, "Did you ever read the American Romantic writers, Emerson and Thoreau? Were they part of your original vision?"

"Oh, sure, Lee. We still haven't caught on to all that those early birds were awakening us to. I was reading *Walden* back in my army days. Their books are always listed in the *Catalog*. But folks like you are putting it into practice, and that's where the new lessons are. This little poem was in the last *Whole Earth*, I memorized it for my talk tomorrow: 'Think of community—/ you think of together:/ being—/ living— / eating—/shitting—/ freaking—/ working—/ it's not like we got to/ get it together/ we got to/ see that we are.' I love it, and you people are living it."

There is actual applause at this, then Lois speaks up, "You'll have to forgive us our kind of forcing on you this invitation to stay, but neither of us wanted to be in some Motel Six trapped between the television screen and the parking lot, then picked up by a department head or his lackey. We're with you, and we really do thank you."

"Hey, let's play that new tape of the Dead." Stewart says. "The guys brought it in just this week, and it's great, so we can all be really grateful." We forgive him his pun, and Chance takes the tape and pops it in. Some of us move over to the couches and light up. Sharon takes Lois by the hand to show her around the place.

At dinner that evening, we talk more about where the whole movement is headed. Stewart and Lois have been to most of the larger communes in the country, and Dick runs down the list, calling them out for us: Morning Star, New Buffalo, Black Bear Ranch, Drop City and the Hog Farm.

"Those last are probably the oldest," Stewart says, "and a couple of the best. We've been to most, big and small, far out wild and down home farm-like. They're each unique, and that's part of the beauty of it all. Like I was telling Lee, one reason we promote communes is that there's no better place to make all the wishful mistakes, to get your nose rubbed in it. And when a mistake works, that's gravy, and you have to pass it along." He looks around. "Lois," he says, "you talk some. Tell them what you dig."

"Well, first of all, I don't think you can really dig the commune lifestyle unless you live it, like you folks are doing here. It's not ice cream to take a lick; you have to eat the whole cone and get your hands all sticky." Susan leads the laughter at this.

"And I'll tell you," Lois goes on, "what draws me is the intimacy, the way you develop a new tribe, a horizontal extended family. Everything is shared, the love and the labor."

Susan speaks up, "We get you, really. Carl and I, we needed to leave the suburbs and find a new way for us and our kids. One night a year ago, we're lying in bed and I'm looking up at the ceiling and I say it out loud, 'There's a crack in it all.' And he sees it too, says, 'The crack is in the system...in the values of this consumptive society.' We lay there seeing it and knowing we had to get out and embrace a better way." She looks around, holds her hand out to Charlotte, "and then we found you and the Farm."

We're quiet for a long moment then Charlotte says, "This may sound cliché now, but I'm going to say it anyway. We need a culture which acknowledges the human body, not just for sex, but to hug each other, and be naked without shame. And we want to honor the body with natural foods, yoga, meditation, herbs, baths, massage, and a deep understanding."

"Wow!" Stewart says, "you said it, Char. And this vision isn't part of the immediate culture we came from, so we have to make it new, and it's happening everyday all around us. We're leading a way out of darkness." We're all nodding at this, when he adds, "But I gotta tell you all that some of these communes aren't too fond about what we're doing at *Whole Earth*. They know we support them, but they think we should drop out, leave the system, and start a whole new one."

"Yeah," I say, "what do you say to them? I mean we're struggling with that too. Most of us are still going to classes, working part-time jobs somewhere else. How do you answer that?"

"I tell them, if they'll listen, that we're changing the system from within, we're not only taking the road less travelled, we're making it into a highway. And they're all part of it, and we're just communicators at *The Whole Earth*, translators maybe for the whole culture."

"This is great," Chance says. "We're part of something bigger even if we can't see it all. But let me ask you, Stu, since we want to survive, how do some of these communes pay their bills?"

"Well, that's a good question. Some run coffeeshop bookstores, some do farmer's markets, veggie restaurants; some make things like meditation pillows, hash pipes, musical instruments. You know, Lois, we ought to write these solutions up in the next supplement to the catalog. Lee, maybe you could research and write it up for us as your first assignment. Lee's going to work for us."

Now this is the first I have heard this from Stewart. I'm sitting on the floor, thankfully, and I can't even swallow so I just nod, my heart in my throat. Finally, I say, "Yeah. I'll do that. Maybe you or Lois can give me some names and addresses."

"You're on," he says. When I look up everyone is smiling down on me.

Chapter Twenty-Three
The Circle Games

Before Stewart and Lois leave, we shake on a contract. I'm to be paid for the length of my articles and some sense of how much time they took for research. I'll be paid by the Portola Foundation, the nonprofit that funds the whole thing. On the way to the airport, he tells me, "Listen, Lee, *The Catalog* is just the first step in this co-evolution we're about. It may cease or it may go on without me, but either way, we have much more work to do." The guy is full of surprises and turns, like this road I'm trying to follow. "Right now," he says, "I'm so into the design and social theories of Buckminster Fuller—not just his geodesic domes, though we're promoting those everywhere, but his theories of cybernetic design and communication. It's all part of USCO's engagement with the techno-centric visions of social transformation."

I'm driving buddha-bug with him up front, Lois and Sharon asleep in the back after our late night of talking, so I have no protection from his bombardment of ideas. I nod and hold off telling him that I have no idea what the hell he's talking about. I figure I'll be researching it all soon enough. At the airport parking garage, I get out first to let off some steam, take Sharon's hand as she climbs out from the back. "My god," I whisper to her. "I love this guy, but save me from his talk, please." She brushes back her hair and leans a kiss into my neck standing there. She has this short skirt on, and her fine legs beckon to me. I take a deep breath and find relief in contemplating the drive back beside her.

We take them right up to their loading area where great hugs are passed around. Sharon and I have really come to like Lois, and I trust that she'll remember all of our understandings. Stewart will keep rolling ...Onward...as they say. Before she boards, Lois says, "Remember, you're one with us, both of you. Peace and love."

Stewart's farewell is simple, "You two, stay together and travel light."

We don't even leave the parking lot before I devour Sharon's oh-so-smooth legs and tender bottom. Her warm lips on my neck, mine on her breast, and we are alive again in our bodies in the Columbus Airport parking lot.

The days go by quick that week, and at dinner Wednesday night, Dick tells us that one of his teaching buddies at the university wants to bring his students out to the Farm. "Jake is teaching my old course in American Romanticism, and he wants to show them a functioning commune," he explains. "What do you think? I'd say we're functioning."

"How would this work out?" Carl asks handing Gracie a hard cookie for dessert; hers have to be gluten free, and so she makes a face.

"Is this it?" Gracie asks looking up.

"Yes, it is," Susan says and looks back at Dick. "So how would this visit go? I'm wondering. Do we have a plan?"

"Well, this is a first for us," Dick answers and looks around at the others. "Any ideas?"

"I say we sit around naked passing the pipe, with some of that Black Russian Stu and Lois left us," Chance jokes, with a mocking face to lighten the mood.

"We could still say 'no,'" Dick says. "I told him I'd talk with the family."

"Well, I like this idea," Sharon says, surprising me some. "We could learn from it, makes us reflect on who and what we are. It could be good."

"Yeah," Chance says, "And we might get more recruits to fill the empty basement left by the void of the Triangle."

"Well," Carl speaks up, "I don't think we need to be recruiters. I hate that term for obvious reasons...though we do have that space available."

"Yes, some new faces and bodies," Ingrid says, and Chance and I grin. "...to help with the work," she quickly adds.

"Okay," I say, "Let's stay with the questions at hand. Do we want visitors, and if so, how would we handle things? Would we just be doing what we always do or would we sit and share with them? How many people are we talking about, Dick?"

"He said it's a small class, junior seminar, about 10, I think. They could come out on a Saturday morning or afternoon."

"Wow," Chance grins, "I'm really digging this! Feels like we're here for something more than ourselves."

"I agree," Sharon adds, pulling out the great Free Farm Notebook. "I'll take notes on this if it's okay."

Charlotte rises from the table, asks, "How about we take a 15 minute break and clean up all of these dishes, then talk it over at the Gathering Space." The Gathering Space is also the Free School, where we've made built-in benches along three walls. They're wall-seats actually that open for storage, leaving the floor space for little tables and activities. Carl's idea really, with Susan's sanction. We agree to meet up there in 15 and all pitch in with the cleaning up.

Sharon and I walk up to the Free School over muddy spring ground. At the crest we look back at the great valley below us. A golden sunlight is spread across the fields like in a Van Gogh painting, and we're speechless before it, yet not immune to each other's touch. Others pause with us at the doorway, take some long, deep breaths of spring air, then enter. The electricity has been in for a month, thanks to Carl, so that all we need do now is throw the switch. Sitting together in the warm light we look around at each other in the little room. We are a unit yet part of something larger, the whole community out there, the alternative wave. Talking and listening we come up with a plan. Charlotte and Chance will welcome them around 11:00. We'll all be working at whatever needs done that day, maybe Susan and Sharon will be up at the Free School, and we'll just let our visitors roam around for a while talking to each of us. Then we'll share a lunch of fresh bread, meatless chili, and a garden salad. The lettuce is already coming along. We'll go scriptless, just be who we are where we are and let things happen. We form our circle, say our mantra, and tonight a bottle of Mateusz wine is shared. Some stay talking inside, while Sharon and I sit on a log outside and watch the sun set.

When I arrive home from work today, Sharon greets me at the back door. "Wait a minute," she says, puts her hand on my chest. "Let's talk outside. I have news from home."

Just glad to be home from work, I take her hand and we walk around the side of the house. At the bench she stops, "Let's sit," she says, and we do. "Don't get upset, no one is hurt, but there's trouble at your folk's place."

"What, what's going on? Is Dad alright?"

"Yes, like I said, he's okay, and so's your mom. It's your brother Dave." I'm pressing her hand hard. "Okay," she says, "I'll just say it, he's home from school."

"It's only late March! What's up?" I wish she'd just say it.

"He's been expelled from Brown."

"Expelled! That's what they do in high school. I think you mean kicked out. How does a brainiac like him get booted from a school like that?" I stare at her face. Nothing. "What did he do? Come on, tell me."

"Well, your mom wouldn't say exactly. She's the one who called, and she was pretty upset. She cried on the phone a couple times, and then she said they need you to come home this weekend...to help out."

This has me spinning, and I simply say, "I'll call her in a little while. I gotta sit with this a minute." I'm feeling winded like when my kid's sled ran into that parked car and knocked the breath out of me. Dave was leaning over me then, and he told the others, "Just leave him alone. He's coming around." Like that, only now it's he who's knocked the wind out of me. "You know," I say to Sharon, "Mom won't even come down here to visit until we're married, and she wants me to run home for Dave's little mess. It's not fair."

She touches my hand, and I almost pull away, when she says, "Oh, honey, you can't ask for fair. Deal with what you've got."

"Listen," I plead, "Think about it. There's nothing I can do. I've got this research I'm working on right now, and those college kids are coming out this weekend."

"I know," she says. "It's hard."

"Damn right, it is. And my going home is not going to fix things, now is it?"

"Oh, Lee, honey, that's not why we go home."

"Well, what is?" I ask.

She touches my cheek, brings her face up close to mine, those clear blue eyes, and says what I both know, "We go home because we love each other."

When I call home, Dad answers, "Hello, Lee, good you called. How are things?"

"We're fine, Dad. Listen, Mom called," I let that sink in then cut to it. "What's happening with Dave?"

A long silence. "He's home now."

"Yeah, but what's up...he in some kind of trouble?"

"Well, yes and no. The school sent him home, suspended or expelled. I don't know what they call it."

"Dad, come on, tell me, for what?" While I'm waiting, my old roommate Tom pops into my head and the way the school mistreated him.

"I guess he was doing drugs," Dad says. "Selling them too."

"What kind of drugs, Dad? Marijuana, LSD, what?"

"Cocaine, they said. He was selling it to other college kids and got caught at a fraternity party. An undercover policeman arrested him."

"Is he facing charges?" I ask.

"No, that's the good thing. It was campus police, and they've kept it there, but he won't be allowed back, so I guess it's expelled."

"Jesus!" comes out of me. "What was he into?"

"Son, I don't know. He'll only tell us so much and won't come out of his room. That's why we thought you might come home and talk with him. We don't know what to do."

"Okay," I say, thinking it through, "I'll head home tomorrow. You guys hold it together. He's a good kid. He'll come around. Tell him..." I don't know what to say, so I say, "Tell him I love him."

*   *   *

It's a long lonely drive back home to Mingo, and I know I'm being mournful and blaming Dave for it all. Sharon and I agree that she should stay and help at The Farm, so it's just me and the FM radio driving north. There's construction on Route 7, so I have to cross over into West Virginia at Marietta. There's a lot of gospel radio still in this part of the Appalachians, and for a while I follow bluegrass songs into a woman shouting the gospel—"Bring it to the Lord" kind of thing. "All your sorrows," she moans twice, "The Lord will make them right. But, dear ones, listen to me. You got to live right," she shouts, "Cast those sins aside," the audience roars, and I am about to turn her off when she says another thing: "I'll warn you now. Don't fall in love with your pain and sorrows, like I did. Oh, no, sweet Jesus, or you will drink yourself blind to all the good that surrounds you." She goes on into a list of sins and paints the hellfire pretty good. I do turn the radio off, but I think about her saying it—how we fall in love with your pain—for the next hour or so, from Marietta up to New Martinsville.

I drive through Moundsville, then on into Wheeling, old river cities struggling to survive, and I pass that bus station where Sharon met me one winter night. At a traffic light, I look around at the people out shopping, an old woman holding the hand of a young boy as they cross Market Street. A doorman stands outside the old hotel talking to one of the town's two taxi drivers. I toot, and they look up and wave, though they don't really know me. At Route 40, I cross the bridge back over to Ohio and come out at the Bridgeport intersection near the Lucky Star Bar and Grille, its welcome sign still glowing. I wave to it and to Gladys inside who's probably still serving burgers and wondering about her boy in Nam. In Martins Ferry, I can't help thinking of its poet James Wright and his mournful and tender poems of our homeland: "My grandmother's face is a small maple leaf/...Locusts are climbing down into the dark green crevices/ Of my childhood. Latches click softly in the trees. Your hair is gray/" something...and then he ends on "the red shadows of steel mills." I'm passing them now, those mills, my hands gripping the familiar steering wheel as I bless our buddha-bug for bringing me home.

I knock then enter the old front door—feels right, even though I've been living away so long. The house seems empty, but there's a note on the kitchen table, "Lee, welcome home. We've gone out to get fish sandwiches for dinner. Dave is up in his room." I look up at the kitchen clock; it's already 5:00. I check the fridge and get out a beer, two of them, then head right upstairs to talk.

Again I knock, this time at my own bedroom door. "Dave, it's me." Nothing. "Come on, I got us some beer. I want to see you." Silence again, but I wait it through. I can hear him rustling around.

Finally, I hear, "Come in," and I open the door slowly. He is sitting on his bed buttoning his shirt. I want to go to him, but hang off.

"Hey, bro," I say.

A weak "Hey," comes back.

"Dark times, huh?" I dare to state. He stares back at me.

"Why'd you come home?" he asks, and his dark eyes tell me I'm a threat. The disgrace of the golden boy casts a different light on me.

"Ah, you're pretty direct," I say sitting down on my old bed. "I guess I wanted to be here for you and the family, that's all."

"Well, you can head right back, because I don't need anything from you. You can't solve this one."

"I know that, believe me," I say and lean forward a little, remembering Sharon's words, "I came because I love you, brother."

He looks right at me, and allows me to read all the hurt inside. I don't speak, I get up and go over to sit beside him, wrap my arm around his tight shoulders. We sit like this for a while, then I say softly, "We'll get through this, Dave. We will."

"It's me," he says, "I created this shitty mess. I have to clean it up somehow." Then through tears, "Oh god, I hurt Mom...Dad...the girls, even you, bro. I didn't mean to. I lost myself to the stuff, started using hard...had to sell to get a supply."

"Okay, I hear you. That stuff can eat you alive. But what's happening for you now?"

"I'm not using, but I cant' sleep, fear and darkness everywhere. I start to get up, but can't get out of this damn bed." He stands up. "This, this sitting up is major."

I don't want to say the wrong thing, and so just say, "It's hard for you."

"Yes," he nods. "Each day I hope it'll get easier, but it doesn't." He shakes his head, "Shit, man, I want to be myself again." I just nod and he sits back down beside me. "I'm glad you're home," he says.

"And I'm glad you're home too," I say.

An hour later, when they come home from Mike's Place with the fish sandwiches, they find Dave and me sitting at the kitchen table drinking coffee and talking. Mom breaks down in tears and hugs both of us really hard. Dad smiles at us like he does at his cars, and the girls giggle and run around laying out the fish and chips. We unwrap the sandwiches, still warm and steamy, lay them and the fries on their papers, and eat together as a family, without plates or forks.

Diane comes and leans on my arm. Janie is getting prettier, looking more like a young woman. They tell me little stories of their lives, and I just listen. "And how's Sharon doing?" Mom finally asks. "You two still together?"

I swallow and pause. "Yes, we are, Mother, for now and forever. We love each other." Enough said on that, I surprise them with, "Dave and I have decided something." They all look up from their sandwiches. "He's coming back with me for a while to work on the Farm."

Dad nods repeatedly as he lets it sink in. "Is this what you want, Dave?"

But Mom breaks in, "Oh, I don't know, Lee. I don't think he's ready."

It's Dave who has the next words, "Listen, everyone. I love you all, but I think..." He begins to choke up but pushes through it, "I think this is really a good plan for me." He swallows and looks right at Mom. "I'm not ready to start school or a job anywhere, and I don't know when I will be." Mom comes over to him, strokes his hair, but he goes on, "Dad and Mom, I swear I'm not using anything, and I don't ever want to again. But right now it's making me so damn sad and helpless. I've made a terrible mess, and I know I'm bringing you all down. I need a safe place for a new start, and..." He surprises me now by taking hold of my hand, "My big brother Lee and his friends are welcoming me in." He's still shaky but these first steps are his own.

No one says anything, then Diane looks around and bursts out with, "Family, let's celebrate. Break out the cake and ice cream, Mom."

I don't let on, but I haven't spoken of any of this with Sharon or the family at the Farm, but my gut tells me it's right and will work. I welcome the drive back together.

Before we head back, Dad takes me to his new body shop on lower Commercial Street, Otto's old car dealership.

Kenny is there working on a Ford Mustang that was in a wreck. "Hey, man" he calls to us in his coveralls. "This one's for you."

Dad shakes his head, waves him off. "No, this one'll be for Dave, when it's all done." He looks over at me, "Is that okay?"

I look back, "Why you asking me? Hey, I'm a VW man. I love my buddha-bug."

They both make faces, but we all laugh it off. "Lee," Kenny says, "I hardly recognized you through that beard you got all over your face. And look how long your hair is, man! Del, you allow him to look like this?"

Dad grins and shrugs, "I've lost control, can't remember when I last had it. But, hey, Lee, come look at this Studebaker we're working on. It's like Grandpa Ernie's."

Before I leave I invite Kenny back down to the Farm, tell him, "Dave's coming back with me now for a while." He looks up and nods.

"Good plan," he says, then in low voice, "You keep a close eye on him, you hear?"

"Got ya," I say, and Dad and I head out.

When we get back to the house, I call Sharon. "Honey, some news. My brother Dave is coming back with me. He'll live at the house for a while, at least till he gets it together."

"Okay," she says and waits.

"He's clean but in a really dark place right now. Can you break the news to the others?"

I can tell it's sinking in, 'cause her voice relaxes. "Okay, I'm hearing you," she says. "And, I'll let this family know. You sure this is best?"

"Yes, I am. He needs a fresh start, Sharon. And like you said...he's my brother and I love him."

"And I do too, Lee. He's a part of you and us. It'll be alright. I'll get the basement ready. There's still a cot down there, and a sleeping bag somewhere."

"Great, he can sleep with the dragon and dolphin," I joke.

And she comes back with, "Beats the snakes and rats, I guess."

"I love you," I say, "I'll be home soon."

Sunday morning after church and noon dinner, we are about to head out. Our bags are packed, Dave's are full of books. His guitar is stuffed into the back seat. "Wait," I tell him. "I forgot to do something. I'll be back in 20 minutes tops." And I head down through the yards, past the old garage where they now park the Pontiac, and over the fence on through Sharon's old back yard. There's been this light spring rain in the night and the grass is wet. Shirley smiles to see me at the door and gives me a nice hug in her house coat. "Get in here," she says. "I just pulled some cinnamon rolls from the oven." The sweet smell is overwhelming, and we sit at the table with coffee.

"The kids are at the movies," she says. *"Black Beauty* is playing. God, I loved that book when I was young...decades ago. Hope they didn't muck it up in the film." And before I can answer, she jumps to, "So, you and my daughter got any plans to tie the knot?"

"Hmm," I say, "We're working on it." I look right into her eyes, "I do love her you know?"

"Oh, hell yes, I know that. You maybe don't realize how lucky you are to already have that. That's a good place to start is what I'm saying."

"Ah, Shirley," I sigh, rising to go. "Everything's moving so fast, but we're doing great and someday we'll get married, and you'll be the...well, the second or third person to know, I promise. For right now I gotta head out. I'm taking my brother Dave back with me."

She nods. "Good, that'll help. Your mom's been pretty upset for days now. We talk now," she says and comes over to plant a kiss on my cheek. "You're a good man, Lee. Give that to my daughter, will you?"

"You know I will," I say and head back through the wet grass to the Bug and brother Dave.

We are almost to Brilliant without speaking, when I ask, "You all right, Dave?"

He lets out a sigh, "Forgive me, bro, but I'm suddenly so sleepy. I haven't slept much all week. Okay if I doze off?"

He doesn't wake till we reach Marietta. Driving him to Athens this way, I feel somehow strange, like a father taking his son to college, or me bringing Mingo to the Farm. A little further down the road, I'll ask him to take the wheel.

Chapter Twenty-Four
Rites and Passages

Dave drives for the last hour and I watch him become excited at the hills and streams, the way the road lifts you up along a ridge and slowly sets you down in deep hollows, green forest all around. "This is really neat," he says, "Reminds me of when we were kids riding our bikes out the old New Road to first bridge." At Millfield, I guide him past Frank's drive-thru, then point the way out of town to Sweet Hollow Road, then home. "That's it?" he asks. "That's the town?" I nod and direct the way up ahead, and he takes us there, each turn a discovery for him, a coming home for me. At our final turnoff he says, "This is what I need, man,...a place far enough away to find myself again."

At the house, Sharon is standing in the yard and greets us with a hello kiss, first Dave and then me. I hold her and don't want to let go. She's been watching for us. "Come on, you two" she says and takes Dave's arm. "It's good to have you here. I saved you some dinner in the oven. Lee, you show your brother around while I set it out. The others just now went up to the Gathering Space." One thing about Sharon, is her ability to be present while moving forward. With me it's always one or the other. I get so focused I can't see around me or beyond.

While Dave relieves himself in the bathroom, she whispers to me, "Honey, the class visit went great. I'll tell you about it later. More important, the family is okay with

Dave's moving in for now. And, hey, he looks better than you described."

"Yeah," I say, "he's looking better hour by hour."

When we head down to the basement, Dave looks around, sees into the corners of the place. "No mold," he says, then stands before the painted murals, arms out and looking back at me. It's a Kodak, and I wait, as he grins. "A hippie haven, just what Mom feared most."

I laugh with him, then I touch his arm. "I gotta tell you something, Dave. We had to ask the last threesome who lived here to leave when we found they were dealing drugs in town. Just to let you know. We smoke and pop some tabs, and a few of us have tried peyote, but we don't sell coke or meth or DMT or STP or any of that shit. You understand? House rules."

He stares back into my eyes. "You honestly think I'd do that here? I'm running from the stuff, man. It's ruined my life." His sharp eyes echo my own.

"Sorry, bro, I believe you. But if that stuff does come chasing you here, you know help is near. You're not off in some college; you've got family here, and by that I mean the whole fucking bunch of us."

"Sweet," he says. "I hear you."

In early twilight we walk with Sharon up the crest to the Gathering Space. Inside are all the others sitting along the walls in the glow of two lamps. Charlotte, who remembers Dave from Mingo, comes over and gives him a warm hug. "This is my brother Dave," I say to the others. "He's with us if you'll have him."

Chance and Carl and Dick come forward. "As part of the Brotherhood," Chance says, "we welcome you." Men hugs are shared. Then Susan and Charlotte, Ingrid and Sharon come next, "As part of the Sisterhood," Charlotte says, "we welcome you." Hugs and kisses are passed all around, and I see lines of happiness breaking in my brother's face.

I look around and ask, "When did all this brother and sisterhood thing evolve?"

"Last night," Chance says, "when we decided to accept Dave into our family. We saw your devotion as brothers, and it felt like what we have here. Makes a kind of heart sense, doesn't it?"

"Hell, yeah," I say grinning, then I try singing the line: "He ain't heavy, he's my...brother." My voice is not that great but suddenly Chance and Carl join in, "The road is long...and many a winding turn..." Dick joins us in crooning till we run out of words and echo, "He ain't heavy, he's my...brother." We laugh, but it's clearly a fine moment.

"Was that Neil Diamond?" Charlotte asks.

"Nope," Dave says, "The Hollies...they had the original on that in '69."

"Hey, a guy who knows his music," Carl laughs. "That could come in handy, brother," and they slap palms.

*　　　　　*　　　　　*

For days and weeks in March, we begin work outside, digging and turning soil, extending the organic garden into the fields. Dave, who often comes to campus with me, and joins in with the labor of the farm. His appetite grows for food and life. Chris stops by from time to time to teach us how to plow with the tractor and to offer advice on crops. Under Charlotte's direction we get in our onions and early lettuce, along with other veggies: beets, Brussel sprouts, cabbage, carrots, cauliflower, broccoli, even some leeks and turnips. Chris helps us lay out the upper field for a May planting of corn. "You're hippie farmers now," he jokes, "You have to watch the weather and seasons along with the rest of us." Everything is so damn fertile, you can taste it in the air.

Sharon has been having bad headaches lately, and so has gone off the pill. We have to use rubbers again and watch closely. I hate that calculation, like rubbing sticks together to start a fire, but I love the touch of her, the taste of her skin, the warmth of being in her. We do what we must to stay close.

*　　　　　*　　　　　*

Spring arrives early by the third week of March with sights and sounds all around us. Fresh green after February thaws, the press of soft earth beneath us, the ripe smell of life among the woods, the birds at mornings and twilight. Standing by our hoes, Dave turns to me, "Hey, man,"

"Yeah," I say taking a break.

"If you guys will have me, I'm going to stay on and take classes here in the fall."

"Hell, yeah, that's great. After we're done here, call and tell the folks."

"I already did," he laughs, and I slap his shoulder. Grinning he says, "I figured, one way or another, I'm hanging around."

The Free School is ready for launching come June, and we've posted fliers around campus and in town at the churches and drive-thru. We only need nine, besides Gracie. At Susan's suggestion we've come up with a "stay dressed" practice during school hours. Since the visit by Stewart and Lois, I've written three articles for *The Whole Earth*, and they're printing them in October. Hell, the government is even cutting the troops to Nam. Things are really working out, and I begin to feel hopeful if not optimistic. At our Sunday gathering, the family makes plans for a Spring Equinox Celebration under a full moon. We agree to invite Chris and Margo to join us.

A golden sun is setting in the west, as we move up the hill. The women are all in flowered dresses with ribbons streaming from their hair. Under their direction, we men have set candles along the crest of the hill and in a circle around our big fire pit. Bright colored eggs have been set out with bowls of sunflower seeds and raisin, dates and figs on the railroad ties we hauled in last month. Pretty much it's the Sisters who planned this. Some things they're just more attuned to, and the spiritual is among them. Chris and Margo have come up to join us. Sharon is lovely in a flowered peasant skirt and a sheer blouse that almost reveals her nipples and makes my heart beat. Somehow her confidence at exposing her body makes me less jealous. Little Gracie looks like a May Queen with flowers woven into her blonde hair. The women stand around the fire as we gather.

Finally the gong is rung and each takes a turn with a spring blessing.

Charlotte lights a candle and begins, "Welcome all. We witness tonight this turning of the wheel and now we invite you each to look to the North...let's breathe it in... and out. Now we turn to the South, breathe again, in,...and out. Now we make our turn to the West, another long breath, in...and out. Oh, sisters and brothers we turn at last to the East with our breath, in...and now out. Our days and nights are equal now, as we face the light." She looks up to the night sky. "We pause together and stand in balance here, to honor and welcome the spring season and to reflect on our blessings."

She passes the candle to Ingrid, who bows to her then faces the fire, "This first fire of the new year is the Spring Equinox, fire of the East. It opens our minds and our hearts to rebirth." She raises her candle to the night. "We plant new seeds of our intentions and bring awareness to our actions."

There is a pause, then Susan bows and takes the candle, "Oh, brothers and sisters, these sticks and branches we've brought for the fire represent what we are releasing ...and what we are inviting. This offering rekindles our inner fire, reminding us of our spiritual purpose." We all stand moved in the glow, listening to the gentle sputter of the fire. It feel like a dream, yet I look around at all that's real.

Finally, Sharon bows to Susan, takes the candle and in her most mellow sweet voice, says, "Family and friends, we invite you to lift your arms up in an arc with me, stretch them upward to the sky...now allow heaven and earth to meet, sun and moon to kiss, press you palms and slowly bring them down before your heart space. Let's do this again," and we follow her slowly three times. At the end of the third, she says, "Breathing in, I find peace...breathing out, I am free. Now open your palms and extend them outward toward the fire...allowing compassion to spread in every direction." We stand like this in deep silence except for the crackling of the fire, the March wind. Even the birds have grown quiet. "Willingly we burn away all that does not serve and invite our deepest desires to surround us during each Earth cycle. We bless the coming light."

And then all five, including Gracie now, slowly remove their clothes, lie them gently on the bushes and stand beautifully naked and innocent in moon and fire light. We men join them. Chris and Margo do not hesitate. The women look to each other and together say, "We are one. Join hands." I am holding Dave's hand and Sharon's hand as we begin to circle the fire, slowly at first till we get our footing, then more surely and steady, again and again. As we dance under the fullest moon that has ever been, we drink its light and fill with warmth. Food and drink is passed around, nuts and berries and juice. Sounds of laughter and joy surround us as slowly we don our clothes again.

Back in our cozy bed and protected only by our love, Sharon and I make love deep into the night.

In morning light, we lie there breathing together a long time, listening for the birds, and then she whispers to me, "I don't know if we started anything last night, but I'd like to keep trying."

Without thought or reason, I answer back, "I do..." And she softly echoes me, sealed with our tender kiss amidst the morning cries of birds.

The Epilogue
Onward

Still learning by going, we've moved on with our shared lives at The Free Farm. The river flows and turns and yet remains. Some things you'd probably like to know, so here's the latest.

First off, the university settled with the teachers they had fired last June. Though no public admission of wrong doing, they agreed to hire any of them back on a one-year term lectureship or they would pay each person a year's salary for the lost work year. Charlotte refused the lectureship, and settled for her cash option of $15,000 and ownership of her research. The cash she put into a banking account for The Free Farm, so now we have an FE number and some security if crops fail. That same week Chris let us know that the tractor won't last much longer. "Hell, man, it was as old as you when you bought it."

Dick wrestled with the options for a while, but in the fall, he'll start teaching again in the OU English department. Oh, and we co-authored an article on "Early Communes in America" for what Stewart's been calling *The Last Whole Earth Catalog*. I pray it's not the last, but he writes that he's taking a break and working on something new that's to evolve as the *CoEvolution Quarterly*. Ingrid's still with Dick, and she's now training for massage therapy at the Hocking College in Nelsonville. She'll have lots of naked bodies to get her hands on.

Dave has found a girlfriend, Lisa, in one of the Free University classes on gender differences. It's funny, 'cause she's as smart or smarter than he is. She's tall with long dark hair and hangs out here often, though she hasn't moved in yet. It may happen, or he may move in with her in town. He has to find his own path, I know, but so far he's following a straight one and knows that he's not alone.

The Free School opened at the end of May with a full enrollment of 10, counting Gracie. It's paying for itself and more, with some folks working it out co-op, aiding Susan as teacher. Sharon loves working with her. They talk about each child like he or she is their own. I help out as aide and general custodian. We're going to add on another room when things settle down some. Carl's designing it, and he's taken a job with a Green company bringing Buckminster Fuller's Geodesic domes to southern Ohio, most for people, some surprisingly for livestock. Carl and Susan and the kids are living in one now at the back of the property near the school.

When Dick and Ingrid togehter went down to check out Stephen Gaskin's big farming commune in Tennessee, he confided, "Hey, Lee, down there, if you're having sex with someone, they consider you engaged. And if she's pregnant, they say you're married." He shook his head in disbelief, but didn't say anything. He also returned with Rupert James and his wife Elizabeth who moved into the spare bedroom. Rupe's helped us harvest some trees and cut timber, and Liz is great with identifying wild herbs.

On the learning from our ignorance side, we lost a good bit of the corn crop. First off Ingrid came running in saying "The corn is down. The corn is down." And it was leaning on its side, so we hippie caregivers went out to help straighten it with our hands. Later Chris shook his head, said "Listen, corn does this, and it will right itself again after a storm." It's true, but not the ones we managed to break off by our overconcern. Next we had the corn earworms

Chance and Charlotte are still together, though no talk of marriage. It's funny how they know each other enough to anticipate every move, every word, and maybe that unspoken bond is enough for them. They just got back from a week at Ram Dass's place up in New Hampshire—lots of chanting, dancing, and listening to the quiet word. They were filled with light and brought back pamphlet copies of *Be Here Now* for each of us, and so the path opens wider. Chance now leads us in kirtan chanting before our silent meditation.

I guess the biggest change is with Sharon and me. On June 22nd, we celebrated the Summer Solstice here—not with moon dancing, because there was no moon that night, but during the early evening before the sun began to set on the longest day of the year. We had set up a ritual around the fire circle, and both of our families were there...the Free Farm and our Mingo families—Sharon's mom, sisters and brother, and my folks. They came for more than the Solstice though, but for another rite, and shared in both. Susan performed the ceremony in a white robe she'd sewn, and we all circled round the fire in light summer clothes. It was great to see Mom and Dad standing there in the glow of the fire, Janie and Diane in flowered dresses.

Sharon was lovely beyond words, and I looked my best. I'd shaven my beard down to a mustache and goatee, and I wore a crown because I felt like a king that day. Chance played guitar while Carl drummed. The rite, of course, was our wedding ceremony. And though Sharon wondered whether people could tell if she were showing at two and a half months, she had nothing to worry about. She wore that same sheer blouse with a full golden skirt, only this time it was she who had flowers in her hair. The others were in yellows and golds, and though no one "gave" anyone away at the wedding, Sharon asked Dad if he would stand beside her, and I had Dave at my side while Mom looked on. What moved us to take this next step was really everything that had happened, lately but really for all of our lives. We felt a part of the great movement of the sun slowly and surely passing over in its path.

Susan began with a blessing on the Earth and on all of those who love, but especially on couples. I have a copy and it goes like this: "I invite you to renew your devotion to each other, just as Nature renews herself this day of our summer Solstice. We come with herbs, incense, and soaps as signs of cleansing. This is a time of fullness, and of blessing and celebration. We honor the love today of two of our family...Sharon and Lee." Someone started an applause, and I know I blushed from the sheer joy of it all. Sharon took my hand and we pledged our vows. First Susan guided us through what she had prepared, "I take you, Sharon, to be my wife from this time onward, to join with you and to share all that is to come, to be your faithful husband to give and to receive, to speak and to listen, to inspire and to respond; a commitment made in love, kept in faith, and eternally made new." I spoke those words while gazing into my love's eyes. Then I chose to recite Theodore Roethke's "Waking" poem which had become our theme song, only I changed the "I" to "we."

We wake to sleep and take our waking slow.

Great Nature has another thing to do
To you and me; so take the lively air;
And, lovely, learn by going where to go.

This shaking keeps us steady. We should know.
What falls away is always. And is near.
We wake to sleep, and take our waking slow.
We learn by going where we have to go.

Sharon and everyone had tears in their eyes, including me. When she recited the vows, I was melting from the pure emotion of it all, then she surprised me and everyone else except Chance when she began singing sweetly and slowly to the chiming of his guitar chords the words to "Come Sail Away." The lines that I remember are: "I'm sailing away/ Set an open course for the Virgin Sea/ 'Cause I've got to be free/ Free to face the life that's ahead of me.// ...So climb aboard/ We'll search for tomorrow on every shore/ And I'll try, oh Lord, I'll try to...carry on." All the women sang the chorus of "come sail away with me/ come sail away with me," and when I looked around Mom was singing too. On that great day, standing together on the crest of the hill, above the long valley of fields and forest, I took my wife into my arms.